The Sculptors

Suzanne Glass was born in Edinburgh and brought up in London. She studied French and Education at Cambridge and spent several years working abroad as a simultaneous interpreter. She is now a highly successful freelance journalist with her own column, 'The Looking Glass', in the *Financial Times*. Her first novel, *The Interpreter*, was published in 1999 to great critical acclaim.

Praise for *The Intepreter*

'What marks out this love story is the depth of under-standing Glass lends to the complex relationships and situations she creates. Multilingual, like her heroine, her honeyed words are seductive in their power' *The Times*

'A heady mix of romance and intrigue which keeps you on tenterhooks to the final page' *Independent*

'A fascinating story of love, passion and morality' *Prima*

'A magical story' *Frank*

'Suzanne Glass's instinctive feeling for words and their layers of meaning contributes to the subtlety of this highly polished first novel' *Woman & Home*

Also by Suzanne Glass

The Interpreter

The Sculptors

Suzanne Glass

ARROW

Published by Arrow in 2003

3 5 7 9 10 8 6 4

First published in the United Kingdom in 2002 by Century

Arrow Books
The Random House Group Limited
20 Vauxhall Bridge Road, London, SW1V 2SA

Random House Australia (Pty) Limited
20 Alfred Street, Milsons Point, Sydney,
New South Wales 2061, Australia

Random House New Zealand Limited
18 Poland Road, Glenfield
Auckland 10, New Zealand

Random House (Pty) Limited
Endulini, 5a Jubilee Road, Parktown 2193, South Africa

Random House Group Limited Reg. No. 954009

www.randomhouse.co.uk

A CIP catalogue record for this book
is available from the British Library

Papers used by Random House
are natural, recyclable products made from wood grown in
sustainable forests. The manufacturing processes conform to
the environmental regulations of the country of origin

ISBN 0 09 927808 1

Typeset by Palimpsest Book Production Limited, Polmont, Stirlingshire
Printed and bound in Great Britain by
Bookmarque Ltd, Croydon, Surrey.

This book is for fathers and daughters everywhere.
In particular it is for you, Dad, and on behalf of my mother
I dedicate it to the memory of her father
William Wollenberg.

Acknowledgements

First of all there was Dr Wafik Hanna, the Egyptian plastic surgeon and my inspiration, without whom *The Sculptors* would not have been written.

Then there were all those who have helped me along the way, namely, Dr Sherrell Aston, chairman of plastic surgery at Manhattan Eye, Ear and Throat Hospital, Dr Frank Vakari of the Children's Memorial Hospital in Chicago, Dr Ala Gheita from Cairo, Dr Danny Schwarz, State Prosecutor Judy Dobkin, Defense Attorney Todd Merer, FBI agent Elaine Smith, and the many experts, sculptors, painters, historians and sailors who have helped me along the way. They are too numerous to mention, but they know who they are.

Also, of course, my thanks go to my editors Kate Parkin and Kate Elton at Random House and to Jo Frank of A. P. Watt. And then there were my friends, my wonderful friends who have made it all worthwhile. Lisa Goldman and Michelle Berman have lived and breathed this book with me. I owe them everything.

I also want to thank Sarah Hartley, Michael Hoffman, Jim Petrakis, Mark de Souza, Jackie Cohen, Lynn Barber, Lisa Quigley, Ilene Landress, Michelle Hirschberg, Mandy Isaacs, Anna Albright, Steven Silver, Franca Tranza, Lesley Piper, Odelia Haroush, Romana Agliati-Manzoni and my parents for their support and for not giving up on me when I disappeared for months on end. Thanks also to Jonathan Harris and, of course, Steve Fox. And my thanks go too to Richard Mackie who has absolutely no idea just how much he helped me.

Art is meant to disturb.
Georges Braque

ONE

Chicago is wicked in winter. Through the window she might lie to you, beckon you, even, with a sky that is bright and a lake that is blue. But once she has lured you outside she will show you no mercy. She will bite and she will whip. She will chafe and she will freeze and as you propel yourself against her so she will push you backwards, testing both your stamina and the strength of your will.

The woman who fought her way forward despite the force of the wind and the flurries of February snow, might almost have been a man. Her defence against the elements was such that from a few feet away no part of her was visible. The length of her body was covered in a shapeless dark-grey sheepskin coat. Her feet were in short black lace-up boots with rubber soles, her hands in thick black leather gloves with the fingers curled underneath the palms as if to protect them.

A heavy black balaclava, with snowflakes caught in the ridges of the wool, hid all but her eyes, so that if you saw her just from the neck up and out of context, you might have thought that she herself was some sort of criminal rather than someone whose life might be touched by the crime of another. She might have been plain and she might have been beautiful. Dressed as she was, everything but her height was left to the imagination.

She was tall and still quite young. In her late thirties perhaps. One could guess that from her gait and from the strength with which she pushed against the chasing driving wind of the Midwest. Inside, some minutes later, framed by the wooden doorway she bent to unzip her boots. Her assistant Emily looked up from her desk. 'You're covered in icicles.'

'I know,' she said as she walked through the heavy oak doors of her rooms, her voice muffled, and she pulled the balaclava over her head adding, 'I couldn't start the car, the bus just didn't come and I couldn't find a cab . . . So, Em, how was your weekend?'

And Emily, pixie-like with shaved blonde hair, winked and said, 'Exciting . . . Now how are your hands?'

In response she pulled off the thick black leather gloves and the thin cotton ones underneath them, and bent her fingers trying to get the feeling back.

Emily reached for the icy hands and rubbed them in hers. 'They're blue,' she said. 'Quick, put them against the radiator . . . You've got a heavy day today.'

She held her hands on the radiator beside the door. Numb fingers curled over the edge of warmth against the wall. One couldn't help but think of frostbite in a climate like this and at the insistence of others she had insured her hands against both accident and illness.

Because they were quite extraordinary hands. Both in terms of the way they looked and of what they could do. She had been told that all her life and though she found it hard to accept compliments, when people said to her, 'You really do have the most beautiful hands,' she knew that they spoke the truth. She knew, inasfar as beauty could ever be objective, that her hands were beautiful. They were soft, unwrinkled and unmarked save for a tiny dark-brown dot just above the wrist bone of her left hand. They were slim with the fingers of a model. Long and delicate. Fingers that might on another woman have tapered into painted nails. But her nails were kept short and unvarnished, both because her work demanded it and because she was not in any case the sort of woman who would have chosen to wear her fingernails manicured.

She hung her sheepskin coat on the back of the door and took a comb from her leather rucksack. In the room, along one wall, there were mirrors positioned at every possible angle:

2

large old-fashioned mirrors in ornate bronze frames fixed against the wall; small silver adjustable mirrors attached by only two hinges; mirrors positioned at eye level for the adults and mirrors positioned lower down for the young child and on the desk a tortoiseshell hand mirror the size of a woman's face.

As for her own reflection, she chose for the moment to ignore it and, distracted, combed her hair, staring out of the window at the collage of towers, the spikes and the triangles above Lake Michigan.

Through the open door Emily called, 'A package arrived for you last night after you'd gone.'

'Oh?' she said. 'I'll be through in a minute.'

Her accent was foreign. Not strong enough for any but the most discerning ear to hazard a guess as to its origin, but foreign nonetheless.

She put her comb back in her rucksack and only then did she get up and glance in one of the mirrors.

Her hair was spiky. Short and black and shiny, and cut behind her ears, in a way that could be worn only by someone with prominent cheekbones. Under her eyes there were slight shadows. These were not shadows of tiredness. They were there even if she had slept well and woken refreshed. All her life they had been there, in stark contrast to the whiteness of her skin and she had long since ceased to wish them away. Visible only from certain angles and in a certain light, at other times they were hidden by the darkness and the thickness of her lashes.

'Who's the package from?' she called.

'I can't read the name,' Emily called back. 'It's in *your* language.'

She walked outside her room to Emily's desk in the hallway. She took the tall brown paper package with its string and air-mail stickers and lifted it, covering the upper half of her body and her face as she went. She carried it back into her room and with the side of her shoulder she pushed the door shut.

She squatted then on the rough carpet in the middle of the floor and ran her fingers over the package. The phone on her desk began to ring. She walked over to it, picked it up.

'Mrs Weiss is here for you,' said Emily.

'I'll be late,' she said and hung up.

She took a pair of scissors from the desk drawer and going back to sit on the floor, with the vaguest of shakes in the otherwise steadiest of hands, she began to cut the string that was wound time and again round the brown paper parcel. 'Looks like once for every year I've been away,' she said out loud to no one, the colour rising to her cheeks as she cut and cut.

Her hands had begun to thaw now and in an instant she knew the shape of the contents of the parcel. She knew, because as she slipped her hand beneath the brown paper and the bubbles of protective wrapping, the tips of her long slim fingers were sensitive enough to see. She knew because her fingertips could read and her fingertips remembered.

TWO

The small girl in her earth-green dungarees stared up at the painting, then looked up at her mother and said, 'Ima.'

'Sarit?'

'That is you and that is Abba,' she said, climbing on to her parents' bed, jumping up and down on the sheets, pointing with her long slim fingers at the painting, touching the thick blue and orange oils in the thin wooden frame on the wall above the headboard. She loved to touch the colours of her father's paintings, to trace the odd shapes of their edges, to feel the bumps and ridges with her fingertips. Once, her parents had taken her to a museum in Tel Aviv and she had run up to a portrait of an old man and touched the thick strands of his mustard-yellow moustache that rose from the canvas in the style of Van Gogh. The hunchbacked museum guard, standing close by, had pulled her arm back roughly from the painting. And shocked, Sarit had cried out, 'But I can touch it if I want to, you horrible man. It's dry. Abba lets me touch his paintings when they're dry.'

On her parents' bed Sarit carried on jumping up and down and chanting, 'That's Ima and Abba . . . Mummy and Daddy, Ima and Abba.'

'Yes,' said her mother, 'I suppose that is us,' and she laughed, a free and unencumbered laugh. 'Yes, Sarit, that's me and Abba.'

'Why haven't you got faces? Abba can paint faces. I've seen them. And why are you all muddled up together like one person?'

'So many questions,' said Gabriella.

'Ima, Ima, I want to know why he's muddled you up together. What are you doing?'

5

'We're . . . loving each other,' said Gabriella.

There is a silence then. The child stares at her mother. Not because she has understood what she has been told, but because she knows from the resolve in her mother's tone she is about to learn something of significance.

'What does that mean, Ima? What?'

Gabriella takes her daughter on her lap on the edge of the bed and strokes her shiny black hair. She supposes that at six Sarit is too young to be told about men and women loving one other. But when Sarit asks her the question, when she says, 'What does that mean, Ima? What?' Gabriella feels an inexplicable urgency to respond. As if she has to answer there and then or else the child might never know the truth in the way that Gabriella would like her to know it. Her husband could tell Sarit about loving, of course. He would try hard to explain it through a drawing or a painting. Max always pre-ferred to explain things to his daughter with a pencil or a paintbrush. But Gabriella knows that the child will always remember this moment, that she will look back on it in her adult life and that somehow it will define the way in which she thinks of her relationship with her mother. For there is almost no one who cannot remember when first they learnt of the force that drives our lives. And there are so few who recall an explanation that is sensitive and gentle.

And now Sarit puts her face in front of Gabriella's and nose to nose against her mother says, 'Ima, tell me. Now.'

'Well,' says Gabriella, resting her hands on Sarit's shoulders and looking into the child's grey eyes, 'that's how Abba and I made you. By loving each other.'

Sarit looks very serious, turns from her mother's face to the blue and orange painting and says, 'But I love you, Ima. I don't understand.'

'I love you too, sweetheart. But it's a different kind of love. What you see in Abba's painting is loving with the heart *and* the body.'

The child throws her arms round her mother's neck and says, 'I love my Ima with my heart and my body.'

Just outside the doorway to the bedroom Max stands looking in. He cannot stand in the doorway, because his head would touch the frame. So he stands just outside and he looks at his wife sitting there with their child on the edge of their bed. He watches them together and he smiles a serious smile. Max's smiles are always serious. Gabriella is the one who knows how to laugh out loud, to let it go, to enjoy life without turning her head to look at what has been or straining her neck to see what it is that will be. So often she has said to Max, 'I know it's hard for you, but if you keep on looking behind you, you'll turn into a pillar of salt.'

Now, standing in the doorway Max says, 'So, Sarit, what are you and Ima talking about?'

'About loving, Abba.'

He frowns and Gabriella looks at him and, a half-smile on her face, she says, 'She wanted to know about the painting, Max . . .' and laughing then, pointing at him, she says, 'Don't blame me. You painted it. You hung it there.'

'True,' he says and then, 'So what did Ima tell you, Sarit?'

The child, when she speaks to her father, is far more serious than when she speaks to her mother. She is not quite afraid of him, but she senses that everything must be far more earnest, that even though she is small still, with her father she must be more of a grown-up than with her mother.

She walks up to him, takes his long slim hand in hers. She drags him over to the bed, climbs on to the sheets and points again at the painting. 'You and Ima,' says Sarit, as though teaching him, 'are making me. It's called loving, Abba. That's what it's called.'

Later, when Sarit is asleep in the children's house, where in the 1960s and 1970s the kibbutz children still spent much of their time, to free their mothers for work in the fields or the factory, in the kitchen or in the laundry, Gabriella and Max

7

lie in bed and talk about their daughter's question. They talk about her asking, 'Ima, why are you and Abba all muddled up together?'

'Max?' says Gabriella.

'Yes.'

'At least now when the next one arrives she will know where he comes from.'

'Do you think,' says Max, for once light-hearted, 'if there is another one, that we can arrange for him to be born on my birthday too?'

Gabriella strokes her husband's bony face. She says, 'We'll work on our timing, shall we?'

'I like it, you know, Gaby,' he says, 'that she and I share a birthday.'

'You should say that to her, Max. She's the kind of child who needs to hear these things. You don't tell her enough how you feel about her.'

'Don't I?' he asks and then, propping himself up on his elbow, looking down at his wife, he says, 'And even if I don't, should a child not take her father's love for granted?'

'Max, she's six years old. She's just a baby.'

'I know,' he says, 'I know.' And he leans over and lifts a wisp of hair from Gabriella's face.

She takes hold of his wrist as if to be sure she has all of his attention for a moment. 'It's almost as if it's too much for you with Sarit. As if . . . as if . . . you love her so much that you can't put it into words. It's because she's the only flesh and blood that you have left, isn't it?'

Next to his wife, Max nods into the darkness.

That night he and Gabriella mirror the blue and orange painting that hangs above their bed. Time and again over the next months they throw caution to the wind, but when they lie there some time later, clinging to each other, beneath the image of themselves, Max whispers to his wife. 'Gaby. Oh, my Gaby, what shall we tell Sarit?'

'The truth in a way that she can understand it . . . and also a half-truth.'

'What's the half-truth?'

'That a child as talented as she is will need all of your attention to herself. That a brother or a sister would have taken too much of you away. In fact, that's not really a half-truth, Max. But it's half of the truth. Don't you think, my love?'

THREE

In the early hours of the morning of Sarit's birthday, in a high-rise close to downtown Chicago, a man whose name she has momentarily forgotten turns to her and says, 'That was great.'

In the dark greyness their silhouettes are separate. Her eyes are shut, her back is turned and when he says, 'That was great,' she says nothing in response.

'This is a bit odd,' he says. 'We're almost strangers.'

'Must have been the Black Russians,' she says.

'Or the Margaritas.'

'Yes,' she says, 'perhaps.'

'I wanna to get to know you better, though.' He reaches a hirsute arm across her mattress on the floor and rests it on the shape that is her back. She slides a little further under the sheets and over towards the door. She has sat on occasion in a restaurant and finished a meal without real hunger, without real pleasure, though its taste per se has not been flawed. And she has pushed her plate aside then and been desperate for the waiter to take it away that very second.

'We should chat,' he says. 'I guess this is the wrong way round. You're supposed to talk first . . . but . . . I would like to get to know you. So . . .' and he inches closer. 'Shall I stay the night?'

'No . . .' she says, and she sits bolt upright and switches on the bare electric bulb and says again, 'No . . . you better leave now.'

'Why?'

'Because I have to be up early and I don't sleep well with a stranger in my bed.'

10

He raises his eyebrows. 'Your call, lady.' He leans down and begins to pick up his clothes from the side of the bed and to dress. He pulls on his white socks and his black shoes.

'Don't take it personally,' she says.

'You know it's freezing out there. Probably minus ten.'

'Yes.'

'So you still want me to go?'

'Yes . . . I do.'

'OK.' And then, 'I'll take your number.'

She reels off a phone number. The last two digits are the wrong way round. He takes the pen from her bedside table. He sees it is a fountain pen and frowns. He unscrews the cap as though poison and not ink will flow from its nib and scratches the number she has given him on the back of a cigarette packet. Next to it he writes her name and spells it *Sareet*. He stands up and finishes dressing.

'Bye then.'

'Goodbye.'

'What? You're not even going to look at me?'

She lifts her head. She says, 'I don't mean to be rude.' She sees his muscles now. The triceps and the biceps she felt before the Margaritas and the Black Russians began to wear off. Thick, hard and heavy muscles that must be the focus of his life. She finds their shape interesting. On his right upper arm is a large tattoo of a distorted starfish. She finds it ugly.

He sees her looking. He grins. 'You got a tattoo yourself,' he says. 'I saw it in the bar.'

He reaches down and pulls the duvet off her to reveal the tiny green omega in a horseshoe on her shoulder. She pulls it back on as if he no longer has a right to see her naked.

'What is it?' he asks.

'What is what?' she says, annoyed.

'That tattoo.'

'Nietzsche's eternal recurrence,' she says and, half amused

11

by her own tactics at getting him to leave, she adds, 'The artistic representation of the idea that life goes round in circles.'

'Yeah, right,' he says and, changing the subject to ground on which he's comfortable, he flexes his muscles, slaps the biceps of his right arm, says, 'I'd be wasting these if I wasn't in security.'

'You could be a wrestler,' she says.

He laughs, then looks around. 'Not a bad place. Could do with some more things in it, though. How d'you make your money, then?'

'Me?' she says. 'Um . . . I'm a moulder.'

'A moulder . . . hm.'

She has relied on him not wanting to appear ignorant.

'Interesting,' he says.

'Can you let yourself out?' she asks.

'Suppose so.' He touches her right hand and he gets up to go. 'Nice hands,' he says.

'Thanks.'

The bedroom door shuts. The front door bangs. She turns on to her back and throws off the duvet to throw off what has been. She stares into the ghastly familiar emptiness of it all. An emptiness that hit her while she was filled with him still. By her bedside where the photo frame might have been, the ringer on the telephone is turned to the highest volume. Once, when the phone had rung in the middle of the night, half asleep and half awake she imagined that she had lifted the receiver, that she had listened to the caller's voice and that she had heard herself responding, giving him instructions on what to do till she arrived. She dreamt that she was getting up, crossing her bedroom naked, mentally splashing her face with icy water as she went. She imagined too that she was getting dressed, grabbing her keys, rushing down to the underground car park, responding to the urgency of the moment. In reality, though, she had barely woken at all. She had tossed and she had turned and had been dragged within seconds into an even

12

deeper sleep. A sleep where she heard the urgent moan of a siren. A sleep where she was moving, focusing and doing what was needed of her.

In the year after her eighth birthday those half-dreams had often come to Sarit. That was the embarrassing bed-wetting year when time and again she would half dream she was climbing out of the little low bed in the kibbutz children's house, that she was hurrying barefoot along the cool concrete floor to the bathroom, only to wake instead with her sheets sopping wet. The first time it happened, in the darkness with all her might she had pulled and she had tugged at the wet sheets till they had come away from the bed and she had dragged them behind her to Ben, the night guard on duty at the door of the children's house. He had brought her fresh clean linen, though rough sheets this time that scratched her skin. He had soothed her and tucked her in. But that happened just once, because in the next bed Odelia had seen and heard it all and word spread fast, so that in the morning in the schoolroom the children had begun to chant, 'Sarit wets her be–ed. Sarit still wets her be–ed.'

After that she didn't bother to tell the guard when it happened. Anything, even the smell and the discomfort, was better than the humiliation. That was the year when she would sometimes wake to see the tall thin shadow of her father standing over her, watching her breathe. She wondered on occasion if it really was Max she had seen or if perhaps she had dreamt him or seen a ghost because the second she opened her eyes, the second she whispered, 'Abba,' and stretched out her hand to him, her father seemed to fade away to nothingness. That was the year when Ben let Sarit's father into the children's house at all hours. Because Ben had known Max since, gaunt and haunted, he had first disembarked the ship in Haifa. A scrap of a young man with no luggage and enough baggage to last him for a lifetime. Ben had known him for more than long enough to understand his pain, his angst, his fears.

13

Even now, even here in the high-rise on the borders of Lincoln Park and Old Town, Sarit's fear was that though she might dream she was awake, she would sleep still through the ringing of the phone. Not that she was disturbed often as she slept. Her work demanded night-time calls only on the rarest of occasions. But still at times she would wake to find her arm draped over her bedside table. Sometimes she would laugh at herself and out loud she would say, 'For God's sake, woman. It's just a job . . . Don't take yourself so seriously. The world would manage perfectly without you.' But her subconscious mind was stronger than her reasoning and so, as Sarit slept, her right hand would be outside the covers, poised there and waiting for the phone to ring.

FOUR

Their faces are swathed as those of Muslim women, though not in black.

Their eyes too are shielded, though not with gold or silver and the mask they wear is no bar to the language they speak with their eyes. So muffled is their world, so refined their art, that many of their words are spoken only by looking.

They are expecting her when she walks in, swathed and gloved as they are. Her smile, her upright posture and the calm in her voice inspire them. No matter what has been the night before it falls to her to lead them. She has chosen them. And they her. And here under the bright lights, with the humming and the ticking, the stakes are high.

She walks round to one side of the pale face that sleeps. A large and handsome face, though one that has worshipped the sun. A face that Sarit knows as it is and as it will be. She might have sketched it to show the woman who she would become. She would have shown her true colours with a pencil in her hand. But she prefers to use the black and white photographs that are clipped now to a tall thin stand by her side. Photographs created as always on her computer screen, images that are so important to Sarit if she is to understand how the sum of the parts will work as a whole. Sarit looks down at the woman. She watches the green shrouds as they rise and fall. She composes herself, glances at her friend, standing waiting at the other side of the table, and in readiness she nods.

A voice close to the humming and the ticking says, 'Music maestro?'

15

'Yes please. You choose, Pamela.' Pamela, with the Chinese eyes, lifts the compact disc from a table by the door and moves towards the other end of the room. Sarit lays a gloved hand on the woman's cheek. She wonders what went through her mind that morning when she looked in the mirror. She wonders if she had second thoughts. Sarit never pushed her. She never said, 'This will change your life.' But she asked, as she always does, 'Are you looking to change your life?' because she wants them to know that they cannot vest her with the power of a deity. She always says to them, 'I can't work on the inside and I can only work with what is there. I can alter and refine but remember I can't create from scratch. There are limitations to what I can do.' And this woman, the handsome shrouded woman, before she made her decision had turned to Sarit and said, 'You mean, you can only work with the materials you are given. What you do is more of a craft than an art, then?'

'I suppose that's what I mean,' Sarit had said and then, the woman's suggestion registering in her mind, she had added, 'An art? God no. Absolutely not. This is certainly no art. Far from it.'

Opposite Sarit, her blonde hair hidden by her head covering, green eyes alert, her friend and colleague passes her a thin piece of silver from the table next to her. Sarit takes it, lifts it to the woman's hairline, traces the curve of her ear, of her jawline, her forehead.

Sarit and Lauren have danced this dance together many times. Their ballet is so rehearsed, so choreographed they anticipate each other's every step. She hands Sarit the fine pieces of silver before she needs to ask for them.

They speak in hushed tones, not now looking at each other, for Sarit dare not lift her eyes. And their conversation could almost be taking place between friends over coffee.

Her long gloved fingers working on the face beneath her, Sarit says to Lauren, 'Anything I should know about?'

16

'I'm giving Todd two more weeks to propose.'

'Well, if that's what you want, you propose to him. If you're sure. This is the twentieth century, Lor.'

Sarit has said, 'If you're sure,' and 'If that's what you want,' because once, at the end of a session when Lauren's head covering had slipped and she had been off work with flu for days before, Sarit could have sworn she saw a bluish greenish area just above her eye. At the time, with the women in the room, she couldn't ask. She couldn't say, like she did to so many of the others, whose faces she touched after surgery, 'Does it hurt at all?' And when a few days later she had seen Lauren, though the mark of bluish green was gone, Sarit put the question to her. She asked, 'Did someone hurt you?' and Lauren looked at her as though she'd lost her mind.

Now when Sarit says, 'Well, if that's what you want you propose to him . . .' Lauren answers, 'Hm, you might just be right, you know,' and then, 'By the way, there's someone I want to fix you up with.'

'Another one?'

'I won't give up on you.'

'Who is he?'

'A shrink.'

'Oh please. I can't stand doctors.'

Sarit keeps her eyes lowered, drifts from the conversation, talks now to the woman beneath her hands. 'I hope,' she says out loud, 'that this will make you happier.' She pushes and she pulls. She stretches and she smoothes. Her control belies the adrenalin's steady flow.

Lauren is quiet now. Her hand and Sarit's reach across the table to one another, back and forwards flashing red and white and silver, fingertips straining, close though never touching. She knows when Sarit no longer wants to speak. When she needs to be alone with the rhythm of her work. Alone with her skill and the sounds of the music. She watches as Sarit begins slowly to move the thumb and the

17

forefinger that hold the silver sliver close to the woman's face.

'The thumb and the forefinger. You see, Sarit, this is how you hold the paintbrush. Just like this . . . Gaby, look, look, she's holding the brush to the paper . . . ! That's good, Sarit, but it would be better like this.' He manoeuvres the thick brush in the child's hand. The hand that has not quite yet lost its chubbiness or the dimples at the base of its fingers. The child's hand that feels the roughness of his skin on hers.

'Hold your forefinger here, Sarit. This way.'

'Max. She's not even three. She has time for this.' Gabriella is in the room now, standing close to them. 'Let her play with the colours. Let her finger-paint, Max. Let her make a mess.'

'She can play. But later. She must know how to hold the brush properly . . . Come, Sarit. Let's paint some squiggles. Round and in and out and round and in. Come . . . with the music now. Can you hear how the music moves? Orange and blue and red.' Their hands, hers and her father's, Max guiding her wrist, leading her, moving the brush across the sheet of paper, dipping the big fat furry brush in paint and saying, 'Grey now, Sarit, and then some black.'

'Not so much black, Max . . . she doesn't need it yet. She has time enough for that.'

And Max looking up at his wife, saying, 'Gaby, why should we let her think the world is pink? I want my child to know the truth,' and then looking back down at his daughter, one hand resting lightly on her head, the other on her hand guiding her thumb and her forefinger as she learns to draw and to paint.

The thumb and the forefinger. Sarit's fingers darting in and out with the silver and the thread. The rest of her still. Only her fingers moving. And the music, the Mendelssohn, with her, in the room and in her head. The lone bow on the strings. Short notes that move with her across the woman's face.

And then suddenly Sarit is no longer in her own world. She hadn't realised it was over. She hadn't felt the moment when her fingers finished working. The woman on the table begins to move. The swathed women gather round, closing in on her.

'It's all done,' Pamela says to her. 'You're going to be a beauty. Such a beauty.'

The bright lights are dimmed. The music is almost played out. Above her Sarit stretches her arms, throws off her gloves, pulls off her mask. 'See you tomorrow,' she says. 'You were great. All of you.'

And she is gone. Anonymous without her mask, in her jeans and her sheepskin, driving along by the side of the branches wrapped in ice, by the side of the pond in Lincoln Park, which has frozen for a lone skater who sinews on thin ice.

FIVE

Kingston Mines is a backstreet blues bar, an after-hours hang-out, a grungy rosewood haunt. At Kingston Mines on Halstead in downtown Chicago, you can choose to sit in the light beneath the stage, in the half-light of its alcoves or in the shadows of its corners. Sociable or anti-social, upbeat or in the depths of gloom, Kingston Mines will draw you in, will render you anonymous as its scratched and beaten chairs, as its confusion of cigarette butts, beer bottles and dark wooden tables. The place knows no age, no class, no colour and no person who does not leave it in a somewhat altered state.

In silky red pants and a top cut lower than low to reveal the matching red lace of her bra against the smooth dark skin of her bosom, her black hair piled high on her head, her microphone a little too close to her shiny lips, a black woman is singing the blues. Close to the small stage at the front of Kingston Mines the singer's cheap and heavy musk joins with the heady bluish purple mix of marijuana, of sweat and of smoke in the air.

They have come, Sarit and Lauren, to hear Koko Taylor, one of Chicago's most famous black jazz singers. She has cancelled and in her place is the shiny-lipped singer with a presence of a sort.

Moving a little with the music, closing her eyes, Sarit says, 'She's OK, Lor . . . She's OK, don't you think?'

'Go on, then,' says Lauren in her tight jeans, her leopard-skin top that clings. She hands Sarit the roll-up. 'No more cutting till Monday. You can chill out. You deserve it, babe.'

Sarit hesitates only for a split second before she takes the joint. She puts it to her mouth, rolls it for a moment against the ridges of her lips, inhales and says, 'Haven't done this for a while. Ages, actually.'

'Since when?'

Sarit sees the outlines of her friends, the gathering around the campfire on the kibbutz in the dead of night, in the light of the flames, in the heat of adolescence. She smells the humidity, hears the lyrics of the songs. In her mind she hums the tune and sings the words, '*Al ha machane yored yareach, ve ha zman cmo gumi mitmareach* . . . The moon falling on our bonfire, time stretching like bubble gum . . .' She feels the scratching of the twigs on her legs, the shape of the joint passed from hand to hand around the circle.

And Dani, his bony arm round her waist, whispering in her ear, his mouth against her lobe in the hot and sweaty blackness, 'Go on, try it. Nothing will happen to you when I'm here. I promise.'

Sarit shakes her shoulders, loosens herself from the tentacles of memory, tries hard to haul herself back into the moment. Because this is where she wants to be. Here in Kingston Mines with the jazz and the dope, the beer and the blues. And to Lauren now she says, 'Oh, I don't know when the last joint was, Lor. Ages ago. I don't know.' And then she asks, 'Is Todd angry that you're here?'

'I said it was your birthday. That you were alone and I felt sorry for you.'

'Oh.'

'When is your birthday anyway, Sarit? It's some time soon, isn't it?' Lauren asks, half talking, half shouting over the sounds of the jazz.

'It was this week,' she says.

'Oh, charming, and you let me forget it. Why didn't you tell me?'

'What's the big deal?'

'What did you do?'

21

'Nothing,' she says, her tone too sharp. 'I don't do birthdays . . . What's the point?' And then, 'It was Tuesday. I think I did a cleft lip, eyelids on that burn case . . . oh, and a nose job in the afternoon I think. Remember?'

'Oh, I remember. Super birthday. And then?'

'Then nothing.'

'You can't go on like this, Sarit.'

'Like what?'

'Like . . .'

'Can I buy you ladies another beer?'

Sarit turns to her left, unsurprised, expecting that at some point from somewhere this question or a similar one would find her. Usually it does. Though she makes no effort to draw attention to herself the drinkers in the bars and clubs are drawn to her, in her faded jeans and the white sleeveless vest top she wears under the layers of sweaters she has shed. They are attracted to the shape and the strength of her shoulders, to her strong slim arms with their hint of muscle and of definition. They are attracted to the expression, not of arrogance, but of self-confidence that makes no excuses for the Semitic nose. They are drawn to the clear-skinned unmade-up face that refuses to pander to their received notions of beauty.

'No thanks,' Sarit says now to the bearded man in his short-sleeved multicoloured shirt who has offered her the beer. 'We're just fine right now.'

Defeated, he retreats.

'And you, Lor?' asks Sarit, making no reference to the inter-ruption, giving it no more relevance than the swatting of flies in heat. 'Are you happy?'

Lauren takes a swig from the bottle. Bolder, braver, more outspoken by her third Budweiser she says, 'I guess it beats being alone . . . when he's calm, that is.'

Sarit repeats her question. She says, 'But Lauren, are you happy?'

From somewhere further back in the room they hear the

voice of a girl shouting, 'No. No.' And her 'No' rises above the talk and the tables, the beer and the blues, her 'No' breaks through the dope and the mist, the smoke and the sweat, and turns heads. But the room is big enough, packed enough, heaving enough so that by the time Sarit and Lauren turn round, though both are sure of the direction from which the 'No' has travelled, neither can pinpoint its author.

'Someone's angry,' Lauren says.

'Sounds that way.' Sarit is hovering on the edge of mellowness, the effects of the marijuana jousting with the astuteness, the alertness that are with her always. She takes the joint from between Lauren's fingers. The fingers with the candyfloss-pink nails. Her weekend nails. She says, 'I wonder what that was all about.'

The girl, hidden in one of the half-lit alcoves twenty feet or so behind Sarit and to her right, the girl who has shouted 'No' into the noise of Kingston Mines, sits with her chin in her hands, a silver cross round her neck. She has calmed down for a moment. She takes a deep breath and says to the man sitting opposite her, 'I don't want this. To be caught up in your . . . your goddamn lifestyle.' She turns her face away from him.

He holds her arm. 'Felicia,' he says.

Her voice angry, sharp, high-pitched, she turns back. 'Do you honestly think I would have started with you if I'd known? I don't want this. It's sick Alessandro . . . It's . . . it's immoral.' And she begins to sob again now, her face in her hands, a twist of her blonde corkscrew curls falling into her beer.

Alessandro draws her hand from her chin, prises open her fingers, interlaces them with his. This is not the first time they have fought over his work. Not the first time she has cried and begged him to clean up his act. In the past he has avoided and evaded, but he knows that if he refuses to listen now, soon she will simply up and leave. She will pack the one suitcase with which she came to him, she will walk out of his swish apartment and she will go, back to the trattoria, back to the

23

relative poverty and the stability of her clean-living family on Taylor Street. He doesn't want that, not just because he loves her, but because, since the day she walked into his 'gallery' on Milwaukee, she has offered Alessandro the most stable element he has ever known in his life.

Alessandro is no stereotype. He doesn't wear a gold chain on a hairy chest beneath an open-necked designer shirt. In his dress there is nothing showy, on his person nothing shiny and in his manner nothing obviously shady. His way is different from his colleagues'. They feel the need to call out to the waiters for the finest caviar and the fattest cigars at Rosebud's or at Jilly's. They feel the need to flaunt it. Not that they want people to know where it came from, but they want them to know it is there and to wonder. But he goes to these places sometimes, to Rosebud's and to Jilly's. He goes with the guys, when they insist on his company, when they say, 'You hiding yourself away again with that white-skinned beauty of yours, Alessandro. Where did an Italian woman get that porcelain skin, then?'

'Sardinian grandparents,' says Alessandro.

'Come on, then, Alessandro. Bring out your Sardinian princess. Let her have some fun.' So sometimes he succumbs, drags Felicia along and drinks with them there, though in truth he would so much rather be alone with her, listening to jazz or to the blues in a wooden alcove in Kingston Mines.

Her head thrown back, her eyes closed, the blues artist is singing 'I can't stay this way for ever . . .' Felicia can't see the singer from where she sits but the irony of the words she hears are not wasted on her.

'I've had it, Alessandro.'

'It will change. I promise, Felix. I swear. I just have to do it slowly. I don't want the others getting jumpy.'

She looks at him. With her eyes she says, 'I'm giving you one last chance.'

'I'll sort it out,' he says. 'You'll see.'

And he means it. Though it's hard to change the habits of a lifetime and he worries about the consequences, of course. He wonders what he will do then, when his life is clean, when he no longer lives on his nerves, when his heart doesn't pound as he watches his worker bees rip open the boxes from the shipment, unwind the protective bubble wrapping, pull out the layers of paper inside the vases and the urns to check if what was stashed behind them, taped to the inside of the artwork, has arrived unscathed. He tries sometimes to envisage what it would be like not to live in fear, not to feel your pulse race when you pretended to stop and browse with nonchalance, certain that the reflection of the man behind you in the shop window was the one you had seen the day before. And Alessandro dreams sometimes of how it might be not to jump when your doorman called to say you had a visitor or two, not to panic and wonder if you were hallucinating or if you really had seen the same white vans that seemed to have no purpose parked outside your home week in week out.

And now, turning to Felicia he says, 'I will break away, Felicia. I swear,' and whispering he adds, 'I just need to do it carefully. That's all. They know I know about them. That they're keeping stuff for themselves. That it's not all going where it should go. They'll be terrified when I break away. You understand. They'll think I'm going to split on them.'

'And will you?' she asks.

'No. Of course not.'

Alessandro can feel the sweat between his shoulder blades and in the hair under his arms. Once or twice before he has tried to fast forward in his head and imagine how his colleagues might react when he said, 'Guys . . . I think we've got to talk. I can't see myself working with you that much longer. I'm going to get a job. A proper job. I don't know what yet, but when I marry Felicia I'll get a green card and . . .' And every time that in his head Alessandro hears their cynical laughter, sees their hard, all-knowing faces, his stomach churns and in his mind he changes the subject to some banality or other.

The singer wraps her shiny lips around the microphone to a Koko Taylor blues number called 'Don't lay your hands on me'.

In the alcove Alessandro puts some dollar notes on the table. Felicia stands up to leave and wipes her hand across her eyes.

In the conventional sense of the word she is a beauty. Youthful, blue-eyed, blonde-haired, full-mouthed with skin so white as to be almost transluscent. A beauty that is unmitigated even by the roundness of her face. As she edges along the seat out of the alcove she grabs Alessandro's arm. She says, 'Look me in the eye right now. It's got to stop. I mean it, Alessandro. I mean it absolutely. This is our last chance.'

'I know,' he says, and then, 'You're so grown up, Felicia . . . and you're still a baby.'

They walk out, he with his arm around the curve of her waist and she exhausted, suddenly leaning into the part of him she trusts. So that from behind as they leave Kingston Mines, as they pass the tables at the front beneath the stage, they look relaxed and lucky. That at least is what Sarit thinks in her slightly altered state as she sees them for just a split second as they disappear outside the door.

'I have to go now,' says Lauren. 'Todd will be wondering. He'll think I've picked up some guy.'

'He doesn't trust you, does he?' asks Sarit.

Lauren shrugs and suddenly seems panicked, in a hurry, desperate to get the bill and leave. She beckons to the waitress with the blonde pigtails. In her beer-stained yellow apron, an empty mug through almost every finger, she pretends not to see them.

Sarit senses Lauren's sudden rising panic. She has witnessed her fear of Todd's reaction to her lateness before. 'I'll go and get the check,' she says and she stands up and walks over to the waitress. She comes back with the bill.

Lauren reaches for her purse.

'No.' Sarit grips her wrist. 'No, leave it.'

'Why should you pay . . . again?'

'I'm overpaid. You're underpaid,' says Sarit, her kibbutz background, with its ethos of socialism and equality, surfacing in her even after all these years.

She leans over, stuffs the twenty-dollar bills back into Lauren's handbag. She pulls her thin grey sweater, her thick black sweater, then her white fleece over her head, and follows Lauren to the doorway. The narrow corridor to the door is thick with people and with coats hung on top of one another on iron hooks. As she squeezes her way out, Sarit is pushed against the wall. In the dim light of the corridor and the hustling of people, a heavy winter jacket falls on to the floor. She bends to pick up the dark worn sheepskin suede jacket and hangs it back on top of a coat. And she and Lauren move towards the door to the bluesy sounds of 'Don't mess with Mother Nature'. Sounds that travel back through the corridor, back past the alcoves and into the farthest corners of the club.

In the shadows of the back right-hand corner of Kingston Mines the chubby waitress begins to feel uncomfortable, as though, merely by going up to the man with the thick silver-grey hair to ask if he wants another beer she had turned into an intruder, an eavesdropper interrupting a conversation. In one sense the waitress is indeed an intruder, for the man that night is so lost in his thoughts, so immersed in his inner world that to address a word in his direction is in fact to invade his privacy. Still, as is her duty, the waitress walks up to him. She says, 'Need anything else, Sir?'

He merely nods and points to the beer mug that is almost empty. He takes a black leather tobacco pouch from the pocket of his denim shirt, he takes out a small piece of white square paper and some tobacco, and between the fingers of his left hand begins to roll a cigarette. He has been coming here to

Kingston Mines for years. For months on end he might turn up twice, even three times a week only to disappear then for weeks at a time. He chooses always to come alone and always to sit in the shadows. Most nights, like this one, he sits back on the wooden chair, smokes his roll-ups, sips his beer and talks to no one at all. On these nights often his face seems almost black. As black as his eyes. As black as once his heavy brows had been.

The waiters and the waitresses are curious about Ramsi Riyad, whose name they do not know. They have tried, each one of them on occasion, to draw him into some semblance of conversation. They have hazarded guess after guess as to his personal life, his background, his nationality. The waitresses have even tried to flirt with him, for though he is past fifty he has about him a certain raw sexuality.

On the occasions when he is not oblivious to his sur-roundings, Ramsi leans forward, his elbows on the table, his chin in his hands: the large, strong, dark-skinned hands, with the strong fingers, the protruding knuckles, the heavily ridged nails and the small patch of uneven-textured skin on the inside of his right palm. And as he leans forward so he fixes his gaze in one direction. Usually the object of his scrutiny is a woman and though from a distance his interest might be misinter-preted, if one were to look closely one would see on his face an expression not of lust, but of interest, of curiosity and of analysis. He would furrow his brows and cock his head from side to side as if weighing up the object of his gaze for some higher purpose. He would never move from his chair, though. He would rarely stand up and approach any of the other drinkers at Kingston Mines. When it came to his professional life, Ramsi had a certain confidence that what was fated to come his way would do so.

On occasion as he stared so he was approached. A year or so before that evening when the singer in the red lace bra was singing the blues, he had stared with great intensity at a

28

middle-aged woman with long thick grey hair, an ample bosom and slightly wrinkled skin above her cleavage. And though all the while she was engaged in conversation with a pale skinny man, she could feel Ramsi looking. She turned back once or twice to see if he was focused on her still and because he was not embarrassed, because he felt his reasons for staring to be quite legitimate, not once had he attempted to avert his gaze. She had stood up, walked over to him, sat down next to him with purpose and said, 'You bin looking at me.'

And for him, for Ramsi, the moment she opened her mouth, the fascination, the illusion that she might be important to him was shattered and he had said, 'Sorry. I thought you were someone I knew.' And the woman, disappointed, got up and crossed the room again, back to the boredom that was her life.

Another time he had fixed his gaze on a girl in profile smoking a cigarillo. She had not noticed him at first, but her boyfriend had nudged her and she had turned and seen him. She had marched over in defiance, puffed smoke at him and said, 'You've been staring at me.'

'Yes,' he said.

'Can't you see I'm with my boyfriend? And I'm much too young for you anyway.'

'I'm staring at you as a work of art, not as potential prey.'

She looked at him, disbelieving, standing there with her hands on her hips, her thumbs in the pockets of her fake black leather trousers with her black crop top and her hair in a dirty blonde knot on her head.

He had come down a level. He had said, 'Have you ever modelled for an artist?'

She had laughed, called over her boyfriend and said, 'Get this. He's an artist. He wants me for his model.'

The pale skinny man stood there, wary, and said to Ramsi, 'You're not serious?'

'I'm one hundred per cent serious. You can come with her if you want. I only need a couple of sessions. All clothes on. It's her face that interests me.'

Excited now, the girl turns to her boyfriend. She says, 'Well, well, he's going to paint me.'

'Not paint,' says Ramsi. 'Sculpt. I will sculpt you if you'll let me.'

'Paint. Sculpt. It's all the same. How much do you pay?'

'Enough,' he says, and then, 'It depends how still you can sit.'

And in truth Ramsi is prepared to pay his models well. On himself he might spend little, but with others he is as generous with his money as he is guarded with his emotions.

And so the girl in the PVC trousers is one of several characters from Kingston Mines whom Ramsi over the years has sculpted and sold in quasi anonymity in New York, in Boston, in Santa Fe, New Mexico and in the galleries of River North, at the centre of Chicago's world of art.

The night of the singer in the red lace bra Ramsi has looked around him, seen nothing of interest and chosen then not to stare, not to care, but to retreat. It is one of those nights when his thoughts are in the past, when his interest in the present is limited to the taste of tobacco and of beer. For the past in any case provides him with more than sufficient material to fuel his art. In an artistic sense the past is much more the making of Ramsi Riyad's success than is the present.

Had Felicia not been hidden that night with Alessandro in an alcove, had he seen the near perfect proportions of her face and the darkness of her distress she might well have interested him as an *objet d'art*. He might have been drawn to her then and had his eyes rested on her high forehead he might have shuddered and seen ghosts. But of Felicia's existence, of her presence that night at Kingston Mines, Ramsi Riyad knew nothing.

Had Sarit been close to him, had he seen her in profile, the thick lashes, the Semitic nose, the graceful neck, the sexy shoulders, he would no doubt have leant forward and considered her. But he saw neither Felicia nor Sarit. Though the three of them, Ramsi and the two women, had sat in Kingston Mines in some sort of triangle shape. He at the back in the shadows, Felicia in the half-light of the alcoves and Sarit in the light beneath the stage.

He jumped when the waitress touched his arm, when the bare electric lights went on, when the chairs were lifted on to the tables. He left the money for his beers and a handsome tip on the table, stood up and walked slowly through the empty littered room towards the door. He lifted his worn brown sheepskin jacket from a hook by the door and, his hands in his pockets, he stepped out on to Halstead and negotiated the cold night air.

SIX

The meanderings of the life line, the head line, the heart line are never alike in any two people. The contours and the curves, the shapes, the slopes and the planes of faces may follow similar paths in brother and sister, in parent and child, but the patterns on our palms are shared with no one. These are the stories that we struggle to co-author all our lives, alternately rejoicing in and railing against the input of chance or of destiny. As we run a fingernail across our palm, we might feel the grooves, the depths and the direction of the lines, but without help we are powerless to unravel them. These lines tell the story in which we are too grown up, too rational to believe. They tell the tale from which we might pretend to turn our heads, yet endlessly fascinated, we cannot help but prick up our ears and focus on the voice and the art of the reader who sits with our palm in her hands.

Sarit would often consider her hands. As a child of five and six and seven she had looked at them and lisping, repeating her father's words to her mother, she had said, 'Ima, I've got special hands. Abba says so. I have got special hands, Ima, haven't I?'

As a professional, though, Sarit was forever critical of her hands. She challenged their skill and their dexterity. She challenged the speed and the nimbleness of her fingers. Sometimes she would rub cream into her hands, more for her patients' sake than for her own, so that when she touched their faces, drawing her thick black eyebrows together over her grey eyes as she did so, thinking about what they had asked for and what she could achieve, her hands would feel smooth against their skin.

Once a well-dressed woman in her seventies with paper-thin skin patterned with her life and with the sun had come to beg Sarit to turn the clock back and had said, 'Doctor, your hands are so soft. Whatever you use, keep on using it.' Sarit had said nothing in response. Except on the odd occasion she spoke little more than was necessary with her patients. From Gabriella, though, she had learnt the art of listening and so at the request of the preened and prune-like woman Sarit kept on using the cream. She kept it in a big pot in the drawer of her desk and on occasion in the evening she would stand at the window that overlooked the city of Chicago and Lake Michigan and rub a dollop of the thick white cream into her hands. Never once, though, did she stop, look down and consider the tomes on her palms. In the whole of her life there had not been a time when she had sat and contemplated the lines of her hands. But at the kitchen table now, long bare legs stretched out beneath an oversize white T-shirt, she drinks black coffee from a chipped mug. She turns the pages of the *Chicago Sunday Tribune*, then reaches for the phone that rings.

'Hello.'

'Morning, Doctor.'

'Lauren. How are you?'

'Great,' she says, her voice high-pitched and excited. 'I have a surprise for you, Sairit.'

Lauren after all this time is still as incapable of pronouncing her name as the bodybuilder with the distorted starfish on his arm had been. Sarit smiles into the phone.

'Lauren, Can you say "Sarit"? Sar to rhyme with far, not Sair to rhyme with stair.'

'OK, *Sarit*,' she says, 'I have a surprise for you.'

Sarit's fellow surgeons, all of them men, found it strange that she would wish to share her confidences with a theatre nurse. For them it was not fitting to choose as your confidante a person of a different rank within your own profession. In their hierarchical preoccupation the American medics had all but forgotten that Sarit came from a place where the dustman and the doctor drank coffee together, where the plumber, a guest at the dinner table of the professor, was unafraid to speak his mind. They forgot that she came from a kibbutz, from a microcosm of communism, from a place where the yardstick of status was effort and not rank. And so, at one and the same time amused and intimidated by the power and the talent of this woman in their midst, in their canteen they might say, 'Aren't we good enough, Sarit? Aren't you going to tell us about the intrigues of your love life?'

A few of her fellow surgeons had spent some leisure time in her company. In the spring and summer they all chipped in and shared a sleek white sailboat on Lake Michigan. But still they did not feel that they knew her and they were both fascinated and infuriated by her impenetrability.

On the phone that Sunday morning Sarit asks, 'So, Lor, what's the great surprise? He's proposed?'

'No.'

'You've proposed to him?'

'Not yet.'

'So?'

'Ever had your palm read?'

'You're nuts.'

'Sure am, babe. I got you a belated birthday gift . . . A session with a palm reader.'

Sarit at first is silent. She sighs. She says, 'Lauren you're a crazy woman . . .' And then she laughs and adds, 'Anyway, if you felt the urge to get me something you could've bought me some of that stuff you smoke.'

'Now listen, babe,' says Lauren. 'Take me seriously. This isn't just some hokey-cokey nonsense. This woman is more than a clairvoyant. She's an Indian palmist. She's studied for years. I've been and I . . .'

Sarit interrupts her. 'Where did you get this lunatic idea?'

'I went. I didn't tell you. I thought you'd find it ridiculous.

You're so . . . well . . . practical. But she was fabulous, Sairit. It was like being in another world I swear.' And then, pleading almost, she says, 'I'm dying to know what you make of her . . . Even the celebs go to her. Her name's Mona by the way.'

Sarit pushes her newspaper aside. She says, 'Cut the sales talk, Lor. You won't persuade me with the celebs. Don't you think we see enough of them?'

Lauren laughs. She says, 'We do. That's true. But please go, Sairit . . . *Please*. It's so much fun. It'll do you good. What do you have to lose?'

'An hour of my life,' she says, and holding the phone between her chin and her ear she walks towards the kitchen with her mug and her plate in her hand.

And Lauren says, 'Do it, Sairit. For me. For you. Go on.'

Despite the levity of the subject Sarit sighs into the phone. 'OK. I'll do it, Lor,' she says. 'If you insist . . . Oh and by the way . . . thanks for the thought.'

'You will? You'll go?' Lauren asks, squeaking almost.

'Yep,' she says, 'I'll do it.'

'Great,' she says, 'I'm sooo psyched . . .' A pause and then, 'But what's up with you? You don't sound all that good.'

The tall brown package stands still only half unwrapped propped up against the white cupboards in the corner of the kitchen. On top of the counter in Hebrew script lies the note that went with it. It reads, 'I was helping your father sort through some paintings in the basement. I'm sending this to you on impulse. Didn't think he'd notice if one went missing for a while. I hope you're doing well, Sarit. Love as always, Dani.'

And now to Lauren on the phone, Sarit says, 'I'm fine, Lor . . . absolutely fine.'

'You sure?'

'I'm sure.'

'Well then . . . I've already made the appointment with Mona for you.'

35

'Don't be ridiculous . . . You're incorrigible.'

'That's a big word for a foreigner,' Lauren says. 'What's it mean?'

'Look it up,' Sarit says and then, 'So what's the bottom line, Lor?'

'You're going this afternoon at three.'

A moment's silence. Sarit shaking her head, having second thoughts, then saying, 'Why on earth would you tell me at the last minute?'

'Because she's just called me. She had a cancellation.'

'And what if I said no?'

'I'd threaten to call in sick on Monday and you'd have to do Mrs Horowitz's chin without me.'

'Aah,' Sarit says, 'that's done it. Give me this guru's address.'

Mona lives in Wicker Park on the opposite side of town to Sarit. An area of Chicago that is home to ethnicity and diversity, to urban grit and inspiration, to aspiring artists, sculptors, writers and musicians. Sarit dresses in her old jeans, her trainers, her white wollen polo neck and her sheepskin. She runs her fingers through her short black well-cut hair and makes her way to Mona's house.

Sarit feels alive in Wicker Park. When she drives her old black beetle through its messy streets, with their tall, thin grey and red-brick buildings, with their offbeat run-down shopfronts, with their ethnic restaurants and cafés, she feels different from the way she feels in Lincoln Park. She is drawn to the coloured graffiti on the walls, to the reggae blaring from under the arms of black men in rainbow knitted hats, to the jazz being played by scruffy hopefuls on street corners. Wicker Park brims with the sights and sounds of creativity. The place is genuine and on the edge – not really an area of the city in which a plastic surgeon far removed from the underworld of art might set up home.

Mona's narrow red-brick house is next to a Lebanese restaurant. She buzzes Sarit in and through the intercom she asks her to wait in the tiny downstairs hallway. The carpet is a petrol blue and the walls are a lemon colour. Not the way Sarit had envisaged the home of a palmist. She had imagined it would be heavier, darker, more oppressive. Sitting there, she wonders if her patients feel this way, if they too sense the weaving of nerves and excitement in the pit of their stomachs as they sit waiting for their first consultation.

On the small round table next to her is a photocopied article in a plastic folder. The title is 'In the palm of your hand'. Sarit has begun to read it when Mona calls for her to come upstairs.

The palmist is in black. Black leggings and a thin black V-neck sweater. She wears rings and bangles of engraved Indian gold and a red chiffon scarf tied in a knot above her head that holds back the long, straight black hair. On her forehead, dead centre, a little above the line of her eyebrows, is a perfect blood-red circle. Sarit cannot help but think that in a different setting a woman like Mona would have complained to her that her chin was too prominent, that her lips were too thin and her eyes were too deep-set. That between her eyelids and her brows there was far too little space and that her nose was far too long. Sarit looks at her and thinks that she is beautiful.

'Would you like a coffee?' Mona asks. Her accent is Indian and heavy. She shakes her head a little as she speaks.

'Yes,' says Sarit.

'Black?'

'Yes.'

'No sugar, right?'

'Right.'

Sarit wonders briefly how Mona could have known that she likes her coffee strong and black.

The sitting room in which Sarit waits, with its high ceilings and its large sash windows, ought to be light and airy. But with the white sunlight that now pours in, half blinding her, comes a fine layer of dust, so that wherever Sarit looks, in front of her eyes there is a mist.

She doesn't notice Mona has come back until she is sitting next to her on the low red sofa, until she puts the gold-leaf china coffee cup on the low table in front of Sarit and says, 'Please take off your watch.' She takes off her silver sports watch. She lays it on the table.

Mona's opera singer voice comes from some place beneath her ribcage. Her scent is that of lemon and tangy spices. 'I draw from a mixture of old Indian systems of palmistry . . .' she says and taking both of Sarit's hands in hers she adds, 'Now let me see, I think, as you are right-handed, this is where I'll start.'

With her dark-skinned fingers she smoothes Sarit's palm. She lifts her hand as though it were a separate entity, as though it doesn't belong to the rest of her body. She takes it with her, leans back to look at it and runs her blood-red fingernail across the middle of the three most pronounced curves.

'*Dhan rheka* . . . the head line,' she says, 'begins here . . . you see the fleshy part here under your thumb. This padded part. We call that Lower Mars . . . And at the top here it's separated from this line . . . the heart line . . . the *jeevith rheka* . . .' She purses her thin red lips. She says, 'Now let me see. It looks like you're not easily swayed when you make decisions. Even if the people around you question what you are doing, even if they think it is pointless for you to carry on, you will follow your own path . . . You have always been determined, no? When you have an idea in mind. Am I right? I am sure you were like that even as a child, weren't you? Sarit, do you remember?'

And Sarit had said, 'Ima, Ima, I'm going to make Abba better. He's sad today.'

They are walking, the child and her mother, hand in hand back from the kibbutz schoolhouse uphill to the dining room. They walk slowly because of the heat. The grass is brown in patches because there has been less rain this year than normal, but still they can hear the water fall into the River Hatzbani, and the trees of the Galilee, the planes, the laurels and the cypress trees alongside them, are still green though it is the height of summer. Sarit and Gabriella are both in white shorts and red T-shirts. Mother and daughter matching each other, walking together, laughing and joking together till Sarit, mixing Hebrew and English, says again, '*Abba nire kolcah atzuv ha yom* . . . My Abba looks so sad today. I want to make him smile.'

'I don't think you will today, Sarit. There are some days when Abba doesn't feel like smiling.'

'I can. I can make him smile. I know I can.' She has let go of her mother's hand now and even in the heat she is dancing up the gravelled hill that is covered with a thin layer of black dust and she is singing, making up a silly tune and singing to herself and to her mother, 'I can make him smile. I can make my Abba smile.'

Her mother chases after her, swoops her up in her arms and runs a little way with her, sweating and laughing. Breathless at the top of the hill she puts Sarit down. She says, 'Come, let's go and eat. We need to put a little bit of flesh on you, you skinny bean.'

They are sitting in the dining room, next to each other, eating plaited bread, chickpeas, radishes, chopped cucumber and tomatoes. For Sarit, this is a treat. This lunch in the grown-ups' dining room with Gabriella. Normally at midday the children eat in the kibbutz children's house, but once a week, when their mothers finish work early, they join them in the canteen where the grown-ups sit on wooden benches at long tables.

The room is huge, the ceilings high, the acoustics those of a music hall, so that when between mouthfuls Sarit calls out, 'I can make my Abba laugh today,' several of the kibbutzniks turn to look at her and smile.

The woman with the cropped grey hair on the other side of Sarit talks over the child's head to Gabriella. She says, 'Gaby, is Max having a bad day?'

'Tomorrow will be better, Dalia,' Gabriella says. 'We have to be positive.'

Sarit turns to look at her mother then. She has inherited her white skin, but not her eyes or her hair. Because of her blonde hair and her light-green eyes Gabriella is used to people asking her, 'Gaby, are you really a Jew? And so blonde? A Jewish nurse? The Jews don't make that many nurses.' Even Max had been curious about that when they first met. He had asked her that while she, a kibbutz volunteer, in her white overall, was pulling a nail from his sole in the wooden shack that in 1960 had still served as the kibbutz medical room. The question 'Are you really a Jew?' still makes Gabriella smile and she answers always, 'Yes, I am. We Americans just have brighter skin and whiter teeth than you Europeans.'

She remembers saying that to Max as she held his foot in her hand and she recalls too how his thin and serious face had broken into a smile and he had asked her then, 'So what brought you here to us?'

And, the tweezers between her fingers, not for a moment taking her eyes from Max's sole, she had said, 'My parents would have wanted this for me. My father died when I was small and I lost my mother three years ago. She dreamt of coming here to live. So I suppose I'm doing it for her . . . and,' she says, as the tweezers prick the skin of his foot, 'and I just wanted to feel at home. Amongst my own people.'

Now in the canteen as Gabriella ladles chickpeas, chopped cucumber and tomato on to her plate, Dalia says to Gabriella, 'What work has Max been doing this week?'

'He's been planting in the orange groves.'

'Is he digging?'

'Yes . . . I keep telling him, Dalia, he should refuse when they ask him to do work like that. He should tell them he will pick or he will irrigate, but digging is not such a good idea for Max.'

Gabriella's voice does not often sound heavy. So that now when it does, Sarit feels its weight and tugs at her mother's sleeve. 'Ima, why shouldn't Abba dig? Everybody else's Abba digs.'

'Yes, Sarit. But digging is not such a good job for your Abba to do.'

'Why not, Ima? Why?'

And Dalia, on Sarit's other side says, 'Abba did that job for a long time, Sarit. In Germany when he was no more than a boy. He didn't like it at all. Now it's time for him to do something else.'

'What did he dig?'

'He helped dig graves, Sarit,' says Dalia.

The child turns to her mother. 'What's a grave, Ima?'

For a moment Gabiella thinks. Then she says, 'It's the hole in the ground where they put people when their bodies are dead. Now eat your lunch, Sarit . . . We'll talk about it later.'

Sarit feels rather as she felt when her mother told her about loving. She knows she has been told something of great importance, but like the tail of the kibbutz cat and the grasshoppers she tries to catch on the porch outside her house, the idea is just beyond her reach. So, her mouth still full, she turns to Dalia and says, 'Well, if Abba doesn't want to dig in the fields he can paint.'

'Yes, of course he can,' says Dalia. 'Your father is a wonderful artist, but he has to do a different kind of work on the kibbutz as well. We all have to work together.'

Sarit still wants to understand about the digging that her father did in Germany. She's going to ask him. She decides that on the way home after lunch. She's thinking about it, quiet beside her mother, when Gabriella says, 'Sarit, don't ask Abba about the digging, please.'

'Why not?'

'Because you are too young to understand these things properly. You will know one day. Anyway, sweetheart, you said you wanted to make him laugh today. I don't think that's such a good way to do it.'

'I know. I know how I will do it,' she says, pulling at her mother's hand, letting go then, when Gabriella cannot keep up, and running alone towards her parents' house. Running past the huge grey stone sculpture of the Queen of Sheba on a camel on her way to Jerusalem. The Queen of Sheba who has no arms. Often Sarit would stop and touch the cool stone, craning her neck, looking upwards at the Queen's stony face, marvelling at the way she seemed to have tiny diamonds in her body when the sun shone. But today she has no time for that. She waves at the sculpture, shouts out, 'Hello,' and races along the muddy path, towards the three simple rooms with the tiny kitchen and the tiny shower room in the flat-roofed house that stands under the parasol of the laurel trees. She runs inside, not waiting for her mother. She doesn't need a key. On the kibbutz everyone leaves their doors open. Her father says it's so that all the kibbutzniks can poke their noses through the front door into their neighbours' business. Sarit finds that idea really funny. She knows she has a long nose with a bump just like her father's, but the idea of a nose long enough to reach the door of her friend Dani's house next door really makes her laugh.

She rushes over to her easel that stands next to Max's. She used to sit on a small chair at a small easel next to him. So that when they worked together she would have to look up at him and he down at her. She hated that and she had said that if they didn't give her an easel like Abba's she didn't want to paint one more picture. She really had to make a big fuss because then, in the late sixties, when Sarit was still small, on the kibbutz it was never just a question of 'I want' or 'I need'. It was never just a question of the child convincing his parents. Every important purchase made was a collective one, every decision was a collaborative one, discussed by the kibbutz board members. They had sat there, a group of men and women, in their muddy overalls just back from their work in the fields, smoking roll-ups, drinking strong black coffee, considering, leafing through a pile of Sarit's drawings that Max had brought to them. And though money was tight, when they looked at her work they had begun to nod. All of them. And around the room the word, '*Kisharon. Kisharon, kisharon* . . . talent, talent, talent,' had fluttered and flapped its wings, batting them against the walls for attention. The word *kisharon*, spoken by the board members in a loud whisper as if they were talking of something both exciting and dangerous at once.

A week later Sarit had run towards her parents' room. By the door she had skidded to a halt. And she had gasped at what she saw there. She had stood and stared in awe at the matching easel in light-brown wood that stood next to her father's. She will not forget that moment in her life. She will not forget the taste of the excitement on her tongue or the heat of the emotion in her cheeks. She will bury the image, of course, but from time to time, when by accident she touches it, the memory of the joy will threaten pain.

On the day that her father has been digging, Sarit climbs quickly up on to the high chair and she reaches for the brightly coloured wax crayons. She knows that he will be back in a short while, so she sketches fast. She knows not to press the wax hard against the paper as the other children do. She knows too that she must tell her story quickly and that there is no time for drawing in the details of eyes and mouths and noses. So in orange she sketches two easels, with two figures beside them. The figures next to the easels are at the same level, though the smaller of the two is sitting on a high chair while the other is standing. By the time her father walks into the room Sarit is drawing his right arm. He comes up behind her, puts his hands on her shoulders. He is dirty from the digging. His face is dark. The child turns round to look at him, says nothing, watches him, waits for him to comment on her work, all the time unaware that she is struggling, as though treading water, holding her breath almost, as we do throughout our lives, waiting for the approval, the admiration of our parents. For without their understanding and their acceptance of our essence we are orphans. But with it, with their blessing, we will not be orphaned even when they die.

The mud on Max's face has already dried in the sun. Around his mouth it begins to move a little when he sees what his daughter has drawn. She watches as the dark mud cracks into a smile and her heart leaps. Her father reaches for one of her wax crayons next to her easel and begins to add his art to hers. Not until he has almost finished drawing the star of congratulations on the bottom right-hand side of the page does Max realise that the crayon he is using is yellow. The thick yellow star on the paper. The yellow star on his right arm. On his sleeve. Sarit sees her father pulling at his sleeve at the top of his right arm, muttering something in German. '*Nein ich bin kein Jude . . . Es muss ein Fehler sein Diese Jacke gehört meinem Schulfreund. Die ist nicht meine Jacke. Nicht mein Stern . . .* No, I'm no Jew. It must be a mistake. This is my school friend's jacket. It's not my jacket. Not my star. Not mine. It must be a mistake . . .' And Max is pulling at his mud-caked sleeve now, pulling at the yellow star that isn't there and calling out in German, '*Nicht meine Jacke. Nicht mein Stern . . .* Not my jacket, not my star.'

And Sarit is shouting at him, 'Abba, what's wrong? I don't know what you're saying. You were smiling before, Abba. I made you smile. Made you . . . made you . . . Abba, Abba, Abba . . .' and the child too begins to sob.

Sarit feels a hand on her right arm. She hears Mona saying, 'You look pale, Sarit . . . Are you all right?'

'Oh er . . . yes, yes. I'm OK. I'm fine . . . Really I am.'

'Let me get you some water.' And Mona stands up, walks over and parts the curtain made of strands of coloured beads that separate the living room from the kitchen. Sarit closes her eyes and takes a few slow, deep yoga breaths. She reaches her hands back to massage her own shoulders. Then she puts the hand that Mona has been reading on her lap in front of her and stretches out her fingers.

Sarit notices when Mona comes back that her feet are bare, that she wears a tiny gold ring on her little toe and that her toenails are painted a blood-red colour that mirrors the circle, the *bindi*, on her forehead.

As Mona sits back down she says, 'The head line . . . the line that I've been looking at, can also tell me many things about your work and your professional orientation. In your case' – and she lifts Sarit's hand from her lap – 'there is a great overlapping between the head line and the heart line. I see so much creativity here.'

Sarit sits quite still, composing herself, heady with Mona's spicy scent and the journey of her mind. And Mona asks, 'Do you consider yourself a creative person, Sarit?'

'No. No, not especially. Not at all, in fact. I'm not sure if I'm supposed to tell you anything about myself but I'm a scientist . . . well, a doctor.' She does not lift her grey eyes as she speaks.

'Surprising. Very surprising,' Mona says. 'Then your artistic talent must be untapped . . . because the lines, you know, they rarely lie to me. Look, look,' she says, tracing a groove on Sarit's hand, 'you see the way your heart line forks, the way it branches off twice from the main head line . . . These are signs of an artist's creativity. You could be a writer or a composer I sup-pose . . . but no, that just isn't what I read here . . . not at all.' She looks up. She says, 'Drink some more coffee, please, Sarit. I want to be able to read from the markings on the inside of your cup later.' And then, moving away from Sarit, crossing her legs lotus-style on the deep sofa, Mona shakes her head and says, 'I just can't get away from the creativity when I look at your hand. I can see it in your heart line too. It's the sort

45

of creativity that ties you to other people.'

For a moment, just a moment, Sarit Kleinmann loses herself. Her tough, clear-headed, rational self. For a second she forgets that Mona is no professional, that she is no more than a palm reader, in whom she cannot possibly believe. And talking to her as though she were a fellow medic or a psychologist, her tone almost aggressive, Sarit says, 'What do you mean it ties me to others? In which way exactly?'

Mona gives a half-smile. This is the point that she waits for in these palm-reading sessions. This moment of recognition from these high-powered cynics as they sit there in her living room. And now to Sarit she says, 'I don't know in which way exactly . . . I can't read as precisely as that. But I think your creativity has bound you with someone in the past, caused you complications, perhaps even heartache, and from the way it looks here, in the future it might do the same. How can I put it, Sarit? Your talent is not meant to be just a private affair. It seems to belong to the outside world,' she says and, looking down at her client's hand, she goes on. 'The heart line, the *jeevith rheka* . . . this one here . . . and the head line have hardly any space between them on your hand . . . do you see that?' She lifts Sarit's hand up away from the dazzle of the sunlight that pours through the leaded windows. And her fingers, her coffee-coloured fingers, lie over Sarit's white hand. A game, a dance of hands in the misty sunlight of the afternoon. 'You see, Sarit. Look here . . .' she says. 'What this means, I think, is that what is important for your head is also important for your heart. Your talent and the affairs of your heart cannot be separated from one another.'

And all of a sudden when Mona says that, when she says, 'Your talent and the affairs of your heart cannot be separated from one another,' Sarit no longer wants to hear this woman, this stranger, sitting there lotus-style with her chipped blood-red nail polish, reading her life, leafing through its pages as if she knew its denouement for certain. Sarit shifts position. She wants to leave. She takes a deep breath and in her mind she says, 'That was really interesting, Mona. Thanks. And now I have to go,' but out loud Sarit utters not one word, so that when Mona clears her throat and in her deep and husky voice begins to talk again, Sarit sighs, sinking deeper into the sofa, knowing that until she has heard the end of this chapter at least, she will be unable to move from where she sits.

From the table Mona picks up a large magnifying glass with a mother-of-pearl handle and a silver surround, and she lifts Sarit's palm and brings it closer to her face. She says, 'I want to have a closer look at the area around your life line . . . These short lines that you see . . . the ones here, like half-rings, above and below your life line,' she says, tracing them with a tapered nail, 'these lines show the influence of your parents in your life . . . The maternal line is here, beneath the life line, the paternal line is above it . . . This one. Now let's see. Your maternal line is strong . . . See . . . and then it fades out. And the paternal line . . . now let's see.' Under the magnifying glass she looks closer. 'The paternal line is strange on your hand, Sarit. See . . . the way it almost cuts into your palm all the way along, but then there's this complete break in the middle of it . . . And it joins here with your life line. Look. See how they cut each other up . . . Come, Sarit, look through the glass and see it.' She lifts Sarit's wrist, puts the magnifying glass in her left hand, tells her to bring it closer to her palm. Sarit sees the bracelets engraved in her skin at the base of her wrist, the rings engraved at the base of her fingers, the branches and the forks that spread from the curves, and in the centre of her palm she sees the faint lines that, when she screws up her eyes, seem again and again to make the letter N. She sees the little chains and crosses at the start of her life line.

So engrossed is she in the map of her palm that she sees through the mother-of-pearl magnifying glass that when Mona says, 'The chains and the crosses that you see can often mean emotional trauma,' Sarit hardly hears her.

She is engrossed and caught up now in the pattern, the sketch of her life on her palm, studying the lines as though she were peering at the lines on a leaf. A faded, withering summer leaf, already crispy at its edges. A leaf that all of the children in her class were asked to copy, drawing its patterns in pencil, sitting in rows at their little desks next to one another.

'Yours is the best,' Dani says to Sarit. 'I'm the best at Maths, but you're the best at drawing. My leaf is awful. I can't do it.'

'Sh, I'll help you,' and she leans over to the desk pushed right up next to hers. 'I've finished mine,' she says. 'Rivka won't notice if I do yours.'

'Sarit, why are doing Dani's drawing for him?'

'Because . . . because I want to.'

Their elbows are touching as they work. The children are concentrated now. They have run since the early morning in the fields and alongside the river. They have picked up the catkins, the black avocados and the green grapefruit that have fallen too early from the trees. They have smelt lime and mint and eucalyptus leaves. They have scratched their ankles on nettles and brambles, and grazed their wrists on rose bush thorns and now they must leave the midday heat and settle down to work in the cool dark schoolhouse.

'Whose is the best drawing?' one of the children asks the teacher.

'They are all good. There is no best. The veins on all the leaves tell a story.'

And Dani calls out to the teacher, 'You know there is a best. Sarit's drawings are always the best.'

'But that doesn't mean the others aren't good, Dani. We all know that Sarit will be an artist. She already is. It's not right to compare everyone else's work with hers.'

Sarit is excited when Rivka says that she's an artist. When school is over and the other children go to eat, she says she has to go to her house to fetch something, but she runs instead towards the medical room that says *ACHOT* (NURSE) in red letters on the door. Sarit bursts in while Gabriella is looking down a fat woman's throat. She knows she's not allowed to disturb her mother while she's working unless it's very important, but she thinks that what Rivka said about her being an artist must be something *really really* important. And Ima has always said you should talk about the important things, the things that make you very happy or very sad, instead of holding them inside you till they make your tummy hurt.

Sarit knows that her Abba is a real artist, even though he's a digger and a fruit picker too. And Abba must be important because a man with a shiny red car came to take some of his paintings away to Jerusalem and Tel Aviv to hang them on the walls. So if Abba is important because he's an artist then she must be important too and what Rivka just told her must surely matter to Ima as much as holding down someone's tongue with a wooden stick, telling them to say 'Ah' and peering down their throat.

At the door of the medical room, lisping, Sarit shouts out, 'Rivka says I'm an artist, Ima.'

'Sarit, please go out of here and close the door. We will talk about it later.'

'But this is a big thing. You said I should tell you big things.'

'Go out, please, Sarit, and shut the door.'

'No, I won't.'

Gabriella excuses herself from the fat woman with the open mouth. She takes her daughter firmly by the wrist and walks her over to a blue plastic chair in the hallway beneath a diagram of the human body, beneath a blend of art and science. 'You mustn't disturb me when I'm working. I've told you that before, Sarit. You can wait for me out here and we'll talk about it when I'm finished. There is a time for everything.'

For the rest of the afternoon Sarit sulks. She bites her lip. She fights the tears that smart in her eyes. She doesn't want to talk about being an artist any more. She doesn't even want to be an artist any more. Not now. Not ever.

In the evening Gabriella says, 'Come, Sarit. Tell Abba what Rivka said.'

'No.'

'Come on.' Her mother tickles her side. Sarit tries not to laugh, but she can't help herself. Not just because of the tickling, but because Gabriella's laugh and her sense of fun are so infectious. 'Tell Abba . . . Come on.' And speaking for her daughter, urging her to join in, Gabriella begins, 'Rivka says . . .' She waits for Sarit to finish the sentence, but the child purses her lips and shakes her head so Gabriella continues, 'Rivka says? Come on, what does she say about you, my Sarit?'

'No, no, Ima.' She pushes her mother's arm. 'I'm not saying.'

'Sarit,' says Max, 'tell me, please.'

Sarit turns to her father and says nothing. She just stands there in silence, avoiding her father's gaze, looking not at his thin frame or his face, but down at his wrist, adding up the green numbers. Six and four and three and . . .

'Tell me, Sarit,' he says.

'Rivka says I will be an artist.'

Her father doesn't often hug her. When he does she sometimes sees how he has tears in his eyes when he pulls away. She finds that really silly, because only children are supposed to cry. She doesn't tell him what she thinks, though, because she doesn't want to upset him even more and she knows that she is supposed to look after Abba. He is thinner than her friends' fathers and even though his hair is jet-black there are more lines on his forehead and round his eyes. She thinks that one day, when he is old, his face will look like a leaf. One day she'll practise drawing it.

Now Max holds his hand out to his daughter and says to her, 'Come on, Sarit. Come for a walk with Abba,' and then in German that she has learnt from him to understand, '*Komm, mein Kind, komm.*'

Down the half gravel, half sandy slope to the green of the

riverside. Down to the river, where they lean over together to look at the circles and the ripples that the fish make in the water. And Max, as if talking to an older child, following his stream of consciousness, says, 'There was almost nothing here when we came, Sarit. Just the sand and the earth and the water from the falls and the River Jordan. We grew everything. We built everything. Imagine that. I built my own easel out of pieces of wood . . . It took me weeks. We had to have every-thing brought in by ship. There was no milk and honey here like they promised. . . . We grew as much of our own food as we could at first. But it was hard to keep the ground fertile enough. You don't know how lucky you are, Sarit, to build your life here without a struggle. To know from the start where you belong, where you will always be. Do you know how lucky you are, Sarit? Do you promise Abba that you will never leave this place? Do you promise that you'll always paint just like Abba does and just like my Abba did?'

'Promise. Promise. Promise. Abba, can I go swimming now?' She is pulling her clothes off already, saying, 'Abba, come, let's go swimming. Come on. Come on. Did you see that fish jump out up from the water? Look, look . . .' And naked, save for her underwear, she begins to tug at her father's shirt. 'Please, Abba, please. Let's swim, let's swim,' she says jumping up and down on the spot.

A little further up the bank an old man sits with his son. He waves to Max and to Sarit, then turns back to look out towards the water, to think about the past, his line cast ahead of him in the river.

And Mona says to Sarit, 'This line . . . you see this one . . . the fate line is long enough to cross all the other lines. Western palmists think it's just a minor line, but I see it as a major one. It's the line that talks of change and life choices . . . Let's see, Sarit . . . it's not only your accent that tells me you have changed countries. Look, you can see it here. There have been dramatic changes in your life. Your fate line is frayed and broken. It disappears when it crosses the head line. To me it looks as if the natural path of your life is blocked in some way.'

She lifts Sarit's empty gold-leaf coffee cup from the table and peers at the shapes of the brown stains on the inside of the cup. The silence is thick with dusty sunlight. At least a minute passes, maybe two, before Mona speaks. She says, 'What I am reading is that somehow you are not free. That at this point you are headed towards the road that is meant for you, but you are not yet there. It seems as if your path has been obscured. Do you have any idea what I'm talking about, Sarit? Am I making any sense?'

The path to the fields was narrow and overgrown. They each carried their easels under one arm. In the other hand they carried their oil paints, their brushes, their palettes in a plastic bag. The way was not light, though now and then the sun flirted with them through the leaves of the trees and of the undergrowth, and though the air was mild it threatened cold. Only at the far end of the path could they see the open endless spaces of the yellow and green November fields. They chose their spot. They set their easels down, unravelled their canvases and began to paint.

Max said to her, 'You will be a bigger artist than me. You will see, Sarit. I will teach you to be better than I am. You will never abandon your genius, will you?'

Engrossed in what she's doing she doesn't answer Max and so he says again, 'Sarit, I asked you for a promise.'

'What are you talking about, Abba?'

She wanted to paint green that day. The green of the fields, the rust, the burgundy and the ochre of the leaves. Max wanted her to paint black. Shiny black. Dull black. Grey black. Any black, but always black. She was only ten but he said, 'There were doctors and lawyers and judges there. It was the camp for the élite. I was a child myself. Not so much older than you, but I looked older. So I dug their graves you know. The officers shouted, "*Schnell . . . Bewegung.*" The men were naked and their heads were shaved. They held guns to their backs and their necks till they climbed into the graves. Then they stamped on their heads with their shiny black boots.'

Sarit was lucky to have Max teach her, here outside in the coloured fields with the wind on her face. She was lucky in a way to have him guide her hand, to have him tell her how to hold her brush. But his stories always changed the colour of her work. So that her work was his as much as it was hers. She hadn't noticed that before, when she was smaller, but now the others would tell her. They would say, 'Sarit, you are a prodigy, the kibbutz prodigy, but you use too much grey and black for a young girl.'

A pattern of black birds flew towards them as they stood there in the field and Max said, 'There is so much beauty in this place, Sarit. For that at least I am happy.' She takes the largest brush. A thick and furry brush that she dips into the grey oil paint. She puts the brush to the canvas and without knowing it, for the artist at ten is unable still to understand her own work, alongside her father, and as if they were the birds that had passed above them, the child begins to paint the thick and heavy strokes of strife.

Next to her now, still on the red sofa, she hears the clink and jangle of Mona's thin gold bangles. The palmist moves her neck, stretches and, Indian-style, as she speaks she shakes her head. She says, 'I think, Sarit, I've lost my touch. My picture of you and the picture of who you say you are just seem so entirely different.'

SEVEN

In the dead of night Sarit was the only child still awake. She had pretended to be asleep, of course, like she pretended every night. When the night guard for the kibbutz children's house, in shorts, barefoot and huge from where she lay, walked between the low beds to check that all the children were settled, Sarit kept her eyes shut and imitated the puffy night-time breathing of the other children. As the guard walked towards the door she prayed that he would leave it slightly open, because she hated the pitch black. She hated it more than she hated dresses and more than she hated vegetables. It made her heart race and her head reel. She wasn't afraid in the same way as the other children, though. She wasn't afraid of wicked men or witches. She wasn't afraid of ghosts or of monsters. And she knew for certain that she wasn't a coward. She was sure of that because she'd heard the grown-ups saying it. Over and over again they'd said, 'Sarit, you're a brave girl. Such a brave girl,' even before she understood what brave meant.

No, Sarit was afraid of the dark for different reasons. She was afraid because of how much she needed the light. Because she and the light had a secret. Because of the light she had stopped feeling left out when the other children's mothers sat on their beds and read them stories before they kissed them goodnight and left them to sleep in the children's house. There was always one mother who would say, 'Sarit, come sit with us. Come and listen to our story.' But she didn't want to sit on Joel's bed with his mother and listen to Joel's story. She didn't want to have to get out of her own bed and sit on top of someone else's sheets instead of underneath her own. It was just that if she stayed in her bed she could lie there and use the voices of the mothers reading stories as background music while she thought her own thoughts. She could think about the light and about how she hoped that later on the guard with the bare feet and the hairy toes would remember to leave the door open. She hoped against hope that tonight he would be the one on duty, because the one who wore sandals almost always closed the door behind him and left her there in the pitch black. When that happened Sarit lay there and fought hard with the night. She clenched her teeth and she pursed her lips and she managed almost always to stop the tears from escaping.

She had tried once to climb out of her bed, to creep over to the door, to stand on her tiptoes and to reach for the handle. And she had done it. The door had swung open and the night lights that protected the kibbutz had flooded into the room, waking the other children and alerting the guard on his chair at his table outside in the hot night air. He had turned round towards her, he had stood up, he had scooped her up in his strong arms, stroked her hair and carried her straight back to bed. Then he had sat on the edge of the bed and whispered to her, '*Kara mashehu*? Is something wrong? Do you feel sick? Do you want me to go and fetch your mummy?' Sarit shook her head and even in the middle of the night, even then, she was clear-headed enough to think that the guard was being really silly and that he must have got her mixed up with one of the other children if he could ask a question like that. If he could ask her, 'Do you want me to go and fetch your mummy?' She always got more goodnight kisses than the other children. Their mothers would bend low or kneel down next to her. They would kiss her forehead or stroke her cheek, they would say something about one of the paintings on the wall above her bed or about her long eyelashes and Sarit would smile with her mouth but not with her heart.

In the beginning she had been scared to fall asleep in case

she didn't wake up till the morning when the light would no longer belong only to her. What she needed to do didn't work in the morning. She had tried it once but she soon realised that there was nothing special about light in the daytime and so now she waited for the nights. She waited till the stories and the goodnight kisses were over. She waited till she had slept a little and woken with the guard's gentle turn of the door handle. And the reason she was no longer scared to fall asleep at the same time as the other children was because she knew for sure that in a second when the guard walked in she would be awake. She had taught herself how. All she had to do was to sing before she fell asleep. She didn't sing out loud of course, she didn't want the other children to laugh at her, but she sang in her head to the tune of the lullaby her father sang to her on Friday nights when he wasn't feeling quite so bad. Her father's lullaby was all about a child dreaming of shapes and colours but Sarit replaced his words with different ones. In her head she sang, 'Sarit, Sarit, lechi lishon, lechi lishon aval kumi be karov, kumi be karov . . . you can go to sleep, Sarit, but wake up soon. Wake up soon, Sarit.' Her song worked and almost every night when the guard came in she would wake and pretend to sleep.

Tonight she was in luck. The guard with bare feet was looking after the children. He walked around the room, bent down over each child and then moved towards the door. He crouched and he pushed the wedge into the crack between the door and the wooden floor.

Then she heard the last creaks of his feet on the wooden floorboards and he was gone. Yes, he was gone and Sarit lay back and waited. She waited till she could no longer see the shadow of his back through the crack. Then she sat up against the little wooden headboard of her bed and invited the light to come in through the door. She left it alone at first, let it move and stretch itself. She let it dance its own dance on the one bare wall ahead of her. She watched while, without her help, it made its own messy shapes and squiggles. She pretended to the light that it left her indifferent. Because she already knew that if you chased a thing too hard it would elude you and refuse to play your game. She had learnt that from her cat. Well, it wasn't really her cat. On the kibbutz nothing was just yours. Everything was everybody's. The men and women picking apples worked for the women in the laundry room. The women in the laundry room worked for the men and women picking apples. The kibbutz was all about a thing called community. Her kindergarten teacher had told her that again and again. And she had learnt that if she wanted to feel the cat's long grey fur against her ankles she had only to turn her head away and make out that he mattered to her not at all.

And so now, only when she was sure that the light was there to stay, did Sarit begin slowly to make it hers. She half closed her eyes and she began to drag little bits of the squiggles and the circles across and to make her own shapes on the wall in the darkness. She was glad there were no paintings on that wall straight ahead of her bed. They would have got in her way, whereas now, with the white expanse in front of her, she had a blank canvas with which to work.

With her eyes half closed, leaning back in her little bed, with the light on the canvas of darkness Sarit began to paint. She painted a curve for the forehead. She painted long, long hair. The strands of lights against the wall worked well for the hair. She squinted and drew a broad stroke of light across for the mouth and a thin one for the nose. And once she had started nothing could stop her. Even if the guard had closed the door, in her head she would still have seen the lights. She used her lashes as filters and lifted two dancing shafts of light from one place to another to paint the eyes. She lifted her own chin, pointed it upwards, to change the position of the picture on the wall. She lifted the corners of the lips and moved the mouth on the wall first into a smile, then into a laugh.

Yes, she had done it. She had made the painting laugh. She remembered that. How she had been able to make her mother laugh. And Sarit was laughing too now. Laughing together with the painting of lights on the canvas of darkness. The painting of the face that danced and moved on the wall in the blackness ahead of her. The painting that talked to Sarit and played with her and disappeared only when the child in the bed next to Sarit woke and began to cry out for her mother.

EIGHT

On the black tar of the jogging track Sarit ran in her ear muffs and her grey fleece. She ran alongside Lake Michigan, from Navy Pier with its huge multicoloured ferris wheel, past Oak Street beach, past the Hancock building with its triangle tip and the neoclassic brownstones on North Lake Shore Drive. As her white skin reddened and she breathed out the icy air, a game of dominoes played itself with verve around her life.

As she moved, Sarit didn't really have a conscious master plan. She was driven, yes, determined, yes, but more by the minutiae, more by each task than by greater goals. Because the greater goals, the climbing of the professional ladder and the growing of her reputation, were incidental to her, born more of rebellion than of her own truth. And the truth, the path that was meant for her, was so thick with thorns and over-grown with foliage that unaided she would never have been able to see it. There was much, though, that Sarit did see clearly. Within that bigger picture were the smaller practical goals that she viewed with great clarity. She had known the day before when the five-year-old boy walked into the room behind his mother, his head bowed low, clutching the back of her long black dress, how she must work on his disfigured mouth and change it before it disfigured his soul further still. Sarit didn't think in terms of greatness. She didn't think, 'Because of my talent it is for me to help these children.' It was simply a part of what she did with her day. Had she allowed herself to reflect too much or for too long on her life she would have been forced to turn and look behind her. She would have felt more often the digging in of nails and the grasping of fingers that tried to pull her into blackness. A blackness that she hid well both from herself and from others. And so it was that Sarit would rarely allow herself the luxury of being, but only of doing.

Sarit said little to the Spanish interpreter who trailed the boy's mother. Just enough to find out that the child's cleft lip and cleft palate had been poorly operated on in Mexico and that his complications were both speech-linked and aesthetic. When the child would not come forward, Sarit had lifted a yellow bear with a red ribbon round his neck from the chair. She had crept round to the back of the mother and knelt down by the boy with the toy in her hand. At first he kept his face hidden in his mother's skirts. And Sarit didn't push him. She didn't say, 'Come, now, won't you look at me, Stefano?' She crouched instead on the floor and began to tell the story of the bear with the mouth that wasn't quite the right shape. Her tone when she spoke to the children was quite different from that which she used when she spoke to the adults.

The adults came to her only for her skill. With them she had little bedside manner. They would say to one another, 'She's a bit sharp. She's not much into conversation and she can't have more than a few years' experience, but when I saw the way she did Mrs Horowitz's chin I just had to go to her,' or they might say of her, 'If only that Dr Kleinmann would be a little more talkative the whole experience would be more pleasant. But did you see Sara Norman's nose? It's just awesome.' Now, with the yellow bear in her hand, crouching next to the boy, Sarit says, 'Stefano, I want to tell you the story of this bear,' and as she speaks to him her foreign accent grows stronger, as if here with this little boy, telling him a story she can lose herself. 'If you take just a little peek, Stefano,' she says to the child, 'you'll see this bear was born with two halves of his lips that don't quite join together. Just take a quick look. See? Now he's often very sad, because he looks different from all other bears and sometimes he can't talk quite the way they can. And they laugh at him and make him cry and he doesn't want to be with them or play with them any more. But he's special and his mummy wants to help him so she's going to take him to a bear doctor who will make him look and feel better. Don't you think that's a good idea, Stefano?'

The child is still clutching the back of his mother's black woollen skirt, but he's staring at Sarit in awe now. His deformed mouth wide open, his interest piqued, his shame forgotten.

'So, Stefano, tell me, do you think it's a good idea for the bear doctor to help the teddy feel better about things?'

The child nods.

And not yet touching him Sarit says, 'Shall we go over to the bed and undress the bear?'

'Yes,' he says, lisping as Sarit once had. And suddenly he holds out his small dimpled hand to her, allows himself to be led over to the corner of the room. Sarit sits on the carpet by the side of the child, by the makeshift operating theatre, with its table covered in white for the toy to lie on, by the bear dressed as a surgeon and the one dressed as a nurse. And in their world of make-believe Sarit and Stefano lose themselves, though all the time as she talks she is examining the child closely, altering and shaping his cleft lip in her head, moving, lifting layers and flaps of skin, without touching him till the end, till she's sure she's won his trust. And the child is laying the toy down, sitting him up, feeding him, dressing and undressing him, first in his trousers and a red shirt, then in his hospital gown.

This game comes to Sarit so naturally. The child Sarit, kneeling on the floor in her shorts, in the heat, her torso bare. She had dressed and undressed her own bear, talking to herself, talking to her toy. She had said, 'Now, Mummy, I'm going to undress you and put you to bed because you're not well. But you'll get better if I do this. I promise you will. I'm going to put you in Daddy's bed and pull the covers over you. That's right. Now sleep, Mummy, sleep. That's good. It makes you better to sleep. You said that, didn't you, Ima? And when you wake up you'll be alive again. You won't be dead any more. I promise.'

Sarit thinks she is alone in her father's house on the kibbutz, in the bedroom with the orange and blue painting of her parents making love above the headboard. She thinks her father is still in the fields picking oranges or apples, reaching his long skinny arms out to the branches of the trees. She is sure that is what he is doing and so she plays the game with the bear and his clothes and she doesn't hear when Max comes in. She doesn't hear him behind her or feel him listening. She doesn't know of the lump that burns his throat or the tears that burn his eyes. She doesn't see how he shakes his head and strangles a sob, but she does hear him clear his throat and raise his voice. She jumps and turns round and he is shouting at her. Yelling at his daughter, saying, 'You can't. You can't do this, Sarit. You are eight years old. Much too old for this. You should be outside in the fresh air, painting. Not playing these crazy games. Do you hear me?'

She drops her bear on the wooden floor and bows her head and bites her lip.

But the boy, the boy in the surgery with the bear in his arms, lifts his head and smiles at Sarit. 'Can I take him home with me?'

She laughs. She says, 'Yes, Stefano. You can.'

'*No Stefano, no puedes . . .* says his mother in Spanish. '*Tenemos uno en casa.*'

The interpreter, a thin pale shadow of a woman, says to Sarit, 'His mother says he can't take the bear home. He already has one.'

'But, Mom, there's nothing to fix on my bear. He's not broken,' and the child begins to cry.

'He can take the bear home, Mrs Mendez,' says Sarit. The interpreter translates.

The mother, all in black, looks humbled and embarrassed.

She speaks and is translated by the shadow. 'I'm so sorry, Doctor. He shouldn't have asked,' and then, holding on to the back of a chair, pale in her long dress, the woman looks at the interpreter, then at Sarit and says in Spanish, 'I want to say . . . um . . . this is difficult to talk about, but how much will this surgery be? We only have Public Aid. No health insurance. And we . . . well, we won't be able to afford any extra. My husband isn't working now. He's . . .'

'There will be no extra,' says Sarit when she has understood what has been said.

'*No entiendo*,' says the mother. 'I don't understand,' says the interpreter.

'If you decide you want me to work with Stefano you will not be asked for extra payment.'

'But what about the rest?'

'Didn't you hear me? I said there is no problem, Mrs Mendez. Let me tell you what I would do for Stefano.' And she proceeds to talk of cleft lips and growth spurts and bone grafts, not once looking at the interpreter who tries to keep up with her, but with fingers gentle on the face of the child, who trusts her now, Sarit finishes her explanation. She says to the mother through the shadow, 'I'm sorry, I'm running late. You'll have to go now.' She turns her back on Mrs Mendez. She turns her back on the interpreter, but she smiles at the child, she ruffles his loose curls. She says, 'Goodbye, Stefano. Please look after that teddy for me. And make sure you change the bandage on his lip, won't you? That's your part of the deal.'

NINE

Relentless, an animal hungry and in pain, the winter wind howls against Sarit's windows. She sits on the ledge, her arms around her legs. She watches the dark grey water form into white-tipped spikes and throw itself in anger, stabbing the wind breaker and the shores of Lake Michigan. She is grateful to the weather for sensing her mood.

She thinks of the morning ahead and swears aloud, curses herself even for succumbing to Lauren's nagging, for succumbing to a blind date with a doctor. Time and again Lauren has repeated what she said in Kingston Mines: 'You can't be alone any more, Sarit. You just can't. It isn't healthy. It's not a life.'

Sarit no longer knows whether she can or she cannot be alone. Aloneness is her status quo. She seeks neither to alter it nor to maintain it. And her loneliness, that ugly, amorphous form that appears at random and at will, that taunts her sometimes just for a moment or that stays for hours, is not hers to master. Yes, she is the modern world's Proteus, a master of shapes with the vision to mould and alter in her head, the talent to mould and alter in the flesh. And yet this loneliness, this shape, this strange ungainly form eludes her and defies her. Perhaps were she to sit and study it at length she might grasp it better. With her long and skilful fingers she might smooth its rough, scarred skin. But to achieve such a feat she would be forced to look her loneliness in the eye, to stare it in the face, to touch it as she does the faces of the men, the women and the children who come to her. Instead, when it intrudes, she will see only a part of it. She may choose to quell that part alone, or on occasion with some faceless man. As for the rest, with a swipe of the hand she will dismiss it and sometimes, like the man in Kingston Mines in the multicoloured shirt, it will obey and retreat in an instant. When it doesn't, when the loneliness is wilful and insistent, she is forced to carry it around with her as though in a sling or a rucksack. With her, but not within her. It is only when others ask her questions that she has little choice but to unwrap her loneliness and to become enveloped in it.

Her blind date, the doctor Sammy Schwarz, invites her to brunch at Savories, a cosy café that looks like someone's old worn living room, on North Wells Street in Old Town on Sunday morning in the cold and the grey. From Lauren she knows that he's a shrink, funny, kind, divorced and on the lookout. He is not in the conventional sense of the word an attractive man. Pock-marked, with thick glasses, thinning hair, he's an anorak type. But then so is Sarit, though she wears her fleece and her anorak in genuine nonchalance. He sits opposite her in an armchair with no springs. He drinks caffè latte from a cup. She drinks her coffee strong and black. She holds the thick white china mug that warms her hands. Hands that he cannot fail to notice right away. He talks at first of his profession, his child, his ex-wife from whom he is still not quite emotionally detached.

Sarit sighs with relief inside and sits and listens, and all the while she studies the psychiatrist's face and changes it in her mind. She implants his chin with silicone, straightens his nose, smoothes out his brow, fills out his lips and she's beginning to work on the contours of his cheeks when interrupting her he says, 'Women always say it's scary to date a shrink. They think I'll see into their heads. Well, I think it must be scary to date a plastic surgeon. When you go out with men you must look at them and think how you could change their faces.'

Sarit starts, then laughs. She says, 'It's an occupational hazard.'

'So how did you get into to it, then?' he asks. 'Changing faces?'

'Oh, it just happened. Just like that, you know. You choose a path.'

'Come on, Sarit. Plastic surgery doesn't just happen. Where did it come from?'

'A professor at the University of Chicago. He looked at me one day when I was a resident. We were doing the rounds, unpacking sterile bandages by the patients' beds and he said something like, "Amazing hands, Kleinmann. Phenomenal manual dexterity. Ever thought of becoming a plastic surgeon?" It just stayed with me, I suppose . . . It was that or paediatrics. So I decided to mix the two. I did a year in paediatric plastics in Southern California after my surgery training here . . . so I do cleft lips and burns on the kids and cosmetic stuff on the adults . . .' and gulping down a mouthful of coffee she looks at him and, half sarcastic, says, 'There now, you have all the details on me you could possibly want . . . It's your turn. Why the psychiatry?'

He says, 'We'll get to that. We have all day.'

She thinks, 'We don't, you know.'

He asks, 'So is there artistic talent in your family?'

'Artistic? Strange question. I'm a doctor.'

He says, 'It's not such a strange question. You must know that many plastic surgeons are also painters or sculptors . . . I know one whose waiting room is full of his own sculptures . . . and lots of them are great athletes too, though I can't quite work that one out.'

She picks up on the athlete bit. She says, 'I run.'

'Oh?' he says and then, 'So if you're not artistic what is it about plastic surgery that attracts you?'

'My medical side comes from my mother. She was a nurse. American, actually. From here . . . the suburbs. That's why my green card was no problem.'

'So you have dual citizenship?' he asks her.

66

'Yes, but I consider myself a real Yank these days . . . I have an American passport . . .' She looks round for the waitress. She says to Sammy, 'I need more caffeine.'

'Me too,' he says and then, 'You said your mother was a nurse?'

'She died when I was eight.'

'I see. That's tough . . . I'm sorry.' An appropriate silence followed by, 'When did you come to the States?'

'When I was twenty. I did my bachelor's here before med school. I had a great-aunt here. My mother's aunt. In Evanston. I lived with her at first.'

'Tough,' he says again, 'to lose your mother when you're so small. . . . But you have your father still?'

'He's still alive,' she says.

'He must be proud of you.'

'What's there to be proud of ? You mean the fact that I'm a woman and a plastic surgeon?'

'It's harder for a woman to get to where you are and you know it. You have quite a reputation, Dr Kleinmann. They say that you're the best with kids. They also say' – he stops and laughs, revealing smoke-stained teeth – 'that your bedside manner with the grown-ups can be a little brusque.'

She smiles. 'I don't have a bedside manner. I'm not into shmooze.' She's comfortable with Sammy's straight talking. She comes from a place where people say what they mean however harsh. The modern Hebrew language wastes no words. They say 'I want' instead of 'I would like.' They say 'Give me this and give me that' instead of 'Could I please have this or that?' Life in a constant state of vigil has left little room for niceties, so that the pleases and the thank yous are more the exception than the rule and the translation of spoken Hebrew into English can often sound quite rude.

Sarit looks at Sammy Schwarz and she thinks, 'I couldn't do it with him. God, no. But he could be my friend. Yes, I think I'd like him as my friend.'

He looks at her and thinks, 'Sexy, strong but very complicated.'

He says, 'So, Sarit, tell me, is he proud of you?'

'Who?'

'Your father . . . He must tell you all the time. I mean what a thing to be able to say: "My daughter the plastic surgeon."'

She shrugs. A few seconds pass. 'I hear you work with children and young adults too,' she says. And this time when she changes the subject Sammy does not attempt to change it back. He is not a shrink for nothing.

He tells her instead how often he sees young adults who want to change the way they look. Unhappy teenagers and young women sent to him by the more ethical plastic surgeons to unravel their reasons for wanting to remove a piece of this or add a piece of that. Sarit listens and she nods. She says, 'Unless there is a deformity or some severe trauma because of the way they look, I don't like to operate until they're twenty-one. I need to be convinced that there's a pressing psychological need for it and that they really understand what they're asking me to do. It's hard to be sure that their desire to change the way they look isn't just transient. That's why I often send them to a shrink.'

And so Sarit and Sammy sit and chat, the different branches of their profession somehow meshing. He walks her home. Outside her building where North Avenue meets Clark opposite the park he shakes her hand. A more pleasant morning than she might have imagined. For her, nothing more than that. He is intuitive. He knows it and he says, 'I hope we can be friends, Sarit. After all we're almost neighbours.'

'We will,' she says.

She walks inside towards the lift past the huge bald doorman with the coffee-coloured skin. 'Hey there, Doctor,' he says.

She smiles at him.

'That smile,' he says. 'It gets me every time.'

She goes upstairs, back again to her window ledge. She

wants to think about the Sunday morning ambience in Savories. She wants to plan her afternoon. Instead in her head she hears Sammy's voice. Once and then in stereo, he says, 'He must be proud of you? So tell me, Sarit, is your father proud of you?'

'Mr Kleinmann,' says the fat woman in the tiny gallery on a Jerusalem backstreet in her strong French accent, 'you must be so very proud of her.' In front of them on the wall tightly packed with other artists' vibrant colours they had hung another of her father's paintings. Sarit didn't like it much. Before he had wrapped it she had seen it and from where she stood it had looked like stick men in a wire cage piled on top of one another and screaming in black and white with wide open black holes for mouths waiting for food. She didn't tell her father, though. She thought if they had travelled all the way from the kibbutz in Qiryat Shemonah in the north of Israel on the hot, smelly bus where people yelled at one another, held on to pieces of leather above their heads and stuck their elbows in each other's sides, if they had done that just to hang this picture on Madame's wall, then even if she hated it, it must be good. So she sat in silence while her father and Madame unpacked the painting from its brown paper and spoke of the influences in Max's work of Giacometti, of Miró and of Munch.

Sarit took out her crayons and her paper from the bag that Gabriella had packed her and she drew a picture of Madame. Round and fat the way she was with all her chins and dressed in a long green silk tent dress. Sarit was seven at the time and she called a spade a spade. 'Let me see, *mon enfant*,' said Madame. She took the paper from Sarit's hand. She leant back and laughed a belly laugh. She said, 'So, who needs a mirror . . . ? Max Kleinmann. You must be so very proud. This child is talented like you.'

When they left the gallery in the Middle Eastern heat her

father gripped her hand. His palm felt sweaty against hers. He said, 'Sarit, you told Madame she was fat.'

'No, I did not.'

'You did. You told her in your painting . . . But still I'm very proud. You are in your realist stage.'

'What, Abba?'

'Never mind, Sarit.'

She says, 'I want to go to the wall. You know, the big one where people stick little pieces of paper between the stones. Ima told me about it.'

'We have too little time.'

'Please, Abba.'

'Why do you want to go?'

'I want to see it.'

'What for?'

The child is clever. She thinks hard before she speaks. She says, 'When I go home I can draw it or paint it for you and Ima.'

Down hundreds of narrow grey stone steps in her red sundress with her skinny arms and legs next to her father in his baggy grass-stained trousers. Once or twice she stumbles. He catches her arm. Down and down and down, she watches her sandalled feet to stop herself from stumbling, till Max says, 'Look, Sarit. Stop.' She stops. He grips her wrist.

Ahead of them a massive light-grey stone wall that makes her stand stock still and takes her breath away. A wall that from a distance has coloured blobs dancing in front of it. A Lowry painting she will think when later on in life she remembers. Neither she nor her father speaks. She drags him down the steps. Ahead of them on one side of the wall hundreds of men in long black coats and high black hats are swaying backwards and forwards in some sort of ritual dance. On the other side the women, shrouded in scarves and shawls despite the heat, are making the same hypnotic bowing movements.

'What are they doing, Abba?'

'Praying.'

'To whom?'

'To God . . . Come, let's go and see.'

'But you don't think God's there? Do you, Abba? Remember?' She giggles. 'You told me that. And Ima was cross.'

'Sh,' he says. He lifts her in his arms and she feels safe. On the men's side they walk into the enclosure in front of the wall. Max thinks that at seven Sarit is small enough still for it not to be considered immodest if she enters on that side, but a man with a high black hat, long black beard and two thick black sidelocks stares at her and tuts and frowns.

Against her father's bony shoulder she hides her little face, then pointing, she whispers in his ear, 'Silly man with those curly hair things on his face.'

Close to the wall she asks her father, 'Abba, why are these men crying?'

'That's what they do at the wailing wall. They pray and they cry.'

'But what are they crying for?'

'Because of the bad things that have happened in the past,' he says to her and then under his breath, as if to himself he adds, 'Because of the people they've lost.'

'Are you going to cry, Abba?'

'No.'

She watches a wiry little man next to them, sobbing, bent and old, scribbling on a scrap of paper that he folds and folds and sticks into a crack between the white stones of the wall.

Her father sees her looking. He says, 'See. He made a wish. Like you and I do on our birthday when we blow our candles out.'

For a moment, as the idea comes to her, she grips her father tighter. Then in a voice too loud she says, 'Put me down.'

Kneeling on the ground, she opens her satchel, tears a piece of paper from her pad. She crouches down so that close to her

71

the bowing dancing men are huge. She presses hard with the crayon on the paper leaning on her satchel. A minute later she taps her father's leg. 'Take me to the ladies' side.'

They push their way through the men in black round to the entrance of the wall with the veiled and scarved and shrouded women. 'Come on, Abba,' she says, pulling him towards them.

He laughs. He says, 'I can't. They don't let men in there.'

'Then I'm going by myself,' she lisps.

'What for?'

'To put my piece of paper in the wall.'

In a 'let me see it' gesture he holds his hand out to his daughter. She won't give the piece of paper to her father. She holds it far enough away so he can't get at it, but close enough so he can see it and she unfolds it to show him what she's written. In big green letters of wax crayon, with a spelling mistake here, another there, it says, 'God, make Ima better for my birthday.'

Max closes his eyes. He nods at his daughter.

'Abba, wait for me right here,' she says. And before her father can utter his objection she moves away from him towards the wall. He feels his gut wrench. He feels his heart sink. He feels a sense of panic seeing her small figure run from him. Through the wall of crying swaying women she runs to the wall of huge white stones. Most of the cracks are overflowing with tiny pieces of paper crammed in, desperate to find their place, to send their messages to heaven. But on her knees on the ground Sarit finds a clean empty crack almost at the bottom of the wall. She folds her wish again, carefully, neatly, into a minute square, then pushes it back and back till it is lost somewhere amongst the other pleas. Then she runs towards the exit, squeezing between the legs, stockinged in black for modesty even in the heat. Back and back she runs through the sounds of murmured prayer. By the gate, a young guard in green uniform stands upright, his gun slung over his shoulder. She stops by his side, looks around in panic for her father. She shouts, '*Abba, Abba, eifo atah* . . . where are you?' He turns round, walks quickly towards Sarit and picks her up. She touches his face. His rough, wet face. She doesn't ask him, 'Why, what for?' but she says to him, 'Abba, you broke your promise. You said you wouldn't cry.'

He takes her hand. He strokes her hair. 'I'm proud of you, my little one,' he says.

TEN

Independence comes quickly to the leopard cub, the lion cub, the tiger cub. He clings at first, of course, for long enough to learn what he must know. Then he is off alone or with his peers padding through the foliage of the bush, the forest or the jungle. The cub does nothing on his journey in defiance of his parents. He does nothing in rebellion against them and nothing to seek their approval. He does not block himself or damage himself in some silent reaction, be it conscious or sub-conscious. He, unlike us, unlike the sons of mothers and the daughters of fathers, moves easily from dependence to inde-pendence through the shades of browns and greens that are the undergrowth. He, the cub, does not define himself by his history or redefine himself because of it.

'I thought,' says Sammy, 'we could go wander around River North. Look at some of the galleries. They've got some fabu-lous stuff at the moment.'

Sammy Schwarz is Sarit's friend by now. She wants no more than that. And he, sensing that no crusade will win her over, is prepared to offer her his friendship. She is enigmatic enough, interesting enough, talented enough, for him to welcome her as a figure on the edge of his life's canvas, even if she will never be at its centre.

'No, Sam. Interesting idea, but galleries are not my thing.'

'Oh come on, Sarit. You work with your hands. You must be drawn by colour and by beauty.'

'I can take it or leave it to be honest. Sorry, I'm a bit of a philistine. I could handle a movie, though.'

And so in late February's cold and pouring rain, they walk,

the psychiatrist and the plastic surgeon, to Old Town's Music Box in Southport to see an art house movie, a French sub-titled film. He holds up a green and white golf umbrella that does not quite protect the two of them and when they arrive at the cinema she runs her fingers through her hair and with the back of her hand she wipes the drops of water from her face. She had paid little attention when, leafing through the culture section of the *Chicago Reader*, Sammy had said, 'Right, I've chosen something. Some low-budget French movie. Supposed to be great.'

All week it is Sarit who has to lead, so, happy for once to follow, she goes with him and doesn't stop to think about the nature of the film.

Sammy sits there, eats his salted popcorn, lets it spill over the sides of the carton, enjoys the entertainment as he might if it were a lighter film. But she, Sarit, unprepared as she is to be exposed to a story of art and love and love of art, cannot avert her eyes from the screen even for a moment.

Often in past years some object of great artistic beauty has crooked its finger, beckoned to her and threatened to draw her back home. But only later in her nightmares does she acknowledge the lure of it. Only then, at the edge of the sheer drop, does she cry out and stretch her arms across the deep black rift between the rocks, towards her father and the palette he holds out to her.

Never to anyone else nor even during waking hours to herself does Sarit acknowledge the need or the muffled pain. And the sheaths of apparent indifference to the world of art that she wears are so multi-layered that when she says to Sammy or has said to others in the past, 'No, art is not my thing. I'm more the sporty type,' the comment is so practised, so effort-less by now, that even she almost believes it to be the truth. She is the sporty type. Over years that is what she has become and how she has come to think of herself. Sarit the cyclist, Sarit the jogger, Sarit the sailor, the blader by the lake.

Sammy leans towards her, proffers popcorn. He nudges but she doesn't turn. Riveted to the screen, Sarit only shakes her head. And seconds later in her mind she is no longer next to Sammy in the plush seven-dollar low-backed cushioned chair in the oldest art house cinema in town. Instead she is in the high-ceilinged whitewashed room with the actress on the screen. Standing there behind her. Watching the young dark-haired woman in a splattered white shirt before her art. Close enough to see the hairs on her neck, as she waits with her for every brush stroke. Watching her, at first a little more detached, musing, dipping, dabbing, stroking, brushing, drawn into her canvas then, driven by it, at one with it, moving fast now, consumed, all arms and legs winding in and out of one another, in and out of the massive brush strokes, as she grabs a wooden chair, pulls it to her, splattering the wood of the chair and the floor with paint, throwing off her shoes, standing on the seat to send her colours flying from the depths to the heights of her creation.

Sarit feels a rush of excitement at first, an arousal then. Intense. Intoxicating. All enveloping. As though the woman on the screen were her and all she might have been. Then a pain in her chest, a shortening of her breath, a sensation of panic, of claustrophobia. In her seat she squirms, pushes her legs against the seat in front of her. A man turns round and glares.

And Sammy whispers, 'What's wrong with you . . . ? You can't sit still.'

'I want to leave.'

'Now? Are you sick?'

She pushes past the people to her right, past the people leaning backwards, tutting. Clutching her rucksack, knocking legs, obstructing views, never once saying she is sorry. And as she runs up the aisle of the auditorium that is lit only by the light of the screen, heads turn, wondering why this tall dark shadow is tearing from the cinema.

Outside the rain is heavy as before. Sarit moves up the street, past restaurants with families in their windows, past bars and cafés with lovers huddled in their doorways, and she runs to the corner not knowing why she is running or from whom.

'What the hell? Sarit?' Sammy calls, panting as he grabs her arm. 'Are you sick?'

'No. I'm not . . . I . . . just had . . . to leave.'

'Why?' he says, out of breath. 'Tell me . . . why?'

The rain has soaked her. Her white sweater clinging, her nipples erect where her thick-lined denim jacket falls away, she says, 'Nothing. It's nothing. I just have to get home.'

'This is some sort of panic attack,' he says.

Angry now, she loosens her arm from his grip and begins to cross the road. 'Don't analyse me,' she calls back and she leaves Sammy standing there staring after her, abandoned and confused.

Confused and abandoned. Just as Sarit finds herself the next day. Abandoned by herself, despite the years of hardened resolve that had faded into denial and to attempted effacement of the past. Effacement that was all but successful. Though the light switch of course has flickered many times, threatened by a nonchalant Gauguin hung on the wall in a patient's penthouse home on Lake Shore Drive, by a chalk fresco of a devil and an angel on a Bucktown pavement, by the paintings on the ceiling of the Palmer House Hotel that had stopped her in her tracks and kept her there for minutes, her head lifted upwards towards the masterpiece. She had been threatened too, some years before, by the artistic expression of a fellow plastic surgery student. A young skinny man who painted pastel watercolours of his patients as a hobby and challenged her to do the same.

'I don't do watercolours,' she had said and had bitten her lip.

And now, propelled by the image of the artist in the film, she is crossing the high footbridge with the February lake ahead of her, walking fast as if with some purpose alongside the water that is busy with wind, walking for miles, the weather beating at her cheeks, past the shoppers on Michigan Avenue, though because of her speed she could in no way be mistaken for one of them. Turning right towards the art district of River North, where she has never wandered before in all the years that she has been here: under the tracks of the 'L', the train that carries city dwellers overground then underground, underground then overground.

And the vibrations of the train now are no disturbance to Sarit, but a complement to her thoughts, to her mind's refrain of 'What am I doing, Where am I going? What am I doing?, Where am I going?'

Under the train track into streets that seem at first devoid of charm. Bleak and bare with uniform, uninteresting grey and red-brick buildings, much less handsome, much less alluring than so much of Chicago's architecture. Streets that once were steeped in industry and manufacture and now are galleries and lofts.

So that in the beginning as she walks through them she can almost fool herself. She can pretend that this is some normal Monday power walk, that she is but profiting from a day away from surgery and consultation, rather than heading towards her life.

On the corner of Franklin and Grant the naked elm trees stand, their trunks encircled a few feet from the ground by large and wooden slatted squares that serve as seats and invite the browser to come and rest a while. As she passes Sarit notices the spot. She sees the couple sitting on newspaper, almost cheek to cheek, the young blond man in his glasses, his head bent over his sketchbook. She feels a pang and hurries on.

Here and there, into the tall window of this gallery and then that she shoots a furtive glance. Past the Galeria Amalia, past the Gruen Galleries, past the Gallery Gwenda J. She looks briefly in the shopfronts. Briefly, not for long enough to really see at first, as if looking just to open up Pandora's box and quickly snap it shut again, saying, 'This might once have been my world to wander round, but not now. Not any longer.'

She stops in the end by the ethnic shop window of Primitive Art Works, which is filled with coloured beads and chains threaded through the branches of a jewellery tree. And even as she thinks, 'Why am I wasting my time?' she pushes against the door frame hung with golden chains and bells that chime as she steps in.

'How are you today?'

'Fine.'

'If I can help with anything please let me know.'

Stones of jade, of coral and of amber are piled high on the tables. The sanded wooden floors are covered with tassled woven rugs of muted reds and blues and greens. Sideboards are strewn with trays of shiny brown eggs found on the bed of Indian rivers and sculpted to bring fertility to all who touch them. A courtyard filled with tiny ponds and fountains and a huge sculpture of Ganesh, the Indian elephant with his many arms. And the walls inside are hung with tapestries of scenes of fields and farms, with batiks of man and woman, father and son, mother and child. The mother reclining against pillows, her child beside her cleaved to her in the crook of her arm, the way it had been in the Middle Eastern warmth of the late afternoon.

'You know, Sarit, that people, you and me and Abba and Dani next door, we are made up of little round things called cells.'

The child looks up towards her mother's face. Her grey eyes wide, she lifts her chin to Gabriella's shoulder. 'What's a cell?'

'A tiny circle with a round black dot in the middle of it called a nucleus. You have millions and millions of them in your blood.'

Sarit thinks hard. She says, 'But when I cut my finger on Abba's painting knife and blood came out it was just all messy like that red paint from the tube. There weren't any circles, Ima.'

'There were. You just couldn't see them. They're so tiny that they're hidden.'

'So how do you know they're there?'

'Because the doctors who study people's bodies find out about these things. They can see them under a microscope.'

'What's a microscope?'

'It's like Abba's magnifying glass. You know, the one with the gold handle that he uses when he paints the birds' feathers or the fishes' fins.'

'Oh . . . he doesn't use that one any more, though. He says that people have to guess they're fishes now . . . Ima, tell me about those things . . . those little cell things.'

'Well, you have red cells and white cells. They help you grow and keep you healthy.'

It is always the same with Sarit. She knows when something big is on its way. She presses herself still closer, hides her face in her mother's white nightgown.

Gabriella holds her daughter to her. 'Some of my cells are not healthy any more, Sarit. The cells in my ovaries.'

'What are ovaries?'

Despite the subject matter Gabriella starts to laugh. A weak laugh by now, though one that still lights up her face, one that Max has often said is the only justification for the colour in his work. And now it is the child's thirst for understanding that is making Gabriella smile and keeping her alive. 'Ovaries, Sarit, are the eggs in a woman's body. And mine have bad cells in them. That's why I am not so strong.'

Sarit ponders a moment. Then she says, 'Is that why I can't have a sister?'

'Yes.'

Sarit thinks and then she says, 'Oh. Well, Ima, Dr Katz will make you better.'

'No, sweetheart. He can't. He has tried very hard. But the bad cells played hide and seek for too long. We didn't know they were there.'

The child is quiet. She is racking her seven-year-old brain for a solution to her mother's problem. 'OK, Ima,' she says.

'Then if Dr Katz can't make you better then me and Abba will look after you for ever and ever.'

The child has thrown her mother quite off course. And Gabriella's strength, at least for now, is spent. She goes to lie down on her bed, shuts her eyes and falls into a heavy wheezing sleep. Sarit slips away and goes to sit on the rocking chair by the door of the house. To keep watch like the night guard does in the children's house, rocking herself backwards and forwards, talking out loud all the while as sometimes children do, saying over and over again, 'For ever and ever and ever. For ever, Ima. Me and Abba will look after you for ever.'

In the gallery in River North the assistant asks, 'Are you interested in the tapestry, Madam? It's beautiful, isn't it?'

'Yes. I mean no,' says Sarit. 'I was just looking.'

Sarit walks for miles that day. She doesn't browse exactly, for to browse implies an absence of adrenalin and of that there is plenty. In her head she has no names of galleries. No names of artists she must see. She has no plan. No firm direction. Sarit knows nothing any longer of the artist's world. And yet, and yet, that Monday she is a child in a sweetshop. A child starved of coloured bonbons, of liquorice sticks, of lollipops. And now in this gallery front on the corner of Franklin and Huron the iridescent turquoises, oranges and pinks, painted on trunks and on tables and chairs, the stone and wooden carved men and women bending, stretching, squatting in the window are all of them crooking their fingers at once.

In turquoise silk camouflage at the far end of the long room, her skin black and flawless, her eyebrows arched and plucked, her back straight, her hands positioned on her hips, a tall cur-vaceous woman follows her customers around the room with her eyes. Her name is Nicole and her intuition is strong. She sees Sarit walk in and move around her world. She wonders and she waits.

Sarit does not look the type to spend on art. In her jeans

and her trainers, in her sweatshirt and her fleece she seems more like a graduate student. But Nicole can sense when her gallery will hold some meaning above and beyond the obvious for a customer.

The long front room is taken up with the stories, shapes and colours of Haiti and to the side of the gallery a somewhat smaller room houses works of art from all over the world that have captured Nicole's heart. As Sarit stands at the entrance before she crosses its threshold, behind her in an accent thick with Haitian French, heavy with its guttural 'R's she hears Nicole say, 'This was the room that I gave to myself to fill not just with Haiti, but with the rest of the world too. I fell in love a little with each and every one of these pieces. Art cannot break you like love can.'

Sarit starts and turns. Then laughs. A laugh that once was Gabriella's. Except that now, standing on the threshold, Sarit is not sure why she laughs.

Nicole notices the beauty of her smile and of her teeth. 'Please, Madame. Come in and take a look. This is my house of sculpture. . . . If you like you can sit and watch,' she says and points towards a chair.

In this room that with no windows of its own is darker than the rest. In this room that lives with wooden, clay and marble women, men and children, frozen somewhere in their lives, Sarit sits in the corner armchair that is covered with a bright blue embroidered throw. She sits still, she watches and is hypnotised. Hypnotised by the sculpture that stands in the farthest corner of the room.

At first, even before the girl's shape, it is her eyes that beckon. Eyes, not expressionless as in those sculptures that let the body speak its mind, but eyes that see Sarit and somehow call her name. Egyptian eyes, painted shocking white and darkest black, shaped almost like a cat's. The eyebrows too, arched and shaped and lifted in the question why. Her nose, almost straight, save for on its ridge the slight Semitic bump.

The lips, small yet full, neither pursed nor open, but just touching one another. Like the priceless lips of alabaster, sculpted by some anonymous Ancient Egyptian. The lips still of a virgin. The face slightly rounded with youth that promises to shed its layers and to reveal a form more oval. The cheekbones high, higher even than Sarit's. The chin not square or pointed, but a slightly rounded shape with strength. And from her high forehead a sculpted mane of thick hair that falls to the sides of her long thin neck. And the whole in wood. And those eyes. Those coal-black and white eyes that call Sarit to look at her. To look not as another would. Not as the untrained eye would do. Not just at the outer petrushka doll, a work of art on the left-hand side on a tall black marble stand in the corner of the gallery. No, she calls Sarit to see her as no one but an artist might. As only a sculptor or a painter could.

For how often when we see an object of great beauty, as Sarit does now, do we stop and think of all that is behind it? A sailboat on a lake. A candle, coloured, curved and fashioned. We might watch the white sails billow and marvel at the sailor's skill. We might revel in the scent or the shadows from the candles. But too often we gloss over the real struggles behind these creations, when in truth there is so much more to know of them.

Sarit might have sat and stared for hours but her reverie is broken by Nicole. 'She is beautiful, *n'est-ce pas*?'

'What?'

'*Nadia*. The sculpture,' says Nicole.

'Yes, She's . . . she's . . . a work of genius,' says Sarit.

'She's like an Ancient Egyptian, like Nefertari really. All the more brilliant because this is not his usual medium. He usually uses clay and casts in dark bronze.'

'I see. And who is he?'

'An Egyptian. A classical figurative sculptor. A master in his field.'

Nicole in her turquoise silk, called by a customer, turns and leaves the room. And Sarit moves over to *Nadia*, looks at her from a foot away, then disconcerted by her gaze she bends to see the artist's name on the flat gold plaque attached to the marble stand. But the plaque is engraved only with the name of his creation. *Nadia. Nadia. Nadia.* Engraved three times in a script that slants towards the right. And then a straight line of tiny hieroglyphic symbols. A thread of running water, a bird, a leaf, a fragile arm, a tiny hand in Ancient Egyptian that make up *Nadia*'s name.

Nicole is back now. Standing in the doorway, hands on her hips again. 'He doesn't sign his work,' she says.

'Why not?'

'He prefers not to be known. Of course I know who he is. I've been showing his work for years. I know him well or as well as anybody does. But he keeps himself to himself. Except when the mood takes him . . . then he'll wander round and watch the artists work in Wicker Park. But I think he's in one of his more reclusive phases at the moment.'

'I see,' says Sarit as she begins to walk towards the door. 'Well, thanks. Your gallery is quite amazing.'

'I'm sure,' says Nicole in her thick French accent, 'that you will be back. My place seems to cast a spell on people.'

And as nonchalant as she can be, walking half backwards towards the door Sarit says, 'Oh, I might be back. Some day. If ever I have time.'

Nicole says nothing, but as she opens the door, on the frame, the bells and chains begin to chime and jangle.

ELEVEN

Is the isolation of the artist essential to his life? Must he really lock himself away not just in body, but in mind and in soul, allowing himself to dip into the real world only now and then? Only to search and scavenge for material, scurrying back into his hole then, back to his graft and to his selfish drive to create? Or does his need for days, for hours, for weeks of seclusion come in the first instance? Is it this need together with the talent in his fingers and the madness in his mind that maketh an artist of the man? The aloneness then that bears the artist, not the artist the aloneness?

And as he works in isolation, is he in truth alone at all? Is it not just the outside world that wanders past, that sees his silhouette against the window and imagines him alone? Is his creativity not his companion and his confidant? Are his characters and his images not his friends, his lovers and his enemies at once? And what of his state of mind? Is it preordained that the true artist can stain his fingers only with his clay, his paint, his ink, but never with a happiness that reaches far beyond the creative orgasm of the moment?

'He prefers to leave his work unsigned,' says a gallery assistant the next time Sarit sees a face that so resembles the girl with the Egyptian eyes in the ante-room at Nicole's in River North. The face, this time, in deep mocha-bronze. Cat's eyes again though this time their depth suggested by shape and not by colour. Full mouth, a nose with dignity, long neck and yet this time, just perhaps no more a virgin, thinks Sarit. Her lips are parted just a little more, her eyes this time are half closed in the memory of pleasure of some sort, her head thrown slightly back.

'Why doesn't he sign his work?' she asks.

The assistant, in her high pink heels and mask of perfect make-up, shrugs. 'They say he wants to be left alone. You know these artists. They make such a big thing about being alone. Very dramatic,' and she puts the back of her hand to her forehead as if to imitate the drama.

'Have you met him?' Sarit asks, and thinks as she speaks how she would like to scrape the layers of orange cakey make-up from the sales assistant's face.

'No,' she says. 'I haven't had the pleasure. My boss has, though. He's on vacation now, but I'm sure he'd be happy to talk to you about the work when he gets back.'

Sarit touches the cool bronze of the sculpture's neck. Her brow. Her eyelids. Her nose. Her lips. And she thinks, 'He does a far better job than I do . . . Far, far better.' She thinks, 'If she, this beauty, came to me for help, I'd refuse to change a thing.'

The gallery assistant asks, 'So, are you interested in the work then, Madam?'

'No . . . er, yes. I'm not quite sure. I would love to know the artist's name.'

The assistant dons an expression of regret. 'I'm really not supposed to tell you,' she says. 'He likes to keep his anonymity, as I said . . . But seeing as you seem so taken with the work I'll tell you. I only know his first name,' and she puts her finger to her lips and whispers, 'It's Ramsi . . . he's an Egyptian.'

'Egyptian,' Sarit says. 'Interesting. Do you have some literature on his work?'

'I sure don't. I'm so sorry. We just don't seem to need it. He has his collectors. His pieces are never on display for more than a month or two and then they're gone.' And the woman with the orange cakey make-up carries on, 'His stuff sells for serious money too,' and then, thinking better of what she's said, 'What I mean is, the sculptures aren't cheap but the prices aren't at all high for the quality of his work . . . And he always wants to know where his pieces are going. If he doesn't like

86

the sound of the client there are certain sculptures he just won't sell. Crazy really.'

'I see.'

'Now this one here . . . hang on a minute. It's part of the *Nadia* series. Beautiful works done in terracotta usually and finished with a dark bronze patina. Let me look it up . . . *Nadia, Nadia, Nadia at twenty*. This one here is thirty thousand dollars . . . My boss says our prices should be much higher. He says Ramsi has no idea of his own worth.'

Sarit looks at the piece and envies the sculptor the luxury of his blank canvas. She envies him his power to play with expression in a way that she in her work cannot. She wonders if he gets his inspiration from photographs or models, or if he has found this young woman somewhere in his mind.

She asks, 'How old is the artist? What did you say his name was? Ramsi?'

'Yes. Ramsi. Now, let's see. I think he's in his early fifties.'

'I think I saw another piece by him in a gallery on Huron,' says Sarit. 'Nicole's. Do you know it?'

'Yes. She carries his work too. I think she is one of the few people who know him well,' she says and then . . . 'But he gives us first choice, of course. We're very lucky. We get his better pieces.'

Sarit turns to leave. The assistant in her pink heels says, 'Here, have my card and do come back. My boss will tell you all about the sculptor. All I know is he's a genius and a loner.'

'I get the picture,' says Sarit.

And she does get the picture of course. Though now in her working world she spends almost no time alone, she is all too familiar with the concept of the artist as a loner.

When she was small, when for the first time she heard the word '*mitboded* . . . loner' she had to ask. Not just because the word was beyond the range of her vocabulary, but because for most kibbutzniks the concept of a loner was alien to their communal way of life. So Sarit had asked her mother, 'Ima. What does a loner mean?'

'It means a person who often needs to be alone, Sarit . . . like Abba. We mustn't disturb him when he feels like this. He's working on an important painting.'

'I want to see him now,' she says and stamps her plimsolled foot. 'I'm going to find him this minute.'

'I don't like it when you behave like this, Sarit. You're a hot-head.'

Lisping, Sarit yells, 'My head is not hot. And Abba does not want to be alone. He needs me with him. He says he needs me and you and no one else, so I'm going to find him.'

'You are not going to see him just now, Sarit,' says Gabriella.

She grabs her child's wrist. And again Sarit stamps and sobs and grunts with the exertion of trying to pull her arm from Gabriella's grip. Standing on the spot at almost seven years old, overtaken by her tantrum. 'Let . . . me . . . go. I'm going to find my Abba.'

Her mother strokes her cheek, pulls her daughter to her. The child has a flash of inspiration. Her sobs grow quieter. Quieter, quieter. 'Ah, I've calmed her,' Gabriella thinks. She lets the child's wrist go and Sarit stands quite still for a moment, for long enough to fool her mother before she tears down the gravel path of the kibbutz, past the tiny flat-roofed wooden houses, past the children's house, the schoolhouse, the dining room, the laundry building, the Queen of Sheba on her camel, along the narrow path scratching herself on the nettles and the brambles, down the short dry mud slope that leads to Max's studio. She knocks. No answer. She knocks again, the wood rough against the knuckles of her hands. 'Abba, Abba . . . I'm coming in,' she calls, excited still, banging at the door. No answer, so she yanks it open, panting with the effort of pushing the weight of her small frame against the heavy door.

Inside the large windows are covered with black cloths

strewn with messy teardrops of white paint and fastened with rusting nails to the cracking window frames to block out much of the strong summer light. The room, though, still feels stifling. To Sarit's left a huge half-face with tufts of hair round it stares at her. Unfinished, but already tortured. Haunting, pleading from the canvas. She stands still at the door.

'Abba.'

He's sitting in the corner of the room, crouched, his head in his hands.

'Abba.'

In his mind he is conjuring up the other side of the face, his mother's face. Creating it in his head, before his hands can create it on canvas.

'Abba. It's me.' She's still standing by the door. 'Why don't you speak to me?'

He's waiting there, his back against the wall, the sweat pouring down his face and neck, ready for the rest of his mother's face to come through him and paint itself on to the canvas. Waiting for the merging of the vision and the ghastly memory of the image, as he, the boy, had seen it at the end. Should he let the flesh hang loose from his canvas in thick and dripping clumps of paint or should he merely suggest? Should he leave her as she is, with half a face, half a haunted face, or should he create the other half, then ravage it with his palette-knife where the Nazis' dogs had mauled and ravaged too?

And Sarit is crying now, calling out, 'Abba, talk to me. Talk to me,' not yet daring to walk up to him, small and still at the door. Max has hardly moved at all, but now he lifts his head, stares at the wall straight ahead of him, clenches his teeth, breathes louder, panting almost.

Sarit runs over from the door to where he is crouched, ready to shake him, to push him, to bang him on the back, to shout, 'Abba, I came to surprise you,' but as in a slow-motion film, just as she reaches him, just as she is about to touch him, propelled towards his canvas he jumps up, lunging almost, leaving Sarit standing there, her hand stretched out towards him in mid-air.

Fired up now, he lifts his palette-knife to create the face's other cheek, to make it whole first so that the Nazis' hounds and the Nazis that hound his mind can ravage it. And standing in the corner where her father has been, where he has crouched creating, Sarit is facing his back and in the heat and the semi-darkness she is playing some grotesque and solitary distortion of peekaboo with him, calling out, 'Abba, Abba, can't you see me? See me? Abba, look, I'm here.'

And later when she has run back home, when the sobbing has subsided, she says, 'Ima, Ima, what is wrong with Abba's eyes and ears? He couldn't see me and he couldn't hear me. And I was shouting at him. This loud. Listen.' And into the air at the top of her voice she shouts, 'Abba, Abba,' to show her mother what has been. 'Abba, Abba, Abba . . . Daddy, Daddy, Daddy,' she cries out, as if the cry were a question, a search and a longing all at once.

'I told you not to go,' says Gabriella as she strikes a match to sterilise the needle that will take the splinters from the wooden studio door out of Sarit's hands. 'He needed to be alone. All artists need that sometimes. They need to talk to the people in their head to make pictures.'

'People in their head? That's funny. I want him to talk to me, Ima. Not silly people in his head.'

Years later, though, *Nadia*'s faces, the wooden and the bronze faces created by the sculptor, stay with Sarit in her head, while she sits alone on the wooden slatted squares around the tree under Franklin and Elm where the lovers had sat. In the way that a piece of art we have seen and loved can stay with us for weeks, so *Nadia*'s expression stays in Sarit's mind while her fingers fly over other features, while her hands touch other faces and wonder how to shape and sculpt their parts.

Sarit, in her artistry, can never be alone of course. Morning to night the voices, their questions, their demands surround her. 'Would you be able to lift my eyebrows without leaving a scar, Dr Kleinmann?'

'Can you get rid of these brown sun marks on my skin?'

'Dr Kleinmann, can you take ten years off me?'

'Sarit. The child has third-degree burns to her face, Sarit. Can you give us an opinion before the trauma surgeons operate?'

'Dr Kleinmann, cleft lip clinic starts in ten. See you there.'

'Dr Kleinmann, when can you operate?'

'Sarit, we have an extra staff meeting Wednesday morning at 7 a.m. Please don't miss it.'

And the sounds of her own voice saying, 'Lauren, pass me this. Pass me that. I'm going to lift this flap. That flap. Watch her heart. Bring her round. Wake her up.'

And through all of this in the week that follows her hours in the gallery district of River North, Sarit sees *Nadia* in her head, conjures in her mind the hands, the fingers of some sculptor in mid-creation. And though his world, this sculptor's world, is that of art and hers to her conscious mind is that of science, still intuition nags at her. An intuition that provides Sarit with the rational excuse for seeking out the sculptor's work and allows her to tell herself that there is something she might learn from him that could help her in her own work. But more, much more than this, it is Sarit's curiosity that is wakened and that drives her. Because for years she has sublimated her true artistic libido. For years in terms of art for art's sake and the love of it she has lived as celibate. And now, perhaps despite herself, perhaps because of herself, because she is ready and is strong enough, she has not blocked this image of true artistic beauty from her mind. So that almost as the faux virgin reawakened and lured back into the world of sensuality, Sarit finds herself in River North again. Her starting point might have been any. But her starting point is this . . . Nicole

91

turning the key in the lock of her gallery door when Sarit goes back. In navy silk this time, that falls over her proud bosom, she stares at Sarit through the glass pane, contemplating whether or not to let her in.

In all of our lives there are these split seconds of keys in locks that might turn one way or another. Moments when someone else's choice to move clockwise or anticlockwise, someone else's choice to move with time or against it, has the power to change it all.

Between the dark skin of her fingers Nicole holds the silver key. She nods at Sarit, decides to turn it clockwise, opens up and says, 'I knew you would come back.'

'Oh,' Sarit says. 'Did you? I can see you are about to close. I just wanted to have a look at a few of your pieces again. Maybe another time.'

'Now will be fine,' and she steps aside to let Sarit pass.

In the gallery, in her grey sweatsuit, her trainers, her white T-shirt, Sarit looks incongruous between the sculptures.

The room feels icy cold.

'The piece you were interested in was in the ante-room, wasn't it?'

Sarit is startled by Nicole's memory.

'I'm afraid,' says Nicole, 'that it's no longer there.'

'Oh. You sold it?' She cannot hide her disappointment.

'No. The sculptor changed his mind. That happens from time to time with him. He creates something, gives it to me and then he can't bear to be without it. He comes in here in a panic and says, "You haven't sold it, have you, Nicole? I must have it back right away." He usually only does that when it's a piece from his *Nadia* series . . . once he even insisted I get it back from a client after they'd paid for it. Now that was embarrassing. But I still take his pieces. The ones he leaves here sell well . . . very well. He's of the old school. A pure artist. A classic figurative sculptor. Left-handed like Michelangelo. And he and I have more than art in common. We share French as our mother tongue . . . Oh, oh,' she says, sounding suddenly so very, very French. 'Now I'm talking rather too much. Please tell me, young lady, how exactly can I help you?'

The feeling, the concept of awkwardness is foreign to Sarit. She was not brought up to watch her 'p's and 'q's, to make excuses for herself, to be afraid of pursuing what she wants, but now as Nicole asks, 'How exactly can I help you?' Sarit's answer sticks to the sides of her throat.

'Yes?' says Nicole.

'Well, I want to know if you could put me in touch with the sculptor . . . I'm impressed by the way he handles form. I feel I have something to learn from him.'

'Put you in touch with Ramsi?' and Nicole laughs. 'My dear,' she says, rolling the 'r' of 'dear' as she speaks, 'My dear, it would be more than my life is worth to give out his number.'

'Could you give him mine perhaps?'

'I don't think I'm making myself clear, my dear. He won't deal directly with the public. He says they get in the way of whatever's going on in his head. He's a bit of a misanthrope, you know. Anyway, why do you want to meet him?'

'I want to meet him because . . . because,' and she says the words slowly as if buying time, as if asking the question of herself as Nicole asks it of her, 'I want to meet him because he may able to help me in my own work. I just think the way he shapes is so extraordinary . . . so . . . so refined . . . and . . .'

'Yes?'

'Well, I'm intrigued by it.'

'Ah,' says Nicole, 'so you're a sculptor too, my dear?'

'No . . .' says Sarit, 'I do cosmetic and reconstructive surgery.'

Nicole looks her up and down in her sweats, her T-shirt and her trainers. 'A plastic surgeon?' she says. 'Aha . . . Hm.'

Sarit laughs. 'I know. I know. I don't look the part.'

And Nicole repeats herself. She says, 'A plastic surgeon . . .

hm. Well, I suppose that is a sculptor too. You know,' she says and thinks aloud, 'the word plastic means to mould . . . It comes from the Greek . . . so yes, I suppose you are a sculptor. I would love to help you, young lady, but I know how he'll react. I'm so sorry. But he has his ways. Occasionally he'll agree to see a struggling artist. But a plastic surgeon . . . ? Never in a lifetime.' And she laughs again. 'He just won't see the connection. I cannot even bear to think of what he'd say.'

Sarit turns to leave. 'I understand,' she says. 'Privacy is important for the artist. My mother used to tell me that.'

And Nicole says, 'Your mother was an artist,' though the way in which she says it, with her strong French accent it sounds much more like, 'Your mozer was an arrrtiste?'

'No, she wasn't. But she understood.'

'You know,' says Nicole, patting the hair piled and pinned up on her head, putting her fingers to her eyes, lifting the skin at the corners, then looking at Sarit from quite a different angle, 'You know, now that I think of it . . . now that I come to think of it, when the mood takes him he'll agree to give a master class at the School of the Art Institute. They say when he's in the right frame of mind his classes are really extra . . . ordinary. The next one should be happening some time soon . . . if he doesn't change his mind of course. If you're that interested you ought to go and watch him work. Maybe you'd learn something from him there. And I suppose you could always try and talk with him then. But,' she says in warning, 'I wouldn't admit to the plastic surgeon bit. Just say you're an artist or a sculpture student.'

And Sarit says, 'Great . . . Good idea,' and she moves to go, as though if she doesn't get out of this gallery now, if she doesn't disappear out of the door and round the corner fast enough, Nicole will come after her and somehow grab the information back.

'By the way,' says Nicole. 'Before you go. You don't have a business card, do you?' and she puts her hands to her face again, and adds, 'I've been thinking for a while of having my eyes done and it is so very hard to find the right person.'

Straight-faced on the outside, Sarit walks back towards her. She says, 'Your eyes, Nicole. Now let me take a look.'

And so the plastic surgeon is standing there at the door of the art gallery with her hands on the smooth black skin of the Haitian woman's face, looking at the fine lines, at the almost imperceptible puffiness beneath her lashes and she says, 'Nicole, I don't have a card with me. But I'll write down my number and if you want to come to me, I'll see you. But if I were you I would leave well alone. You're striking as it is. I'm sure you must already know that.'

Nicole grins. '*Merci, cherie*,' she says. '*Merci* . . . but let me go and fetch a pen and write down your details just in case I lose my fight with gravity.'

TWELVE

Since 1893 two massive lions have protected the façade of Chicago's Institute of Art on the broad boulevard of South Michigan Avenue. The two, a male and a female lion in greenish bronze, have never looked directly at one another. Stared at, talked about and touched by strangers, they might have a been a couple in a room full of partygoers, a couple so confident in their togetherness that they were able to stand apart, able to withstand the onslaught of freezing winters and boiling summers. In the year 1999, the year when Sarit walked up the stone steps of the Institute for the first time, when she pushed her way through the revolving doors, crossed the marble floors and asked the obese woman with mauve streaks in her hair at the information desk for directions to the Institute's School of Art, in that year one of the lions was ripped from his base for restoration to his tail, leaving his partner bereft and waiting. Beneath the lion's feet, amongst old sweet wrappings, a filthy blue glove and empty cigarette packets, on a lined and crumpled piece of paper a passer-by found a two-line poem in faded black ink which read, 'This talent. Yours to tempt and taint me, to draw me and withdraw from me. This talent of yours that is mine.'

As she turned to her left along the cool, carefully lit high-ceilinged hallway, along dark wooden floors, Sarit knew nothing of the poem found several weeks before on the crumpled piece of paper. Nor, had she known of the anonymous verse, would she have drawn parallels between the black ink words and the circumstances of her own life.

In the two weeks since Nicole in her navy silk, about to

lock the gallery door had said to her, 'He sometimes gives a master class to students at the Institute,' she had not been back to the galleries of River North. She had gone about her business, in her surgery in the Bloomingdale building on Michigan Avenue. She had gone about her work at the Children's Hospital, in the operating theatre with Lauren and her other colleagues. And she had gone home to her high-rise with the arched windows that framed the lake and the tiny kitchen with the painting that had stood there for weeks in its brown paper wrapping propped up against the wall, uncovered only at the corners and at the top where Sarit had slid her hand in and felt the contours of the art.

So though she called the Institute's School of Art to find out about the sculpture master class, though she still saw *Nadia*'s face beneath her fingers as she worked, though she saw her too, once her grip had been loosened by the red wine, the marijuana and by Lauren's conversation, in some downtown jazz club, in Sarit's conscious mind nothing much had changed.

But once the water on the ceiling of the cave has begun to drip, does the shape of the stalagtites remain unaltered? Once the air has grown moody, does the rumbling storm retreat and change its mind?

The staircase down to the Institute's School of Art is narrow, the steps uneven, the way to room 6a along the basement corridors is poorly lit and poorly signed. Sarit stops a tiny Indian girl hurrying past her. She says, 'Room 6a. The sculpture master class. Do you know where it is?'

'I'm on my way there. It's right at the other end of this labyrinth. It's already started. You can come with me,' she says, beckoning to Sarit to follow her. 'Are you a student or just an observer?'

'An observer,' says Sarit, feeling tall and old and out of place: an unfamiliar feeling for she almost never feels self-conscious. With a tinge of envy in her voice that she doesn't hear herself, she says to the girl, 'You're an art student.' Not a question, but an affirmation.

'Yes. I'm just observing today, though. But I'm in my first year of sculpture. Actually, I'm lucky. I've just had my first exhibition.'

'That's exciting,' says Sarit. Along the corridor their footsteps and their voices resonate. Sarit looks at the *bindi* on the student's forehead. Blood red against light brown. She thinks of Mona and of the *bindi*'s meaning. She knows it signifies that the girl, if not yet married, is at least betrothed. And she wonders as she walks how anyone can be sure enough of love to paint it on their skin.

The girl says, 'Yes, my exhibition was exciting . . . I wish my parents thought so, though. They'd rather I'd studied medicine or law. I'm the black sheep.'

'So am I,' says Sarit before she can think of what she says.

'Oh. What do you do?'

'I'm a doctor.'

The girl laughs, a laugh that echoes all the way along the corridor, all the way to the grey steel door that she leans against with all her weight to open. But her laughter that has followed them into the room is cut dead by the tense silence of the high-ceilinged echoey studio they have entered.

The students, a dozen of them, are standing stock still next to their work. Standing like sculptures of themselves rooted to the spot, next to their art in its varying stages of creation, all of them in their clay-caked grey aprons turned in the same direction. Turned not towards the young blonde woman, who sits in the centre of their circle, still and naked, head bowed, legs crossed above the knees on a piece of red velvet on the cold grey concrete floor. Turned not towards her, but towards a rough unfinished torso of that same young woman fashioned on to a frame of wire mesh. The students, themselves almost immobile, are drawn by the only perceptible movement in the room. The movement of the rough-skinned hands of the

98

sculptor on the beginnings of the likeness of the young woman's body. Dark-skinned hands with large knuckles and strong fingers that add and stroke and slide and shape on one side of the grey clay image. Hands that command silence as they work on the student's piece of art. Hands as those of Galatea that hint at wakening the inert woman from her slumber and bringing her to life.

And he, the teacher, utters not a word, does not lift his eyes to welcome or even acknowledge the latecomers in his master class. He, the sculptor, sculpts. Attended or not by his students, he doesn't seem to care. With a wooden tool he cuts away at the neck and the shoulder of the student's half-sculpture, of the model who sits quite unmoved on the floor. The model whom Sarit believes at first glance to be a true blonde till she shifts position just a touch to reveal the clipped black hair between her long thin legs. For five minutes or ten or for longer the sculptor is absorbed, undoing, remaking, creating, closing one eye, measuring proportions in the air with his index finger, while the student on whose art he is working stands there corrected by her bucket of clay as she sulks. He has not asked for silence, though in his presence, as always, silence has come. He straightens his back. He stretches both arms above his head. He bends and unbends his fingers and he looks round not at the students who stand there and watch him, but at the half-finished figures that stand by their sides. He circles the workshop around the twelve students and the two observers till his almost black eyes land on a point in the room. Till they land on the large round pine clock that says ten to five and that by chance, quite by chance, is just inches away from the place where Sarit in her white fleece stands watching, her back to the wall.

His eyes, his hot, cold eyes, stop then on her face. And for a few long seconds they take Sarit in, right there where she stands. Unflinching, unblinking, his eyes pin her there to the wall, till they leave and move back to the class and the sculptures. Till Ramsi bends to the floor to work on the curve of a heel and the bend of a toe.

The young naked woman on the red drape shivers and shifts position. And Sarit, as she recovers, notices the model move.

'Now she's ruined his angle,' she thinks a split second before Ramsi says, 'Keep still, would you, please. You'll confuse the angle. Let me know first if you need to move.' His accent is foreign, thick and heavy, and somehow not unfamiliar to her. His voice is deep and strong and commanding. A male version of Mona's is what Sarit thinks.

A red-haired male student calls out to Ramsi, 'How long do you think it's reasonable to expect a model to sit still? I can never work it out.'

'Twenty minutes. Maybe more,' Ramsi answers. 'She needs to tell you if she wants to move, or you need to know how often she's going to take her breaks. That is what you pay her for. To sit still and help you work. And you should be marking her pose with tape when she has a break, so that you don't lose it.'

'When you work, if the model takes a break do you find you can keep her in your mind?' asks the redhead.

'Sometimes,' he says. 'Not always. That's why we so often sketch or take photos. That, as you know, is also why we make maquettes. All the greatest classical sculptors worked with maquettes. That's what you would be doing too if this programme were more rigid.'

'So which did you use with that series you sculpt? A model or memory or maquettes? You know, that beautiful girl. The one at different stages of her life. The one who holds herself like a princess . . . With those Egyptian eyes.'

Ramsi lifts his hand towards the circle of student sculptors. No more questions, says his gesture and the students are silenced. He avoids the red drape as he crosses the circle, walks over to a heavy-set mousy student, a pale girl with her hair scraped back, the beginnings of her sculpture modelled on

100

the thin wire mesh armature beside her. 'How many sessions has it taken you to do this?' He, with his strong presence, his deep voice, his clipped speech, is allowed to ask the questions, to break the silence he imposes as and when he chooses. Here in this room he is allowed to say and to do whatever he wishes. They knew how he would be when they begged him to come. They invite him not because they love him but because they know what he can show them. Of his personal story these students know nothing whatsoever. But on that afternoon, one of Ramsi's students whispers to another, 'Typical artist's temperament.'

And the second student answers, 'I'd bet my bottom dollar he's got some tragedy behind him. He's so . . . so . . . closed off.'

Ramsi says to the heavy mousy-haired student, 'Three sessions it took you,' and not changing his expression he looks at the model, then at the half-life-size half-sculpture of clay on the wire. 'A loop, please,' he says. Three students at once hold out their wooden-handled tools with the little wire-looped tips. He chooses from some young man's hand. He crouches down beside the clay half-woman and the students to his right, to his left and behind him creep up to him, gather round him, close in on him, tiptoeing almost, keeping quiet, playing grandmother's footsteps, afraid they'll be stopped if he feels that they've got quite so close to his body.

Only Sarit does not inch forward. Only Sarit stays alone, no longer standing close to the Indian girl. Sarit, a circle unto herself at the back of the room, taller now than the sculptor who crouches, but several feet behind him. So that she cannot see his hands at work. So that she can see only the back of his head with its thick silver-grey hair and a part of his profile obscured by the beard and the five o'clock shadow that darkens the rest of his face further still. His shoulders move slightly, though hardly at all, so that she knows his work must be all in the flat of his hands and the tips of his fingers. Three of the students are on the floor beside him now, watching, squatting, their faces so close to his that they must almost be able to feel one another's breath. Weighing up Ramsi's movements as though they were animals in the bush, they sense the danger of rebuff, they smell when he will allow them to approach and when he won't.

They stiffen and relax according to his rhythm. The language of their bodies mirrors his.

Knees bent in his loose blue artist's trousers, still squatting, he moves backwards, to look at his own work imposed on the blonde girl's creation, imposed on the half-fashioned woman in clay. He looks from the left, from the right, from above. He circles the piece and he nods. No smile. Just a nod that says to the student, 'Now carry on. You're on the right path.'

'Thank you,' says the heavy-set girl. 'I learnt something.'

'That's what I'm here for,' he says. He walks over to the big white clay-stained, paint-streaked artist's sink against the grey stone wall. One or two of the students, the braver ones, ask him a question, the answer to which is a word, a short sentence or the shake or the nod of his head.

The students begin to prepare their creations for the night. They cover them with wet grey rags, then with thick and heavy plastic sheets. The model has stood up and in an accent that's Southern and a voice that's high-pitched and whiney she says, 'My robe, where's my robe? It's pink. It was here.' Standing there, she covers her breasts with her hands and crosses her legs. An artist's model, a professional, bold and nude only moments before, off duty, the young woman is naked and exposed.

Only moments before the people around her were artists, students of sculpture, sketching her figure in clay. Now they are men and women looking at her body and its parts. The heavy-set girl fetches the model's pink robe from the room at the back, brings it to her, holds it behind her. She slips into it, ties the silk belt and before she disappears into the small hidden ante-room, she goes up to Ramsi and says, 'The school said you would pay me and they'd pay you back. That's three hours . . .Thirty dollars, please.' He fumbles in his pocket, finds two twenty-dollar bills, hands them to her.

She says, 'I'll go and and get your change.'

'Forget it,' he says.

The students stand together, chatting in low voices, happy to dawdle for a while, but Ramsi has already tied the laces of his old beige suede shoes and is walking towards the heavy iron door as the 'thank yous' and 'see yous' echo and slide off his back.

And Sarit is still standing there, against the wall, close to the spot, to the clock where Ramsi's hot cold eyes had found her.

One of the students, freckled, red-headed, elf-like, comes up to Sarit, begins to ask where she comes from, why she came. Not normally one for small talk, she might just have made the effort here, but suddenly, mid-sentence almost, she has to go, walking fast through the labyrinth, along the dark, wooden, windowless corridors, with the bold bright student art that lines the walls on both sides. The stretch ahead of her is empty, but as she nears a glass door, around the corner she hears the echo of his step. She turns right, sees the back of the silver-grey head. She walks faster, is a few feet from him now, moving closer, like the students before her, playing grand-mother's footsteps with him.

'Excuse me.'

'Yes?' He turns round, abrupt as if interrupted not just in his passage but in his thoughts.

And Sarit, who never says she's sorry, says, 'I'm sorry to dis-turb you . . . I . . .'

'Yes?'

'I've seen your work in River North. I think it's brilliant. Your faces are superb.'

'Thank you,' he says as if untouched, as if he has heard this a thousand times before. And he starts to moves off towards the door ahead of him, but something in the angle of her cheekbones piques his interest and so she has time only for an instant of disappointment at his dismissal of her, before he turns back to her again in the labyrinth and says, 'You wanted something?'

'To see how you work. Your techniques. I know I just saw you teaching, but I mean your own work. That's what interests me.'

'Why? Are you a sculpture student?'

'No . . .' and she ignores Nicole's advice. 'I'm a surgeon. A plastic surgeon.'

He stares. He laughs out loud. A laugh that is cynical and deep. 'A plastic surgeon and she wants to see me work,' he says. 'That's funny. Too funny.'

And then it's cut dead. That laugh of his. Cut with a razor like the laugh of the tiny Indian girl with the blood-red *bindi* entering his master class. Stony-faced, the sculptor stands there and looks at her.

Uncomfortable now, as uncomfortable as she can ever be, Sarit says, 'So can I watch you work? I mean, you must have a studio or something.'

He takes her in. The length of her. The strength of her. The bones of her cheeks. The planes of her face. He says. 'You can model for me if you want.'

It is her turn now to laugh. He notices her mouth. Her teeth.

Behind them they hear footsteps. The students from the studio. Sarit and Ramsi begin to walk ahead. Striding beside her, a little ahead of her, he says, 'I'll sculpt you. You can see me work that way.'

'I don't think so,' she says. 'Not quite my style.'

'Shame,' he says, on the way up the stairs towards the exit of the Institute. 'Shame. You have interesting lines to work with.'

They are in the light of the ground floor now, walking

alongside one another, past the Indian artefacts, Mexican arte-facts, Egyptian artefacts in glass cases that line the way towards the main door of the building. She notices as they walk that she's taller than he is.

'Behind the red engraved door on Wells Street in Old Town . . . That's where I live,' he says. 'In case you change your mind.'

'Unlikely,' she says.

'Fine,' he says. 'Your choice.'

At the exit of the museum, by the revolving glass doors, as though she has asked, he says, 'I can't say when I work. I sculpt when the mood takes me. If you change your mind, come when you want. If it's a bad time then I'll tell you.'

And Sarit, already half hidden in her own glass section of the revolving door, moves as if away from him, then turns and says, 'I doubt if I'll come. But anyway, what's your name? Ramsi what?'

Outside now, on the steps, he asks, 'Does it matter? I mean, if you're not coming.'

They walk down till they are level with the lion waiting and alone. In a parting gesture Ramsi lifts the hand in which he holds his black scarf. He says, 'See you whenever.'

On South Michigan Avenue he turns right. She turns left. He doesn't even know her name.

THIRTEEN

The views that fall to the bay in Palermo ought to inspire even in the native the sharp intake of breath that they provoke in passers-by. But just as the striking woman might miss the truth of her own face, just as she might take it quite for granted, so in that part of Sicily, Alessandro was not in awe of the landscape or the archaeological heritage of his birthplace. Nor was he able to allow the natural beauty of the town to engender in him the peace and serenity that precludes wrongdoing. For here and there turmoil lurks in beauty. Snowstorms. Lightning bolts. A streamlined beast approaches.

Behind a Greek church with its grey stone statues and a baroque one with its coloured mosaic floors, in the late nineteen eighties in a small workshop on a cobbled side street two men sit on dark wooden stools, their heads bent over their work. The sounds of tapping and chiselling that move from the half-open door of the room and fall into the shadows on the street outside, have about them a certain dissonant harmony. As though the two brothers, the ceramicists, were composing music in wordless synchronicity rather than creating tactile, tangible works of art. 'Tap, scrape, scratch, chisel, scratch, chisel, tap, scrape,' the ceramic vases, coloured mosaics, mirrors of the floor of the baroque church behind them, reach from the cool dark ground to the level of the artists' gnarled hands as they sit on their stools. From the size and the width of the vessels one might imagine them displayed in some grand high-ceilinged room filled with tall pale-green grasses that compliment them without detracting from the drama of the art itself.

'*Quando saranno pronti?* ... When will they be finished?

*Dovete sprigarvi. Domani a le tre la barca é in partenza e c'e da fare prima . . .*You need to hurry.The ship leaves tomorrow at three and there's plenty to do before then.'

The tone of voice of the young man who stands at the door of the workshop, the man not a third of the age of the ceramicists, is one not of gruffness, but of pleading and of urgency.

The brothers in the blue overalls lift their heads. The left-handed brother says, '*Saremmo pronti, ma non poi sbrigare l'artista . . . a il suo proprio ritmo . . . Dovresti già sapere questo . . .*We will be ready, but you shouldn't hurry the artist. We work at our own pace. You should know that by now.'

The boy, for though he's in his twenties he is more boy than man, turns away from the brothers, shuts the ill-fitting door of the workshop behind him and walks downhill. Fast, down the steep slope in his sleeveless shirt in the winter sun towards his car, responding to a '*Buongiorno*' here, another there from men in flat peaked caps and women in long skirts and heels even on the cobbled stones.

He drives towards the docks, through fishing villages, through traffic lights there to be ignored, indicating neither right nor left and worrying as he always does about the delicacy of timing. The timing of the scheduled arrival in Palermo of the cargo ship from Vietnam, of the completion of the vases and of the departure of the ship for the United States of America. He worries too about the timing of his arrival back in his village for lunch for, first and foremost, he is the son of a Sicilian mother. He is there when he should be, on the dot of noon, in her kitchen with the blinds pulled down to block out the midday sun. He sits alone at the table while she waits on him, serves him his *farfalle al carne*, his pasta butterflies in meat sauce, with a salad of *radicchio* and *arugula*, and his glass of full-bodied red wine from the blue ceramic jug made by the brothers.

Hovering over him, the strings of her apron straining, she says to him, 'Is everything on time, Alessandro?'

He wolfs down his food and does not answer her at first.

'*Alessandro, ti sto parlando* . . . Alessandro I'm talking to you.'

'*Ti sento, Mamma, ti sento* . . . I hear you, Mama, I hear you.'

'How do you know the brothers will be on time? Did they say so, Alessandro? Because if you don't get things right you'll never make anything of yourself, Alessandro. You need to climb the ladder. You hear me, son?' she says. She leans down, kisses the top of his dark head. 'Off with you now. Back to work.'

He rolls his eyes to the heavens, wipes his mouth with the linen serviette that she will launder in readiness for tomorrow as soon he is gone. He stands up. As he heads for the door, she calls after him, '*Mi voi ancora bene* . . . Do you still love me?'

'*Sì, Mamma, sì* . . .' as he walks back up the hill to check on the brothers yet again.

The large white cargo ship from Asia does draw into the bay of Palermo on time. The brothers do stay up and work throughout the night on their streamlined urns, their earthenware vases and their coloured jigsaw of ceramics. So that when the ship's cargo is unloaded the ceramic vases and urns are ready and waiting for the nimble fingers of Alessandro's young workers to sit and line them with the tiny plastic bags of valuable white powder. The boys, the three or four of them who work for him, are no more than thirteen or fourteen years old and for their effort Alessandro gives a full packet of cigarettes to each one. The lining secured, they stuff the inside of the art with sheath after sheath of brown paper, they cover the outside in layer after layer of bubble wrapping and pack the work in massive straw-filled wooden crates, for this work that Alessandro is shipping to the States is in truth the most valuable of art.

The French say '*Plus ça change, plus c'est la même chose* (the more things change, the more they are the same)' and so it is after a decade with the brothers' work. So it is with the substances that line the vases and the urns, although by now, some ten years later, the bags contain a substance black and sticky instead of one that's white and fine.

And Alessandro is in his thirties by now, with a sprinkling of grey at his temples. He no longer sees the sea from where he lives, but from the luxury of the Lakeview penthouse condominium that his salary allows him, his view is of Chicago's skyline. He has been sent here from Palermo for his good behaviour, because he has earned the trust of his Sicilian bosses and trust is the essence of this trade. They need to be sure they can trust you before they send you across the waters to manage their conspiracy with integrity, to manage the unpacking, the distribution and the sale of their unique artwork six thousand miles away. And so they test. They request of their employees all manner of things. Over the years Alessandro has carried out their orders to smuggle in, to unload, to supervise the artists, to line their artwork, to load, to smuggle out. When it comes to executing orders Alessandro doesn't fail. And so, in the late nineties when they suspect that the managers of their Chicago front, their art gallery on Milwaukee Avenue, need to be pulled just a little into line, it is Alessandro whom they send for intensive English tuition. It is he whom they begin to prime for export, to be their envoy, to be their eyes and ears in his capacity as Chicago-based manager of their US Midwestern operations.

FOURTEEN

Old Town wears the scent of history. On a bronze and engraved plaque by the district's black gate, Chicago's mayor has declared the neighbourhood's historic triangle a conservation area. The streets are lined with maples, elms and linden trees. In spring they are dotted with the dusky pink of cherry blossoms. The barefaced red-brick houses look down their noses at the newer mimosa-yellow, powder-blue and white ones. The front steps of the red-brick houses are slated, the front doors have gravitas and in the panes of their tall, thin, lead-rimmed windows suggestion lurks.

Sarit has wandered and explored there. She has sat in the coolness of the pews in St Michael's Church. She has stood in the warmth at the back of the Buddhist monastery. In the communal hall she has turned away from the children's scarecrow sketches on the walls. At the Farmers Market in the park she has bought fresh corn, fresh basil and fresh garlic.

In Old Town the wanderer is in Europe, in Antwerp, in Lille or Amsterdam. In Old Town the buildings have interesting lines to their faces.

On the steps of the Art Institute Ramsi had looked at her and spoken of interesting lines. 'Shame,' he had said to her. 'Shame. You have interesting lines to work with,' and as he'd said that, as he'd turned away she'd felt a rush and she'd surprised herself by wishing that his compliment had been for her as a woman and not as an *objet d'art*.

In the trance of her work on the mouth of a burnt little boy some days later, she hears Ramsi's voice in her head. The voice that is deep and is thick with the gravel of decades of late night bars and nicotine.

'Shame,' he had said to Sarit by the side of the huge green stone lion that should never have been there alone. 'Shame. You have interesting lines to work with.'

In the days that went by not once did she say to herself I will or I won't. I need to see him again or I don't. Instead she kept her distance from the decision, let it do its own work, let it come to her in its own time. Like the independent cat on the kibbutz. Like the strands of light that she needed for the image of her mother's face on the wall of the kibbutz children's house. But the way that it came was both unsettling and strange. The way that it came, quite of its own volition.

The theatre that afternoon with the child who was burnt and would always be scarred had been fraught. And walking out, beads of sweat on her lip and on her forehead, despite her usual cool, despite the coolness of the room, her jaw had been clenched and every muscle in her body had been tense. She pushed the button on the wall and ran her ID card across the sensor to open the door that would let her through to the area that led towards the theatre staff's changing room. As she walked, on the white sleeve of her coat she felt a tug. 'Doctor,' was all that the man at first could manage. 'Doctor. I am Anthony's father.'

The waiting room for relatives was in quite a separate area and Sarit wondered how he had got through into the theatre reception, this tall, strong and pathetic man. She wondered too how he recognised her still behind the mask that she had forgotten to remove. She looked at the man, at the father, and untying the strings of her mask right there on the spot she said, 'It might be quite painful for a while. So make sure he takes his medication when he comes home. We want to avoid post-surgical infection at all costs.'

She begins to move away. But the man, the burnt boy's father, makes a coughing noise. A noise that twists Sarit. A sound that she remembers. The sound of someone's father crying. 'The burns, Doctor?' he says. 'How will my son look?'

'Scarred,' she says. 'But if he wears the compression masks we should stop the skin of his mouth shrinking too much at the sides. I've done what I can, but I can't re-create nature,' and then, in a gesture unusual for Sarit she adds, 'I'm sorry. I really am sorry he has to suffer this.' And she moves towards the changing room, to tear off the paper cap, the white and sexless clothing that hides the shapes of her just as her sheepskin coat does in the dead of winter.

As she leaves that day she thinks of the face of the boy and feels dissatisfaction's nag. She feels as the artist who knows that the canvas on the wall, the figure on the shelf, the story in the book is not quite as it should be. And upset, uptight, to divest herself of the tension on the car ride home she begins to visualise herself in her sweats and trainers running by the lake.

At the Art Institute close to the revolving doors, Ramsi had said to her, 'Behind the red engraved door on Wells Street in Old Town.' He hadn't given her the street number or tried to make it easy for her. And she hadn't said, 'Oh, that's odd. I live so close. On the edge of Old Town myself. Wells is just behind me. I live parallel to you.' She hadn't said that, but for a moment she had thought it, then dismissed it, for who cared if she lived near or far? Yes, he was intriguing and there was something both in his voice and in his accent that drew her, but his suggestion that she model for him had after all been quite ridiculous.

The light over the lake this early evening holds a soupçon of scorched pink that later will be poppy red. The boaters for the most part are still in hibernation, but there is one ahead of her in her line of vision as she runs. A sleek white sculpture, so that as she moves alongside the pointed silver slices of the skyline, the scorched pink of the sky's streaks and the bold white of the yacht vie for her attention. That evening, though, it is neither the silver, the white nor the pink that arrests her, but the subdued red of the wooden door on Wells Street engraved with men on horses and with abstract swirls and curves. The door that she has passed a hundred times before on her way to brunch at Savories on Sundays, or to buy her lunch on Saturdays from Cobey's where Mitch the white-haired owner would say each and every time, 'Sarit, the mysterious Sarit, you've got to try my Tina cake. We need to put some fat on you,' looking at her with a different eye then, adding, 'But that's some muscle definition you got there, though, Miss sexy shoulders.'

The subdued red engraved door on Wells Street that had never stopped her in her tracks before, despite the intricacy of its workmanship. But now on this scorched pink evening, still sweating, panting in the cold in her navy running gear, Sarit bends over, hands on knees, stops to catch her breath by the wall next to the red door against which she will stand and stretch her runner's legs. By accident perhaps or maybe not she has ended her run right here, close enough to touch the door's engraving. Just as it so often is when we have learnt the meaning of a new and obscure word and stumble across it only hours later in some quite unexpected place. And scoffing at ourselves we dismiss the power of our subconscious mind and pass it off as mere coincidence.

Sarit pushes the black iron handle on the outer door. Ahead of her through the bars of an iron gate she sees the reddish brown slates on the ground, the uneven building, like some gingerbread castle with its wooden carved banisters even on the outside and its leaded stained-glass windows. She stands with her face between the bars of wrought iron so that from close up she looks like a prisoner desperate to break loose. On the wall to her left she sees the silver panel. Six bells. Five names. She doesn't stop before she pushes the bell that bears no name. She rings and, pressed against the iron bars again, she waits. Inside she can discern no movement save for the trickle of water and the slinking of a cat. She rings another bell.

'Hello?'

'I've come to see Ramsi.'

'Who?'

'The sculptor. Ramsi. I think he lives here.'

'Ring his bell. It's the one with no name.'

'I have. There's no reply. Can you let me in?'

'He might be out.'

'He might be in.'

'He won't be happy,' says the voice . . . 'He doesn't like visitors.' Even through the intercom Sarit can hear this woman sounds half asleep. As though in the early evening she has just fallen out of bed.

'He's expecting me,' Sarit says.

'Who are you?'

'Sarit . . .' And this time she remembers Nicole from the gallery. 'I'm a sculpture student.'

'Push against the gate when you hear a click.'

'Thanks.'

As if the click of the iron gate has beckoned dusk, it grows darker almost in an instant. She walks up the stone steps to her right, runs her fingers along the engravings of the chocolate wooden banister, wonders how the oak survives the winter. Up the stairs in the courtyard is a backless marble bench by a tiny fountain that drips into a small pond of gold and rainbow fish. The grey brick walls creep with green, that in this light is almost black. Here and there a shiny tile in rust or butterscotch or cobalt blue wakens the stone floor.

A woman in pyjamas, a dressing gown and black sunglasses emerges, shaking with the cold, from a wooden door beside the pond. 'You rang my bell. You want the sculptor,' she says, standing in the light from the old-fashioned brass lantern above her door and she coughs, a hacking smoker's cough. 'His studio's round there to the left. The dark-blue door. Good luck. He's not known for his hospitality.' And she turns to go.

114

But Sarit says to her back, 'This place. It's unique. Who did these engravings?'

'Some guy called Mills,' she says and rubs her eyes under her glasses and coughs again. 'He worked on it in the thirties and then upped and left. Went home to the Rockies and gave up art. The owner brought him out of retirement when he bought this place. He got him to create these stained-glass windows,' she says, gesticulating upwards with a cigarette in her hand. 'Apparently he just sort of came back to life after years in hibernation. Anyway, why am I telling you this?' she asks, pushing her sunglasses up over her head to reveal eyes heavy with sagging lids and the regrowth of grey hair from beneath the peroxide blond. 'I'm sure,' she says, 'your charming sculptor friend will provide you with the background information.'

'Thanks,' Sarit says and walks towards the dark-blue door with no name on the plaque by its side. She knocks. And a minute later knocks again, then leans against the wall and waits. She never questions whether or not he will be in, for instinct has a truth all of its own. But still he startles her. Standing there in front of her in the crevice that he has made between the door and the hinge. Standing, looking with his hot cold eyes and an 'Ah, so you decided to come, did you?' written on his face. He says, 'What made you think this would be a good time?'

'You said you'd tell me if it wasn't,' she says.

'No time is the right time. But as you're here . . .' And he opens the door wider. She steps inside, follows him along into a huge room with vaulted beams and skylights. He walks around the room from corner to corner switching on the tall thin lamps. He says, 'You'll have to wait. I'm working.'

'That's fine. That's why I came. To see you work.'

He laughs. A laugh like the one in the Art Institute's corridor. A laugh that says, 'So you're used to getting what you want, are you?' and he walks away from her. Not turning to add some pleasantry, not inviting her to feel at home, he walks with purpose all the way to the other side of the room and disappears behind a thin muslin screen.

Within seconds he has raised the volume of the music, that before had been so faint she'd hardly heard it. So that now, separated from him by the screen and by the lyrics that she recognises as French, she feels free to look around and to guess at his life from the objects in the room. The thin embroidered rug in muted colours on the dark wooden floors. The huge surreal Daliesque batiks hung on an exposed brick wall. And on another wall the black and white framed photographs of a place in some strange way familiar to Sarit, but that she can't quite name. Beneath them a soft, high-backed, mushroom-coloured sofa. And floor to ceiling on a third wall are books. Piled into the bookshelf anyhow. Spilling over on to piles on the floor. No order, rhyme or reason as far as she can tell. Books that as she gets closer she sees are written both in French and in a script that for a moment stops Sarit. A Semitic script she recognises as Arabic, but that could almost be her own, though for years except for Dani's occasional notes she has read nothing in Hebrew. Next to the bookshelves is Ramsi's bed. Not quite a mattress on the floor like Sarit's but a low bedspread with a rough red hessian throw that almost covers the sheets and the blanket. Sarit averts her gaze. Against the third wall, in a place that matters, a young woman sits alone. In profile, yet turned slightly towards Sarit, as if about to turn all the way to greet her. In her own world, her upper body in shapeless modest clothing, cast in deep coffee-coloured bronze, her hair caught up behind her. And Sarit recognises the girl in an instant as another version of the sculpture she has seen at Nicole's. She studies her. She takes her in. The sculpture's beauty moves her.

Ramsi interrupts her appreciation of his work. He says, 'You're still waiting? I thought you would have left by now.'

116

His hands are clean now. Scrubbed of clay. She hasn't even heard the water run.

She says, 'Of course I'm still here. I didn't come to leave after ten minutes . . . before we'd spoken.'

He isn't going to ask her to take a seat. She walks over to the sofa. She needs no invitation. He stands halfway between her and his bookshelf.

She turns her face towards the muslin screen. She says, 'I'd like to see all your other sculptures.'

'I don't do circus acts. Do you have people come and watch you while you operate?' he asks. 'But as I said, you can model for me if you want.' And he looks at her. 'You have a face that might look interesting in bronze. I'd have to sketch it first and see.'

'You think I've come to model for you, don't you?' She laughs.

'I see no other reason for you to be here. Why else would you have come?'

'I told you at the Institute. I was drawn to the faces you sculpt. I want to see how you work.'

'Please,' he says, walking towards the door and opening it. 'I don't have time to waste. You can see my work in the galleries.'

She looks at him standing by the door, holding it open, letting in the cold evening air that she feels on her face and on her hands. She says, 'What is it you want me to do?'

'Just sit there,' he says.

In her mind she sees the model from the Art Institute on the floor, on the red drape posed and naked.

He has shut the door again and is walking back over to the muslin screen.

'Do you have a robe?' she calls.

'For what?'

'To cover myself when we take a break. What do you think?'

He walks behind the screen again, comes out, a sketchbook

and a pencil in his hand. 'Keep your clothes on. It's the lines of your face that are interesting to me.'

'Oh,' she says, 'Oh,' and turns and points to the sculpture behind her and says, 'Mine aren't as interesting as the lines of her face.'

Ramsi offers no response, no reaction in words, but she sees in his coal-black eyes, in his closed-off expression, that there is nothing he wishes to divulge.

Despite Ramsi's expression Sarit wants to go on talking. To speak not about the lines of her own face, but the lines of *Nadia*'s face as she saw them in Nicole's, as she saw them in the gallery with the pink-heeled sales assistant and as she has seen them here. She wants to ask him who the model was. How long he spent studying her face. How well he knew her. How he has animated her so.

'You're from Egypt, aren't you?' she says.

'Yes.'

'Which city?'

'Alexandria.'

'Ah, yes. On the sea.'

'Yes.'

'I love the sea,' she says.

'Have you ever lived by the water?' he asks.

'No . . . but I . . . I used to go there as a child.'

He's standing at the other side of the room, leaning against the wall, sketching the outline of her from afar. No chair. No easel.

The paper and pencil are after all not his true medium, but just another way to help him see her in his mind. She wonders how he can see the lines of her face from such a distance.

For a moment she imagines herself, the muse, the model, the nude lying on the floor or on his sofa. She imagines how it would have been if he'd wanted to sketch all of her. 'How can you see me properly from there?' she asks.

He puts up his hand as if to silence her. Just as he had done with the students in the Institute. He does that and Sarit is not offended. And she is quiet after that, not as the girl reprimanded, but as the girl who knows the artist. Max had said that to her, before the painting stopped. He had said, 'Sarit, I want some quiet now. Stop talking for five minutes, my little one.'

Now she cannot help but move her eyes towards the muslin screen. She is forced to move them there, both because she is curious and because she cannot keep her eyes on Ramsi. She tries, but even though the light is dim, even though Sarit is in her clothes, turned in his direction she is naked. Through the screen she can make out shapes and figures. Behind one another, staggered all the way to the back of the room. At least she thinks she can make them out. Perhaps the room behind the screen is in her imagination. She only knows she wants to go there, to know what is behind it.

'You moved,' he says. 'Could you face me?'

'I can't see what I can learn from you like this. I really wanted to see you sculpt. To see your techniques.'

'So that you could turn your women's faces into pieces of art,' he says.

'Something like that,' she says. 'You could help me.'

'Why would I?' And when he asks the question, when he says, 'Why would I?' it is not Ramsi's intention to sound rude, but rather to question the reasons for her presence in his home, his place of work, his life.

From the other side of the room in the dim light he carries on sketching. Time passes. She asks him, 'Will you sculpt from that sketch?' She finds it hard still to look up, to look him straight in the eye. Sarit never finds it hard to look anyone straight in the eye. She doesn't care enough what they think of her.

Where the light falls she notices the bones of Ramsi's wrist.

'I sketch just for the ideas it brings,' he says. 'That's all. I

119

don't sculpt from the drawings alone unless I know the face well.'

Sarit wants to look behind her now, to see *Nadia* again, to wonder who she is, if she lives here in Chicago or only in his mind.

Ramsi asks her, 'Do you sketch before you operate?'

He doesn't know her name yet, who she is or where she's from. He doesn't seem to care, but he has asked her this question. This one about the sketching. Though he has no idea, of course, where this question goes to. He has no idea of the way that his words stretch back through the whole of her life.

'No . . .' she says, 'I don't sketch. I work from photographs.'

He nods. He carries on. A little later she looks up at the darkness through the skylight window. She says, 'It's getting late. I want to go now.'

'As you wish.'

'Do you need me again?'

'Do *I* need you again? Now that's a strange question.'

'I mean,' she says, standing up from the sofa, 'if you've decided to sculpt my face.'

'I would say the decision has been rather thrust upon me, but yes, if you want to come again, then come. I can't promise I'll be free.'

She stands up and walks towards the door. He doesn't move. Just stays there leaning against the brick wall, with the French music in the background. Ramsi standing there, in his checked shirt with the rolled-up sleeves, waiting for Sarit to leave.

She means to. She considers no other option but leaving until the moment that she stays. Until the moment when halfway across the wooden floor she stops and lifts her head to look at him.

This is her decision. Just as it was her decision to go back to Nicole's. Just as it was her decision to go to the master class and to walk through the engraved red door on Wells. And yet as she looks at him, straight in the eye this time, as she surprises him with this boldness of hers, in the half-light with the books and the batiks, with the veiled sculptures and the sketch of her face in his hand, she has no sense of making a decision. No sense of being guided by her head. Nor does she have a sense of how he will react, for though there is nothing between them, no chairs or tables, Ramsi stands behind a wall thicker, more opaque than the muslin screen, whilst around her, for the first time Sarit wears not even the flimsiest of clothes. She remembers little of this. Only once before has she known a feeling similar. With Dani on the kibbutz. And it wasn't this. Not raw, exposed bareness. Not this madness, this otherness that took over from one moment to the next. For Dani had always known her. Always seen her from the time they sat at school together.

With the security guard with the tattoo of the ugly starfish on his arm, and a few others besides, she had thrown off all her clothes of course, but she had not been naked. Now she was, though Ramsi was not, even with his clothes beside him on the floor. To the onlooker it was Ramsi up against the rough stone wall in his studio close to the black and white prints of Alexandria.

She who held him there, though of course that was not at all the way things were. Because, even against her, even though he was skilled, though he knew how to take her out of this room, out of her head, out of herself, against her, naked he was clothed. Clothed, as he took the gift of her body, as the rough skin of his face moved over the tattoo on her shoulder that he barely noticed in the heat of the moment. On the wooden floorboards then, uncovered where they were, close to the rug but not on it, so that later she would feel the splinters in her hands. Hands that she had protected from cold and ice and snow. Hands that she could not protect from the splinters or from this. So that though she heard herself cry, though she was pierced and drowning in the sound of her own voice, no sound had escaped from her lips.

No sound at all till she heard herself say, 'I must go. Now I really must go,' and she pulled on her trousers, her fleece and her trainers and ran, laces half undone, down the uneven steps to the red engraved door out on Wells Street.

FIFTEEN

The room is still. On the hessian bedspread on the low bed Ramsi lies facing the ceiling, his breathing light, his eyelids flickering, so that he might be asleep or he might be awake. Half dressed he lies there, the buttons of his checked shirt still unfastened, the coarse hair and dark skin of his chest exposed. The natural light is gone now and the room is lit only by tall thick honeywax candles that stand on large rust ceramic saucers and replace the lantern-style lamps he has used in the late afternoon. His sketchbook is on the floor. His creativity is spent. There is nothing now for him to do but to lie there and to sleep or to think.

Through the high open windows a breeze plays with the thick grey and yellow flames of the candles, tipping them towards the west, then towards the east. Towards the direction of his home. Engaged in its game with the wind the candle-light flirts with the *objets d'art* scattered around his room.

The books on his shelves are almost in darkness. Too much darkness, at least, for an onlooker to discern their titles. Except for a few seconds here or there where a flame licks the spine of one work or another. For a brief moment the candlelight closest to the bookcase reveals his battered paperback copy of *La Porte Etroite, Strait is the Gate,* by André Gide. He himself doesn't notice of course. His eyes have opened for a moment but he is not turned in the direction of his bookcase. *Strait is the Gate,* the book Lucie had given him soon after they first met in their late teens in the early sixties in Délice, the high-ceilinged teashop with the coffee-colour wooden surround-ings and the delicious little pastries on Alexandria's Ramleh

Square where the trams and the horse-driven carriages stopped and a bent little street vendor sold white and pink candyfloss on the corner. For hours they would sit in Délice, in the rooms where the sons and daughters of the cultured French-speaking high society met one another over *éclairs au café* and *mille-feuilles*, over *chocolat chaud* and *thé épicé*, though by then, by the early sixties, the concept of Egyptian high society had already begun to fade.

In the pages of *La Porte Etroite*, Alicia all but loses her mind as her nerves fray and then break with the ravages of loss – in her case loss of love. At the time when Lucie, just out of high school, fresh-faced, intellectual and bespectacled, pulled the book from her bag and handed it to Ramsi there were no parallels to draw. Not till many years later in Nice, when Ramsi held the book to pack it in a trunk, did the irony of the thing strike him hard. The irony of a woman who loses her mind to the ravages of loss. He opened his hand then and let the book drop where it fell amongst the others in his trunk. He let it fall next to his paperback copy of *La Sculpture inspiré par notre Héritage Gréco-Egyptien* (*Sculpture inspired by our Greek and Egyptian heritage*).

'It must have crept from the Karnak temples and the carvings of the tombs and the rocks in Luxor and Abu Simbel into your blood, Ramsi,' his mother used to say to him. 'Because it's not from me or your father, this passion of yours. That's for sure. Your father thinks you should concentrate more on your schoolwork, so you can get a real job. What do you say to that, my son?'

'No, Maman. Not yet. I love to sculpt. It makes me forget everything else.'

'Forget?' She laughs, her skin dark and Egyptian, her long thick hair already grey, though she is only in her forties. 'Forget? What's there to forget at your age, my son? But who knows? Maybe later in life it will be useful for you. There are always things to put behind you. I wish we could forget now, but there is not time for that.' She stands by the huge bay windows that the sea has painted grey and white and to her son she says, 'We're lucky to have been in Alexandria for this long. It can't last for ever, Ramsi. You know that, don't you? . . . Did you notice the sea is grey tonight? Have you seen it, my son?'

The sea is grey too where the light from the tall candles in Ramsi's room dances on the glass of the black and white photographs that Sarit has recognised as Middle Eastern. For hours as a boy, in the mid-fifties, he had walked along Alexandria's corniche, along Sidi Beach at Abu Kir with his Greek friends, his Muslim friends, his Armenian friends, his Italian friends, his Copt friends, his Jewish friends, all from the French Lycée. They had ridden the open trams along the Corniche. They had walked by the beach, living in the moment, throwing flat stones into the sea, watching as they skipped and skimmed across the water.

Ramsi's parents and their friends, in their circles of hushed conversations at their card tables and their chess tables, would talk about how things in Alexandria had changed. How Nasser was stripping Alexandria of its physical beauty and its cultural diversity, how he was letting buildings crumble and artistic and academic institutions flail. They would talk of how it never used to matter if you were Greek, Egyptian, Armenian, Muslim, Christian or Jewish, for that mixed heritage was, of course, the very essence of the place, the very spirit of the city of Alexandria. And ever since Ramsi could remember understanding the spoken word, he had heard them talk of emigrating. They were leaving all through his childhood. All through his years at the Lycée. They were leaving all through his adolescence, through his years of days and evenings spent finding the faces hidden in marble, in wood and in stone, sculpting the faces in clay, in the tiny dusty room at the end of the long corridor in the atelier, the workshop where he learnt the art of sculpture. They were leaving through all of those years. All of his teenage years. They never did leave, though: Not until they were made to. For them, for Ramsi's parents, the memories of what Alexandria had been until so recently were too tenacious. Alexandria was soothing. Alexandria was spicy. Alexandria was home. And now Alexandria was threatening.

His mother moved from the tall window overlooking the sea. 'Shall I switch the light off in here, Ramsi?' she had asked him.

The wind had picked up and the candles were flickering more furiously now as they lit the gold tip of the *hukka*, the water pipe that lay on a table in the corner of Ramsi's room. As they lit up its red and green snake tubes, the curves of its bowl, empty now of water and tobacco. It had been a while since he had pursed his lips to breathe in and taste tobacco through his water pipe, though on occasion still he would light up. When that happened it was almost always in the self-imposed inactivity that preceded creativity. Alone in his room in the silence or perhaps in the company of voices that sang in Arabic, in French or in Italian and filled the space. Or listening to a recording of *La Bohème*, *La Traviata* or *Madame Butterfly*, the operas that he had been to see with his mother in the heat of the Egyptian summers when the European companies visited Alexandria on their tours.

In the cafés and bars in the narrow shady backstreets of Alexandria and at times in Cairo, where his father had taught him to smoke, the lyrics of the music had always been in Arabic. They would sit there in a row, the men in long white cotton robes or in Western clothing, all classes, all cultures facing the cobbled street and puffing on their water pipes. And once in the sixties not long before they abandoned the rocks of Alexandria's rugged Corniche for the Corniche of the Côte d'Azur, Ramsi's father had said to him, 'I never thought it would matter, Ramsi, that your mother is a Christian and I'm a Jew. It doesn't matter to me. It never has. But it matters to them. Look, almost all of the Jews have left already since Israel was established. They're not wanted here any longer. And you will have to leave too, son. Yes, you're an Egyptian Christian, Ramsi. But you have my blood in you too. So we will all have to go. You understand that, don't you, my son?'

And still they did not leave. Not till his mother's music pupils were told they must no longer come to the big white house with its picture windows overlooking the sea. Not till Nasser sent his men to Ramsi's father's printing press to ask his policy on printing books related to Israel and Judaica. Not till 1967 when the Israelis invaded Egypt and Ramsi's father no longer knew whether to call himself an Egyptian or a Jew, did they drag the heavy leather trunks down from the attic and begin slowly to fill them till the shiny black grand piano stood abandoned and alone in the room. And his mother, who was quite young still and had been strong and fit, bent over like an old woman with every piece of linen, with every picture frame she placed inside the trunk. She did not want to leave her home.

But Marc, Ramsi's father, said, 'We are lucky. Nobody has tried to shoot us or to gas us here. We will be safe in France. You will see. At least we know the language where we're going. And we'll still have the sea.'

Their story was similar to Max's in its way, to the story of Sarit's father more than twenty years before. But then again it wasn't. It was, in fact, entirely different, because they, the Riyads, had time to pack their bags. They were allowed to take with them at least some of the belongings they loved. And a few of the people they loved too.

Ramsi did not want to join them straight away. He was twenty-two. He had a life of his own. He had his tiny studio at the end of the dusty corridor in the atelier. He had his talent and his professors. He had Lucie.

He lived alone in the big house after his parents left, but within weeks the quasi emptiness of the place, the fading echo of his parents' voices and his mother's music, began to haunt him. And so he and Lucie began to pack what was left. To take down curtains. To board up the windows. He asked her if she would leave with him for France. She asked her parents and they asked one another. They were liberals. Artists too. They trusted Ramsi to look after their only child.

Aboard the ship on the high seas Lucie blamed the early morning nausea on the winter waves of the Mediterranean. At sunrise she would stand there, blaming her sickness and her retching on the elements as she held on to the railings of the deck, till the red light of dawn cracked over the sea.

Till the red light of dawn where it merged with the flames of the honeywax candles fell on the sculpture of Nadia's face. As Ramsi lay there, in a deep sleep on the hessian spread in his high-ceilinged studio where Sarit had been with him only hours before.

SIXTEEN

Change is such a hypocrite. So constant itself, yet so insistent on movement in others. So sure that no matter if it is joy that it brings or havoc that it wreaks, its place will never be usurped.

Change never stirs, but slouches instead in a plush padded chair with gold-studded armrests and a harem of workers around it. Change employs water and wind, pleasure and pain, animal and human as harbingers of its intent. It employs truces and wars, coronations and coups as its pigeons, and as its infallible foreman change employs time.

In her work Sarit has developed a privileged relationship with change. In her game she jousts, she teases and she challenges it. The talent in her hands is such that though she too in the end might lose to the potency of physical change, with the skill of her fingertips, in the wrestle between the two of them, she is able to hold it at bay for years at a time. It is for this that the adults among her patients come to her. Because of her privileged status with change wrought by age, women and men too clamour for appointments to sit opposite Sarit. To look at her in her black trousers and her white open-necked shirt, to stare at the unmade-up face and to wonder how she dares.

'Dr Kleinmann. How are you?'

'Good, Mrs Grossinger. And you?'

'Ready to get these bandages off. Believe me, darling,' says the Viennese Jewish refugee in her heavily accented voice.

'If you can come over here, Mrs Grossinger. I'll remove them under the lights and take a look.'

'OK,' she says as behind Sarit she waddles to the padded

patient's chair. 'So I've been thinking, Doctor. If I'm happy with my chin, you know there are a few other things we could do. There's no point looking young just around the jawline, is there?'

'Could you sit still just for a moment? I can't take the bandages off while you're talking.'

Mrs Grossinger keeps quiet just long enough for Sarit to remove the layers of gauze beneath the outer bandages. Then she says, 'So, how does it look, Doctor?'

'It will look good.'

'Will look good? It doesn't look good already?'

'I told you the skin will be red for a while. Maybe even a few weeks, but we've suctioned the fat away. You have a much firmer line. Here . . . wait just two minutes and I'll give you the hand mirror. You'll be able to see for yourself.'

Sarit in her thin rubber gloves unwraps and wipes and soothes. She reaches for the mirror and as she hands it to Mrs Grossinger she smiles to herself just a little in anticipation of her patient's pleasure.

'Ah. Doctor. Amazing. The sagging's gone.' She turns the mirror sideways. 'No more chicken neck. I can't believe it . . . But it's very red. Will the redness go?'

'I just told you it would. Give it time.'

'So there's some other stuff I'd like to do. I don't like how age is changing my face. Do you think we could do a lift now?' she asks.

'First of all you have to let this heal. Then we can talk about it if you want. But there's no hurry. Let's take one step at a time.'

'How much younger would it make me look?' she asks.

'How much younger do you want to look?'

'Well, you know my friend Mrs Feinberg. You did her face and it looks like her husband snatched her from the cradle. I'd like to look as young as she does.'

'Cosmetic surgery should not be about having a better car

than your neighbour. Think about it, Mrs Grossinger. You have a nice face. OK, you don't look thirty years old. But it's a nice, strong face.'

'Anyone would think you didn't want the business, Doctor.'

'It's not that. It's just what I always say. You have to think about it carefully because I can't change what's on the inside.'

'But, Doctor, you . . .'

'Call me Sarit. I've told you that before.'

'Sarit. Of course I'm old enough to be your mother, aren't I, darling? But you know,' she says, gesticulating with her wrinkled, sun-flecked hands, 'you do change what's on the inside. Maybe not with an old woman like me so much, but what about the other stuff you do? You don't change things when you fix the face of a young kid with a deformed mouth? Sure you do. And not just what's on the outside either.' It was there, with the cleft lips, the burnt faces, the diseased faces that change had vested Sarit with her greatest powers. When her opinion was sought by the trauma surgeons on the burns unit, when diseased adolescents, shamed by their appearance, wanted to give up on the world and small children grew baffled by the taunting of their classmates, change gave Sarit the greatest opportunities to counteract the ravages it had caused.

On a huge screen in a conference hall on the Rive Gauche in Paris a tall, thin, balding American professor of reconstructive and aesthetic surgery in a black suit and orange tie points at the slide of the burnt and mashed-up face of a teenage boy, a car crash victim. He says, 'When they brought him in to our hospital several weeks after his accident his confidence was as shattered as his face. You can see here. Some scarring from second-degree burns, some third-degree burns. Some shattering of the mandible here. There was a team of doctors working on him. First the trauma surgeons worked on him, of course, till his condition had stabilised. He had several operations after the first year. Incredibly skilful skin grafts and reconstruction . . . and you can see, this is how he looks now

. . . There's still considerable scarring here, but the change is remarkable really. It was a collaborative effort but he owes the greatest debt to the one female reconstructive surgeon on our team. A fairly young woman. Actually, I'd call her more of an artist than any of the rest of us. She's been criticised for dedicating a considerable amount of her time to cosmetic surgery with adults, but I think she brings her talent and much of what she's learnt in that area to the field of paediatric plastics. We wanted her to come and lecture to you, but she prefers to stay behind the scenes.'

It was only right, of course, that Sarit should been vested with some powers to reverse sudden, dramatic and unwelcome change. Because change of that ilk had run up much in the way of debt with her. Hadn't Mona said that when she sat in the room with the misty sunlight with Sarit's hand in her own? Hadn't she looked at the branches of her palm and said, 'Your fate line is broken in so many places. There have been many dramatic changes.'

Gabriella had tried to talk to her child, to prepare her for change, as much as a child of seven can be prepared for the unspeakable. On a bench at the top of the grass verge which, strewn with the velvet of yellow and purple pansies, sloped down towards the stream where Sarit had stood with her father and watched the old man fishing, Gabriella sat and played with the straps of her daughter's denim dungarees. She buttoned and unbuttoned them, whilst Sarit made patterns out of twigs and pussy willow buds. 'Sarit.'

'Yes.'

'I want you and Abba always to be friends.'

'Abba is my friend,' the child says tentatively, looking up at her young mother's heavy eyes, her thinning hair, her yellowing complexion. And then she adds, 'He is my friend . . . sort of.'

'What do you mean, "sort of"?' asks Gabriella.

'Well, sometimes he shouts at me . . . You never shout at me, Ima.'

132

'But he loves you, Sarit. So so so much. You know that, don't you?'

'Then why does he shout at me?'

'Do you love Dani?'

'Yes.'

'Do you shout at him?'

'Sometimes.' The child giggles. 'Only when he cheats in hide and seek.'

And Gabriella thinks, 'Ah, my daughter. She's so clever. She's given me my cue.' And she says, 'When he hides, even if you can't see him you still know he's there, don't you?'

'Of course I do. He chooses such babyish places to hide.'

'So how do you know he's there when you can't see him?'

Sarit answers, indignant as a child is when he feels that an adult talks down to him, 'I know he's there, because . . . because I just do.'

'So, if ever you can't see me, you'll know I still love you, wherever I am, won't you, Sarit?'

'Iiiiiima! Why do grown-ups say so many silly things?'

'Because only children say things straight.'

In front of the schoolhouse in the children's garden Sarit is on her knees. The hard mud scratches her skin, but she's busy and she's happy and she doesn't seem to care. She is in her blue-grey T-shirt that Ima has said matches her eyes. She is planting sunflower seeds in an S pattern in the earth when for the first time in her life she is accosted by dramatic and unwelcome change. Rivka comes to her, bends down and takes her hand.

Sarit pulls it away. 'What are you doing? Leave me alone. I'm planting.'

'You need to come with me, Sarit. I need to talk to you.'

'But I've done nothing wrong this time. I promise.'

'I know that, sweetheart. You've done nothing wrong at all.'

The gentleness of Rivka's tone, her choice of words, alarms Sarit. The child stands up and follows Rivka out of the wooden

133

gate, the mud still on her hands and knees. They walk over to the corrugated-iron laundry building. Rivka sits down, pats the ground beside her and the two of them sit there beneath a cypress tree. All around them huge white sheets hung out to flap dry in the wind, so that whenever Sarit remembers this scene, she will see those huge white sheets flapping. The blank, terrifying canvases of the unknown. The *tabula rasa* of her future.

'Why did you make me come here?' she asks Rivka. 'I want to plant my sunflowers. I was planting the seeds in an S for Sarit,' she lisps. 'I don't want to talk to you now.'

'But I want to talk to you.'

'About what?' Sarit asks, impatient. She stands up to leave.

'About your mother.'

Her back to Rivka, in her blue-grey T-shirt with the mud on her knees, Sarit stands holding her breath, rooted to the spot, playing musical statues in a vain attempt to freeze her childhood. 'What about her?' she says, not turning round.

'Sarit . . . your Ima . . .'

'What?'

Rivka starts to cry and Sarit runs off down the path calling, 'Ima, Ima . . . my Ima, where are you? Ima.'

From time to time after that Max still lets her be a child. But the unpredictability of it all is too great. He hardly speaks for weeks at first. In the afternoons when she goes home he is lying there with the orange and blue painting of himself and Gabriella muddled up together above his bed. The painting that he will rip from the wall one afternoon when the pain of the constant reminder is too great. On some days Max lies with his eyes open and stares at the ceiling. On others he lies in a position almost foetal with a pillow against his face to block out the truth.

And Sarit at eight years old watches him from the wooden rocking chair at the foot of the bed. She rocks, she watches and she waits for him to move. In silence she sits there till one

134

afternoon, almost in a whisper she hears herself say, 'I want my Ima.'

Max sits up and looks at his child from the bed. He says, 'Sarit. Come to Abba.'

She hesitates a moment, before she walks from her chair and climbs on to the bed beside Max. He says, 'What would there be without you, Sarit? What would there be? I will make it all right for you, my little one. I swear I'll try. You'll see. I promised Ima.' He pulls her to him. Holds her in his grief.

Like the sculptures of two figures, as a circle with no end and no beginning, their heads touching in bronze or in wood, so these two are curled up in one another. So that the child's refrain of 'I want Ima, I want Ima' might almost have been her father's.

'I want Ima. Ima. Ima,' calls Sarit. 'She's here. She's playing hide and seek with me. She said she would be.'

Only on two or three afternoons do they lie there like that. On others, ignored, she sits in the rocking chair and stares at him in his misery, while their wooden easels stand neglected in the next-door room. While their brushes lie dry and their oil paints lie untouched.

But as a man may be roused from a coma by the touch or the tone of the voice of a loved one, so Sarit knows of one way and one way alone. So that when one afternoon in early March, Max opens his eyes and turns to look at her she is sitting in front of the window on her high wooden chair at the easel she has dragged in from the living room. Sitting there and painting a portrait that begins with her father lying on his bed. He props himself up on his elbow.

'Oh, Abba. Now you've moved,' she says, pretending to be cross.

For the first time in weeks his thin grey face cracks into a smile.

'Keep still, Abba,' she says.

She uses too much of the bottle of turps to mix with her

135

paints so that the watery black and the blue spill over into tiny puddles on the floor. She says, 'This will make you feel better, Abba. You'll see.'

'I'm pleased to see you paint, my little one,' he says.

'No, but this will really really make you feel better.'

'Why is that?' he asks.

She says, 'I'll tell you when I've finished.'

For a child of eight her concentration span is long. Fifteen, maybe twenty minutes later Sarit calls out to Max, 'Finished, finished, finished.' She doesn't lift her eyes towards her father when she speaks, but she climbs down from her chair and she walks over to him with the thin paper that sags in the middle from the wet paint held on the palms of her hands as though it were an offering. The wet painting that he takes from his child. That she holds out to him saying, 'Look, look, Abba. Here. See. I've brought her back.' And Max holds the picture there, looking down at himself next to Gabriella in her red dress, while Sarit stands waiting, squeezing her muscles in tightly, counting to herself under her breath. Her father stares at the painting in his hands, looks at his daughter. Then he lowers his head towards her picture and begins to sob.

His sobs that stain her painting. Her painting that stains sheets and clothes and skin. Gabriella's death that stains lives and souls and psyches. And the child saying to her father, 'Don't cry, Abba. I brought Ima back. And that's her favourite, that red dress. Did you know that?'

Max begins to paint again, though now only in shades of black and grey. The splashes of Chagall greens and yellows and Picasso blues have gone with Gabriella. His balance too is gone. The left leg of his easel wobbles. Only from time to time does he bother to steady it. In his behaviour with his child he wavers too. In this way as well Sarit is made to endure change. Max says to Rivka and her other teachers, 'I don't want her so tired by the end of the day that she can't paint.'

'But Max, on Mondays and Thursdays we have art class in

school. I think that's enough for her for one day. She doesn't need to paint when she gets out of school. She needs to play.'

His face grows red. He says, 'Whose child is she?'

'She's a kibbutz child. She's part of all of us. And we say there has to be some balance in her life. Not everything can change for her. The child needs a little peace now.'

In the north of the country, where streams gather at the foot of the Lebanese mountains, which overlook the kibbutz and flow into estuaries and brooks and rivers, peace was always threatened. In that region, the northernmost tip of the country, known as the 'Finger of Galilee' for its shape, the children of the kibbutz had no fear. There, where the hills drop towards the town of Qiryat Shemonah, towards the Great Rift of the river, these kibbutz children, like water babies born by the sea, like mountain babies born in snow, were war babies born to strife.

They watched the boys and girls, the kibbutz adolescents, come and go in their murky green army uniforms with their guns slung over their shoulders. They watched the older men even in times of relative peace as they left each year to serve their *miluim*, their obligatory annual month-long duty in the reserve army. This would be somewhere further along their path too. They knew it and they were unafraid. In peace on the kibbutz, they practised for war.

'Listen,' screeched Sarit. 'Listen, it's the wobbly waily sound. We get to go in the shelter. Come on, Dani . . . Come.' She's tugging at his arm, ready to run from the schoolhouse.

'Sarit, stand still. You know the rules. You wait for me. We get in line,' the teacher shouts.

'Come on, come on,' Sarit calls to the younger children. 'Let's get into the shelters. It's great for hide and seek in there!'

Out of the schoolhouse, past the little red plastic table and chairs in the courtyard of the kindergarten, past the sunflowers that have been planted in the form of an S not quite finished in the spring of each year, since Sarit had planted them the

137

day of Gabriella's death. Along the gravel path, past the rough granite sculpture of the man arched backwards, looking up towards the hot and heavy sky. Walking fast, running almost, towards the shelter.

'No running, Sarit. Do you hear me?'

Her hand, delicate, with its long slim fingers, clammy with excitement in Dani's hand. Dani, pale and small for twelve, his spindly legs in denim shorts too baggy for him. Another child calls out, 'It's just a practice you know.'

And Sarit shouts, 'Who cares? Who cares if it is? It's still fun, isn't it? Come on, faster.'

Behind the low, flat-roofed library building with its dog-eared books in English, Hebrew and French and German. Behind the grown-ups' social club that smells of smoke and coffee, black and bitter, past the rickety corrugated-iron door to Max's studio: 'That's Abba's studio,' calls Sarit and points as they half walk half run past it, and a little out of breath she says, 'I'll paint there one day you know.'

'I know that,' says Dani, still clutching her hand. Down an uneven path, shaded and overgrown with foliage, to a thick and heavy silver soundproof, blast-proof door.

Rivka pulls hard on the handle. 'Children, help me get this open,' she says between gritted teeth.

Five or six children rush to her aid. Together they yank the handle down. They clatter down silver steps in darkness. 'Feel for the light, children.' Sarit trails her left hand along the rough walls. She is the first to find the switch. And there is light then in the big dark shelter with the rows of bunk beds. Three and four steel bunk beds on top of one another and the thin mattresses, with the rough green blankets folded at the foot of each.

'Now,' Rivka calls, 'we need to talk about the rules.' Above the siren, above the squealing and excitement of the children's voices she has to shout. 'We need to count how many children are here. One, two, three, five, six, seven, eight . . . I'm coming to find you, Dani. Come on, everyone. Let's go and find Dani. He's under one of these beds.'

And the children are moving on their stomachs, crawling on all fours under the bunk beds on the cool stone shelter floors in search of Dani. At twelve and thirteen, unexposed to glamour or sophistication, even the older ones are prepared to play as children. Hiding underground, climbing, crawling, sliding in this new place. That's what the shelter is for. It's for hide and seek, so that Sarit and Dani and their friends can play hide and seek with the smaller ones. They are used to the wailing sounds of the sirens. They have heard them many times before, in the Six Day War of 1967 when they were small and in all the practice runs since then.

Dani turns to Sarit. He says, 'You know it's for real this time. We might be in here for ages. You'll need your easel and your brushes.'

'I'm not going to paint today. It's Yom Kippur. No one works today.'

'They might not let us out.'

'They will at night.'

'Shall I sneak out?' asks Dani. 'Shall I go and get your paints for you?'

'No. Don't be silly. Anyway, you know if we're in here long enough my father will bring them.'

'He won't. Not if he's fighting.'

Since she was tiny, Sarit has seen her father in the green uniform that hangs on his thin frame. She has seen him called away once a year for a month to serve in the reserves. She remembers from when she was small the way Gabriella would hold her by the door of the dining room waving goodbye to Abba carrying the great big pointed gun that looked like it would weigh him down. She remembers how Max would call to her from halfway down the path, how he would say, 'Hands up all those girls who love their daddies.' How he was able to do that, to call out those words when he was far enough away from the door. And she remembers too how she would swing both her little arms backward in the air and laugh.

Though too much time has passed by now for Sarit to recall this, once as Max's uniform had faded into the landscape Gabriella had said out loud to no one in particular, 'Fighting will never be for him. He's been through enough. He would never survive it.'

'They're not fighting,' Sarit says now, sitting cross-legged looking down from the top bunk of a bed in the shelter. 'It's just a practice,' she calls to Dani above the wailing of the siren.

'It's not.'

'It is.'

'It's not.'

'I swear it is.'

'Who cares?'

She calls the other teacher, a man called Eli with a red birthmark on his cheek. 'This is just a practice, isn't it?'

'I don't think so, Sarit.'

'But it's Yom Kippur. No one will feel like fighting today. They haven't eaten a thing. Anyway, my father won't go.'

Eli is not really listening to Sarit. He's standing in front of her with a small black wireless, trying to tune it, lifting it to his ear. She walks up close to him. She says, 'Let me hear.' He puts it to the side of her face. She hears nothing but a thick fuzzy underwater buzzing. The radio stations had not been geared up to transmit that day. The broadcasters, the more observant ones, many of them have been called from their prayer between the wooden pews of the synagogues. Some have shed their white prayer shawls for green uniforms. Others have been ordered to transmit news to the people as best they can. They have been ordered to eat, to obey the army and to disobey God.

Even most of the secular Jews on the kibbutz, once they are beyond the age of thirteen, abstain from food or water on this day. They do so, if not in belief of God, then in belief of superstition on a day when the heavens are said to judge their actions, or they do so at least out of respect for the fasters in their midst. If they eat, they eat in secret. If they drink, they drink behind closed doors. All of them, that is, but Max.

'Abba,' she had said the year before when she was eleven. 'You can't do that. It's embarrassing.'

'Embarrassing? Please. What's embarrassing about it? If I want to eat a banana I'll eat one. If I want to drink champagne today I'll drink it. You don't want to walk with me? So don't. I'll see you later.'

She carries on walking with him, by his side through the kibbutz. She takes her father's right arm on the way to nowhere in particular, because on the Day of Atonement there is nowhere for them to go. 'Wouldn't you be embarrassed if Rivka saw you now or Eli or . . . ?'

'Or God?' he says.

She pulls on her father's arm and stops him. 'What do you mean, Abba?'

'Nothing, Sarit, nothing.'

'No, what do you mean? I want to know.'

He stops. He looks. He hesitates, then says, 'God has hidden himself from me, Sarit. I don't know where he is. Maybe you know better.'

'God,' she says, 'is . . . God is . . .' and she laughs. 'God is in my paintbrush . . . the big thick furry one you hardly ever let me use.'

And now, on the following Day of Atonement in the underground shelter, Eli lies to the children. He says, 'Nothing bad is going to happen, children, but tonight we have to stay here in the shelter.'

'Goody, goody, goody.'

'I'm hungry,' calls a freckled child.

'Yes, we're hungry.'

'We're hungry, we're hungry, we're hungry,' the children chant in the bunker, with the sounds that resonate from its cold walls. In the artificial light they look at their watches. They count down till they know that outside the real light has begun to redden. Till the Day of Atonement is over. They feast then on sugared apricots and figs, on chocolate and on biscuits that Eli and Rivka have fetched from the store cupboards at the back of the bunkers. The children hold out their hands for more. They stretch out their arms.

At the Suez Canal where Israel and Egypt face one another, in desert sands that have always known of conflict, Max and his colleagues are plotting change – observing the other from their vantage points, convinced that they are hidden and protected. They think that, but they are wrong. As chessmen on a board, the Puten and the Russian tanks plan to make their moves. But this game, this one, is played at speed. As if in some sick and dissonant song, shells scream, lights blind and illuminate faces all at once. Lights that have shone through barbed wire in Max's face before: in another time; another place; another hell.

On both sides of the border life after life is changed. Half in, half out of the turret of his tank, Max stands, watches as his regiment colleagues prepare the barges for their first crossing of the Suez. And the ugly lights glare still in his face. Glaring and blinding till his scream, Max's scream, loses itself in the scream of shells, as the tracks of his tank miss the safety of the barge and rearing and raging, it swerves, turns over and is thrown with him at the water's edge. Choking, gasping, they pull him, crushed and torn, from beneath its broken frame. And the nothingness then. The blackness in which he lies unconscious, as they lift him on to the stretcher, bloodied and ripped open, with his right arm hanging useless from his shoulder, just as the flesh of his mother had hung ravaged from her face.

And in his studio the new tubes of jet-black oil paint lie there unopened. Because with one arm, with his left arm, for himself he has no desire left to unscrew the tube. Nor would there be any sense in it. No sense at all now, without his right arm.

The arm that even as a memory, even as a phantom has the power once more to change his daughter's world. Because her life, Sarit's life, is Max's life. They talk about it on the kibbutz, Rivka and Eli and Dani's parents. They say, 'He will suffocate that girl with his love, his pride and his ambition for her.'

Max doesn't ask Sarit to care for him. He is not in that sense a selfish man. He learns to tie the laces of his shoes and to fasten the buttons of his shirt with his left hand. He says no, always, if she asks, 'Abba, shall I cut that up for you?' In that way he would rather struggle. Not to elicit pity or admiration, but because his eyes burn with the fierce independence born of necessity and mistrust of the world. To dress or to eat he wants no one to be his right arm. But to paint, because he believes Sarit's talent to be his and his to be hers, why should he sweat and struggle with his left arm to create an amber sunset or a purple sunrise or to sketch the kibbutz librarian's lined and haggard face? That Sarit can do for him. For him. For her. He runs to the teenagers' house to wake her, because angst has robbed him of sleep and so he has seen the light greens, the mauves and the yellows of the early morning. The air is crisp. The jasmine and the mint smell sweet. He wants to capture them in oils and so he wakes Sarit. He tiptoes into the wooden teenagers' house, walks over to her, ruffles her messy black hair, shakes her right arm, bends down towards her, says, 'Sarit, you have to see this. *Maher, maher, boy iti* . . . quick, come with me.'

She allows herself to be dragged, stumbling after him, three-quarters asleep still but awake enough to know that she's been here before. He stops on the grass outside his house where he has left paper, paints, brushes and a palette.

He stands beside her. He points up at the sky. As though it is a photograph, he says, 'You can't miss this one, Sarit. It's an Expressionist's dream . . . Hurry, in a few minutes the colours will have changed. Here.' With his left hand he pushes a brush

143

into her right hand. He says, 'Mauve, this mauve with a little blue. But just a spot. The light-blue. Here. Thicker strokes, Sarit.' He passes her a different brush. A flat and fan-like brush. He points, he says, 'You can use a little of this purple. And look, there's the sun. Use some white for the light. Use thinner strokes now. A touch of the yellow.'

She is still not quite awake, in her blue pyjamas on the grass, painting the rising of the sun. It matters little, though, that she half sleeps, because as she works she doesn't need to think at all. Max does that for her and once the sun has risen he says to her, 'My genius. Now go back to sleep,' though since the Yom Kippur War, since his right arm has gone, he does not always speak to her that way. Instead at times the tone of his voice is dark with angst and anger. Anger that he vents with all that he has left to lose. 'What's that you're painting, Sarit?' he asks when she is seventeen.

She's at the back of the communal dining room. It's early evening in the winter. For once a dark, dull, grey evening. The kibbutzniks are eating at the long wooden tables. She sees them as rows and rows of heads of different shapes and heights and sizes, lighthouses bobbing in a sea of white.

'What is that you're painting?' Max asks again. This time his voice is louder.

'Sh, Abba. You can see what it is.'

'Yes, but what are you saying with it?'

'Abba, please, I need to concentrate. I don't know that I'm saying anything . . .' and then, 'Well, maybe something about anonymity. All these people. These heads. All eating the same thing in the same place, under neon lights.'

'It's empty, Sarit. It looks meaningless to me. No point to it. Here you should do this.' He reaches over to lift a brush from the tray next to her palette,

'You can't do it, Abba. You know you can't. Now leave me alone.'

'What do you mean I can't do it?' He's raised his voice now.

144

The heads Sarit has been painting have stopped eating. The bobbing white heads that have turned round to watch are still now.

Max asks her almost under his breath, 'What do you mean I can't do it?'

'With your left arm, Abba,' she says in a quiet voice. 'You can tie your shoelaces, but you can't paint properly with that arm. You might learn. I wish you would, but you can't do it yet. I've seen you try. I watched once through the window when you didn't know I was looking.'

And in a moment with a crash everything changes. He shows his daughter not what his left arm can create, but what it can destroy. The heads she has been painting are trodden and messy on the floor as they stare in disbelief at the scene behind them, as they turn round from their meal and gape at the discord behind them. The brushes, the paints, the turps, everywhere. The easel with one leg gone, the other battered as he kicks it and kicks it.

'Abba. Abba. Stop. You're crazy. Why are you doing this?'

'Max. Stop it. Now, please. Come on, Max. It's all right now. It will be all right you'll see. Sarit, are you OK?'

From the table Dani, in his khaki trousers, has run over to her, his mouth still full of food. 'Sarit.'

He holds her while she sobs. He says, 'Why does he do this? I can't bear to see him do this to you.'

She gulps. She says, 'He doesn't mean it. I swear he doesn't mean it. You don't understand him. He wanted to help me and he couldn't . . . he just couldn't . . . he . . .'

Max accompanies Sarit now on their trips to see Madame in Jerusalem. In the uncomfortable buses with the torn red plastic seats and the brown leather straps above their heads, he travels with her every time. In the summer she looks at him, as the sweat pours down his face and he hangs on with his arm to the leather strap. 'Abba, I'm sixteen. I can go by myself. It's too hot for you.'

In winter she looks at him, straight-backed but shivering in

145

the corner of the bus. They step out on to the thin layer of icy snow that covers the Jerusalem cobbles. He almost slips. She catches him. She takes his arm. 'Abba, it's too cold for you. I'm seventeen. I can go alone to Madame next time, you know.'

'You need me here,' he says and there in the bus she breathes a sigh of relief, for he is right. The part of her that's still a child both needs and wants him there.

Madame greets them into the warmth of the gallery with hot cinammon tea and home-made ginger biscuits on a white china plate with crinkled edges. Sarit smiles to herself. Every time she sees her, Madame seems to grow fatter, the pile of hair on her head seems to get taller and taller, and she seems to have grown an extra chin. Madame points to the red velvet couch. Father and daughter sit there side by side. 'I unpacked your latest stuff, Sarit,' she says.

Max looks up. Sarit looks up. Madame says, 'I called you here for a reason. I think it is time we gave you your first solo exhibition. What do you say? I don't want the child to become arrogant, Max, but this country doesn't have many like her. And she owes it to herself. And to you. Yes, it's her talent, but your dedication, Max, *n'est-ce pas?*'

Sarit says nothing. Max says nothing.

Madame carries on. 'Do you remember, Max, when you had your first show here? Remember that orange and blue painting of you and Gabriella that you made me take down from the wall at the last minute? God I was angry with you. We'd already had an offer for that painting. You've done an incredible job with Sarit. In some way her art is just like yours, Max. The way both of you mix the realist and the abstract. The way people who come into the gallery want to touch your paintings. Almost as if they were sculptures . . . Anybody would recognise her work as Kleinmann art. But she has more colour in her work than you've ever had, Max. She dares more than you did. So what do you say, Sarit? It's

146

your turn now. *Ha col mishtane, nachon?* . . . Everything changes, doesn't it?'

In Sarit's body the place where she feels change most is in the soft hollow just below her ribcage. When it grips her in the throat she recognises panic. When it burns in her ears she recognises rage. But change does not need to grip her or to burn her to make its presence felt. She knows it all too well.

And so now, the day after Ramsi has sketched the interesting lines of her face in his studio, now when Sarit can still feel the splinters embedded in the tips of her fingers where she has pressed against the wooden floor, she senses the tightening and the twisting, the movement in the soft hollow beneath her ribcage and she feels the calling out of change. The inevitability of change that is the same yet wholly different from any she has felt before. So that at the end of her day, as she sits alone in her darkened surgery, turned to face the night lights of the city, she leans back in her chair and in that place at the top of her stomach, in that soft place, she thinks of Ramsi and the studio and begins to feels the shapes that change can sketch. With her fingers on the flat of her stomach she traces its circles and its ripples. One foot pressed against the window, one hand over her eyes, she follows its swirlings as they spiral downwards, abstract and erotic. And as she relives the day before, the whole of her that night is overwhelmed by the heat, the movement and the madness of change.

SEVENTEEN

Fingerless black gloves round a glass of steaming tea. Fingertips that hint at strength and nicotine. Nails, smooth first, then ridged, scrubbed clean of stubborn drying clay. Strong hands that cup the glass of hot and sweet black tea in its tarnished silver holder. 'I put honey in it. You taste it there, Ramsi?'

'Yes, thanks, Albert. It warms you up.'

'Crazy having this cold in April. I'd never have left Egypt if I were you.'

'Oh, you would, Albert. You would.'

'This the piece then?' he asks, pointing at the cold stone floor, to a knee-high bundle, pinkish clay peeking through layer after layer of bubble paper that wraps it and protects it.

'Yes.' Ramsi lowers his glass, takes off one of his fingerless gloves.

'You going to work on her a little yourself, are you?'

'Yes, as far as I can.'

This is age old, this exchange between the two of them. This charade that Albert and Ramsi play. The way they pretend that Ramsi has come here for Albert to cast his sculptures, rather than to cast them himself with some conversation here and there to keep him going.

'What's new with you, Albert?'

He raises his eyes to the heavens, this big albino man in his blue overalls, and says, 'It's crazy. Take a look around you. There's so much work, I don't know what to do with it. Suppose I shouldn't complain, though, but take a look at the place.' The space is huge. Wooden tables covered with rusting pots of water, of varnish and of wax, with brushes, knives and bottles. On chairs and on the floor discarded busts and plaster casts of abstract forms. Dusty workbenches hidden by rags and towels and torches, drills and cloths and wax models of art in progress. Yet the clutter and the chaos lend the place its charm.

'You'll get yourself sorted out, Albert. Everybody wants to come here. They like being around you.'

'I guess.' He smiles. His teeth are yellow and crooked. 'I'll clear some space for you,' he says.

He begins to move some of the tins and pots and plaster moulds from the wooden table where they stand. 'You been down Kingston Mines lately?' he asks Ramsi.

'Yes,' he says, taking off the other fingerless glove. 'I've got my own corner there. I sit and watch the world.'

'Good idea. Excellent idea,' and then, 'Hey, Ramsi.'

'Yes?'

'There's . . . em . . . something I've been meaning to ask you . . . I . . . er . . . Now look, don't take this the wrong way, because you know I love your work. I think your work is great. But you know.' And he wrings his hands, shifts his weight from one large foot to the other. 'Well, they used to say my stuff was great. So . . . well, what I wanted to ask you was this. And you know I'm happy for you and everything, but, well, why . . . hey?'

'Go on, Albert, ask me.' Ramsi's tone is patient, almost gentle for a moment.

'Well, it's just, well, why d'you think you've made it and I haven't?'

Ramsi doesn't have to stop and think. The answer to this question has been on the tip of his tongue for ever. 'Nadia,' he says. 'You know that. Because of Nadia. If I've made it, as you put it, then that's why.'

'Oh, right. Yes, right. I never thought of that. Because she has . . . I mean she had a great face, didn't she, or I mean the face she would have had as a teenager and a grown-up and the way you bring her to life . . . it would have been a great

149

face . . . beautiful, you know. I like the other women you sculpt too, don't get me wrong, but the Nadia stuff . . . it's, well . . . well, you know . . . it's amazing.'

'Thanks. Thanks a lot, Albert. I'd better get started,' says Ramsi, his voice muffled as he pulls his thick black flecked woollen sweater over his head.

'Yeah, right,' Albert says. 'Yes, good idea to get working. You know where everything is. Of course you do. You can holler if you need me . . .' and then, 'Do you want some overalls?'

'That would be great.'

Albert disappears for a few moments, then strides over with another pair of blue overalls and hangs them over the back of a chair. 'They're clean,' he says, 'just some paint stains.'

'Thanks.' And Ramsi bends down and begins to climb into them. Above and below his beard that day he is unshaven and his thick silver-grey hair falls over his eyes.

He is doing up the buttons of the overalls, straightening up, already in his other world, when Albert calls out, 'Who the hell is that now? I can't take one more goddamned artist today. I'm done.'

From the other side of the room a banging and its echo resound on the iron door. Albert crosses the room. Goes out into the building's hallway. On the threshold of the foundry, a woman in a thick navy fleece, a grey scarf and a grey woollen beret says, 'Hi . . . I came to see Ramsi . . . Is he there?'

Albert looks shocked. No one has ever come here for Ramsi. No one has ever even called, though at times he's spent days, even nights in a row here, sleeping on the couch. Oh, there have been women of course. Albert has known that. He has even asked him in the past. He has said, 'Ramsi, have you found yourself the love of a good woman yet? It would help those creative juices.'

'A good woman. Yes, perhaps. But love?' Ramsi has said in his accent that is heavy with French and with Arabic. 'Love. No, Albert. What on earth would I do with it?'

Ramsi speaks to Albert as he talks to no one else. As though this foundry, this huge, draughty space of craft and creativity were a haven. Because between the two of them there is an unspoken agreement that if Ramsi becomes the talk of the sculpting world it will not be because of Albert's indiscretions. And the other sculptors do speak of him. The fine arts world of Chicago celebrates Ramsi's work, gallery owners fight to represent him and the local artists are both fascinated by his aura and angered by his obsession with privacy. They are frustrated by his reserve and drawn by his mystique. So that sometimes they turn to Albert and they goad him. They say, as they watch him working on the casting of their sculpture, 'Come on, Albert, tell me Ramsi's story.' And, his eyes fixed all the while on his knife or on his torch on the wax as he works, Albert says, 'You know what? Ramsi doesn't tell me a thing either. He's the most private person I've ever met.' And he leaves it at that.

Mostly it is the women who ask about Ramsi. The men are interested in his professional life. The less successful ones are jealous. But it is the women who insist on knowing who Ramsi is and where in a metaphorical sense he has come from. Now Albert is walking back into the room, his white eyebrows raised, with Sarit a few steps behind him. 'You've got a guest here, Ramsi,' he says.

His hand on the bubble paper he is about to unwrap, Ramsi starts. From where he stands by the table he says just, 'Seems you're an expert at surprises.'

Sarit smiles, walks in his direction, between the tables of art and art tools. With her mind she tries to slow her heartbeat and she moves towards him as if nonchalant, not to greet him with a kiss but to stand at a safe distance from him. Four feet away or maybe five.

'How on earth did you know I was here?' he asks.

'I dropped by to see you at home. To see if you felt like starting the sculpture. I saw your neighbour. The woman who

151

always wears pyjamas. She said she'd seen you walk out with your work all wrapped up. She assumed you'd gone to the foundry.'

'So you thought you'd follow me,' he says.

'Why not?' she asks, though as she speaks, as she says 'Why not?' she wonders yet again at her own drive, both powerful and unfamiliar, to be in Ramsi's presence.

He looks at her and thinks, 'She's right. She followed me. Why not?' He thinks too that the round-rimmed black glasses that she wears today make her look young. He says, 'But how did you know it was this place?'

She says, 'She told me it was a foundry on the West Side. She knew where it was. So I came.'

'What for?'

'You asked me that question at the Art Institute.'

He laughs. A real laugh this time. Not cynical as his laughter had been in the labyrinth of the Institute when she told him what she did with her life. And he just says, 'We could have talked some other time. This is not the best place,' and he lowers his head and starts to pick on the tape on the wrapping of his terracotta sculpture.

'This is a good day for me,' she says. 'I don't see patients on a Saturday. Unless there's an emergency.'

'I see . . . A good day for you. Hm.' And then, 'So please do tell me. What exactly made you come?'

'I wanted to,' she says.

Impressed by her lack of inhibition he smiles. 'Aha,' he says. 'Aha.'

And Albert comes across. He says to her, 'What was your name?'

'Sarit.'

Incorrectly he repeats it. He says Sairit like the man with the starfish tattoo had done, like Lauren often does, he says, 'Sairit, you going to be here for a bit?'

'Yes.'

'You want some tea?'

'Some coffee. Strong and black No sugar.'

Still a few feet from Ramsi, Sarit pulls up a chair. She says, 'I want to stay a while and watch. I've never seen a sculpture being cast.'

'Oh, you do, do you?' he says and adds, 'I warn you. This casting business is a long, slow process. I might not do it for a few days. It doesn't happen overnight.'

'What does?' she asks, daring at first, looking straight at him, lowering her grey eyes then, overcome by an unfamiliar wave of shyness and saved by Albert standing over her with a glass of strong, hot sugarless coffee that she drinks once Ramsi's gone.

EIGHTEEN

Black tar is thrilling and threatening. Black tar is sticky and potent. It sticks to skin. It sticks to flesh. It sticks to lives. On the streets of Humbolt Park and Cabrini Green on the near north side of Chicago, where night is scary and police car sirens wail, the bulbs from uncovered tower block windows glare at treeless streets with used condoms, used-up young girls and used syringes in gutters and on street corners in the ice of winter and the sweat of summer. Behind a tall dustbin on the corner of Division and North L'Arrabee a young black man steadies his own hand that is hot and shaking in the night. The sleeve of his heavy denim jacket is worn and rolled up. He barely notices that his stomach is empty or that his throat is parched. He thinks only of filling his veins. In the semi-darkness he feels for the swollen blackened ridge on his right arm and into it he plunges the thin sharp silver sliver borrowed from a friend. He sits down on a low wall and before he begins to see cars inside out, tower blocks on the move, and people huge as giants, before his heart begins its paranoiac race to nowhere, as he shudders on the wall behind the dustbin that smells and spills with waste and filth, he wonders about the chain of people and of events that has led him here.

He thinks about the black tar that his friend has cooked and heated to a powder in his battered silver saucepan on the boiling oven ring. He thinks with a fleeting sick sensation of the watches he has ripped from wrists, the handbag straps he has slashed from shoulders, the old woman he has mugged to pay for it. He thinks of the street corner where he and the man in the black fur jacket have negotiated for the stuff almost

154

in sign language. He wonders about the life of the man in the fur jacket, he wonders where he goes to get the sticky black tar that wrapped in paper fills his trouser pockets. And as his hallucinations grip, as the heroin carts him off to terrifying territory, he thinks of the unmarked shopfront, the all-night bar where the professionals are said to trade with one another. Where the dealers in their turn go to haggle with the big boys, without whom none of the potent, expensive sticky stuff would have been unloaded in the Southern States and then sent in trucks to New York and Chicago. He thinks of the dealers, swigging their spirits, playing poker for an extra ounce or two. And as he needs them so he curses them, for often when his mouth begins to foam and his heart begins to pound he fears for his life, never imagining that they too might fear for theirs.

The heroin addicts on the street corner, though, know nothing of the Italian gallery on Milwaukee where the ornate Italian ceramic urns and vases, once emptied of their lethal load, are sold as works of art that have been turned by the hands of the Sicilian artisans. He knows nothing of the identity of Alessandro and his colleagues who chain-smoke and hop from foot to foot as they watch their workers unravel layer after layer of bubble wrapping, as they stand over them, breathing down their necks, as they remove sheet after sheet of newspaper from the urns and from the vases waiting for that first glimpse of the sealed bags of tightly packed sticky black tar. For they, the big boys, Alessandro and his team, will never soil their own hands with the drugs. They stand instead and hold their breath, they clench their fists, they watch and wait while workers in their rubber gloves remove the drugs and weigh them in their plastic bags on the old-fashioned weighing machines, to check that no criminal, no impostor, has filched a few hundred thousand dollars' worth en route. And as they watch so they mutter under their breath, calculating, biting the ends of their pens, jotting numbers down on

155

scraps of paper. '*Quante milioni, Alessandro? . . .* How many million you got there, Alessandro?'

'*Sedici* . . . sixteen.'

'*Strano. Io ne ho quindici milione dollari* . . . That's odd, I make it fifteen million dollars,' says Maurizio, standing close to Alessandro by the sink in the kitchen at the back of the art gallery at night.

Maurizio looks at Pino. Pino glares at Alessandro. With just a hint of menace in his voice he says, 'Alessandro, your maths never was much good, was it? We make it fifteen million exactly. That's the street value. Fifteen million. You get it, don't you, Alessandro? Fifteen million, right?'

'OK. Fifteen. You're right,' says Alessandro.

He remembers the first time he had had a similar conversation, how he had leant back against the sink, how he had looked at his colleagues, with their hairy chests, their gold chains, their ostentatious wristwatches, how he had breathed in the smell of their cigar smoke and thought, 'The family . . . They're stealing from them.' He remembers the sick feeling in the pit of his stomach, he remembers how he had felt, knowing that there was no safe haven. That between Pino and Maurizio and his bosses in Palermo he was trapped and that they had all overestimated his toughness, his resilience. Sandwiched between the two, knowing that Maurizio and Pino knew all too well that the family had sent him over to Chicago not to reduce their workload as they'd said, but to supervise their 'art' transactions.

And Pino had repeated then, 'I think your maths is no good, Alessandro. And your memory. You remember the last time we spoke about your maths? We thought you understood. You must be having too many late nights with your pretty blonde, Alessandro,' and each time he had said his name he had poked his hairy index finger into Alessandro's chest. 'Our figure is right, Alessandro,' he had said. 'You tell that to Palermo. Yes? Then you can go and play with that girl of yours. Beautiful girl.'

Alessandro had looked away. He had said, 'I'll tell them.'

156

'Good,' said Pino.

'Good,' said Maurizio.

And Alessandro had closed his eyes, thought of Felicia and had said to himself, 'I'll tell them it's fifteen million. I'll have to. For Felicia.' And he had wondered where they kept their rake-off and what they might have done with it. As Alessandro walked from the kitchen Maurizio and Pino had both come after him. They had slapped him on the back so hard that they had almost winded him and Pino had said, '*E un vero piacere lavorare con te, Alessandro* . . . It's a real pleasure to work with you, Alessandro.'

The scene, with tiny twists and subtle variations, had played itself over and over again. Occasionally it took place in Alessandro's stylish cream brick 1930s apartment on Lakeview. The three thousand square foot apartment with the intricate cornicing on the ceilings and the fireplace surround, with the leather suite like butter, the thick pile carpets, the well-stocked bar and modern artwork.

'*Non ti conoscerai, Alessandro* . . . You won't know yourself,' his boss had told him back in Palermo. 'You'll get a place to die for. In the greatest part of the city. And you'll keep a tight rein on things from there. *Capisci?* The women will flock to you with a pad like that,' he had said and laughed a raucous laugh. 'Just be careful you don't make too many American babies. You hear me, Alessandro? You hear?'

But Felicia, with her blue eyes, her porcelain skin and her blonde corkscrew curls, was the only woman with whom Alessandro had any interest in making babies and she, though she had moved in with him into the Lakeview apartment, had not till recently realised the extent of his involvement, and now she refused point blank to accept the three-carat princess cut that he had bought her. He had sat on the edge of the bed, while she lay there, arms above her head, eyes closed, defiant, half girl, half woman. 'It's dirty,' she had said.

He had leant over, tried to kiss her, had said, 'Felicia, please. Don't do this.'

157

She had pursed her lips and when he moved away had said, 'I don't want it, Alex. Don't you get it? I don't want to be left with a huge great diamond and your dead body.'

'Felix, you're talking like a crazy woman.'

'Alessandro. This is a dangerous game you're playing. It's not just immoral. It's scary too. You don't see it, because you're on the inside. I want you out. I won't tell you again. I won't threaten you any more.' And then, lowering her voice, she props herself up on her elbow, turns to him and, more gentle now, she says, 'Look, this just is not the life I want. If you can't leave them, then I have to go.'

Again and again, in the huge high-ceilinged grey granite kitchen, in the off-white bedroom with her childhood stuffed donkey that lay on the bed beside her, she had repeated the same sentiments, the same pleas, the same threats. Usually they came after she had taken Alessandro home to her family's trattoria on Taylor Street. He would notice how her facial muscles tightened and she looked suddenly older when her father slapped him on the back and said, 'So, how's the art business doing, Alessandro? Earning enough to keep my little girl in style I see. Don't know anything about that world myself. I stick to my spaghetti alla carbonara.'

This time in the granite kitchen Alessandro looked at her. He looked at the round face, the white skin, the blue eyes and the full lips. From the window he saw the naked trees and he imagined being in the apartment, in Lakeview, in Chicago or for that matter anywhere without her. He picked up his thick black woollen jacket and his dark scarf from the chair and he said, 'Felix, I'm going out for a while.'

Outside he hides his hands in his pockets, but he holds his head up high. He lets the wind hit his face again and again as though he were a masochist, as though he knew it were admonishing as it blew over towards him from the lake. He hails a taxi and gives the address of the unmarked shopfront in the area called The Patch, on West Grand Avenue.

158

He pushes the bell. In the cold dark air he can hear the sounds of drinking, laughing men. The iron flap in the middle of the door opens. Through the peephole he sees a dark-brown eye with tiny black flecks in its iris. The door opens. Pino slaps him on the shoulder. 'Alessandro.'

Inside the scene is familiar. The room is packed with men he knows. Men with weathered faces sitting at dark tables or standing around them in the yellow light. Men involved in their drinking, their card playing and their gaming. The slipping of the plastic bags from one hand to another goes almost unnoticed.

'What's up, Alessandro? *Cosa bevi . . . ?*' Pino asks.

'I'm not staying long.'

'*Perché, cosa ti prende? . . .* what's wrong with you?'

They are standing close to the door. 'Nothing. Nothing's wrong at all. I just need to talk with you guys.'

Pino looks at him. He frowns. 'Sure. Let's talk. I'll get Maurizio . . . Hey, Maurizio. *Vieni qua . . .* Over here a minute.'

Maurizio is leaning over the pool table. He doesn't lift his head, but calls out, '*Aspetta . . .* wait. I'm about to blow this guy away.' With a stab, he slams the 9 ball into the top pocket, then punches the air to salute his own achievement. Fat face flushed with excitement, he takes the hundred-dollar bill from his opponent, turns to Pino and says, 'Right. I'm with you. What's up?'

'The *boss* wants to chat with us,' Pino says, and pushing their way through the groups of men they walk up to Alessandro.

Maurizio raises his hand in a greeting.

'I want to talk to you both,' Alessandro says, suddenly queasy and uncomfortable. 'But maybe not here. Somewhere more private. Can you come to my place tomorrow?'

Pino turns to Maurizio. 'You free to go to the Lakeview palace tomorrow?'

'Sure, why not?'

'Around six,' Alessandro says. 'I'll get Felicia's dad to send in some of his *risotto ai funghi*. It's the best.'

'Sure, Alessandro. And make sure that princess of yours is home. We haven't seen her in a while.'

'*Bene . . . A domani*,' and Alessandro turns to leave, lifts the iron bar from the door and walks out into the street.

At home he calls out, 'Felix . . . Felix, I have to talk to you.' Suddenly he is excited by his strength and his resolve. 'Felix . . .'

'I'm here,' she calls.

He finds her curled up with a copy of *The Agony and the Ecstasy* on the beige suede sofa in the living room. He goes over, sits beside her, takes her hand. 'Bookworm,' he says.

'I have my exams,' she says.

He touches the thick book on the life of Michelangelo. 'Why *Agony and Ecstasy*?' he asks.

She looks at him. She says, 'Because being an artist of his calibre was a tortured life.'

He doesn't ask her how or why. He changes the subject and blurts out, 'Felix, I've asked the guys to come here tomorrow night. I'm going to tell them I want out. And then I'll tell Palermo.'

'You're what?' she asks, startled as someone who has kept on walking, kept on stepping down a flight of endless steps only to find that suddenly the ground beneath their feet is flat.

'I'm going to tell them straight. I'm going to say that I can't stay here and be the ham in a sandwich any more. That I can't do this any more. They might even be pleased, you know. I think,' he says and he laughs a nervous laugh, 'they might even pay to see the back of me.'

'And "the family"?' Felicia asks.

'I'll call Monday. That's going to be hard, I'm telling you. We're going to have to get out of this place . . . you know that, don't you, Felix?'

'I don't care,' she says, sitting up, burying her face in the side of his neck. 'I do not care. Don't you know that much about me, Alessandro? We can get a little place in Bucktown or Wicker Park on . . .'

In a quiet voice he says, 'Yes. But I guess I won't be that broke.' He takes her hand and holds it between his. 'And you can wear that goddamned ring,' he says.

'I might just do that,' and she gives a half-smile.

'But I don't want you here tomorrow night, Felix. I don't like the way they are with you. Go to your parents. I'll come and join you when we're done . . . I need to spend a bit of time with your dad anyway . . . get him to think of me as the future son-in-law, instead of the devil who makes his little girl live in sin.'

She laughs at him, says, 'Yes, we need to work on that, but I don't need to go out tomorrow night. You don't think I'm big enough to stay here and handle the guys, do you?' And then, joking, 'You're not jealous, are you?'

He grins, then says, 'I promised them we'd order in some of your dad's *risotto ai funghi*. I guess it's like my last supper with them.'

'OK, fine. I'll organise it. I don't really want to be around them anyway. They make me sick with that macho attitude of theirs. Perhaps I will go out . . . Perhaps I'll go to my parents and bury myself in this book.'

'My little intellectual,' he says. 'How are you going to spend your life with me?'

'I'll get you into books.'

'And your dad will get me cooking.'

'I'll call now,' she says, jumping up from the bed, 'and tell him about that risotto for tomorrow before I forget. What time do you want it?'

'I asked them for six. Let's say six thirty.'

'You can't leave risotto standing. I'll make it seven in case they're late.'

On Taylor Street in the kitchen of his trattoria, Felicia's father puts his heart and soul into his art. For this risotto, his *specialità di casa*, he stands by his huge old-fashioned black stove in a splattered white apron that strains over his stomach. He seasons, he stirs, he salts and he spices. He tastes again and again, till, his eyes closed, he leans back out and with his deep and operatic voice he calls out for his wife, 'Giovanna, Giovanna, *siamo pronti, questo è un risotto buono per un principe* . . . we're almost ready. This one is good enough for a prince. Tell that delivery boy to get a move on.'

In the far corner of the kitchen at the old worn wooden table Felicia sits and studies Michelangelo's misery, her head over *The Agony and the Ecstasy*. She loves to sit at that table, to feel its worn grains, to smell the aromas and hear the sounds of her father cooking, just as she did when she was small. But this evening she is weary from the long day of study and the small print on the page has begun to blur beneath her eyes.

And so when she hears her father call out, 'This one is good enough for a prince. Tell the delivery boy to get a move on,' she closes her book, stands up, walks over to her father, to the heat from the ovens that surrounds him and says, 'Papa, I'll take it. I'm going to go now.'

He turns round, puts his big hands on her face. 'Stay a little. Don't go yet. Mama wants to talk to you.'

'Papa, I'm tired,' she says. 'I'll come at the weekend. Come, give me the risotto. I'll take it home.'

'Home,' he says, 'home!' And then half serious, he adds, 'She lives in sin with some *paesano* for a few months and she calls it home, instead of here where she's grown up, and where she should be.'

Felicia laughs, reaches up to kiss her father on the cheek and waits while he packs up the risotto. She takes it from him, goes to say goodbye to her mother and muffled up against the cold March night she walks to her car and heads east towards Lakeview with the *risotto ai funghi* in a box on the passenger seat. Had she stopped on her way west, she would have hit

162

Cabrini Green, where the young black man behind the dustbin, weakened by the cold and by lack of food, is rolling up his sleeve and preparing for his next fix. But instead she drives straight on, zipping her way between the lines of early evening traffic, for she wants to make sure the risotto is still hot when she arrives. About the same time as Felicia stops at a traffic light, her foot tapping on the accelerator, raring to go, in Cabrini Green the heroin hits the young black man's veins and his body clothed in the worn jeans and denim jacket convulses and suddenly, instead of its usual pounding and racing in protest at the sticky black tar, his heart gives out and stands stock still.

In Lakeview, Felicia pulls up outside the ornate apartment block. On the palms of her hands, through the silver paper, she feels the warmth of the food that she carries. She walks inside towards the doorman. 'Delivery' – she laughs – 'for Alessandro Rinaldi.'

The doorman in his grey cap smiles. 'Prettiest delivery boy I've ever seen. Eating in tonight I see.'

'Yes, from my dad's kitchen. If Alessandro and his friends don't finish it I'll bring you down a taste. Have they arrived, by the way?' she asks him.

'Sure have. They went up about an hour ago. Looking forward to that food. Love Italian food,' he says as holds the lift door open.

That night, though, neither Felicia, nor Alessandro and his colleagues, nor the doorman taste the risotto. That night it grows stone cold and stays sticky and uneaten in its carton. Because by some bizarre coincidence only minutes after the final convulsions of the young black addict on the street corner in Cabrini Green, in Lakeview in the fifth-floor apartment, in an altogether different way, sticky black tar refuses too to release its hold over Alessandro's life.

For as Felicia approaches the apartment she and Alessandro

163

share, through the criss-cross iron grating of the lift she recognises first the front, then the side, then the backs of Maurizio and Pino as they rush from the apartment door, as they stumble over one another almost and run towards the flights of steps that lead out of the building.

Felicia yanks open the iron gate of the lift. At the door of the apartment she balances her package against the wall, rummages for her key in her bag, fumbles to fit it in the lock. Inside, on the threshold of the kitchen she gasps, is stunned at first, then screams at what she sees. Seconds later she runs sobbing down the stairs while the carton of risotto she has dropped swims in Alessandro's blood on the kitchen floor.

NINETEEN

In the antique oval mirror, its glass brushed here and there with bronze, Sarit's body stands reflected. The image of her figure is in its way anachronistic. For whilst both the frame and the glass of the mirror are detailed and old-fashioned, her body itself is tight and lean and modern, altogether unadorned save for the tiny green tattoo of Nietzsche's eternal recurrence that lies etched into the curve of her left shoulder. In a physical sense Sarit knows her own body well. She knows it as one person might know another. She knows its likes and its dislikes. Its methods and its messages. Its responses and reactions. She is experienced and she's practised. She knows little inhibition and can ask for what she wants. Her behaviour in a way is enviable. For who would not wish to be quite so unself-conscious, who would not wish to care so very little about being vulnerable in the eyes or beneath the hands of a lover?

Till now at least, till the art class at the Institute, till the studio and the sketching, for Sarit there has been in this knowledge of her own sexual desires an element of detachment. As if she and her body were not one, but two almost entirely separate entities involved in conversation. As if she could stand outside herself, a detached observer of her own pleasure. And if her mind at times had become involved, her heart and her soul had not. So that here, in front of this mirror, confronted by an unfamiliar longing, Sarit's body is suffused with change. Quite still she stands there, slightly at an angle in front of this bronze brushed picture of herself. Neither admiring nor self-critical, but unmoving and aroused by the unfamiliar mesh of sex and self. Overcome by the oneness, by the mingling of herself and her reflection.

In her leisure, as a skier, as a sailor, as a sprinter, no muscle and no tendon is unknown to her. In her work her hands know every crevice, crease and crinkle. But as an artist, only once at seventeen had she sketched the naked human form.

'Will you, Dani? Would you let me do it? My father's hardly going to teach me to sketch naked bodies, is he?'

They are in a shack on a hill on the outskirts of the kib-butz, beyond the apple fields, beyond the orange and the grapefruit groves, close to the tree house where as children they had hidden.

'Why do you want to?' Dani asks, hovering, his hand in his messy blond hair.

'Just because. I've painted everything else. And everything I do is for some stupid exhibition or for someone to hang on a wall in some stupid gallery.'

'Why do you speak like that, Sarit?' he asks her.

'Because it's true. I never paint anything without someone looking over my shoulder. I've had enough. I want to paint what I want to paint when I want to paint it. That's why I need to do this. This will be different. Just for you and me. No one else will know about it.'

'All right,' he says, 'I'll do it.' He says 'All right,' not because in truth he wants to be painted in his pale and naked adolescent awkwardness, but because Sarit has said, 'Just for you and me.'

And so tripping over his jeans, struggling with his shirt as he pulls it over his head, Dani takes off his clothes and lies in their shack on a yellow rush mat, in the evening, a teenager, white and skinny, all knees and elbows, not looking at Sarit, but letting her sketch him. Knowing that he is her first. 'Can I talk?' he asks.

'Yes.'

'What do you think about what that fat Madame said at the opening of your exhibition?'

'Which bit?'

'That you'll be one of the country's famous artists. That it's in you. That you're a real Kleinmann and that you and your father have almost exactly the same style.'

She stops sketching, holds her hand there, the sharp point of her pencil still touching the paper. 'I don't care, Dani. Don't you see? I want to paint my own stuff. Why don't they just leave me alone? What are they going to make me do in the army next year? Be the army artist? Have you heard them talking that nonsense?'

'Yes, I heard it the other day. They were talking about privileged positions for talented kids. Something about sending your paintings abroad and letting you attend exhibitions.'

Still sketching she says, 'I don't want special treatment. I want to be like everyone else.'

'You might want to be,' he says, from his pose on the rush mat, 'but you're not, Sarit.'

Her head jerks up from her paper. Her pencil points towards him and she stares. With her expression penetrating as it is, her face angled as it is, Sarit looks fierce. The air is charged and dangerous. Dani covers himself with his book. She says to him, 'You see, you're just like the rest of them, Dani. Why can't you all just let me be? I'll end up running away from this damned place if everyone doesn't leave me alone. I mean it.'

Wide-eyed he says, 'You'd never do that.'

She carries on sketching. For some time she works in silence. He lies back. After a few minutes he breathes out and begins to watch and to relax.

'Dani, can you move the book, please?'

'I can't.'

'Why on earth not?'

'Why d'you think?'

She laughs out loud and clears the air. She says, 'So what? It would be fun to draw that.'

'Are you crazy, Sarit? Don't be ridiculous. What if someone finds this drawing?'

'No one will. We'll hide it here. We'll stick it to the underneath of the mat till we come back and finish it.'

'Sarit?'

'Yes.'

'Why do you want to sketch me like this?'

'I don't know. I just do. When I was small I saw my father paint my mother naked.'

'He let you watch?'

'No, I peeked through the keyhole.'

'How old were you?'

'Oh, I don't know exactly. Five or six I think.'

On tiptoes trying to peek through the keyhole at five or six on a winter's afternoon. She knew on a Saturday afternoon, on the day of rest when Max and Gabriella's bedroom door was shut, that she must play in her own room or the living room and wait till her parents came to her. The rule was sacred and she never broke it. Sometimes from behind their door she heard voices and then sounds that didn't seem as if they came from people at all, but on this Saturday there was silence. She thought they must be asleep and wondered why on earth grown-ups would want to go to sleep in the middle of the afternoon. She couldn't reach the keyhole so she crept into the living room and struggled back with Max's biggest, fattest art book, that was almost as heavy as she was. She placed it by the door and climbed on top of it. She liked the feeling of the shiny cover of the *German Expressionists* beneath the soles of her feet. She put her right eye to the keyhole. She and her friends had worked out together how to squint through keyholes and spy on grown-ups but this time she was shocked by what she saw. Full bare breasts with large and swollen nipples, a bare flat stomach, a triangle of strawberry-blonde hair. Her mother's body still and naked on the other side of the door. Sarit forgot herself then. She was frightened by the stillness, frightened by the nakedness that she had not seen in this setting. She was confused by the fact that she could see only her mother's naked body and not her face.

She pulled down on the handle and ran into the room, almost knocking over her father's easel. She ran to her mother, threw her arms round her. 'Ima, Ima, you must be so cold. Why haven't you got your clothes on? Look, you've got goose bumps,' and she moves away and pulls her mother's red dress from the chair and brings it to her. 'Here, put this on. Put your arm through here. It's not nice to sit like that anyway, with your bottom showing.'

Gabriella takes the dress. She bites her lip, trying to suppress her laughter but she cannot help herself. While Sarit stands and stares at her mother, from behind her she hears her father laughing too. Astonished, she turns round to stare at him. She has rarely heard him let go like this. He and Gabriella laughing now in harmony. He picks his child up, holds her to him, and says, 'You are a funny one, my little artist,' and the three of them are there laughing till their sides ache in their little flat-roofed house on the kibbutz. Sarit has no idea what it is that her mother and her father find so funny, but she doesn't care. She just clings on to her father, rubbing her small hand against his rough cheek and in the mirror on her mother's dresser she catches sight of the three of them and she revels in the rarity of the moment.

Alone now, her face to the bronze brushed mirror, Sarit moves forward, till inches from the glass out loud she says, 'He could sculpt you like this, you know. You could ask him to.' There is no vanity in her thought. She hasn't looked at her body and considered it in any way an *objet d'art* or the body of a muse, but she has thought of Ramsi. She has thought of him, of his aura, of his hands, and of how it might be were he to sculpt her naked.

169

She leans forward, presses her forehead, her lips, her palms, her breasts against the glass of the mirror. 'You could ask him to sculpt you like this,' she says out loud again and then, shaking her head at her own reflection, half smiling half bewildered, she says, 'Sarit Kleinmann, what the hell's got into you, woman? What on earth do you want from him?'

TWENTY

The rare artist casts his pieces entirely alone, as Ramsi does. Without the casting, the polishing and the finishing, the raw promise of the work would remain, but the sculpture's full potential would be stifled. A woman almost beautiful. A blue almost indigo. A beach almost deserted. To cast and to finish is a craft in its way as precise and as refined as the art of sculpting. For while the nascent sculpture aspires to the demands of the creator's imagination and his vision, the casting and the finishing aspire to the demands of both the sculptor and the sculpture he has fashioned. The process is the final separation of the artist from his creation, and ought to be the prelude to the sculptor's letting go.

Sarit arrives at the foundry door ostensibly to watch the casting. A little breathless, a little nervous once again at the thought of seeing him, she hides her emotion well.

Inside, nothing yet is unwrapped. Ramsi's hand is still on the sculpture's covering when he looks up at her. A different sculpture from the one he had started to work on the last time she was there. That one he had abandoned for its flaws and imperfections, so that now with a new piece this is but the beginning. And she, Sarit, has never before been the observer. Not, at least, since she was small. But now she turns the paint-stained wooden dark-brown chair back to front and sits in her jeans, her legs akimbo, her arms resting on the frame, her chin on her interlaced fingers, as Ramsi begins to unwind the cellophane, then the cloths from his sculpture. She watches and she says, 'Do you always cast your work yourself?'

'Cast my work myself?' he says slowly. Not imitating, not

mocking, but as if asking the question of himself. 'Do I always cast my work myself? Good question.'

'Well, do you?'

He's kneeling down now unravelling the cellophane. And again out loud of no one in particular he asks, 'Do I cast my work myself?'

The piece sits on the floor. Her face the same as those Sarit has seen in River North, but different. Sculpted, but this time unfinished. A promise in a pinkish terracotta clay that later will be cast in the coffee-coloured bronze that Ramsi chooses as the finish for *Nadia*'s face. The features are the same: high forehead, full lips, the nose with the slight bump on its ridge, the arched brows, the long thin neck. Somewhere between an Egyptian and an Ethiopian woman in her look. But the expression is different from the other sculptures Sarit has seen. On her lips there is no smile, her eyes are cast downwards and the beginnings of a frown hint from between her brows. This time it is the sculpture's nose that draws Sarit. She thinks, 'I can create perfect symmetry. But he can create perfect beauty.'

She says, 'What kind of clay do you use?'

'Usually terracotta.'

'Is that the smelly stuff?'

Despite himself he laughs. His beard is trimmed today and she notices his mouth, though not yet its resemblance to that of the young woman in pink terracotta clay. He says, 'No, that's oil-based clay. This is water-based.'

'Where d'you get it from?'

In a big white bucket he mixes silicone rubber to paint on to his sculpture. Without the black fingerless gloves one can see the strength of his hands, the breadth of his knuckles and his fingers. He looks downwards and doesn't seem to hear her question.

'What's that? What are you mixing with?' she asks.

On to his sculpture he begins to brush the silicone plaster. For a minute or two as he paints, as the piece again begins to

172

hide itself, he says nothing at all. But when the sculpture is covered in white, without looking at Sarit, brushing on a second coat he says, 'What is this? The Spanish inquisition?'

'Something like that. Where do you get the clay from?'

'A supplier.'

'Where do they get it?'

'Do you ask your patients this many questions?'

'No . . . but where do they get it?'

'From the Great Lakes.'

'I don't think I've ever touched clay,' she says to him. Then to herself she says, 'I wonder what it feels like.'

In his hand he holds the thick brush. His sculpture now is covered in a heavy white mask. Around it he paints a clear protective layer that looks to her like Vaseline. This time she doesn't ask, for though her interest in the craft is real in truth, despite herself, her curiosity for the art is greater still.

She waits till he has finished. Then she says, 'What now?'

'I'm going to leave in a minute,' he says and takes a sip from the glass of tea that's cold by now. 'The plaster has to dry,' he adds by way of explanation. Briefly she wonders if he finds it strange that she has uttered not a word about the sculpture. The questions she has asked that mostly went unanswered have been about the casting and the clay. Briefly, in her head she hears her mother's refrain, Rivka's refrain, the Old Testament refrain, '*There is a time for everything . . . For everything there is a time . . . A time to love and a time to hate . . . A time to speak and a time to be silent.*' She senses, as she has before, that she ought not yet to broach the subject of his sculpture. Guided by her intuition she is misguided by her imagination. In her conjecture Ramsi's model is or was his lover. No other possibility exists.

In those first minutes in the foundry she has not suffered from the distance between herself and Ramsi. In truth she has almost forgotten why she came. But now as he pulls his black-flecked sweater on over his head, if her mind has almost forgotten the why of it, then her body has remembered.

From behind her Albert says, 'You can stay and look around if you want, Sairit. Is that how you say it, "Sairit"?'

'It's not Sairit. It's Sarit. Ah, ah, ah,' she says, opening her mouth as though she were teaching him phonetics.

'Ah, right,' and with no change in the way he pronounces her name he says, 'Right, Sairit.'

She thinks of Lauren and her mispronunciation and smiles to herself. She thinks of the security guard with the tattoo of the starfish on his biceps and she frowns.

Hovering, big and clumsy in his overalls Albert says to Sarit, 'You can stay and have a look around. And you could watch some of the casting process when Ramsi's next here if you want. For someone who's never seen it before, it's quite something,' he adds, thinking all the while that this woman with her high cheekbones and her upfront manner is interesting to have around.

'Oh . . . thanks, I . . . well, yes. I might do that. I'll come and watch.'

'You be back tomorrow, Ramsi?' Albert asks.

'I'll be here,' he says.

He looks at Sarit then as if he doesn't understand. He doesn't ask, though. He doesn't say, 'Why would you want to watch me at work?' nor does she say, 'Would you mind if tomorrow I came back and watched?' And in that split second she thinks that perhaps she had just imagined him sketching her face in his studio. Perhaps she had dreamt the scene that followed or perhaps it had happened with another man. Because between Sarit and Ramsi there is not exactly a coolness but a strangeness. As if what had been between them were illusory and now in this foundry the slate is almost blank.

From a tall iron coat-stand Ramsi lifts his worn brown sheepskin. Ramsi says, 'I'm leaving for a while. I need some air,' and he looks at Sarit for just a second longer than he needs to before he turns towards the door and leaves.

'Make yourself at home,' Albert says to Sarit. 'You can snoop as much as you like in this place. People always do . . . Nothing to steal here,' and then, embarrassed by the implication of his comment, he laughs an awkward laugh and says, 'I didn't mean . . . I . . .'

Still in her grey beret Sarit begins to move around the playground. And as she moves so she touches. She runs her hand along the back of a twisted aubergine bronze snake. She lays her palm on the broken plaster cast of an old man's head. She scratches the dry yellowy, orangey wax from the corner of a table next to a large, thick, furry artist's brush. The brush Sarit ignores, not consciously but as if by instinct, as if its bristles might burn their way through the thin white skin of her hands.

The wax still in her hands and under her nails, she wanders. Past newspapers, stiff and brown and yellow in their piles, past mounds of magazines, of rags, past wire racks and iron frames, towards the sink piled high with chipped and coloured mugs. The knee-high bags are on the floor close to the sink. Huge transparent plastic bags of clay, one grey, one pink. She leans down, fights her way into the thick strips of cold grey clay. She grabs a lump of the material that feels hard and bumpy. With her knuckles she presses the clay. She pummels it. She smoothes its surface. She irons out the pockmarks of its skin. She cannot move away. She cannot seem to help herself. She manipulates it with ease, with her fingers and the drip of water she takes from the sink, in a minute she changes the face of it and irons out its wrinkles. She loses interest then and all but throws it back down on top of the untouched grey mound in the plastic bag.

Beside it stands the other bag, as yet unopened. She doesn't think to call to Albert, 'Could I? Can I? Would you mind?' She unwinds the wire tie instead and opens up the bag of terracotta clay. She is not yet ready to take in her hands and fashion it, but next to it she kneels on the floor. She sits there at first doing nothing, staring into space. Then she widens the opening of the bag and starting with the base of her wrist she presses hard and imprints her palm and her fingers in the delicious, dark-pink, grainy clay. Then she stands up and she quite simply walks away.

She hears the dripping of another tap, the humming of a pipe, the distant sounds of a radio. She calls out, 'I'm going now. I might be back tomorrow.'

At the door Albert catches up with her. He says, 'Ramsi usually comes late morning. Around twelve. But you're welcome to be here before and hang out with me. I have to leave by one, though. Going to visit the mother.' And Sarit as she leaves wonders if his mother also has white hair, white lashes and white brows.

Though it has stopped snowing, the air is icy. She pulls her grey scarf up over her mouth. She is not ready to get into her car and drive home. She needs instead to walk and to think. The streets are wide. On either side are warehouses, corrugated-iron garage doors, workshop fronts with rusting paint and coloured 'Love You's, 'Fuck You's and 'Hate You's sprayed over their ridges in huge uneven letters. The cars too are rusty, bashed and broken, some with their tangled entrails hanging from their bellies ready for repair, others disused and abandoned. Sarit is on the South Side in the roughest neighbourhood of town. She doesn't care, though, that she is alone in an area that's tough. She is no stranger to fear.

As she walks she never contemplates her own connection with this side of town. She doesn't think of the knived, slashed teenage faces from these parts that she has mended in the past. She is not quite sure where she is walking to. She is probably looking for a café. Somewhere to sit indoors away from the cold. She asks a young black boy, bareheaded in the cold. He points ahead of him towards the end of the road. 'You can git a hot drink there,' he says and stares at her. White women don't walk alone much on the South Side.

She crunches her way to the end of the road. On the corner is the café, dirty yellow on the outside, with wooden benches on the inside. She sits on the hard wood, her hands in her pockets, looking out of the window as though there were some spectacular view ahead of her instead of just the icy air against the greyness. She sits there, closes her eyes for a moment, watches the images of the foundry, the images of his hands as they form themselves in her mind. The bar owner in his stained overall laughs. 'This is not a park bench, lady,' he says. 'You can dream, but you have to order something too . . . I need to make money from your daydreams.'

She orders a black coffee to take away. He hands her the polystyrene cup. She gets up to leave, and she notices as she pulls on her gloves in the doorway that she can still feel the wax under her nails, as though it were the wax of crayons. The wax that must be piping hot, boiling almost before the first coat can be poured into the glove mould of the sculpture. The wax that warms up not in an instant but slowly degree by degree, till it is ready to be poured, to become involved in the creation of the finished sculpture.

Walking down the road Sarit again feels strange. As if there were another version of herself, her shadow walking next to her.

Unusually introspective and forthcoming at one and the same time, the night before she had said to Lauren, 'I'm not making my life happen any more, Lor. My life seems to be happening to me.' Sarit had driven from the foundry to Rinali's in Lincoln Park and sat with Lauren at the red checked tablecloth over thin-crust pizza with black olives, extra cheese and anchovies.

'What are you on about, Sairit? Because I'll tell you one thing. You are acting strange, girl.'

'Strange how?'

'Did you smoke a joint or something?'

'On my own? Don't be crazy. But I could use one.'

'I don't have one here.' She laughs. 'Oh, and by the way, you have tomato sauce by your right ear.'

'Damn,' she says and laughs.

'Sairit, for God's sake,' she says and shakes her friend's arm, 'you're acting too weird. What's up with you?'

'Oh, just sex.'

'Just sex?'

Sarit puts down her fork. 'I don't know.'

'What do you mean you don't know?'

She begins to play with her pizza. 'I mean . . . I mean,' and she gives a half-smile. 'I mean I don't quite know, Lor.'

'Key question,' Lauren says, 'do you want him out of your bed in the morning?'

'There hasn't been a morning.' Sarit thinks back to his studio in the early evening.

'Well, if there was,' Lauren says. 'Would you want him out?'

Sarit swallows a mouthful of pizza. 'No, Lauren . . . No, Lauren . . . if there was a morning I don't believe I would want him out.'

Lauren shrieks through a mouthful of Margarita. 'My God, it's Schwarz, isn't it? It's that shrink I set you up with?'

'Are you out of your mind? No, it is not Sammy. I told you . . . Yuck . . . I never could. We're friends, though. I've already told you that.'

'So who is this guy? What does he do?' and she laughs. 'I don't mean in bed. I mean what does he do with his life?'

'He sculpts.'

'So do you.'

'Yeah, right.'

'How d'you meet him?'

'Long story.'

'Tell me.'

'No.'

'So what's the deal?'

'I went to watch him cast yesterday, at this great foundry on the South Side. He's doing the wax bit tomorrow. Then the bronze bit after that. I want to see it, but he might think

178

I'm some crazy woman if I go back there again. Like I'm stalking him or something.'

'Tell him doing a nose is like casting a sculpture and you want to see how he does it. Actually it's true. D'you know how many plastic surgeons sculpt? Anyway, since when did you ever care what anyone thought of you?'

'Now that,' says Sarit, 'is absolutely true.'

Before the wax can be poured the artist or the craftsman has to break the plaster mould away from the clay. The mould that is not easily separable from the raw art must not be cut too soon. Not until the clay has fully set, for if it is, if it cracks in the wrong places, the damage might be irreparable. She watches him, when she goes back, bent over the plaster with a rough file in his hand. His hand movement is slow and precise. In her mind she cuts with him, her hand on his.

He changes from the rough file to the knife they call the grinder. He focuses, applies pressure and as he prises the plaster from the clay, without looking up he says, 'This is called the glove mould or the mother mould.'

She starts, not because he has spoken, but because for the first time he has answered a question before she has asked one. 'I can smell the wax,' she says.

'They all have different scents, the waxes that we use. What do you think it smells of?'

She gets up, walks over to the silver pan on the stove that is set into the huge work table. So that she is standing close to where he is. Inches from him she leans down and sniffs the honey-coloured wax. 'It's . . . it's sort of minty,' she says. 'No, not mint. It's eucalyptus. That's what it is.'

Next to her, as though his focus were on the plaster in his hands, he asks, 'So have you smelt real eucalyptus leaves?'

She closes her eyes. Looking up from where he is, cleaning the vestiges of stray plaster from the mould, he watches her. He notices the length and thickness of her lashes. 'Yes,' she says, 'I have smelt eucalyptus.'

'Where?'

'Oh, around.'

'Not too many eucalyptus trees in Chicago.'

She smiles. Her smile in one sense is as her mother's was. More fleeting certainly. Less frequent too. But real and in its way infectious. Infectious and beautiful because of its shape and because of the whiteness of her teeth.

'So where?' he asks.

'Where what?'

'Did you smell the eucalyptus trees?'

'As a child at home I suppose.'

'Israel,' he says. He doesn't ask it. He doesn't say, 'Israel?' He merely states the country as a fact.

Again she starts. 'Yes,' she says and moves back a little from the table.

He begins to spray the plaster with water. 'You're surprised I knew.'

'How did you?'

'Your accent.'

'I don't have one . . . any more.'

He laughs. 'You do have an accent,' he says. 'Not half as thick as mine, though. Not one that most people would recognise. But it's still there. But it's not so much that. It's more your manner.'

'What do you mean?' she asks, defensive.

'Oh, come on.'

'But I've been here for ever. I'm, well . . . I'm American,' she says.

'Sure. Sure you are.'

'Really. My mother was American.'

'Uhuh.'

He has stopped pouring the wax from the pan into the mould now. Instead he brushes it in layer after layer, in great thick dollops.

She watches him and has to stop herself from saying, 'Can I have a go?'

'Tell me,' he says, 'first you want to see me sculpt. Then you want to watch me cast. So where's the fascination?'

When he asks the question, when he says. 'So where's the fascination?' he is not fishing in any way for compliments. He simply wants to know the truth of why she's come.

She takes a deep breath. 'I was operating once, on a nose,' she says, 'a hooked nose. Sort of like mine,' she adds and laughs. 'Anyway, I had to break the bone of course. And when I was setting it afterwards, you know when I spread the plaster over it and shaped it,' she says, moving her fingers with the recollection, 'I remember thinking it must feel something like this to cast a sculpture. And I don't know . . . I just wanted to see. It fascinates me . . . it's . . .' And her voice trails off, the rest of her answer floating wordless, the rest of the reason why she has come somewhere here within the walls of this huge high-ceilinged foundry, but as yet unspoken.

'Ah,' he says as though satisfied with her response, which he knows in truth is incomplete. And just as she has decided not yet to ask about his model, just as she feels the subject is taboo, he decides then not to push his line of questioning. Because in a moment of insight he is sure that his question 'Where's the fascination?' is one that Sarit herself does not yet have the tools to answer.

Now, as he works, he glances at her hands. He notices, of course, as he has done before, how extraordinary they are, though when he utters the sentence, when in his thick Egyptian accent he says to her, 'Your hands are exceptional,' he almost does a double take as though the words must have come not from his own mouth, but from someone else's.

She too is taken aback. Not by what he has said. A million times before she has heard those words about her hands, but she is startled by the fact that he has said it.

'Thanks,' she says. 'They're pretty useful in my business,' and then, to deflect the focus from herself, she points at his work and asks, 'What next?'

'Same story as the plaster. I fill the mould up coat by coat with the brush to avoid air bubbles. Then the wax has got to dry. It takes at least a day. So there's not much I can do while that's going on.'

'Oh.' She cannot hide her disappointment.

'Anyway, I don't suppose you'd have been around here tomorrow. You'll be breaking someone else's nose.'

And as if by some bizarre serendipitous intervention, as he says that, as he says the words 'You'll be breaking someone's nose', he hears an unfamiliar sound. Not the dripping of the tap or the humming of the pipe, nor the bubbling of the wax left in the pan. But a strange and distant repetitive bleeping sound.

Sarit stands up. She puts her hand to a small black box attached to the belt of her jeans and switches off the sound. She says, 'Where's the phone?'

He points to the far right-hand corner of the foundry, close to where she had found the terracotta clay. As she walks in the direction of the phone he watches her and imagines not just her face, but the whole of her in sculpture.

A minute later she is back. She stands by the table, looking straight at him now. And as if it were a question she says, 'I have to go?' As if his reaction were crucial.

'Ah,' he says, smiling, 'so you're going to go and do an emergency facelift?'

'Yes. Right,' she says, taking her old leather gloves from her pocket, putting them on. She says, 'I'll leave you my number. When you want to do the sculpture let me know.' She scribbles her number on a scrap of paper that she takes from her pocket and hands it to him. This time the last two digits are the right way round.

He says, 'So, are you going to lift a face?'

'No. They're not going to bleep me to do that, are they? . . . It's a child. A little boy. Facial and chest burns. Tipped a pan of boiling water over himself. They want my opinion.'

182

And as soon as she says that she feels the sense of urgency. The urgency that in a second has pulled her too far away from him for her to notice the draining of the colour from his cheeks and from his lips. She turns to walk towards the door. She doesn't say 'Thanks' or 'It was nice of you to let me watch.' She just calls, 'Bye.' He manages a smile.

After she has gone he waits a minute or two. He needs air. His heart is beating fast. And so he sets down the wax-filled mould, he takes his coat from the stand and, lifting the keys from a hook, he walks outside through the heavy iron door. He walks along the road in the direction in which she had walked the day before. The ice has begun to melt and is mixed with slush. The water stains his shoes. On the corner in the yellow-fronted café he says, '*Salam.*'

The owner replies in Arabic, '*Salam*, Ramsi . . .'

'You have some whisky there?'

'Sure . . . Sit down, sit down. Make yourself at home.'

'No thanks, I'll take it with me. I have to get back to the foundry.'

'Work. Work. Work. You need a life, Mr Riyad. Whisky to take away, in a plastic cup? It's crazy.'

Ramsi pays him. Takes the shot of whisky in the polystyrene cup and leaves.

In truth he does still have much work to do on this sculpture, though not today. The casting process is a slow one. The creation of the glove mould, of the wax mould, are but the beginning. A sculpture is not cast till the artist has spent time with the wax figure touching it, refining it and honing it, learning to work on it not as the creation over which he has some power, but as an outside figure. A figure that is not cast till the wax has been dipped time and again in slurry made with sand, then coated in thick and dripping, boiling liquid bronze. And at the end the polishing must come. The finishing, the patinage that artists study for a lifetime. The finishing that can take for ever, till the beauty of intent or of accident transpires.

183

Back in the foundry, Ramsi begins to tidy up the cloths, the tools, the pans. He takes them to the sink, turns on the tap that splatters and begins to wash them. The gushing of the water blocks his thoughts. On a threadbare dark-blue towel he dries his hands and as he turns to walk away his leg brushes against the plastic bag of grainy terracotta clay. For some reason he looks down. At first he doesn't move from where he is. He stands quite still and stares at the deep imprint of her wrist, her palm, her long slim fingers in the clay. Then he too kneels down. Right there. Beside the terracotta clay. And on to the surface of her hand he brushes the imprint of his own.

TWENTY-ONE

For days, though she has shed not one tear, Felicia has barely slept, barely spoken, barely eaten. Her state of shock has been such that whilst no detail of the chaos and the disarray has slipped her memory she simply cannot bring herself to speak of it. With psychologists, with her family and with her friends she has nodded, she has shrugged and she has shaken her head. And she has clung to her shock, clutching it as the branch above the abyss, sensing, as one does in some vague and distant place, the inevitable plunging into grief that will follow on the heels of its exit.

Sitting next to her at the table in a corner of the kitchen of her parents' trattoria on Taylor Street in the old Italian neighbourhood, Juliann, a handsome, tireless woman, a successful woman with short dyed red hair, dark-brown lips and matching nails, decides she must approach her task from quite another angle. From behind her in the kitchen the cutting, the chopping, the clanging, the sound of Italian voices involved in the culinary process inspire her too to creativity. 'When you were small,' she says to Felicia, 'did your parents let you help them here?'

Her head on the table, her eyes half closed, Felicia nods.

'Was it a treat?'

She shrugs.

'So what was a treat, Felicia? Where did your parents used to take you?'

She talks to Felicia not as though she were a woman of twenty, but as though she were speaking to a child. She talks to her as though she has sustained some physical injury or damage, though in truth the damage is all in the shock and in the psyche of the girl. And she turns to her and says, 'Come on, Felicia, just tell me a place that you loved as a little girl. I really want to know.'

Felicia does not lift her head from the table. She does not look in the direction of this feisty middle-aged redhead who has spent hour upon hour with her, sometimes in silence, over the previous days. She is simply far too scared and far too weary, but the third time Juliann asks the question, the third time she says, 'Where did they take you as a treat?' through the mass of thick blonde corkscrew curls that half hide her face, in a small voice, Felicia says, 'The zoo.'

'The zoo . . . the zoo, a genius of an idea,' and Juliann pounces. She springs from her chair, in her smart black trousers and her tight-fitting burgundy jumper, and she says, 'Let's go, Felicia. You're coming with me, girl. Where's your coat? We're going to the zoo. You'll feel better there. I know you will.'

To Chicago's Lincoln Park zoo, set in the midst of green and on the edge of blue, there is a certain timeless magic. To the springtime butterfly pavilion within it, there is a rainbow brilliance. To the botanical gardens, indoors and out, there is an aura of Zen. The observer at the zoo will never question the motives of the adult in the company of children. He, of course, has come to watch the excitement of the child before the antelope, the gazelle, the lion or the tiger. He has come to watch the child's learning and his awe. But the grown-up, alone or in the company of others, has some deeper reason for his stroll amongst the shades and textures of the animals.

The outside observer could not in his wildest dreams have guessed why these two grown women were walking slowly past the gazelles, the zebras and the antelopes. He could not ever have imagined that the older woman, with her talent for lateral thinking, had brought the younger one here in an unorthodox attempt to distract her and to open up the sluice gates. Because years of experience had taught Juliann that settings and images from childhood were a catalyst. In her company the most hardened of witnesses had wept and dropped their guard before photographs of their parents. The most conniving of fraudsters, the most gruesome of murderers had revealed long searched-for truths on the whereabouts of hidden bank accounts and bodies. So that Juliann has long since understood that words that seemed vaulted and unreachable in one environment might gush and spill in another. And this is Juliann's trademark amongst her colleagues, this wacky and unorthodox method of getting witnesses to open up. For this she is one of a handful of women to be promoted to the position that she holds.

As they watched the salmon flamingos stretch and curve their necks, Felicia said nothing. Nor did she forget herself before the antics of the two apes who stroked one another's faces and then began to fight. But as they stood in front of a massive lion, who, laconic, splayed out beneath his branch, just lay and fixed his gaze, without coaxing, without prompting, Felicia bent forward and with no warning at all began to shake and through her sobs to tell her story. Juliann took her arm and led her off to a bench at the back of the wildcat pavilion. She sat her down in the slightly darkened area with its smell of raw meat and straw and damp and, ignoring the children who pointed and the adults who stared, she sat still and listened to Felicia's story, afraid that were she to suggest they leave and seek out some more private place, she would stem the flow of the young girl's words. The two must have been there on the bench for half an hour, maybe more, when Felicia whispered, 'Don't you understand how terrified I am? How would you feel?' and crying still, she says, 'This is just a job for you. I'm just another case where you can triumph and show your skills to the prosecution. That's it, isn't it?'

Juliann lays her hand on Felicia's. She notices how it feels ice cold. She thinks, 'She's too smart for her own good. Poor girl, no wonder she's afraid. I do want that conviction and we don't have a case without her.'

For days prior to this walk with Juliann, despite the evidence of the doorman, Felicia had refused to admit she knew anything of Alessandro's murder. Even through the grief, the fog and the despair, Felicia was terrified by the danger she might face were she to testify against Maurizio and Pino. As though in a horror film, time and again she had relived the trauma in her head. First the men as they ran from her apartment. The sick feeling in her gut as she fumbled for her key. The scream then. The scream inside her and out loud, 'Alessandro, Alessandro, Alessaaaaandro . . .' as she stood in the doorway to the kitchen. And the blind white terror. The urgency to get out. Anywhere. To run. And the guilt that came later. The guilt that she had not stayed with his dead and bleeding body. Her anguish at the loss of Alessandro, fighting for space in her head and her body, fighting with the fear for her own life.

She's in her own world now, here in the wildcat pavilion, replaying the video again when Juliann says, 'There's no need for you to be afraid, Felicia. We're here to protect you. It's our job to look after you. You do know that, don't you? You'll help us and we'll help you.'

And in truth Felicia was priceless as a witness in this drugs conspiracy, this ring of corruption, that for months the FBI had been trying to crack. Often in Chicago's drug cases Juliann had the upper hand. Extorting a testimony from a witness was so much easier when he himself had been involved and stood to spend decades under lock and key. To divulge the hows, the wheres and whys was in his interest then, as mitigation of his own position. Such a witness had not a thing to lose. But in this case, in her weakened pitiful state, innocent as she was, Felicia had the upper hand and to ensure her cooperation there was little Juliann would not have done to encourage, to coax and reassure her. There was little that Juliann would not have promised her.

'What if you don't get them?' Felicia asks.

'What do you mean, if we don't get them? We have them.'

'I mean,' says the girl, exhausted by her own emotion, 'what if you don't get them . . . put away?'

'We will, Felicia . . . and that's why we need your help.' She might have added, 'Without you there's no case, Felicia,' but a comment of that nature would have been most unwise. She might have said, 'You're the prosecution's only real witness in a case where for months we've taped and tapped and wired and followed in the hope of finding concrete evidence and now, left with only you and the doorman, we're not about to let you go.' Instead she hands Felicia another handkerchief and says, 'I give you my word that you'll be fine. I'll see to it myself.'

'I won't. I won't. They'll find me. This is just horrible . . . awful. It's . . .' And again she starts to cry.

The light was beginning to fade as they got up to leave. So that the stripes of the zebras, the humps of the camels and the trunks of the elephants became contours, shapes and patterns in their own right. The two walked out on to Lincoln Park West, the older woman's arm on the younger woman's shoulder.

TWENTY-TWO

Sarit's and Lauren's visit to the zoo had been quite unconnected with Felicia's. There was no serendipitous quasi crossing
of paths as there had been the night when Sarit was only feet
away from Felicia at Kingston Mines. Nor this time was there
any coincidence of timing. They had come with Sammy
Schwarz on a whim some days before one Sunday morning.
They had brunched at Nookies on Wells and were walking
across the bridge towards the lake. The end of the early April
snow still lay on the ground.

'Come on, we're turning back. We're going to the zoo,' Sarit
had said.

Lauren and Sammy had looked at her, then at one other.

'What's got into you, Sarit? You regressing?' asked Sammy.

'No.' She laughed. 'I just feel like some fun . . . Isn't that
allowed?'

And Lauren, turning round, following Sarit, says to her, 'We
know exactly what's got into you, don't we?'

Sarit shoots her a filthy look. Then she says, 'Come on, guys,'
and in between the two of them, the tallest of the three, she
turns back and pulls them by the sleeve. 'We're going to the
zoo.'

Her doll-like face full of Sunday morning make-up, her
matching bright-pink lipstick and nail polish applied with a
certain expert touch, Lauren says, 'Sammy Sam, if the surgeon
says we're going then who are we to argue?'

Sammy holds out his hands in a gesture of acceptance and
says, 'OK, girls. Why not? I haven't been for years. I'm game.'

And so the three of them, escaping from their lives, lose themselves that Sunday morning amongst the apes and the orang-utans, the chimps and the baboons. 'Hey, Sarit,' Sammy calls, pointing at an orang-utan with attitude and drooping jowls. 'This one could do with some of the magic in your fingers.'

Sarit studies the animal's face. 'Yes, there's something of Mrs Horowitz in those features. We could work wonders on him, couldn't we, Lor?' she says and then, in mock fear as if she might be overheard, she looks around her and she adds, 'Oops. I'll get sued for talking about my patients like that.'

Lauren laughs. 'You're such a cynic, Doc,' and then, more serious, she says, 'Sometimes I wonder why you bother with the adults at all. Actually, why do you?'

'I . . . I suppose I learn from what I do with them,' says Sarit, a little surprised, a little troubled by Lauren's question, which has come out of the blue, here in Lincoln Park zoo with its covering of spring snow now thin on the ground beneath their feet. 'Yes,' she says again. 'I do learn from the cosmetic stuff I do.'

And Sammy says, 'I think you do it for the artistry. You can be more creative with cosmetics than with paediatric plastics.'

And Sarit, fascinated suddenly by the huge white bear in its cage in front of her, says, 'Artistry? Nonsense, Sam. You stick to the minds of lunatics. They're easier to figure out than mine . . .' and then, changing the subject, she points at the bear. She says, 'His expression's almost human.'

'You know,' says Sammy, happy that the mood again is light, 'the animals look like us and we look like them. Everyone is like an animal.'

'Speak for yourself,' Lauren says and elbows him in the ribs.

'No, it's true. I mean it,' he says, taking off his glasses, wiping the lenses on a grey handkerchief that he takes from his pocket. 'I often think that when I'm working. I talk to a patient and I can't help but compare him to some sort of beast. There's something about that in the Bible. I think it was Jacob who blessed his sons by comparing them to different animals.'

191

'What an intellectual you are, Dr Schwarz,' Lauren says and then, 'So tell me, what kind of a beast am I?'

'You,' he says, looking around and beaming to reveal his yellow teeth. 'You, Lauren, are without doubt a bright-pink flamingo. Don't you think, Sarit?'

'No question,' says Sarit. 'And if you're a flamingo, you need to be with a gentle, graceful creature. What sort of animal is Todd, then?'

Lauren for once looks serious. 'Animal? Yes, he's an animal,' she says. 'Sometimes a deer . . . and sometimes' – and she lowers her voice – 'a tiger I suppose.' Sarit raises her eyebrows. Lauren looks away, makes it clear she won't be drawn.

Sarit senses this and stores the information for some future time and place, and in a light and airy voice she says, 'And you, Sammy . . . What do you say, Lauren?' The two of them look at him, the way he saunters, the way even now in his early forties he is ever so slightly bent over in his red anorak.

'I think . . .' says Lauren, 'he's sort of like a camel.'

'Mmhm . . . a camel. That's it, Sammy,' Sarit says, walking over to him, 'Lauren's got it spot on. You are without doubt a camel. A brilliant one.'

'Charming. Thank you both so much.' And he does a sort of mock bow.

'And me?' asks Sarit. 'I don't suppose you'll spare me. So what am I?'

She is between the two of them again. Though not now the tallest. They each hold her hand and from time to time they swing her in the air in her little green duffle coat and she laughs. This is her first ever visit to the zoo, her first ever trip abroad. Every five years the kibbutz sends each family on a trip of their choice. And so she is there in the zoo with them in Regent's Park in London, swinging between her mother and her father and calling out, 'And me, and me, what am I? What kind of animal am I?'

Gabriella and Max don't consult one another, but they call out their answers at once. 'A jaguar. A black one,' calls Gabriella.

'A gazelle,' calls Max. And over the child's head they look at one another.

'A what? A what?' asks Sarit, laughing, turning from one to the other. 'Ima, what am I?'

'Well, Abba thinks you're like a gazelle and I think you're like a jaguar.'

'What's a gazelle, Abba? What's a jag . . . a jaguar, Ima?'

They stand in front of the long-legged, streamlined gazelles that are somewhere between graceful and lanky. Sarit puts her face up to the cold black bars of the enclosure. 'Why am I like those funny things, Abba?'

'Because you've got long legs and you can run fast. And because you're delicate in an odd sort of way.'

'Oh . . . But Ima says I'm a jaguar,' and the child lets out a mock roar.

'She is, Max. She's a jaguar. A black one.'

'Why, Ima?' She's tugging on Gabriella's arm. 'Why am I one of those things?'

'Because . . . because,' and Gabriella laughs.

In front of the wildcat enclosure the three of them stand and watch. Two of the jaguars are dozing in the shade, but the third, the largest, is roaming on the sandy ground. Undistracted. Powerful. Alone. 'Why am I a jaguar, Ima? Tell me now.'

'Because you're strong and independent.'

'What does inpendendent mean?'

'Not inpendendent . . .' says Gabriella, trying hard to keep her face straight. 'In . . . de . . . pen . . . dent.'

'What does it mean, Ima?'

'Tell her, Max.'

'It means a person who can do things on her own.'

'Oh,' she says. 'Abba, Abba, I don't like the jaguars. But shall we draw the lion?'

Max looks at his wife and smiles. 'You see, Gaby. You always say I push her, but she wants it as much as I want it for her. Come, Sarit, let's get your wax crayons from Ima's bag.'

And Sarit, in anticipation of creation, begins to jump up and down on the spot. 'I'm going to draw a great big strong lion with that furry stuff round his face.'

'It's called a mane.'

Gabriella hands her the sketchpad and the crayons, and Max, crouching down, lifts her on to his knee. She perches there. For a moment she says nothing. She just looks. She is not yet six but already she knows how to contemplate her subject. She cocks her head and she begins. Not with his face as most children of her age would do for instant recognition of their subject on the paper, but prepared to delay the pleasure for the sake of her art, she begins with the outline of his back and of his tail. And to her father she says, 'Do you have my plain pencil? I want to get the shape right. This silly yellow one is much too thick.'

Gabriella hands Max the pencil. Max hands it to Sarit. She jumps off her father's knee. 'Where are you going . . . ?' he asks. 'You need my knee to sit on. Otherwise you won't get your drawing straight.'

'Oh no, I don't. Thank you, Abba. I'm fine . . .' And then, looking at him, lisping as she speaks she says, 'It doesn't mean I don't love you, you know, if I don't want to sit on your knee.'

And Sarit is standing alone then in her green duffle coat and her white trainers, a little in front of her mother, her sketchpad and her pencil in her hand, her gaze fixed on her page, then on the lion, then back on the page. Behind her now her parents stand over her and watch her, though not once does she check to make sure they are there. Already Max has taught her perspective, shade and texture. For the lion's mane and for his tail she turns her pencil to the side.

A couple come and stand close to Max and Gabriella. The

woman carries an overweight toddler in her arms. She points to Sarit, says to Max and Gabriella, 'Is she yours?' Max nods. 'Some artist you have there. I hope my little one turns out like that.'

Over the next minutes the scene in various forms repeats itself twice or three times, with people coming, nodding, staring, watching until Gabriella says, 'Sarit, sweetheart, we have to go now.'

The child does not look up from her work.

'We have to go, Sarit.'

'No.'

'Yes, darling, we have to. We'll miss the bus.'

Sarit ignores her. And Max, knowing what it is to be wrenched from one's art mid-flow, says, 'We'll bring you back tomorrow and you can finish your drawing. Come on, Sarit. We need to catch the red bus.' He takes her by the arm. She pulls away. Her pencil scratches across the paper, defacing the lion's back, his face, his mane and Sarit begins to scream a high-pitched scream. 'No, no, you ruined him. You ruined my lion. Leave me alone. You ruuuuuined him.'

Max picks her up, grips her as she screams and kicks, holds her as she sobs, 'Put me down. Leave me alone.' Screaming and sobbing, 'My lion. You spoiled him. You ruined him. My lion. My lion. Ima . . . Ima . . .'

And later, in the Bed and Breakfast in Regent's Park as Gabriella is putting her to sleep in the little low camp bed, she strokes her daughter's forehead and she says, 'I was right, Sarit. You are a wildcat . . . You'll need a very strong man to handle you one day.'

'I don't want any silly man. I only want you and Abba . . . and my paints . . . and Dani . . . I miss Dani,' she says, lisping. 'I want to go home, Ima.'

'We're going tomorrow, sweetheart . . .' And then, 'I think you'll be too strong for Dani.'

'What do you mean, Ima?'

'Well, Dani's a . . . Hm. Dani's a deer or an antelope.'

She giggles. 'You're silly, Mummy.'

'Yes, you're right.' She kisses Sarit on the forehead. For a few minutes she sits in silence on the bed. Then when the child, exhausted by the day and by herself, has fallen into a deep sleep, Gabriella whispers to her, 'I think you'll need another wildcat like we saw in the zoo. Someone very very strong. Even stronger than your Abba, don't you think, Sarit?'

TWENTY-THREE

Chicago has a kaleidoscope of faces. The first a Midwestern face, scrubbed and unmade-up. Open, smiling, naïve and even-featured. A candid and provincial face on big shoulders and a strong thick neck, that will make believe there is no other, until with a toss of the head both sudden and dramatic, older and wiser she looks at you straight on. Lined this time with European wrinkles in her skin, interesting and erudite with architecture, with politics, with symphony, with art and with history. A kaleidoscope that will pick its moment, then turn the other cheek, to show, ethnic and uneven, the face of the city's artsy other world.

To know Chicago is to know more than one or other of these faces. To know the city is to embrace all her moods and her expressions. So it is with a lover. With true desire comes a longing to touch not just the body, but the face as well. The brows, the cheekbones, the jawline and the lips.

The face of Chicago's Wicker Park at night is rough, thick-skinned and pockmarked. On the streets plainclothes police pass for drug dealers. Drug dealers pass for artists. Artists and bohemians pass the plainclothes policemen and the drug dealers on the way to backstreet restaurants and bars that brim with possibility. On Milwaukee Avenue, Soul Kitchen has been there for ever. At the half-moon-shaped wooden bar the drinkers sit and sip, and wait for friends and lovers. Loners sit and wait for no one or for anyone at all.

The dark walls are hung with art deco paintings of Parisians lounging. The booths, next to the street-level windows, are lit with stained-glass art deco lamps and hung with old-fashioned plum-coloured velvet drapes. The place exudes intimacy, intrigue and intention.

At first when she walks in Sarit does not see him. Over by the bar she looks for him. That would, after all, have been the normal place to wait. At the extreme right end of the half-moon bar she takes the one high wooden stool that is free. She takes off her jacket, her thick cardigan and sits in her jeans and sleeveless black polo neck. The men stare. The women look her up and down, admire and are jealous of her independence and the definition of her arms all at once. The bartender leans over the counter. He wears countless silver earrings in both of his ears. His right eyebrow too is pierced and when he speaks Sarit notices a glint of silver on his tongue. He says, 'Do you know what you'd like?'

'I'll have a Black Russian,' and she reaches, as she does on the odd occasion, into her bag for a cigarette and matches.

From where he sits in the booth in the furthest corner of the room, Ramsi can see her, unperturbed as she seems by her aloneness at the bar, not bothering with superficial conversation.

From so far away her features and her colouring are not distinct, but he recognises the contours of her face. As she sits on her stool, glass in hand, he watches. He sees her then step down, struck suddenly by the thought that he might be elsewhere in the restaurant, that he of all of people would not be sitting waiting at the counter in full view of the bar's clientele. Carrying her Black Russian she walks the length of the place before she finds him. She passes by the side of all the other curtained booths looking each time to her right. She reaches his. The last. She stops; she says, 'I was waiting over there.'

He says, 'I knew you'd find me.'

Opposite him she slips into the booth. 'Good place, this.'

'Yes. It's been here for ever.'

He looks more scrubbed, of course, than on the other

occasions they've been together. This is the first time she has seen him away from sculpture, away from wax and clay. She does not know him this way.

Where his worn dark denim shirt is open at the neck she looks at his skin that is neither taut nor wrinkled and she wonders about his age. He might be fifty-one, fifty-two or fifty-three perhaps. The layperson would guess him to be younger but Sarit is an expert at judging age by skin. She takes a sip of the Black Russian and without quite looking him in the eyes, she asks, 'What are you drinking?'

'Whisky as usual,' he says and then, leaning back against the leather of the booth, he says, 'You were surprised by my call.'

'Yes.'

'To be honest,' he says, 'I surprised myself by calling,' and then he adds, 'I have my group of models whom I sculpt. I sometimes take on new ones but it's rare these days.' He says it not as if he's doing her a favour, not as if she should be grateful for his attention, but just by way of explanation. She wants to ask him, 'And what about that girl you sculpt, that Nadia you sculpt at different phases of her life?' But before she can begin to form the words he turns towards the window, he points over the street and says, 'See that building over there.'

She looks at the strange almost Toblerone-shaped building of white brick, with its tip on the corner of the street. 'Yes.'

'That's the Flat Iron building. It's full of artists' and sculptors' studios. They live and work in there.'

Sarit looks at the building's upper floors interspersed with lights. She stares. She sees the silhouettes of sculptors sculpting, of painters painting, or at least she imagines that she does. She recalls the art house film she saw with Sammy and the young woman half naked on the chair as she painted. Something compels her to ask Ramsi, 'Can anyone go and paint there?'

'If they rent a studio I suppose so . . . Why, thinking of abandoning your lucrative profession?'

'Yes, sure.'

The background music at Soul Kitchen that night is ethnic world music that envelops the listener in its echo. The lighting is subdued. Ramsi says to her, 'I know nothing about you . . . I decided that if I'm going to sculpt you it would be interesting to have some vague idea of who you are in a different setting . . . That's why I called you.'

When he says that, when he says 'To have some vague idea of who you are . . .' just as she had done in the foundry, Sarit wonders if she has dreamt up the scene with Ramsi in his studio. But she realises then, in that moment, that he is right, that what happened against the brick wall and on the wooden floor was somehow separate from their meetings in the foundry and their meeting here. And in truth, save for in the biblical sense she knows him not at all, this man whom she wants to touch. This man with the beard, the thick accent, the scent of clay, of nicotine and cedarwood sitting in the booth across from her.

'So.' And he leans forward just a little. 'Are you going to tell me who you are, Sarit?'

'Who I am? I haven't thought about that for some time . . . Well, I'm a surgeon . . . of a kind, as you know. And I was Israeli as you pointed out.'

From his shirt pocket he takes a packet of thin white cigarette papers. He takes out a worn leather tobacco pouch, begins to roll the strands between the fingers of his left hand. She watches him. He sees her looking. He says, 'There is nothing remarkable about my hands. Sad but true.'

'Ah, but what they can do,' she says and realises then the double entendre of her words. In the muted light she feels the unfamiliar heat of blushing.

'Am I imagining it,' he asks, 'or are you changing colour?'

'You're imagining it,' she says and laughs at herself.

The waitress with her blue-streaked hair and a snake ring says, 'Can I get you something else?'

'Another Black Russian for me.'

'I'll have the same,' says Ramsi and then to Sarit, 'Why do you say I was Israeli and not I am Israeli? I left Egypt decades ago, but I still consider myself Egyptian.'

'Do you go back?' she asks, deflecting.

'I did once. But not for ages now. It's a different world. It was so European when I was growing up. But that went fast with Nasser. He took so much of what I loved away. The last time I went back it depressed me. The natural beauty is still there. But the place is so neglected and run-down. The spice has faded . . . Like a beautiful woman who has lost her looks,' he says. 'And you? Do you go back home?'

'Home?'

'I mean to Israel.'

'No.'

'Never?'

'Never.'

This time, after the waitress has brought their drinks it is he who watches her, hands clasped round her glass.

'They would be almost impossible to sculpt,' he says to her, as if she should know exactly what the 'they' refers to.

'What would be impossible to sculpt?'

'Your hands.'

'Because?'

'To re-create that delicacy would be hard,' and then, as if already working in his mind, contemplating her fingers, fashioning ridges, knuckles, nails and skin, he moves his head to one side and he says, 'But perhaps there is a way . . . I'd have to stay away from the alcohol for a few days before I attempted it.'

She smiles at him, glad that he is focusing now on her hands and not her mind. As if she and her hands were somehow separate.

The respite, though, is brief. He says, 'So why do you say I *was* Israeli?'

'I don't know . . . I mean, I've been here for years. I went

201

to medical school here at U of C. I have an American passport. This place is home.'

'Is it?' He's looking straight at her now. Curious about her in a slow and heavy sort of way. 'Is this really home? Isn't it just the place where you live, Sarit? Isn't home where your roots are?' he says.

She drinks some more. The ice rattles in her glass. 'No, this is home. Really. This is home. Absolutely.'

'I see,' he says. 'Well, your manner is very Middle Eastern as I told you.'

'What's that supposed to mean?'

'You know exactly what it means. No airs and graces. You get straight to the point.'

'And you?'

'Oh me, I'm Middle Eastern through and through.' He sips his Black Russian, then says, 'I spent years in Nice, though, so there's lots of French in me. And I went to the Lycée in Alexandria. French was my second language after Arabic.'

'I wish I spoke,' she says, her chin now in her hands.

He inhales his roll-up, turns to the side to blow out the smoke. 'It opens up my world in terms of literature and music,' he says.

'Yes, I saw the French books on your shelves and I heard the music was in French.'

She has not referred before to the evening in his home except by accident and nor has he. So that now in the darkening bar, with the loosening and the melting that comes with the alcohol, with the talk of books and language and the music in the background, a myriad of possibilities fans out before them. Possibilities that float, vague and fuzzy at the edges, between them and around them in the booth. More relaxed, less on their guard, they watch the shapes there in the reddish light, wondering now, not so much unsure as leisurely.

He says, 'I often think in French. Or dream in it.'

'You're lucky . . . I love the way it sounds.'

'Do you dream in Hebrew?' he asks her.

'I don't know. I don't think there are words in my dreams. Only pictures.'

He notices the terseness in her voice and chooses not to touch it. 'We all dream in languages as well as images,' he says.

'So then I suppose I must do. Perhaps in English. Or in German.'

She doesn't pick up on his surprise, not because of the semi-darkness, but because her surprise at her own words is greater.

'In German?' he asks.

She lifts her glass to her lips and tilts her head. She drinks the melted ice. 'Yes . . . snippets of it . . . not often, though.'

'Have you lived there?'

'No.'

'So who spoke to you in German?'

'Oh, neighbours on the kibbutz where I grew up. Lots of them spoke German.' She looks down as she speaks.

'Holocaust survivors?' he asks.

'Some.'

'Your mother or your father?'

'My father.'

'Is he alive?'

'Yes.'

'But you said you never go home?'

'No.'

'So you bring him over here to visit?'

She shakes her head. 'A long story,' she says.

Between them there is silence. The light has grown orangey. The air has grown heavy. She looks up at Ramsi and he at her. For the first time since the Art Institute they hold one another's gaze without speaking. She wants to turn away and yet she keeps on looking till it hurts.

Because there are moments in life when caught off guard we sense a person has in some way seen through us, moments when our normal reactions, the strong habitual reactions that have been practised over years and years, begin to falter. Reactions that have been fine-tuned and honed, till our face becomes the mask, our mask the face, so that the first of the hairline fissures can be so shocking and so painful. Because to sit opposite a man who is all but a stranger, not to have time to read your own body's warning signs, to put your hand up to your face and suddenly and unexpectedly to find it hot and flushed and wet as if it were the face, the skin, of another is alarming. To be in a place so unfamiliar, in a strange bar with a strange man with the mask cracking, when you know yourself as a controlled, together woman, is in its way quite shocking. And here in Soul Kitchen between the waves that threaten tears, the waves of awkwardness fight for their place. But both are ousted and are beaten, because in the end Sarit is calmed not by her inner strength alone but by the warm, strong and unexpected hand that had made its imprint on hers in the terracotta clay. The hand that reaches out, now, across the booth to stroke the length of her neck and the side of her face.

TWENTY-FOUR

We are sculpted, each one of us. Malleable in the hands of our first sculptors, we are shaped according to their art. Their work is limited at times, enriched at others by their talent, their own teaching and the clay between their fingers, but their power is immense. As we feel them fashion, we will join them, changing or moving with them, then bringing other sculptors into play. Brothers, sisters, friends, first loves. At some time their fashioning will slow and our silhouette will stand alone. And though we ourselves will glaze or smooth or soften, their groundwork is unalterable. And later, much later when the art has tarnished here and there, when the elements have covered certain curves and hidden others, with a new artist we might work together if we dare. We might rediscover the curves the elements have tarnished. We might, through his eyes, discover in ourselves the slants and slopes we carry with us but have never even seen. It is not for this alone, but for this above all that we invite into our lives another artist's eyes.

The night of Soul Kitchen, Sarit looks up at the Flat Iron building and, tentative, she says, 'I suppose we could go in and look.'

'Why not?' he says. 'They have open house on Friday nights. We can wander around and watch them work.'

Sarit hesitates on the street corner where, spider-shaped, the other roads move in to meet the tip of Daimon on which the grimy Toblerone-shaped artist's building stands. This point, this divergence of paths, is the very last at which either way might be open to her, though of this of course Ramsi is unaware. So in her conscious mind is she. Ramsi doesn't push her. He just stands, his hands in his fingerless gloves in his pockets, and waits for her decision, though he feels suddenly that he would like to prolong the evening in her company. Not so that they can be together in his studio. For that, for once, he is not yet ready. The last time, the first time, she had been a total stranger to him and so it had been easy, but the landscape now is different and he knows it. On the corner of the street in the cold he lets her think.

'All right,' she says. 'We'll go for a bit. Why not?'

They wait for the light to turn green. He touches her elbow, guides her in the right direction. They cross the street. The entrance to the studios is a doorway in disrepair between two shopfronts. The stairway is wide and smells of art and age and peeling paint. She follows him up the stairs. Beneath her hand the banister is rough. Here and there the wood is broken off and rotting with woodworm and neglect. A woman trips down the stairs past them. Even in the poor light Sarit notices her cropped dark hair and her shirt that is splattered with paint. At the top of the second flight they begin to walk along a corridor lined with doors. Some are closed and in total darkness. Some have light that seeps beneath their frames. And the doors of others as they walk past are flung wide open in a celebration of the work within. Close to a photographer's studio Sarit and Ramsi slow to the same pace. She follows him in. Black-and-white photographs taken with an old-fashioned camera line the walls floor to ceiling, with natural and artificial light thrown at them from every angle. In the middle of the room a thin young man with a shaven head sits on a black stool. He holds a strip of negatives up to the light, then swivels round to face them. Ramsi nods at the man and begins to wander around but Sarit stops where she is and asks him, 'Is this your work?'

'Yes,' he says, in a heavy accent that she guesses might be South American. 'Please just ignore me. Go ahead and wander. I'm finishing up some stuff for a show, but if you guys have any questions I'm here . . .'

206

'Thanks.'

The images in faded black-and-white old-fashioned print are self-explanatory. In the first, a self-portrait, the man stands alone, his shaved head bowed. In the second too he is alone, but crouching, the camera held in front of his eyes and beneath it one can see his mouth smiling slightly at the beauty of the moment he is poised to immortalise. The moment in which he again is there, head slightly forward, laughing, hands clutching the bare ankles of the child held on his shoulders. The child in her thin light cotton skirt that moves in the breeze. The child whose face, not in the photograph, is all the more vivid in the mind. A face that hidden is so much more visible to Ramsi as he stands before it. The face of a child at four or five or six, somewhere along the sand by the dark-grey sea in the early seventies on the Côte d'Azur.

And her strong young father is running with her as she calls, '*Papa, plus vite. Plus vite* . . . Daddy, faster, faster.' He moves with her on his shoulders faster in the wind, till laughing, out of breath, he stops, he crouches and drops her to the sand.

'*N'arrêtes pas, Papa, n'arrêtes pas* . . . Don't stop, Daddy, don't.'

'Horses need to rest, you know,' he says, laughing, lying back in the sand and she climbs up to his chest then and with her little fists begins to bang and then to tickle. '*Ça suffit, Nadia . . . ça suffit. Arrêtes* . . . Enough, Nadia. Enough now . . . Stop.' But she carries on and so he says, 'Well now, if we're going to talk about tickling,' and he sits up, holds her with one hand and tickles with the other under her arm.

With pleasure and in mock horror she squeals, '*Papa, arrêtes, arrêtes* . . . Daddy, stop, stop . . .'

'Not until you tell me how much you love me.'

'*Je t'aime. Je t'aime, Papa,*' she says, giggling, squirming. 'I love you, love you, Daddy. I love you.'

'Are you sure, Nadia? Quite sure?'

'I'm sure. I'm sure, Papa.'

He lets go of her. Their breathing, erratic at first from the running and the laughter, begins to slow. In the warmth of the early evening, suddenly exhausted, the child pushes her father back into the sand, so that he spits it out and goes, 'Puu, puu, it's in my mouth. Puu.' She laughs again, then lies down, her head on his chest, and closes her eyes. A few minutes later he lifts his head, looks down at Nadia sleeping and marvels at the way in which a small child can be so wired and wild one minute and the next in a deep and heavy sleep. He would like to stand and stretch now, but he doesn't want to wake her, so that without moving the rest of his body he has to crane his neck downwards to see her face. A perfect face he thinks.

From where he lies he sees the side of her high forehead, the olive skin, the beginnings of her cheekbones with a small beauty spot that is almost black just below her right eye. He thinks of her in front of the mirror scrubbing at her face with a flannel. He hears Lucie saying to her, 'Enough, Nadia. Why are you scrubbing like that? You'll hurt yourself.' And he laughs, remembering how Nadia, indignant, had ignored her mother, carried on scrubbing harder and had said, 'I want this horrible black spot off my face. I'm going to rub till it goes away.'

And now in his mind looking down at her Ramsi takes a photo of the side of his daughter's face. Smooth, flawless, almost coffee-coloured skin. Smooth and warm in the heat of the late afternoon summer sun. Hot skin. Boiling even. Boiling, burnt and blistered. Sticky, brownish, red and yellow. Weeping skin. Lids swollen. Lashes gone. Eyes forced shut, huge blisters stuck to a screaming mouth. Nadia's screams. Her mother's screams. 'You . . . you . . . Ramsi, you . . . You left her. Yoooooooou left her alone.' Hysterical screams by the bedside of their child too burnt to writhe in pain. Endless chilling screams. Hers, Lucie's screams, outside and his inside. 'You, you, you . . .' and then just a high-pitched 'Aaaaaaaaaah' as though she were being attacked, so that the nurses come and touch Lucie's arm and say, 'Madame Riyad, we understand your distress, but we have to ask you to stop. You're disturbing the other patients. We can give you something to help.'

But Lucie carries on screaming, 'My baby, look at my baaby, my baaaby,' not ever calming down enough to say yes or no to help. And her screams stop suddenly, not at first when Ramsi holds her. No, not then. Then she is hysterical still, but seconds after the jab of the needle into the flesh beneath her pretty floral summer skirt. Startled, eyes staring, Lucie looks around her. By her child's bedside they sit her down in the visitor's chair. For a week she will sit there nodding off from time to time. And he, Ramsi, will just stand over Nadia and watch in horror and in anguish till he can bear it no longer and in sheer exhaustion and despair he will lie down on the floor and sob next to his daughter's bed.

TWENTY-FIVE

The night after Soul Kitchen, after the Flat Iron building, they might have touched. Instead in the early hours of the morning they had parted ways. The aura, the electricity, the desire was there, but their boldness in the face of the unknown was replaced by a holding back in the face of the unravelling. Over the next days she carried the thought of him with her in a way that both excited and drained her at once. The anticipation of him was with her in a way that she had not known before and it was with her too as though she had not yet known him. The progression of them, of the two of them together, was not linear but moved as in the way of two artists, two guarded, wounded adults who brought their paintbrushes in a slow, hot, broken swirl across the canvas.

She had asked him, a couple of weeks or so after Soul Kitchen, how he made room in his mind for a new piece of work as it burgeoned. And she had learnt that it was not as another artist might do, by seeking out a log cabin in the forest or a cliff above a wild and desolate stretch of coastline. Instead he had said he might saunter alone through cobbled back-streets in search of inspiration or thread his way through people at galleries and museums. He had told her that he might close his blinds, unplug his phone and sit there in the darkness. He might smoke his coloured *hukka* or his roll-ups and drink some good red wine or a shot or two of whisky, or he might go and sit in Kingston Mines, the Green Mill or the Hideout and sink into his other world, held there by the jazz or by the blues. Or if before he sculpted he wanted to visualise the clearest of images, the sharpest of pictures, sometimes he would make his way to Hyde Park, to the museum that, built like an ancient temple, juts out into a peninsula. And from there, as the water flowed right up to the narrow grey stone steps on which he sat, he would stare out into the lake. It was as though at one and the same time he was looking at the past and cleansing himself so that he might begin again.

At other times before he began a new piece of work Ramsi would seek refuge in the sanctuary of the Baha'i temple in Wilmette on the outskirts of Chicago. And now, outside the temple spring weaves itself in and out of late winter. Inside, Sarit and Ramsi sit in the perennial coolness, in the vast and lofty silence. This is the first time he has come here in company and they sit there, the two of them, a Christian and a Jew by name, an Egyptian and an Israeli by birth, not members of the Baha'i faith in any official sense. Two artists in this sculptured place devoid of icons where Baha'i followers come to search for peace of mind.

For some time on the chairs with their dark coverings in the dim light neither of them speaks. On the muted mosaic floor their feet brush with artists of the past. She looks up at the white engravings that, both bold and intricate at once, sweep across the ceiling and through the cupola of the temple and remind Sarit of hands being held and long slim fingers intertwined.

She whispers to him, 'Why the hands?' He follows her gaze upwards and with the eye of an artist sees exactly what she means. 'Maybe it's a symbol of peace,' he whispers back.

'Can you find it here?' she asks.

'Almost.'

'Does it last?'

He shrugs. 'And you?'

'I don't think about it . . . Too much to do.'

She closes her eyes. Next to her, he smells of clay, of cedarwood, of tobacco and of strength. Sarit inhales.

He has not sat this close to her before, in profile. He studies her face. He notices how her lashes make shadows on her cheeks. He notices the tiny blonde hairs above her lip. In this of all places he is meant to be only in the present moment. Instead in his mind he catches himself in his studio, with his hands on clay, with Sarit somewhere close to him. And when she hears him draw in a breath between his teeth, she can imagine where it comes from and she revels in the sensations that he sends her. She keeps her eyes closed now, but moves to let him know she knows.

Close to them they hear footsteps and turn their heads to see a squat olive-skinned man carrying a small blonde child. He walks past them to the front of the sanctuary. The father with his child in his arms. Still, even now, Ramsi's need to stare is as great as his need to look away. Over the years so many fathers with their children have turned from the intensity of his stare.

As they pass Ramsi is tethered, while in the mix of white and coolness, of spirituality and of art, Sarit feels somehow freed. Some minutes pass. She leans towards him, smiles and whispers, 'What am I doing here with you?'

He points upwards. 'He must know,' he says. 'If he's there . . . he'd say you have some higher reason for being where you are.'

'And you?' she asks.

'I suppose he'd say I have a reason too.'

'What is it?'

'You,' he says and then serious, half whispering still, he adds, 'But Sarit . . . This is not what I do well . . .'

'I know what you mean. I'm not so great at this myself.'

'Because?'

'I've never wanted to. It hasn't been there in this way. I don't know . . . All of the above.'

'Interesting,' he says, his voice carrying just a little too far. She puts her fingers to his lips. She whispers, 'Shh.'

Alone, Sarit and Ramsi might not have dared to broach the

subject of their reasons for being where they were. But the Baha'i temple lends them the illusion of protection. Inside its walls fear and inhibition seem quite out of place. Almost as if the spirit of the temple were a third person, a counsellor or an acquaintance asking in a friendly tone, 'So tell me, what's your story?' or 'How long have you two been together?'

She asked herself that question as she sat there close to him. '*Am* I with him? Does *he* think we're together? Does desire and connection and feeling mean there is direction to this thing?' and then she stops herself, scoffs at herself. 'Sarit, I've never known you to think like this before. You sound like all those normal women.'

She looks at Ramsi as if to check that he has not been reading her mind. She clears her throat as if to clear away her thoughts. She whispers, 'I need to stretch my legs. I'll wait for you outside,' and she gets up and walks back to the huge, high, sculpted doors.

In the gardens she reaches for her gloves in the pocket of her thick denim jacket. Here too in the promise of the croci, the tulips, the pansies, the wild roses in their beds there is a peacefulness. She stands by a bench, rolls her head from side to side. She stretches her fingers. She raises one arm, then the other. She arches her back.

'Good place to do yoga,' he says from behind her.

She jumps. 'I didn't expect you out so soon.'

They walk along the path between the trees and the flowerbeds.

At the entrance to the grounds, as though choreographed, at the same second and with the same step they both turn back to look at the temple.

'Magnificent. Just magnificent,' she says.

'Maybe that's why there's only one on each continent,' he says.

'How do you mean?' she asks as they walk fast towards her car.

213

So that slightly out of breath he says, 'They only allow one Baha'i temple on each continent. Maybe they think exquisite beauty shouldn't be re-created too often.'

'You mean because it makes it commonplace?'

'Perhaps. And maybe what is commonplace is no longer as beautiful.'

'Tell that to some of my patients.' She laughs. 'Do you know how many of them want the same noses and the same lips? The younger ones at least. They come to me with pictures of Hollywood stars. They want Brad Pitt's lips and Nicole Kidman's nose.'

'They're not really Brad Pitt's lips they want,' he says. 'They're those beautiful alabaster lips from the eighteenth dynasty. That full mouth . . . Did you see them at the Egyptian exhibition?'

'No,' she says. 'But I know which ones you mean.'

'But you do what your patients ask for, don't you, Sarit?' he teases. 'Mail order lips and noses.'

'Sometimes,' she says. 'Not always. I have to know they're of sound mind. I have to get their point.'

'I see.'

They have reached her car, her old black beetle. He walks round to the passenger side. She gets in, lifts the piles of paper from the passenger seat, leans over to open the door for him. She turns the key in the engine that spits and cranks and chokes a little as it starts. She puts her foot on the accelerator.

He leans towards her. Slowly he runs a finger down the bridge of her nose. He asks, 'Do they ever want to know why you keep this?'

'My Barbra Streisand nose?' She laughs.

'Your Cleopatra nose,' he says.

She smiles. 'Sure my patients want to know,' she says. 'I tell them my nose is me. I say I like it this way.'

'Do you?'

'Uhuh,' she says, 'I think I do.'

He likes her confidence. For a moment in her company he feels younger, almost carefree. He says, 'You know, Sarit . . . I find you beautiful.'

'Flatterer,' she says. 'You just want to sculpt me.'

'That, yes. But I mean it.'

'Beautiful no. Interesting perhaps.'

'Beautiful yes. Interesting too. Alluring. Different . . . Sort of like an amaryllis . . . a blood-red one.'

She feels the beating of her heart. 'An amaryllis?' She laughs. 'What do they look like?'

'Ah,' he says. 'Well . . . they're tall, powerful flowers. Nothing wishy-washy about them. Amaryllis means splendour in Greek.'

'You hot-blooded Middle Easterner,' she says. 'You'll make me crash the car.'

Next to her he laughs, puts his hand on the back of her neck.

She asks, 'So if you like imperfection why don't you ever sculpt the odd irregular feature then?'

'I do,' he says. 'Do you think I sculpt every model as if she was flawless?'

'You sculpt Nadia that way,' she says. 'Or almost.'

A silence then. Just the sound of the engine and the weight of the unspoken in the car.

And Sarit listening to herself as she tries now to sound casual. So completely casual. Though as she changes gear, in the tone of her own voice she feels and hears the rising of its pitch and looking at the road she says, 'So I take it Nadia was your lover. One of your harem?'

'No, Sarit,' he says. 'Nadia was my child.'

TWENTY-SIX

The sculptor at work before his muse bears a marked fascination for the onlooker. In etching after etching Picasso created engravings of a sculptor, himself perhaps, perhaps another, naked and in the throes of intense concentration. On sheet after sheet he etched the sculptor bemused, the sculptor prepared, the sculptor involved in creating the image of his model. That the model should be naked comes as no surprise; that the sculptor too should be without his clothes suggests not only an element of sexuality, but the need for freedom from the constraints of clothing so that he might liberate his mind and his body as a prelude to the creative process. The sexual suggestion is not in itself extraordinary. Often moments of tension will weave their way into the sessions between a sculptor and his model. Moments when creative and sexual energy brush with one another, confuse one another, each struggling hard to find their proper place.

'Lauren,' Sarit had said as they had sat in Margie's, the oak-panelled, mirrored 1920s ice cream parlour in Wicker Park, 'he wants to sculpt me.'

'All of you?' she asks, mascara-laden lashes fluttering.

'I don't know . . . I doubt it. He's sketched my face, so it's probably just that.'

'Why don't you ask him?'

'No, I'll wait.'

'You should let him. You've got a great face and a great bod. Take a look at yourself there,' she says, pointing at the mirror next to them in the booth where they sit, smudging her pink lipstick as she shovels the chocolate fudge sundae into her mouth, while Sarit eats her fruit salad. Her words half inaudible, she adds, 'You should show that body off, Sairit. D'you know how many women would die to have a stomach as flat as yours, girl?'

'Haven't got boobs like yours though, Lor. But what do I care?'

'You could get them done . . . I'm sure one of our friends would be happy to oblige.'

'Not in a million years.'

And Lauren says, 'It's not such a big deal. It only hurt for about a week and Todd loves them.'

'Lor, I'm not about to change my body and I certainly wouldn't do it to please some man.'

'Thought not . . .' Lauren says. 'Anyway, you should know the score with him by now . . . what's his name Romsi, Rimsi . . . ?'

Sarit has to laugh. 'It's Ramsi,' she says.

'Ramsi, whatever. You should know the score with him. You've been to his place before, haven't you?'

Sarit in that instant is not quite sure whether Lauren is calling her bluff or whether she had told her she was there in Ramsi's studio, but she says, 'Yes, I have been once. But that was different. I sort of asked to go last time. Now he wants me there.'

'What's it like, where he lives?' Lauren asks.

'Beautiful, I suppose . . . In an unplanned sort of way. Middle Eastern. Sort of.'

'My God,' she says. 'You look weird. Like nervous. I've never seen you like this. Not even before surgery.'

'Give me a break, Lor. I'm not nervous.'

'Then what? Not in control for once?'

In his studio on a Saturday morning in April, she says to Ramsi, 'You have to understand. I'm not officially on call, but that means nothing. If they bleep me I'll go.'

'I know. I've seen it before. Give me your jacket.'

217

She takes off the denim jacket. Underneath she wears a thin long-sleeved white sweater, a pair of faded jeans with a worn brown leather belt and an old pair of trainers. He hangs her jacket on an iron hook at the back of the door, asks her, 'Do you want coffee?'

'Yes.'

'Strong. Black. No sugar,' he says.

'How do you know?'

'I remember . . . from the foundry.'

He disappears behind the muslin screen. She looks around. The room is as she has remembered it from weeks before, except that opposite the chaise longue, where the low dark table with the *hukka* had stood on a Persian rug, he has cleared a large space. And in the middle on a wooden plinth stands some wire mesh, shaped roughly like a head, with a pile of metal sticks that lie beside it on the floor. She thinks of the students at the School of the Art Institute. She thinks of the model on her red velvet spread. She wonders where and how he will want her to sit.

He walks towards the chaise longue with the coffee, hands her the earth-coloured ceramic mug. His behaviour is slightly formal. As if that's the proper way to be now that she's his model. 'So it's up to you, Sarit,' he says. 'I can sculpt just your face or I can sculpt your body too.'

'You're the artist. Whatever you prefer.'

'No. It's what you prefer. It's how much time you have. To sculpt your face I might only need you for half a day. Then I can work from the sketches I did last time. For the whole of you it'll take much longer. If we stop you need to be able to come back. You can't leave me in the lurch once I've started.'

'Would I?'

'What do I know? Would you?' he asks, as though putting the question to himself as he puts it to her. 'Would you? I don't know you well enough to say. You might.'

She laughs. 'You're right, you know. I might, if I'd had enough of sitting here.'

'Great,' he says, half serious, half joking. 'Just great . . . so is it worth me starting at all?' And he looks at her and adds, 'Sarit, it's not as easy as you think to stay in one pose for hours. You don't have to do this, you know. You can still change your mind.'

'I know I don't have to,' she says. 'I never do anything because I have to. But I want to.'

'Because?'

'Just because.'

'Because what?'

'You sound like me interrogating a patient,' she says and laughs. 'I want to just because I do. Why not? I'll get to see you work this way.'

He doesn't ask her the question about her face and her body again. He says just, 'When you're ready.' And as though he's taking photographs he opens and closes his eyes, watches her move around while they try out different places in the room. Sarit in her clothes sitting on the rug. Sarit propped against the bookcase. Sarit in a low, worn green armchair with Ramsi taking pictures in his head.

And each time, on the rug, against the bookcase and in the armchair, he shakes his head. He says, 'No, not right. Not right. Not right,' till without a word she walks back towards the chaise longue and, turned away from him, stretches her arms above her head and begins slowly to undress.

He watches her from behind. He thinks, 'Sort of like a Bonnard but no pastel-coloured woman this.'

Her back to him she calls out, 'Do you have a piece of material? A throw or a sheet or something?'

From a heavy rounded drawer in a large Indian chest by his bed he brings out a piece of purple raw silk. He stands behind her. 'Here,' he says.

Without turning, she reaches a hand back, takes the silk

219

throw. He walks back to his wire armature and for a few moments busies himself. Sarit reclines on the chaise longue, her head against the armrest, the purple silk across her like a skirt from the middle of her stomach to halfway down her thighs, her arms resting on the material of the throw.

He doesn't show surprise. He doesn't say, 'Oh, so you decided to let me sculpt the whole of you.' Instead he goes to stand at the foot of the chaise longue and he looks. Not at her. Not yet at Sarit, but at the model and her pose. He says, 'I need to move the material.' And he moves the purple silk with care so as not to uncover her. He turns it round on her skin, lifting it from where it hangs to the floor, so that lengthways and thinner now, like a scarf, it begins just below her belly button and it falls covering her between her legs and draping beyond her feet, over the edge of the chaise longue. Looking at her, noticing on her shoulder the tattoo of the tiny horseshoe inside the curve of the omega that he had not mentioned before, he says, 'Now you're confusing me. Are you a bohemian or a plastic surgeon?'

'It would seem,' she says, 'that I'm a sculptor's model.'

In a split second he can change from being Ramsi the sculptor to Ramsi the man and back again. He says, 'Don't move now,' and with her lying there he lifts the chaise longue at its foot, then turns it lengthways so that she is facing the centre of the room. Back by the wire mesh and the clay he stands, his hand over his mouth in contemplation. He shakes his head. 'No, I can't. I can't do it,' he says, 'not like this.'

'Why not?'

'Put your left arm behind your head,' he says. 'Like this . . . Leaning on it. That's right. And the other one under the throw . . . No, a little higher. Flat. By your thigh.'

'You don't want to sculpt my hands?' she asks.

'I can't. They are a sculpture on their own . . . or part of a bust, with your face resting on your palms like this,' he says, showing her the gesture. He pulls up a chair next to the arma-ture. 'I need to do a couple of sketches of you.'

'But you did. The other week.'

'That was your face. And anyway you weren't lying back like that. It changes everything.'

'Go for it,' she says. 'But first some music, maestro.'

He might have lost his cool, the artist given orders on the threshold of creation. Instead he stands up. He says, 'I have just the thing.'

He crosses the room, takes a long-playing record from a worn sleeve, lifts the needle to it on the record player. She thinks of herself in the theatre preparing for surgery. She thinks of Pamela placing the CDs in the player on the wall. As he sits back down and puts pencil to paper the sounds of guitar strings, the clapping of hands and of castanets fill the room. 'Abed Azrié,' he tells Sarit. 'He's Syrian. His music mixes East and West. You'll hear his lyrics are in Arabic and in Spanish.'

Lying there on the beige velvet, with the purple silk cool against her stomach's warm white skin, she says, 'I won't under-stand a word of the lyrics.'

And half smiling, Ramsi says, 'If you're quiet for a little bit and don't move I'll translate them for you afterwards.'

'Ah,' she says, 'my prize.'

He begins to sketch her. Slowly at first. Carefully. Then faster. Sheet after sheet of white paper falling to the floor as he walks round her, considers, discards, embraces angles for her, shapes of her, curves of her. As she lies there, her head against the armrest, her eyes closed, listening to the music, she visualises a belly dancer in gold and turquoise in her head. For an hour, maybe more, he sketches. From time to time she looks across at him. She cannot see his face, nor his left hand, with which he draws, because of the way he holds the sketchpad, but in the movement of his arm she senses his con-centration, his frustration and, for a moment here or there, his satisfaction.

This part for him is more graft than pleasure. She can feel that. Here, as he draws, he is the actor backstage, rehearsing in the wings, waiting for the curtain to go up, mouthing his lines to himself in preparation. Lying there she is neither bored nor restless. The music and the imagery lend her patience. The turquoise belly dancer in her mind, transposed with the next tune into a flamenco dancer with the mixture of *olas* and *olés*, the slow strings, the accordion and the pathos of the Spanish lyrics that she feels without understanding. She thinks, 'A mixture of classic and modern. Sort of like him.'

'We can take a break,' he says.

'Are you done?'

He laughs. 'The beginning's over. That's all, Sarit.'

'My clothes,' she says.

'I'll lend you a robe.'

From a cupboard by his bed he brings out a thin fern-green cotton kimono. Lying there still, she slips it on. It smells of cedarwood and earth. It smells of him. She stands up, letting the throw fall to the floor.

He lifts it, holds it in his hand. 'You must be hungry,' he says.

'What do you have?'

'Pita. Some tehina. Tomato and cucumber salad. Oh, and some falafel.'

'Great,' she says. 'Where did you get it?'

'From Old Jerusalem, you know . . . the Palestinian restaurant up the street.'

'Yes,' she says, 'I've eaten there.'

Cross-legged they sit at the heavy low brown table in the corner of the room. He pours red wine into her glass without asking. She catches a glimpse of the label and sees that it's a French Gevrey Chambertin. 'He knows how to drink,' she thinks.

He sees her looking, says, 'Comes from my time in Nice . . . the obsession with good wine . . . believe me you'll need it. It's going to be a long session,' and then he adds, 'I'm sup-posed to pay you for this, you know. Models get up to fifteen dollars an hour.'

Her mouth half full, she tries not to laugh. She says, 'Yeah, right. I'll charge you more. I'll charge what I do for a chin.'

'It'll take longer.'

'OK, a chin and a lift.'

'A deal.'

They shake on it, hands speaking as they touch. Sarit feels her nakedness beneath the kimono.

After that they eat in silence. Not because there is nothing to say. But because in his head Ramsi is working and she knows it. She recognises the expression on his face.

He leaves her sitting there and goes to work on the frame of metal sticks on which he will sculpt her. Even though she has refilled her glass, even though there is time for her to read the newspaper that lies there, afterwards when he asks her to come back to pose she remembers exactly how she had been lying, so that now she manoeuvres herself into the same posi-tion as before and lifts the piece of purple silk to the right place without his help.

'What's your policy on talking while you're working?' she asks.

'I can listen,' he says. 'And there are times when I can talk. You'll work it out. And yours?' he asks.

'What do you mean?'

'Oh. You'll make your own decisions about talking too,' he says as he bends down to lift the first of the loaf-shaped pieces of pinky, grainy terracotta clay from the bag. 'There are so many places you can go to in your head while I'm working. I think that's the only good thing about posing for a sculptor. That and maybe the fact that you can learn discipline and inhibition I suppose . . . You can go where you like in your head while I'm working. You might not feel like speaking.'

About to start, he remembers something. Goes to change

the music before he starts. A deep, adamant, mature woman's voice singing in Arabic comes from the speakers. Sarit hears a lone flute. She hears drums and tambourines. He says, 'It's Remetti, an Algerian nomad. She's singing about the life of the artist. It was a scandal for an Arab woman to follow a creative life. Still is in some places.' He bends down to lift a piece of terracotta clay from the pile. With a long piece of wire he slices it and begins to pad a piece of it on to the armature. With another piece of clay he fills it out, lifting his head then bending back down again, looking up again, while Sarit gives herself over to the beat of the music, to the tambourines and the indignant wail of the singer. He walks over to her, kneels down beside her calves, looks at the way her feet are crossed, the way her soles arch, the interplay even of her veins. Then, back with his clay, with his left hand he makes the strong curve of her calf muscle. With the tips of his fingers he sculpts her long slim feet and the arch of her sole. With a knife he cuts into the clay, then rolls tiny pieces to create her toes. With the pads of his thumbs he shapes the toenails.

'Smooth skin,' he says to himself, 'I have to make the skin smooth.' He pads the metal on the other side, begins to work with his palm on the movement of her hip. Without asking she has taken a couple of five-minute breaks, as if by instinct she knows when she can sit up and pull her knees towards her without disturbing the flow of his work. Though it has been over an hour, till now neither one of them has spoken.

Till he says, 'You have to stay this way until I've finished your legs. Can you?'

'How long will it be?'

'A while.'

She nods at him. Only then, only when he speaks, does she realise how stiff her neck is. She rolls it from side to side. She asks him, 'How did you start sculpting?'

'In the sand,' he says, looking at his piece. 'With my mother. For hours at the beach in Abu Sir in Alexandria. The other kids buried their friends and their parents in the sand. But I copied the people instead of burying them,' and remembering something he laughs out loud.

She asks him, 'What's so funny?'

'I got myself into big trouble,' he says, 'for building two huge big mounds of sand, sticking pebbles on the top of them and saying in front of everyone that they were my mother's breasts.'

'I like that,' she says, 'I really like that.'

'And you, Sarit?' he asks, working, cutting, curving, chiselling with wooden tools and with his fingertips to refine the narrowness of her ankle. 'How did you start sculpting?'

'Very funny,' she says.

'Go on, tell me. I want to know.'

The music turns instrumental. She looks upwards towards the skylight in the vaulted roof and admires the way the ivy grows across the glass. She says, 'I was a first-year resident. We had to do the rounds with the doctors in the mornings. Everyone was nervous. I think it's an American thing to be so nervous of authority. I wasn't afraid at all. Either I could do what was asked of me or I couldn't. You know what I mean?'

He nods.

She doesn't see his expression, but she feels him listening. She carries on. She says, 'I remember we had to tear open the bandages and dress the wounds. We were under time pressure and the other residents' hands used to shake. But the practical part was the easiest part for me. Easier than dealing with the patients . . . Except for the children. I just did what I had to do and this professor watching me said . . . how did he put it? He said something like, "phenomenal manual dexterity, Kleinmann," and he wanted to recommend me for the surgery specialisation. It went from there.'

Not looking up, concentrated on his clay, Ramsi says, 'Do you think you made the right decision?'

'I don't question it. I just do it.'

She sighs. He is far enough away not to hear, but he does hear or at least he thinks he does. In Arabic the nomad starts to sing about the free spirit of a woman. And Ramsi is shaping the clay for the joint of Sarit's knee. He walks over, looks at her knee from the side, goes back again. He says, 'But why here? Why not Israel? Did you leave before the army?' and he lifts more of the pinkish clay to begin to create the movement of her torso.

'No, not before the army.'

She doesn't change position, but her eyes move around to look for a clock. Surely it must be mid-afternoon by now. The time when the light begins to change. The time when a change in mood is imminent. Mid-afternoon in spring when the sun has passed its prime. Outside at the long table on the kibbutz, on the grass not far from the statue of the Queen of Sheba they sit there and celebrate the army's selection of Sarit as an élite officer in intelligence. She's in her green uniform. The murky colour green shirt and trousers, the black beret attached by a strap to her shoulder, the heavy black shoes. Her hair is cut shorter than short, shaved almost, so that her cheekbones seem to protrude through the thin white skin. In her mind in Ramsi's studio she sees herself as she was then.

He pulls her back. He says, 'So did you leave in the middle of the army then? Did you abscond or something?'

'No, not in the middle. I had done my two years. The obligatory years,' she says. 'But I hated it. They treated me as if I was different.'

'Are you different?' he asks.

'They thought I was. They gave me all this free time to devote to my art. They said that my painting was important for the country too.'

His hands resting on the beginnings of her image, he is still. 'Painting . . . ?' he says. 'What painting?'

She shuts her eyes. She says, 'I haven't told you about it.'

'No,' he says, 'you haven't.'

226

She says, 'I am . . . I was . . . an artist. A "child prodigy" they called me.'

'I had no idea, Sarit . . . an artist. I had no idea at all. It makes sense but . . .' He looks at her from a different angle, as if all that he has so far sculpted of her needs now to be changed.

A minute passes. Maybe two. He says again, 'I didn't know, Sarit.'

'I was sort of trapped,' she says. 'I didn't want to spend my time hauling guns about, but I didn't want special treatment either.'

'But you . . . you wanted to paint?' he asks her.

'I didn't want to.' She says the words slowly, separating them, repeating them. 'I didn't want to paint. I had to. I couldn't help myself. I could have run away then, given the whole thing up . . . the exhibitions, the galleries and all the pressure that came with it. On any of the weekends when they sent me home on the bus from the army base I could have just absconded. I fantasised about disappearing. But I suppose the painting was like a drug. I'd crave it and resent it at the same time . . . My father . . .' She clears her throat. 'My father was always there at the entrance to the kibbutz waiting for me when I came home. He would guess when I might arrive. I think he some-times stood there waiting for hours. I remember once after he'd lost his arm in the Yom Kippur War, when I came back for the weekend I saw him standing there against the back-drop of the black mountains. All brown and black and grey. He had got someone to cut and stitch his shirt where his right arm should have been. It sort of looked as if it was meant to be like that after a while. He was an artist, of course, wasn't he? He couldn't bear having anything that wasn't aesthetic in full view of other people. Stupid, really, the way I'd get emo-tional when I saw him like that. I mean, I was a soldier. But he was so . . . so, well, proud of me. The time I came home when they'd decided they definitely wanted to make me an officer, we were walking past the orange groves towards the kibbutz buildings and he had his arm round me. I remember we kept passing kibbutzniks on the way. Rivka, my old school-teacher, came up to us. She had a red scarf tied round her head. She came up and hugged me and she said, "Whoever would have thought? The naughtiest girl in my class. We're so proud of you," and my father said, "At least it means we'll never lose her from this country. And we'll still have her here at weekends. And Bezalel say they'll take her afterwards." . . . Bezalel,' she says, 'was the best art school in Israel.

'He had it all planned out for me. I think he'd always been afraid I'd want to go and see where my mother came from and that I'd never come back and I'd neglect my painting.

'He was so excited that time when I came back from the army. I hadn't seen him like that since before my mother died. And while we were sitting at the table outside celebrating he just kept saying, "Wait till you see, Sarit. Just wait till you see." I was twenty and sometimes I felt he would talk to me as if I was still a child. He just kept on saying, "Wait till you see, Sarit. Wait."

'"What till I see what, Abba?"

'"You have to wait till the morning."

'"Why?"

'"Because of the light. It looks different. Everything looks different in the morning."

'He woke me up very early the next day. Like when I was younger and he used to get me up to paint the sunrises. And I remember we walked down to where his old studio had been. Neither of us said anything. I just remember hearing the birds waking up. Behind his studio there was this disused shack. It belonged to a sculptor who'd died – the one who'd sculpted the Queen of Sheba – and it had just been left there for years. At the door, behind me, he put his hand over my eyes.'

Remembering, Sarit brings her own hand up to cover her eyes. Ramsi watches. He loves the pose. He wishes he could sculpt her just like that. In his mind he takes a photograph. She carries on. She says, 'So he had his hands over my eyes and he said, "Ready?" sort of like he'd do on our birthday before I saw the presents he'd laid out for me. I nodded and he opened the door. And the light just burst out and hit me. The way he'd fixed the studio up was so . . . so beautiful. It was like . . . like the Creation. He'd been working on it for me for months. Everyone had helped him, of course. But I remember someone saying to me afterwards, "It's just amazing what Max can do with one arm. He'd do anything for you, Sarit." The floor of the studio was tiled. Those cool, reddish terracotta tiles. The walls were whitewashed and he'd painted the skirting boards and the window frames turquoise because that was my favourite colour. It was like a private joke between us. He always used to say I overused turquoise, so it was sort of like his concession to me. It was as if turquoise was his recognition of my coming of age as an artist in my own right. You earn very little on a kibbutz but he'd saved up to pay for the studio for me and I remember standing there on the doorstep and he said, "It's yours, Sarit. All yours. The kibbutz board passed it. Everyone's so proud of you." Then he ruffled my hair and he said, "Do you know how much I love you?" I don't think he'd actually said anything like that to me since before my mother died. Expressing emotion was never really his thing . . . Maybe I inherited that from him.'

She says, 'It was all so weird, though. My whole life I'd dreamt of a studio like that and now I felt as if someone was standing and choking me with their hands on my neck.'

Standing by his work, Ramsi's hands are on his clay, but still. No longer sculpting, blending, moulding, he says to Sarit, 'So . . . so you left him. You left your father.'

She lifts her right hand to her left from underneath the throw so that they are close to one another, her smooth white skin against the purple silk. Her eyes are still closed. She is no longer thinking of what she is doing. Of why she is there. Ramsi reaches behind him and picks up his sketchpad.

She says, 'I went in there, to the studio, late that night, when the whole of the kibbutz had gone to sleep. I remember I had to take a torch to find my way. He must have known I would come again that night because he'd set up my easel and there was a tray with oil paints of every single colour you can think of. And knives and brushes and palettes. It was a grown-up version of what he'd done for me as a little girl. I went straight for the black and grey and murky green, and I painted him from memory, the way he'd been standing that afternoon against the mountains of the Lebanese border. At first I painted his left arm and the rest of him with his shirt stitched back like that to keep things tidy. And then I don't know what happened to me or how it happened but when I stood back and looked at the canvas in place of his right arm there was this other arm. On his body there was a young woman's arm. A strong bare arm attached to my father's clothed body. And a hand with long slim fingers . . . It was so . . . so surreal. My father's body with this imaginary arm growing out of it. I couldn't believe it had come from me. This young woman's hand with long slim fingers. I'm not sure I understood what I was saying. It sort of came through me and I . . . well, I left it there, on the easel,' she says.

'Your farewell letter,' Ramsi says and then, almost talking to himself, he adds, 'He must have wept when he saw that.'

'Yes,' she says. 'Yes. My letter I suppose. Though I did write one too.'

Sarit says nothing more then. She keeps her eyes closed. She feels tired suddenly. So terribly, terribly tired with the emotion, the exhaustion that comes with revelation and reliving. She forgets to put her left hand back behind her head, her right hand back under the throw. And so they rest there, on top of one another, just above her breastbone.

Her head begins to drop. She sleeps and Ramsi works. He

turns for a few moments again to his pencil and paper and, while she sleeps, he steals her hands. He sketches them from the front and from the side. Then he goes back to the sculpture of her figure in the grainy terracotta clay that seems darker, heavier as the light begins to fade. With the palm of his hand, with the inside of his wrist bone, he shapes her stomach. With both of his hands together, the whole of his hands, he curves the sides of her, squatting there, moving around her as he works. With his fingers adding, smoothing and refining he creates the dips of the tight-toned runner's muscles. With the thumb and the forefinger of his left hand he creates the raised circle of her belly button, his mouth for a moment in a half-smile as he works. With the sides of his hands he textures the raw silk of the purple throw. He fashions the half-circle of her thighs and touches the pink of the clay for her breasts: small, cheeky breasts; runner's breasts. The breasts, he thinks, of a woman much younger than Sarit. He traces their curve round from her arm, from the side, to the dip of her throat. To the soft nipples, full and shaped between his fingers. The nipples taut then, and sculpted. The curve from there to the top of her long neck. Skin, he thinks, that would be so much better in marble than in bronze. And her face . . . that he has not even begun to explore. She's waking now. Half asleep still. And his hands are wet from sculpting her. The purple silk throw has slid from where it was so that it is half on, half off. Only just part of the image now, where it rests against one leg. And his fingers, his strong sculptor's fingers, wet from the smoothing and tracing of lips.

'Like that. I like the way it looks like that. From here. Curved and thick and open.' His strong fingers shaping. 'Here. This way. Like this. On the edge. There. Inside the curve. At the top. Try this. Now this. And this.'

The clay that dries. Hardening. Hands roughened. The soft throw over her eyes. Her face not yet sculpted but involved. Wet too from the clay. From his hands. Her hands behind her head. Wrists held still the way she wants them. The shaping of things. One way and then another. Over and over again. Not just delicate, intricate, fluid sculpting, but strong, rough sculpting. Rough, sensitive, creative, changing the way things look. 'Do you like that?'

'Yes . . . Yes . . . Oh yes, I do . . . And you?'

'Yes . . . I thought . . . you would. I felt . . . you would.'

'Yes, this is how I like it. This way. Just this and this. Till this happens. And this. And this. And this.'

uses the Baha'i temple or the gardens at Hyde Park. He has not sailed for years, not since the South of France, so that now he is surprised at himself for having said that he would come.

Joking, just in her white sleeveless T-shirt now, she calls to him, 'You're daydreaming and I'm working, Mr Riyad.'

'Ah,' he says, 'but, Captain, I'll provide your sustenance.' He points to the hamper beside him on the quay.

'Oh,' she teases, 'that kind of sustenance. Better than nothing, I suppose.'

The covers are off the boat. He looks on to the deck, the slightly faded teak seating, the dark wooden steering wheel and the curves of the sailboat's sides. '*Narcissus*,' he says, 'is a beauty.'

'Isn't she . . . ? She's my favourite thing.'

'But you're not really a thing person, are you? You have almost no things in your apartment.'

'I'm a kibbutz girl,' she says and bends as if to tie the laces of her shoes.

'A kibbutz girl, huh? Come on, Sarit, you're a left-wing plastic surgeon to the rich and famous.'

'Remember,' she says, 'your life is in my hands today.'

This is the first time that, unquestioned, unprompted, even in a joke, Sarit has made reference to her roots. Since the afternoon he sculpted her Ramsi has wondered about her as an Israeli brought up in strife, brought up on the borders, albeit in a left-wing socialist environment. He has thought about her as the daughter of a Holocaust survivor, the daughter of a pioneer of Israel's independence, maimed fighting for his country. In his time away from her he has contemplated these things for long enough to feel that he might understand why she has never brought up politics with him. And he senses that it is not just because she has spent so many years away from her birthplace, not because she is Israeli and he at least in part Egyptian Christian, that she makes no allusion to the troubles and the conflict, but also because she herself has turned her back on Middle Eastern politics. Precisely because she is the daughter of a pioneer. Because of the daughter part. And Ramsi has understood that for Sarit to identify with the struggle of her father's land would be exactly that. It would be to identify with the struggles of her father. He understands that and he is almost sure that of all the things that might come between the two of them, between himself and Sarit, it will not be politics. Not just because of Sarit, but because of his own struggle. Ramsi's personal battle, his war with his own past, that has left no room in his head or in his heart for the collective wars of a people or a country.

Now, while he stands close to the edge of the slip, while he jokes with her about being a left-wing plastic surgeon to the rich and famous, he reaches across and hands Sarit the hamper. 'Shall I untie the lines?' he asks her.

'You'll have to hand them to me and then jump on.'

He unties the lines, throws them to her. She holds out her hand to him. He takes it and jumps on to the boat.

Draping the lines, looping them, tying them around one another to store them, she asks him, 'How did you know to wear white rubber soles?'

'I knew,' he says.

The morning is not yet hot, but heat is on the horizon. She climbs around the boat, attaches the main sheet to the sail, attaches the rope, readies the jib lines. She leans over the side of the boat, pumps the water from the bilge.

He watches her move. Her agility, her strength, the rising and falling of the muscles in her arms. Slightly out of breath she says, 'Let me show you where the life vests are.' She leads him down to the cabin with the tiny silver kitchenette and the berths on either side. From the wicker hamper she unpacks the cut meats, the black bread, the green olives, the strawberries and the Chablis. And she feels a flicker of contentment as she arranges their lunch in the tiny fridge. As if each olive, each strawberry, each sip of the wine he has brought in some small way signals his moving towards her.

Standing up, she touches the side of his neck, which several hours from then will feel unshaven to her touch.

'Let's hope for a rain storm,' he says. Tempted, she laughs.
Again he notices the beauty of her teeth.

She says, 'You never know. It can change out there from
one minute to the next.'

As she climbs back up on to the deck she points to the
right-hand bunk. 'The life jackets are under there,' she says.

'So, what are my orders?' he asks her.

'I'll start her with the motor. Can you steer then while I
raise the sail?'

'Of course,' he says. 'And music? What about it?'

'I almost forgot . . . what can I offer you?'

'I have my own offering,' and he removes a cassette from
the side pocket of his jacket.

'What is it?'

'Gilberto, Brazilian jazz and later perhaps a little Ravel . . .
depending on the way the wind blows,' he says. 'No foreign
words this time to torture you. Just instrumental . . . Where's
the tape deck?'

'Downstairs . . . above the starboard . . . I mean the right-
hand bunk.'

He goes down the companionway into the cabin, puts the
music on, comes back up. As they move out of the slip, out of
the harbour towards the grey stone breakwater, the laid-back
lazy jazz accompanies their passage.

Sarit steers and turns her face to the light wind. 'South-
west,' she says. 'Perfection.' And then she adds, 'Ready, Rams?'
for the first time shortening his name.

'Ready.'

He comes and stands beside her at the helm. In the wind
he smells the perfume that she wears. 'What is it . . . ?' he asks,
breathing her in. 'Your perfume . . . I've never noticed it
before.'

She says, 'I've never worn it before.'

'Spicy,' he says. 'It suits you.'

Her face away from him, turned out towards the water, she smiles to herself. She says, 'OK, now I want you to steer for me. Just the way I've pointed the boat. Straight out there, towards that catamaran,' and she lifts one hand from the helm to indicate the parrot-green and orange sail ahead of them somewhere in the distance. 'Can you manage?' she asks him as he takes the helm from her.

He smiles a wry smile. 'I think I can just about deal with a straight line.'

Behind him Sarit unties the lines for the main sail and the jib. The sails unfurl.

He hears the flapping and turns round. 'That's gorgeous,' he says, looking at the shape and the whiteness of the sail unfurled.

'I'm going to open it right out,' she says, almost to herself.

'Daring of you.'

'I'll watch it,' she says.

She walks over to him, lays her hand on the head of silky, thick, grey-silver hair. 'Your job is over. Let me tell you what's going on.' And it crosses her mind suddenly that she has watched him teach, that she has watched him sketch and sculpt and cast, but that he has never seen her work at any skill at all. From behind, a little taller than him, she puts her arms round his neck, she lets her hands fall beneath his T-shirt on his chest. 'The wind is coming from the south-west and we're heading south . . .' she says. 'And by the way, you know if I have to change the position of the sail you have to duck. The boom can knock you out.'

This time he is kind. He doesn't say, 'I knew that for myself.' He just nods in front of her and she lifts her hands and touches his face from where she stands behind him.

In the light wind their sailboat takes on its own momentum. Sitting opposite one another now, she on the port side from where she sees Chicago's skyline, he on the starboard, she asks him, 'How well d'you know the city?'

He comes and sits beside her in the warmth. Hip to hip they sit. He has one arm round her. Pointing with the other, he says, 'You testing me? OK . . . Sears Tower, the Drake Hotel over there, the John Hancock Building, Lake Shore Drive, Northwestern campus . . . over there to the right some of the most beautiful intricate twentieth-century European-inspired architecture in the city . . . and then . . .'

'Enough.' She laughs and puts her hand over his mouth to stop him from going on. His voice muffled, he points and says, 'Now in that direction . . .'

'Stop.' She laughs again.

He takes her hand that is over his mouth, takes each finger, one by one between his lips.

'Hey,' she says, 'someone's got to captain this boat.'

'OK, OK,' and then, 'Just one last thing . . . the Mies van der Rohe buildings over there. They're my favourite. He was a genius that man, wasn't he?'

She says, 'I don't know much about him.'

And Ramsi says, 'He was head of the Bauhaus movement. A German-Jewish refugee from Berlin. Originally an artist, I think. I'm surprised you didn't know.'

She turns away. She looks towards the lake.

The sounds of the jazz, lazy, laid-back and fluid floating over the water. Sarit stretching out her legs. Time passing.

The figures of the joggers and the rollerbladers along the waterfront grow smaller. A tiny sailboat with a burnt-orange sail moves in their direction. She says to Ramsi, 'I've never asked you why you came here . . . I mean, why Chicago?'

Her question is an easy one to answer. Easy enough so that he doesn't have to move his arm from round her neck, for his level of comfort shows almost always in his body language. He begins to talk and she dares to lean back against his arm as for years she has not leant back against the arm of another. 'My work had begun to sell here,' he said. 'I was in my mid-thirties. Still young for a sculptor. There was a collector who'd come and bought a few of my pieces in Nice. It was the eighties and River North was just beginning to grow. It was starting to get a reputation as a serious art centre . . . It used to be full of industry and warehouses. Anyway, my pieces sold. She ordered more and it just went from there.'

'I see,' she says.

'So this was as good a place for me to come as any. I knew there was an Egyptian community here and a French one, so I thought I'd try. Nothing much to lose.'

Not meaning to be rude, just talking straight, as they are sailing out she says, 'What did you care about the French and Egyptian communities? You don't socialise much anyway. You're a loner, Ramsi Riyad.'

He laughs. 'That's true. Even this is strange for me. You must have worked me out by now. Mostly I've been used to hibernating during the day and going out at night.'

'An owl,' she says.

'A skunk,' he says.

She asks him, 'Why did you leave?' Behind her this time, with this question, she feels Ramsi's arm stiffen.

'Egypt . . . ? I've told you. There was a mass exodus from Alexandria when King Farouk was ousted. The government started to take control of my father's printing press. Nasser stripped the place of so much of its beauty and possibility. By the time I left, in the sixties, Alexandria's soul had been quite battered.'

She lets him finish. Then she says, 'I didn't mean that. I meant why did you leave France?'

Out there on the vast sheet of the lake the wind has picked up slightly. He moves his arm from round her neck. He reaches into the pocket of the jacket by his side for his sunglasses. The lenses are large and very dark. So that with them on, and with his beard and the thickness of his hair, Sarit can see little of his expression. She does not move from where she sits, against the side of the boat, but she brings her legs in towards her and hugs her knees. She says, 'I know why you left Egypt. But why did you leave France?'

Ahead of them the water is a clean pale blue with growing ripples. Then, the seawater, the water of the Mediterranean on the Côte d'Azur, had been navy striped with white. To their right, the grey and raw and rugged cliffs had dropped in sharp dramatic lines to join the side of the Corniche in Southern France above the speck that was their sailboat.

At first Ramsi doesn't answer Sarit's question. He answers one she hasn't asked. He says, 'We had a sailboat too.'

Without showing her surprise, she says, 'What was it like?'

'Smaller than this,' he says. 'But lovely shiny wood. I almost wanted to sculpt something from it. The wood was so wonderful to touch. I bought it from a fisherman and restored it.'

'What was it called?'

'We called her *Poupée*.'

'What does that mean?'

'Doll,' he says. 'It means a doll.'

She says, 'What an odd name for a boat . . . You can't have chosen that.'

'No, it wasn't me,' he says. He leans against the side of the boat. He nods his head. He says, '*Poupée, Poupée* . . .'

In his mind he hears her say, '*Papa, Papa, c'est dimanche aujourd'hui* . . . ? Is it Sunday today?'

'Yes, Nadia,' he says, his arm across his daughter as she lies under the covers in the warm dark triangle between Ramsi and his wife.

'*Dimanche . . . Bâteau à voile.* Sunday sailboat, Sunday sailboat.' Nadia sits up and she chants.

Her mother says, '*Nadia, va jouer un peu avec ta poupée* . . . Nadia go and play with your doll a little bit till Daddy and I are ready to get up.'

And Ramsi, his face hidden in the pillow, says, 'That sailboat is her doll, Lucie. We're going to have to call it *Poupée*.'

'My doll wants to go on the sailboat,' Nadia says. 'Ask her, Mummy, ask her.'

'You go and ask her.'

And Nadia climbs out of the bed, away from the Sunday morning haven, and she rushes into the next room to discuss the day's plans with her doll.

The smell of salt hits Ramsi as soon as he nears the harbour of the small sleepy town of Beaulieu. He has grown up in Alexandria with the smell of the sea. Later in Chicago, when he is close to the freshwater lake, he will imagine the sea's salt in his nostrils. He will dream he can still smell it. But in Beaulieu as his wife walks beside him in her own thoughts, he doesn't need to dream it. He doesn't need to dream it as he carries Nadia on his shoulders towards the harbour. She wears a little white plastic rucksack with her doll's face peeking out from the corner. And Ramsi then is strapping the orange life jacket on to his child when she says, 'Can we put a life vest on my doll, Papa?'

'We haven't got a spare one, Nadia. You'll just have to hold her tight.'

On the wooden seats on board *Poupée* Nadia's mother holds the child on her lap in her little orange life vest. The wind that Sunday has a voice. But Ramsi knows the ropes. He has sailed since he was small and his father has taught to him how to tack and reef and jibe and read the weather vane. He climbs around the boat. He directs it out of the harbour at Beaulieu. He says, 'Hang on, girls, this bit should be fun.'

And Nadia on her mother's lap, her long, thick, dark-brown hair blown, covering her tiny face, begins to sing, 'I love it. I love it. I love the wind. My doll loves the wind. We love the wind, don't we, Maman?'

Lucie looks up towards the Corniche and pointing to the modernity of Monte Carlo she says, 'D'you think that's what the skyline in America looks like? In New York or Chicago?'

His silky jet-black hair blowing over his face, to his wife he says, 'Perhaps. One day we'll go and see.'

And Nadia, straining on her mother's lap, calls out, 'Chicago, New York, Chicago, New York . . . *nous allons à Chicago*, New York . . . we're going to Chicago, New York.'

'No, *chérie*, we're not,' Ramsi says. 'We're going to Ville-franche for lunch.' The boat begins to rock with the wind.

'I love it. I love it,' Nadia calls. 'Maman, can I see the waves?'

Lucie moves with the child towards the edge of the boat. She holds her tightly to her in the fastened orange life jacket. 'I want to swim,' the child calls out. 'Maman, Papa, can I swim?'

'Of course not, Nadia. It's dangerous. You'd disappear in the waves.'

'I would not.'

'You would, *chérie*.'

'My *poupée* can swim. See,' says Nadia and, by way of demonstration, throws her stringy blonde-haired rag doll into the rocking, foaming waves. 'She's swimming . . . see, she's swimming. Now let's go and get her.'

Lucie turns back to Ramsi, holding the child. She calls, '*Ramsi, c'est la fin de la poupée* . . . it's the end of the doll.'

And Ramsi, still wearing his dark glasses on the sailboat on Lake Michigan with Sarit, comes back to her then for just a moment. He says to her, 'Nadia turned round to me then. I still remember that look of pleading, of helplessness, of "Daddy, you can make it all right, can't you?" on her face, before the shock set in. At five you still think your daddy can do everything. That there is nothing beyond him. I walked to the edge of the boat, leant over and of course her *poupée* was gone in the waves.

'In Arabic I said to Lucie, "I'm going in for it." We always spoke Arabic if we didn't want Nadia to understand. And she said, "You are crazy. No way. It's just a doll." There was a note of hysteria in her voice.'

In the cockpit of *Narcissus* Sarit is sitting away from Ramsi now. Watching him move in and out of his other life. Her eyes closed for a moment, she is listening to the soundtrack of his voice, visualising his story as though it were a film. 'I didn't dive in to get her *poupée*, of course,' he says. 'I took her from her mother's arms and held her and she said, "Please, Papa, please. She's all by herself in the water. She'll be so lonely there."

'"We'll buy a new doll, Nadia."

'"No, I want my old one . . ." She put her little hands up to my face. She said, "Papa, you can get her."'

The wind on Lake Michigan begins to stiffen. Sarit feels goose bumps on her arms. She moves fast to pull the line that reefs the main. Ramsi this time doesn't offer to help her. In the building wind that with the suddenness of its advent poses a risk to all but the most experienced of sailors, Ramsi says, 'That's the last clear picture I have in my mind of her face before . . . before . . .' His voice trails off and then, as if to no one, 'I have spent twenty years trying to re-create that face. So I could watch her grow up . . . That's what I do with my life.'

There is a split second, just a split second, when Sarit is struggling with the lines of the boat, when they threaten to burn her skin, when she is fighting to flatten the mainsail, to regain the sailboat's balance, unsure of who will win in the fight with the wind. But the muscles of her arms are strong, her hands never let her down and just as she is about to ask for Ramsi's help she masters the sail. So that she may have heard him say, 'I have spent my life trying to re-create that face,' but then again the words may have been lost in the gust of wind that comes in her direction.

As she straightens up, arches her back, she feels the cold spray from the waves on the bare skin of her arms. The boat begins to sail towards the west. And above the wind Ramsi calls to Sarit as if she were a judge and he were pleading his case, 'I was trying to make it up to her. I so wanted to make it up to her. I promised her a new doll.

'I remember her mother turned to her and said, "And Nadia, guess what. This afternoon when Maman's at her music class Papa will show you something very special. You know the pastry dolls he's made for you before ... Like Grandmaman used to do with him in Alexandria when he was small. The ones you want to learn to make yourself. Well, this afternoon, maybe, if you're a good girl and you ask Papa nicely, he might show you how to shape them and bake them into biscuits. And you and Papa will be ready to surprise me by the time I come home."'

The child, wet-cheeked, red-eyed, wide-eyed, interested though not yet placated, says, 'When will we buy my new doll?'

'Tomorrow.'

'Let me go,' she says to her father. He sets her down in the cockpit of the boat. She puts her chin in her hands and she says, 'Hm, I'll have to think about it.' And to the right and the left of Nadia, headed for the painted fishing port of Villefranche, Ramsi and Lucie fight hard not to laugh at their five-year-old perched there between them in her orange life vest considering their proposal. She looks first at her mother. Then her father. Then she says, 'Oh, all right then. We'll bake ... but I'm the one who gets to taste the biscuits first.'

The child is fickle. By the evening her old blonde rag doll with the stringy hair is all but replaced with the promise of the new one. The child is fickle because at five a whole afternoon is a percentage of her lifetime. Already she is contemplating naming the new doll of her imagination. She kneels on her chair at the kitchen table. The oven is heating, in preparation for the baking of the sculptured pastry. Delighted by the magic of his fingers Nadia watches her father shaping the sweet white dough into short fat little people. She leans over Ramsi, standing on the chair behind him, her chin on his shoulder. She says, 'A boy or a girl, Papa?'

'What do you think?'

'A girl of course.'

'Why?'

'Because if she was a boy,' she says slowly, 'if she was a boy you'd have to make her a you know what . . . and then,' she giggles, 'then I'd bite it off.'

'Nadia Riyad.' He tries once again to stop himself from laughing and he fails. 'I'm glad your mother can't hear you talk like that.'

'It's my turn, Papa. I want to make the pastry people by myself now.'

'Come, let me help you first,' he says. 'Look, see the person is made up of all these different bits . . . let's take one bit of pastry for the body, two for the arms, two for the legs, one for the head. Look, you roll them like this and then you make them flat and . . .'

Nadia pushes her father's elbow. She says, 'Papa, go away now. I can do it all by myself. I want to show you.'

He moves his hands away. He says, 'OK, I'll sit and watch you.'

'*Non, Papa* . . . I want to do it on my own.'

Ramsi drops his head, fakes sadness. With her floury hands she strokes his face. 'Papa, don't be sad. Go and do your work. Make your own people. That makes you happy. Go on, Papa, go on . . .'

He smiles, stands up. He says, 'Surprise me then, *chérie*. Let's see what we can show Maman when she comes home.'

She is happy, alone at the kitchen table, knowing that her father is in the next room. She is content listening to the grown-up music, the Mozart concerto that Ramsi puts on and then turns down to call to her, '*Ça va, chérie?*'

'*Oui, Papa*,' she calls. She is happy rolling pieces for arms and legs and faces. Clumsy, lumpy, sausage-like pieces, because Nadia does not have her father's talent in her hands. She has her mother's talent in her body, though. Her gift for rhythm and for movement. So that as she rolls the dough, as she tries to shape it for the feet of her pastry people, she moves her little body with the music from the next room.

Ramsi comes to the kitchen door. He asks, 'How's it going, Nadia?'

She shoos him away. 'Papa, I'm not finished. Go away. I'll call you when I'm ready.'

He smiles at her and leaves the room. With the palm of her hand she flattens her biscuits on to the silver tray. She hurries. She's going to surprise Papa. She lifts the tray of clumsy mis-shapen people on to the chair where she has knelt. Out loud she says, 'Mustn't drop them. Mustn't drop them.' She lifts the tray with the skew-whiff pastry people from the chair. Her arms spread wide, she carries the tray over to the oven. She puts it down on the floor and with both arms, with every ounce of the might in her five-year-old body, she pulls at the door of the oven as she has seen her maman and her papa do. She lifts her tray from the floor then and, concentrated, intent on her task, she pushes it into the oven, and wanting to make sure, to be quite sure that it is far back enough, Nadia climbs with the tray into the huge old-fashioned oven. To the back where the blue gas flames blow all around her, till the door almost snaps shut behind her, till the skirt and the bodice and the sleeves of her flowery yellow dress are aglow, till with the sound of explosion, the sound of her screams and then the chill of silence that he hears, Ramsi comes running from his sculpture to find his child alight.

TWENTY-EIGHT

The difference between time spent alone and time spent on one's own is huge. Without a lover in one's life, times not spent with friends or family is time spent quite alone. And even in a relationship, in one that ails, that is, so often the hours with that person, across the table from them, or in their bed, is time spent in desperate isolation. But when, for all its complications, love begins to bring a sense of joy and of direction, the hours without one's lover are often spent not alone but on one's own. These are the hours when the strength that comes from knowing love engenders even greater independence and brings the courage to explore.

And so on a Saturday morning, after an evening watching Ramsi sculpt and a night with him where she felt for the first time both passion and a sense of peace at once, Sarit has left him outside the red engraved door. A parting in the early summer heat, so very different from the one that day outside the Art Institute. This time when he turns left and she turns right he walks only a few steps, then calls her name. 'Sarit,' he says.

'Yes.'

'You inspire me,' and, his arms full of sculpture, he turns again and walks to his car on the way to the foundry.

The smile is on her lips as she goes to buy bread and fruit, as she stops to buy a copy of *Streetwise* from a homeless person with dreadlocks and a mangy dog. The smile is on her lips still as she almost passes the black gate that divides the cobbled streets of historic Old Town from the main road. She notices the group of people standing just inside the entrance. She catches a side view of the first booth in a row of stands. She sees the banner, with the words 'Annual Old Town Art Fair' written in red on white. She sees the words but not till she has walked a few steps past them do they register in her head.

A few months before would she have stopped there in her tracks? Would she have turned back and ventured to the entrance of the Art Fair? True, she had sought out River North. She had walked into Primitive Art Works and then Nicole's, but that was almost in a trance and this was not.

So that seeing her turn back and walk towards the Art Fair, one might have asked if it was love then that had engendered this courage and this growth. She might not have waited had the queue been long, but though there are crowds inside the gates, ahead of her at the entrance, where the heat seems to rise up from the cobbled stones, there is just one family. Sarit does not see the father roll up his sleeve. She does not see him hold out his arm to the young bald man at the gate and say, 'Here. Look. We've already paid. We just went out to get something from the car.' The young man standing by the makeshift table waves the father and his family through. They walk on. Slowly. A father, a mother and their two boys, one small, one in his early teens. Walking together towards groups of people. The elder boy holding the younger one's hand.

'A one-day pass?' the man at the black gate asks Sarit.

She nods. He says, 'Six dollars.' She reaches into the pocket of her jeans for cash. She wears a white cotton sleeveless vest. With her right hand she gives the young man a five and a one.

'Thanks,' he says and with the thanks, without a word, he takes the wrist on which she's hung the bag of bread and fruit, and he lowers the rubber stamp towards her. The guard at the gate stamping the numbers on to Sarit's wrist. Green ink numbers. Numbers 84111.

She doesn't move. He says, 'There you go.' Still she stands there, quite still with her black rucksack on her back and the white plastic bag hanging from her arm. Till he says, 'Go ahead . . . I've stamped you.'

She walks between the stands. She looks but doesn't take in the figures sculpted into trunks of trees, the photos woven into collage, the images of Chicagoans of last century dressed for snow. She sees only a painting of black stick men piled on top of one another with gaping open mouths and a painting of a half-face in thick oils of the grandmother she never knew. She feels faint from the heat of it. Not from the sun or from the shopping that she carries. But from the paintings in her head and the skin on her wrist. From the way the numbers burn as she moves. To her left and to her right the faces of the vendors are hard. Their cries of 'Come and take a look' are orders. Their casual clothes are uniforms. She passes and they turn their heads. She passes and their eyes follow her. Her throat feels parched. She catches sight of the boy, the young teenager who had stood with his family by the gate. He's on his own now. She looks around for his parents. In the heat and the fuzziness she scans the crowds. As if she were him. As if they were her parents lost somewhere in the crowds. As if there were a chance that standing on tiptoe she might find them for him. As if scouring the crowds their outlines might be clear instead of vague and blurred and fading and . . . she feels the plastic cup put to her lips. 'Don't worry, dear. Drink this now. It's the heat and the crowds. Too many people here. You must just have got yourself dehydrated.' The woman's hand is on her arm. Soothing. Stroking. On her wrist. As if wiping away. 'You're getting your colour back. Do you feel a little better?'

'Yes . . . Thanks.'

'No problem. None at all.' She puts a hand behind Sarit's back in support, then helps her to her feet. Pale and gaunt herself, the woman wears a red scarf on her head. She asks Sarit, 'Is there anyone I can call for you? I have a cellphone here.'

'No, no. Well, yes, there is. But no, I'll be fine. The dizziness is passing.'

'But you shouldn't be alone.'

'I live just across the road . . . and my . . . my boyfriend lives just up the road . . . but he's out . . . so I'll just go home.'

'I'll walk with you,' the woman in the red scarf says.

Perhaps love had given Sarit the courage. Perhaps in the absence of loneliness, her bravery and her daring had been enhanced and at first she had found the strength to go towards the Art Fair. Fortified by the presence of a significant other in her life she had not been on her own at all.

And yet Sarit's togetherness with Ramsi had been unable to protect her from her subconscious mind. From images of a past that had shaped her life. Images that she herself had never even seen.

TWENTY-NINE

Sarit's days are filled to bursting in the month of June. As if the strong sunlight has exposed her prospective patients' physical flaws in their own eyes, they have come to talk of change before the onset of high summer. In the afternoons in her surgery after the theatre of the mornings and her children's clinic, Emily will say, 'I've squeezed in an extra patient here and there, Sarit. They begged me.'

And Sarit will nod. She'll say, 'You're the boss, Em,' though in truth with the combination of her surgery at the children's hospital and the extra hours in her private practice as the season progresses Sarit is pale and drawn and stressed with overwork. In the last week of June, in the last hour of her day on a Friday afternoon, she sees four prospective patients. The first a man in a toupee who hates the bulging and the sagging of the skin beneath his eyes. The next an elderly woman with a purple rinse who hates the brownish sun flecks on her cheeks. The third a strong-looking woman with short red hair and deep-brown lipstick and nail varnish, dressed in black trousers and a burgundy jumper. A woman who says she may well be interested in a facelift and asks Sarit, 'Do you think that plastic surgery is just about creating a disguise?' She asks the question as the camera clicks and clicks from every angle with Sarit taking polaroid photographs of the woman's face with which to work.

A few feet from her, Sarit asks, 'What exactly do you mean by that?'

'I mean, am I disguising who I really am by doing this? And if I go ahead with this will I become the person that you make me?'

On an impulse Sarit pulls up a chair next to her patient, sits with her chin in her hands and thinks. 'Perhaps it is a disguise,' she says. 'Yes. Perhaps you're right. But then after a while you become the disguise and the disguise becomes you. So then it's no longer a disguise, if you see what I mean.'

The woman laughs. She says, 'I want to do it. I want to be the best that I can. But I worry sometimes that it's not the truth . . . But then this isn't the truth either, is it?' she says, gripping a tuft of her red hair. 'Nor is this or this,' she says, pointing to her dark-brown lips and her mascara-laden lashes.

'Perhaps,' says Sarit, 'the truth can change and evolve. The physical truth, that is . . . But then it's so bound up with the psyche. I always tell my patients I won't operate on them if they're coming to change the circumstances of their lives. But you know,' Sarit carries on, 'ironically the surgery often does change those circumstances because the patient gains confidence and reacts differently to the outside world so the outside world reacts differently to him. That's much more the case when someone is disfigured, of course, than when someone just comes to me for cosmetic enhancement. It's almost impossible to separate the psychological from the physical in that sense.'

'I don't think,' says Juliann Stocker, holding Sarit's tortoiseshell hand mirror to her face in the bright and unforgiving sunlight that streams in through the floor-to-ceiling windows, 'that I am trying to change the essence of who I am,' and she laughs. 'I just don't want to look like a grandmother.'

'Professor Stocker,' says Sarit, 'you can go away and think about it. There is absolutely no pressure to make a decision just because you've been to see me.'

'Tell me, Doctor,' she says, 'if you don't mind the indiscretion. Would you ever have anything done yourself?'

And Sarit, enjoying this irreverence, says, 'I take it you're referring to my nose.'

'OK. Your nose.'

'No, I wouldn't.'

'Why not? If I might ask. Not that I don't like it. Actually, I think you look like Barbra Streisand, but . . .'

Sarit laughs. She says, 'I wouldn't change it because I don't know a doctor whom I would trust to do it.'

'No, seriously, Dr Kleinmann. Why not? Perhaps it will help me answer my own question.'

'Because,' she says and, in an unusual gesture, takes the mirror that the Professor has put down on the table and looks at her own profile from left and right, 'because it's part of my identity, I suppose.'

As she speaks, referring to her Semitic nose she says, 'Part of my identity.' The irony of Sarit's own words is lost on her and she wonders why she is philosophising with the Professor when the sun is waning and in the room next door another patient waits. And yet there is something about Juliann Stocker that draws Sarit in, that makes her want to sit and talk.

'Where are you from, Dr Kleinmann?' Juliann asks her.

'I'm American.'

Juliann needs the truth. She needs it absolutely. She needs to know that Sarit is honest to the nth degree. Under the table she crosses her fingers. She doesn't want to have to go through this again. 'But originally?' she asks.

Sarit stands up. She says, 'I was born in the Middle East.'

'Ah, right,' she says, relieved. 'Yes, there's just the tiniest bit of accent left.'

'Yes,' says Sarit, 'I'm not the greatest linguist.'

And Juliann, serious now, forgetting for a minute that her visit is not a personal one, says, 'You are a linguist. The language you speak is all in your fingers.'

'Let's hope so,' says Sarit and then, 'Look, I've taken pictures here. We can sit and go through them and we can discuss what I could do for you if you do decide to go ahead.'

The tilting of her head, the angling of bright lights, the

positioning of mirrors at angles to her face. Discussion of ageing and healing, surgical procedures and realistic expectations until Sarit says, 'Go away and think about it. I don't think there's any pressing need for a decision here. You seem very comfortable in your own skin.'

Juliann picks up her scarf from the back of the chair. She says, 'I'm sure I will be back soon. I know I will, in fact. I just need a little time to think.'

Sarit would have liked the time to sit in her swivel chair and think when Juliann Stocker left the room. She would have liked to have stared out over Lake Michigan and pondered, but the last patient of the day had been waiting for almost an hour.

And so Sarit is forced to focus her attention on the face of a big broad-featured German banker, unhappy with the shrinking and the thinning of her lips, unhappy with her extra chins. Sarit is forced to stand and hold mirrors at different angles close to the woman's face, when in truth that day she would have been so much happier to stay a while with her previous patient. To sit with Juliann Stocker and contemplate the need for and the nature of disguise.

THIRTY

If we choose to stay closed, if we choose to stay guarded we
will live unspoken lives. Our pain and our past and our stories will stay hidden. Like a talent for music or for painting
that is stifled, we will never know the effect that the gift of
our secrets might have had on the world. We might leave our
stories as they are, cocooned and beyond the straining fingertips of others, unaware of the confidences they might become,
if only we will let them. Confidences that are powerful, life-
changing even, and that by their very nature bring us closer
to our friends and to our lovers. For confidences are the cor-
nerstone of intimacy. Without them how can love be knowing?
And not knowing, where can it find its depth to last?

Santa Fe, where Sarit and Ramsi have come in the height
of the summer, spills over with its stories and its secrets. The
secrets of its history that seep through the red mud of the
casitas on to the canvases in the galleries of Canyon Road.
The secrets of its artists that spill from the terraces into its
shady sculpture gardens. The pain and struggle of its peoples,
poured into the waters of the Rio Grande that flow down
towards the town, and are carved into the red and pink rock
formations in the mountains that watch over it. And above it,
above Santa Fe, in the pueblos that surround it, the past and
the pain and the secrets are told still by American Indians,
native storytellers with jet-black plaited hair who speak their
stories, dance them, sing and act them out through the generations, with small clay puppets, miniature sculptures made
by tribal artists, made to mime the stories of their lives.

From the Inn of the Turquoise Bear, a Bed and Breakfast

shrouded in vines and ivy, where D. H. Lawrence wrote, where Robert Frost slept, Sarit and Ramsi walk through the cobbled side streets of Santa Fe. In their togetherness here, in the brushing of their shoulders, the touching of their hands, there is the newness of the lovers' first trip out of town.

Sarit, for once, is not in trousers but in a dress of grey-blue linen a little lighter than her eyes, so that Ramsi stops and says, 'You're a different woman in a dress.'

'How so?'

'Not a tomboy.' He stands back and looks at her, there in Santa Fe on the pavement by the side of the road. 'You look . . . more sophisticated. Just another of your faces, Doctor.'

She smiles and looks around her. She says, 'Is it the tint on my glasses? Or is everything really red here?' and she gesticulates towards the flat-roofed red adobe houses. 'They're more like cakes than houses . . . Do you know how they built them?' she asks him.

'Cakes,' he says. 'Hm, not exactly . . . they're mud, baked in the sun and covered with clay. They're supposed to keep you cool,' and walking beside her, just one sculptor amongst many now in this town that is the artists' haven, he wonders how they got here, how for the first time in years he has agreed to leave his studio and his sculptures, to leave the city with his foundry, his jazz bars and his blues bars, to leave the only place where he feels safe, even though except for the confidences he shares with Albert, he speaks so very little with the people that he knows. And as he is wondering, wandering towards the red historic plaza, past the pink symmetrical face of the cathedral of St Francis that chimes the hour as they approach, Sarit too is struck by the surreal nature of it all.

Over the years she has taken breaks from work. Ski trips, once with a group of medics and many times alone. To travel by herself has been no punishment for her. She has been happy to be in the stillness, in the snow where the air is thin, high up between the fir trees. She has been happy to be anony-

257

mous in big cities. In Savannah, San Diego, San Francisco, Boston and New York, the towns that she has visited over the years. Again alone. It was, in truth, despite brief interludes the only way she could be. Till now. Till him. And next to Ramsi, squinting in the sunlight, she touches the dark skin of his arm almost as if pinching him, checking that he's really there, that they really are together here in Santa Fe.

As they walk towards the Palace of the Governors, where underneath the arches along the pavement Hispanic and Native American Indian traders sit in a row on rush mats, play Chinese whispers, telling stories, selling turquoise and silver wares, Ramsi reads her mind and says, 'Was this your idea or mine?'

'Yours of course,' she says and smiles.

'No, yours.'

'No, yours,' she says and thinks, 'It doesn't matter. We're here. I'm here with him. We're here together.'

At first it had been her idea. On the telephone she'd said to him, 'I can't stitch one more stitch. I have to get out of here for a few days. I need a break.'

And he, shocking himself even as he spoke, had said, 'So where are we going?' Perhaps this time it was the telephone that had made it easier. Telephones for Ramsi were for the essential. For monosyllables almost. For finding out when and where and how. So they said no more about it there and then, and between the time they spoke and the time they saw each other, he walked around his studio touching photographs and books, saying out loud to himself in French and then in Arabic, '*Ya Rabi, ana basalhak rayha fein?* . . . My God . . . I asked her where we were going? I really did. Well, Ramsi Riyad, where are we going then?' He thought of seclusion, he thought of sea and then quite unrelated to both he thought of Santa Fe. Yes, Santa Fe, New Mexico. Somehow if he travelled with Sarit that was the place they should go. He knew, for he had understood enough, that the idea of going to a

at all. For, in truth, so much that we know of people we link to the places we have found them.

As they walk along the pavement, as she looks to her left in the front courtyard of a gallery, she sees a life-sized sculpture of a young woman, propped up on her elbows, buried save for her head and her feet in shiny black and grey pebbles. And on top of the pebbles that cover her, as if mimicking the sculpture's breasts, are mounds of sand. Sarit laughs out loud. With the excitement of a child she says, 'Look, look over there.' But Ramsi doesn't laugh, just stops there in his tracks and stares. And even later, after they've moved on, for the rest of the morning he is quiet and withdrawn.

'Like my mother,' he tells Sarit that evening outside over white wine in the courtyard garden of the Santacafé, which is lit by oil lamps and shrouded with green and yellow vines. 'That sculpture so reminded me of her.'

She remembers then what Ramsi has told her and she says, 'Yes, you told me you used to sculpt images of your mother in the sand.'

'I did. At home in Alexandria when I was small.'

He has spoken to Sarit of his mother here and there. He has made allusions to her vitality, her culture and her music, and Sarit knows of course that she is dead, that she passed away in the South of France a year or so before his father, though she does not know how or why, and later that night after dinner, pouring wine she asks, 'How did your mother die?'

A silence. A pregnant silence until Ramsi says, 'You know, Sarit, I think I killed her.'

He sees shock register on Sarit's face and in her body and almost laughs. He says, 'Oh, not literally of course, but in a way . . . My mother wasn't old when she came to Nice. Only in her late forties . . . But Middle Eastern women, you know what they're like,' he says. 'They give themselves over so completely to their family . . . and to food. They sacrifice themselves. They get old before their time, don't they?' Sarit nods and Ramsi carries on, speaking now in her presence but as if to himself and if some hours earlier he had seemed ageless to her, now on his high forehead she notices the deep furrows. As he speaks from beneath his beard, from behind the years of silence, she hears his deep, rough voice grow pained. Where they sit now in the gardens of the Turquoise Bear, an American Indian flautist in full folk dress is strolling through the grounds, playing some sweet incongruous tune, so that for Sarit listening to Ramsi's story with the music in the background will be like looking at a jagged surreal object painted against a backdrop of soft-focus flowers and gentle pastel slopes.

As he speaks he does not reach for his tobacco and roll a cigarette but chooses to abstain instead, as if to smoke might be some sort of profanity, as if each puff would interrupt his train of thought. 'We wanted my mother to carry on playing the piano in France. We thought it would distract her. Stop her from longing so much for Alexandria. We bought her a second-hand black baby grand with money from the first sculpture I sold to the States. She ignored it for months, but one evening she surprised us by sitting down to play. She was at the keyboard with a Mozart score in front of her. She was there for what seemed like hours and we waited, sitting there by the side of her, my father, Lucie, Nadia and I. No one said a word and after a while she lifted her hands, poised to play.' Remembering, he lifts his own hands.

'Then she let them drop,' he says. 'She closed the lid and she just stood up. She said, "It's over, children, don't ask me to play again. I left music in Alexandria," and then her face lit up and I remember her exact words. She walked over to . . . to Nadia, picked her up and said, "Who needs the piano anyway? I have something else now. Nadia is my life. She's my music."'

Ramsi lifts his glass, gulps his wine as though it were water. And his hand movements that normally are slow and careful, measured almost despite the creativity of his spirit, grow quick and agitated as he talks. 'When it happened,' he says and clears his throat. 'When it happened I gave the hospital strict instructions not to let my mother in. Every day the nurses came to me. They said, "Mr Riyad, your mother's here to see the child. Mr Riyad, you can't be so heartless. You have to let her in . . . for Nadia's sake."' He bows his head. He says, 'And every time I made them turn her away . . . they'd say, "Mr Riyad, she's crying at reception. Please, she wants to see her grandchild." And I remember once I lost my temper with a nurse, a beautiful young Armenian woman who was a saint with Nadia, who changed her bandages with such care . . . I . . . I lost my temper and I yelled, "No. Don't you understand?" I said, "No. Send her away right now and don't you dare ask me again."

'Once when I went home for a change of clothes my mother was there in the house. We bumped into each other on the stairs and she just grabbed me by the sleeve.' Remembering, he tugs at his own sleeve. He says, 'She was begging me, but still I wouldn't let her come. I said, "Maman, it will kill you." How ironic that I said that. I think it was then that she started screaming. She screamed and at the hospital Lucie screamed. It seemed like the screaming went on for ever. My mother and Lucie shouting at me in stereo, "Why did you leave her alone? My baby. Our baby." I can still hear them,' he says and there on the terrace he sits and holds his hands over his ears. The hands that had taught his child how to sculpt the little pastry men. The hands that had lifted her alight, the black burnt pastry stuck to the remnants of her dress and of her skin. His hands and his wrists too burnt and swathed in bandages themselves for him to touch his daughter in the hospital.

And in the light of the oil lamp set down by a waiter, Sarit wants to reach out and touch Ramsi now, to touch his strong rough sculptor's hands and his shock of silver-grey hair. She stretches out her arm towards him so that as he begins to talk again her long slim hand, that has not quite reached him yet, is suspended in mid-air.

'Sometimes,' he says, 'I don't know which of the screams

263

belonged to Lucie and which belonged to my mother. They seemed to go on for ever . . . And then they stopped. Just like that.' With the edge of his hand Ramsi slices the air as if cutting something dead. 'First Lucie's when the sedation got heavier and heavier. She was a zombie after the accident . . . after Nadia . . . after it happened. She would just walk round and round the house, up and down the stairs, as if she was looking for something. She couldn't even shed a tear. Sometimes,' he says, 'sometimes I would watch her almost trying to cry. It was pathetic really . . . First her screams stopped and then my mother's. At the kitchen table with my father, she sat there staring at her food, playing with it like a child day in day out. As if she had become Nadia. And then one, two, three and that was it . . . she was gone . . . A month after Nadia, with a massive cardiac arrest,' he says, his voice thick, his throat tight and strained as he clears it again and again, as he struggles to go on.

And as he talks, watching his face, hearing his words, Sarit thinks that it sounds as if the pain of his mother's death is unconfronted territory. As if till now in the pain of Nadia's death the loss of his mother has been subsumed and overwhelmed.

He carries on. He says, 'Lucie was with me at my mother's funeral. I mean with me in body. She was so doped up. I remember she had a stupid smile on her face, like she was making social niceties at a cocktail party or something . . .' He puts his wineglass down. He nods his head, he says, 'Oh yes . . . in some way I suppose I killed my mother too.'

And in the 'too', in that one syllable at the end of the sentence, in the 'I think I killed my mother too' there is so much that Sarit begins to understand.

Forming the shape of a tiny headstone with his hands now, in the semi-darkness, Ramsi says, 'Nadia's gravestone is next to my mother's in Beaulieu. I suppose that's why I was finally able to leave there. I felt as if my mother was looking after her . . . That's still the way I feel . . . at least in the better moments . . . in my best moments, though, my daughter isn't really dead.'

Sarit has never before heard Ramsi refer to better moments. The better ones that of course imply the worse ones. At first she cannot speak. She bows her head. Then, in a quiet voice she asks him, 'And her mother? Nadia's mother? What happened between the two of you?'

'Nothing . . . Nothing ever happened between us after that. We were like ghosts passing each other on the stairs for a while. She ended up going into an institution of her own free will. In her more lucid moments she asked for a divorce . . . Her love for me died with Nadia,' he says.

That night on the patio Ramsi finishes off the first bottle of the Chardonnay and half of another. Sarit holds a glass to his lips, coaxes him to drink water to stave off the next day's hangover and in their room with its exposed low wooden beams, slowly and with a patience she didn't know she had she helps him to undress. She pulls the sheets over him, but on her side of the bed she stays uncovered. In seconds Ramsi sleeps, but she lies there, her eyes wide open looking upwards into the pitch black. And when sleep will not come and thoughts are too heavy, she turns in her mind to her patients. To Mrs Grossinger with her sun-stained hands and strong Viennese accent, to Stefano, the little Hispanic boy with the cleft lip, and then to Juliann Stocker, the amusing and unusual red-haired professor with whom Sarit had debated the nature of disguise.

Ramsi does not complain the next morning about his head, but as they dress he asks Sarit, 'Did I drink too much last night?'

'Just a bit,' she says.

'How did I get undressed?'

'With much coaxing,' she says.

'Thank you,' he says, as embarrassed as he knows how to

be. And then as if he's not quite sure what they should do with the leisure time ahead of them, 'Well, where would the doctor like to go today?'

'Let's wander,' she says, 'and maybe later take a drive.'

He nods. Looks up, catches her eye, looks back towards the bed beneath the vaulted ceiling. 'I think I need to make up for last night,' he says.

Not till the midday sun beats down do they walk through the hot leafy streets, in and out of this house and of that, for the galleries that from the outside are red and rounded look little different from the private homes. Following her up the path with an arrow and a large gold embossed sign saying 'Sculpture Garden' he stops in his tracks. He says, 'You can go in here without me. I want to walk a bit.'

'No,' she says, 'come with me.'

'Why?'

'I want you to.'

They walk at first not into the garden, but into the main room of the gallery. In the room rich with artistic offering, Sarit does not see the eyes at first. The slanted eyes that call to her. Not till she lifts her own eyes towards a broad grey marble shelf on which the dark bronze bust sits, finished in a shiny chocolate-brown patina, does she see the expression of the sculpture's face. She turns then to Ramsi and she says, 'You never told me.'

'Why do you think I didn't want to come in here?' he says, '. . . But anyway, I thought they might have sold it.'

And Sarit, suddenly light-hearted, says, 'Come here. Come with me. Let's have some fun, Ramsi Riyad.'

They walk together to a large antique desk, where a middle-aged woman with silver hair sits, her half-rimmed glasses on a beaded chain halfway down her nose. She lifts her head from her reading, says, 'Welcome. How can I help you both?'

And poker-faced Sarit says, 'I'd like to know a little about the sculpture on the ledge . . . that one over there.'

266

'Ah yes,' she says. 'Let me bring it over. It's a beauty.' She goes over and lifts the heavy shiny bust from the marble shelf, brings it to the desk and says, 'Isn't she just gorgeous?'

Sarit touches the sculpture's face. She says, 'Do you have any literature on the artist?'

The woman sighs. She says, 'I wish we did. He refuses to allow it. But I can tell you what I know about him. He lives in Chicago. Been living there for many years, but he's originally Egyptian and spent quite some time in France . . .' She strokes the sculpture's head as if smoothing out her hair. She says, 'The sculptor's very well known. Or I should say his work is well known. We have been trying for ages through our agent to get him to come here to Santa Fe, but he's always refused. He's one of those purists, you know, old time artists who couldn't care less about publicity. People say that he rarely gives anything away and that he's this really gruff, unfriendly type . . . It's strange. His work is so . . . so fine. In contradiction with what they say about him as a person . . . I'd like to meet him. His talent astounds me every time we get a new piece in.'

At the other side of the desk Sarit takes Ramsi's hand and squeezes it. She says to the gallery owner, 'Well, thanks. I'm going to have a look in the sculpture garden now,' and she and Ramsi turn and walk away, both unable to suppress laughter, with the woman in the glasses puzzled, staring after them.

And in his laughter, in Ramsi's laughter that is so rare as to be almost extinct, there is both great beauty and great depth. As they walk towards the sculpture garden Sarit feels a fleeting happiness that comes from him. She takes it to her and as if it were a present she holds it there.

There is great beauty too in the gallery's sculpture garden, which sprawls and shades with the dark pine of its fir trees, with the paper-thin leaves of its poplars and its silver birches and with the long-stemmed wild daffodils playing with the sun. The sculptures are figurative, most dark bronze and mostly life-size. Sarit and Ramsi smile at the bronze pigs, the dogs, the ducks, the elephant in the middle of a pond with a fountain pouring from his mouth. Ramsi studies the faces of sculpted children playing. By the side of the image of a teenage boy Sarit says to him, 'Yours are better.'

'Different,' he says. 'Less playful.'

They pass a sculpture of a mother and her child, life-size again, sitting on a park bench. Sarit bends to see the name of the piece engraved on a copper plaque. '*The Facts of Life*,' she says to Ramsi.

'Who taught you?' he asks.

'My mother.'

'How old were you?'

'Oh, I must have been six or so. I still remember it, though. I asked her about one of my father's paintings. I couldn't understand what the man and woman were doing . . . He had sort of blended them together,' she says, moving her hands, remembering. 'Anyway, she told me all about it,' and Sarit smiles. 'I think she called it "loving".'

'And,' he says, looking her right in the eye, 'is it, Sarit?'

'It can be,' she says, not returning his look, 'and it can be about other things too.'

'As we know,' he says.

And as he sits down on the grass, as he pulls her down beside him, brushes the side of her neck with his mouth, he says, 'What happened to the painting?'

'I have it,' she says, still not making eye contact with him. 'I've had it for a while. An old friend from the kibbutz sent it to me. But I've never unwrapped it properly. It's in a closet now.'

'Why there?'

'Because . . . just because. What's the point? If I hang it I'll have to look at it. It's part of another world. Another life. You should be the first person to understand what I mean.'

He nods and then, 'Sarit.'

268

'Yes.'

'I want to know why you and your father don't speak . . .' She jerks her head. 'Why?' she asks.

'Because I am . . . I was a father too.'

A silence then, that she breaks and says, 'No, Ramsi. Not now. I don't want to. I can't.'

In Shidoni, the park filled with sculptures high above Santa Fe, where Sarit walks with him but says almost nothing, Ramsi points out the emaciated Giacometti-like sculptures. 'Brilliant,' he says. 'Like Holocaust survivors,' he thinks. In the far corner of the garden he points to a lion in green bronze and laughs. He says, 'Looks almost like the second of the pair in front of the Art Institute.'

'Yes,' she says. 'Almost, but not quite. The ones in front of the Institute look more serious.'

'You look serious today,' he says. 'What do you think of it here?'

'I like it,' she says, defensive. 'Why do you ask, though?'

'To get an answer from you.'

Between them there is almost a role reversal that evening. Sarit is serious and pensive, and Ramsi seems relaxed as they sit and eat in the tent that is Maria's, the Southwestern restaurant, described to them as 'a hole in the wall with great food'. As they order their fajitas with guacamole, red hot peppers and chili, Ramsi seems as close to happy as she's ever seen him. 'You're different here,' she says.

'How so?'

'I don't know . . . you're . . . you're . . . somehow a little freed,' she says.

THIRTY-ONE

Ramsi is not, of course, completely freed. With thick and heavy ropes that burn, he is tethered to his history, but Sarit is right that here, with her, away from everything, the ropes seem somehow loosened. As if the spirit of Santa Fe and the distance from his studio have afforded him some respite. The spirit of the place, the distance from his studio and, of course, the confidences he has shared with Sarit. Because the past spoken, the past out in the open, even if its telling causes pain, cannot help but lend the storyteller at least a window of catharsis, however brief. A leaded window of the Palace of Governors, through which the next day Sarit sees an old ornate grand piano, a heavy silver Torah, part of the exhibition on the Jews of New Mexico and their trek via the Santa Fe trail, via the Camino Real, to this town of art and artists in the late nineteenth century. Sarit asks Ramsi, 'Will you come with me to see it?' and in the dimly lit room with touching testimonies of German and Eastern European Jews who have come dragging their belongings to start a new life here, in the darkened room with detailed portraits of displaced men and women with Semitic features, Ramsi senses that Sarit is in some other world. Beside a picture of a thin and sharp-faced man in the biography of his life it says, 'He came to Santa Fe, having trained in painting in Germany and gave his life to the community and to art.'

Sarit says, 'Come. I've had enough. Let's go for a drive.'

A drive through black and pink mountains, through forests green and dense still in the height of summer, green even in the desert. A drive past a lake, a respite in the New Mexico

270

desert on the way to a foreign world. The world of the New Mexican Indian, who in his pueblo, his village above Taos, in his close and tightly knit community, lives today with his language, his folk art, his storytelling almost as he lived a hundred years ago. On their way to Taos Sarit says to Ramsi, 'Let's go and see the pueblo. It's supposed to be fascinating, the way they live.'

'Why not?' he says.

As he drives, along the high road forged between the mountain range of Taos, forged between the layers of pink and black and orange sandstone, she puts her hand at the back of Ramsi's neck. She says, 'I feel dwarfed by all of this.'

He nods. He says, 'The joke is, we think we can create beauty, you and I. It's nothing in the face of this . . . and no man's touched it.'

At the entrance to the pueblo, the butch bald Native American guard standing at the barrier doesn't want to let them in. His tone hostile and aggressive, he says to them, 'The pueblo closes in five minutes. We're not here to be ogled at all the time, you know. We have our lives to live.'

And Sarit says, 'We've driven all the way up from Santa Fe. Actually, we've come all the way from Chicago. We just want to have a look around for five minutes.'

And the guard says, 'What do you care about us? Are you one of those journalist types?'

'No,' she says. 'It interests me because they say it's beautiful here and . . . I'm . . . I'm an artist.'

The air is still. The air is hot and heavy. Ramsi stares at her. She clears her throat. She says to the guard, 'Well, what do you say?'

'I'll take you through,' he says, 'but quickly.'

They walk, shoes scuffing along the sandy ground, past the tiny gated crumbling church, past the village cemetery filled with tall uneven grey stone crosses. The place seems empty, eerie almost. But the guard says, 'This is still a community. No

271

one else lives like this these days.' He turns to wave to the village chief.

Under his breath Ramsi whispers to Sarit, 'I'm not surprised no one lives like this.'

In the heat, in her white cotton shift dress, Sarit shivers. They walk towards the tiny, low, curved-roofed red adobe homes, so sunken into the ground that one has to step down several inches into the desert sand to walk inside them. They watch as a native, short as he is, is forced to bend his head low to walk through the front door of his home, as if entering a doll's house. His tiny adobe house, with its slatted wooden front door painted bright turquoise, as are the doors of all the others. And Ramsi asks the guard, 'Why turquoise doors?'

The guard answers him with disdain on his face as though Ramsi were stupid not to know, as though he ought to have done his homework before coming here. 'Don't you know blue keeps the evil spirits away? Didn't you see all the bright-blue roofs on your way up here?'

Sarit steps down towards the front door of a tiny house with boarded windows and lays her palm on its splintered turquoise wood.

Bright turquoise. Turquoise painted wood. The bright turquoise painted wood of the door with the ripped-off piece of canvas that she had stuck to it where Max would see it. The ripped-off piece of canvas on which she had written in pencil, pressing hard to be read and understood, after she had sat there on the floor for hours in the dead of night. For hours after she had finished the Daliesque painting of the man, of the father with his daughter's arm attached to his right side. The piece of paper that had read,

Abba, this studio is incredible. I don't want you to think I don't appreciate it. I know how many hours you and the others must have worked and how hard it must have been for you to save for this.

But I can't do this any more, Abba. I can't. I'm nearly twenty and I feel as if my whole life has been planned for me, by you and by the kibbutz. I can't breathe. I'm choking, Abba. I don't want to be an officer in the army. I don't want to go to art school. I don't know if I want to paint any more . . . at all . . . ever. I don't know what I want. But I need to try other things . . . Do you understand? Stupid question. Of course you don't understand, because painting is all you've ever wanted to do and all you have ever wanted me to do. I know what you would say to me now. I can hear it. You'd shout at me and say, 'Sarit. You don't want to go to art school? Are you crazy? Do you know what an opportunity this is? Do you know I would have given anything to go to art school in Berlin, but I couldn't because of the Nazis and now you have it all laid out on a plate.' I can hear you saying all of that but, Abba, I'm not your little girl any more. I want change. And I want to see where Ima came from. I want to meet Ima's Aunt Lily. I don't remember her from when I was small. I want to know that part of my heritage too.

Please don't hate me for this. I don't know how else to leave. If I asked your permission you would never agree. So I'm going to go on my own. I will write to you and I will be home. I promise you that. But then you'll never believe my promises again, will you? But I don't want to be trapped any more. I need to see another world. Please try to understand me, Abba.

With all my love
Sarit

Sarit, . . . Sarit, sitting head back against the chair almost in the same spot where Ramsi had sat and spoken of his mother the night before, turns to him now and says, 'By the time I finished writing that letter the birds on the kibbutz were waking up. I remember as I went to my room to get my backpack, putting my fingers to my lips and saying, "Shh . . . shh," while they were singing.' And she laughs at herself. 'I was scared they would wake people up before I left. I had been in my army clothes all night. I changed into jeans and I left my uniform there on the bed, laid out as if I was coming back for it. Dani told me he left it there for weeks, like parents did with the uniforms their kids were wearing when they were killed in action. I remember passing Dani's room as I walked out. Oh, I've never told you about Dani, have I? He was my childhood sweetheart. My best friend. He wasn't there, but I stopped outside his door and looked into his room. I can still see it . . . with my paintings, unframed and plastered all over his walls. I didn't leave him a note. I waited and wrote to him from the US. He already knew, of course, and he was heartbroken, but somehow not surprised.

'I'm not sure I quite understood what I was doing, but at the time it felt like life or death. As if I had to go catch my breath, to find out who I was without the painting. And to find out who I was without . . . without him . . . I don't mean without Dani. I mean without my father. Because . . . because . . . do you know what it is to feel so needed and so loved that you're . . . you're suffocating? Do you know what it's like when someone is so proud of you, so sure of your capabilities that you feel that in the end you can only ever let them down?'

After that, after Sarit sits there with Ramsi and says, 'In the end you can only ever let them down,' for a minute or so she simply can't go on. She tries, but in the meeting of her mind and her heart there is no room left for her voice.

Ramsi doesn't push. He waits until she's ready, until she says, 'I didn't have much money, but I had some. The general kibbutz philosophy was that everything went into a communal pot. There was no such thing as individual success that wasn't for the common good . . . But for the first time in my life after I finished the first two years of the army they let me keep the money from one of my paintings. It was seen as a sort of graduation present. But I also knew that I had a small inheritance from my grandmother in the US. My aunt had written to me about it when I was eighteen. She advised me not to take it immediately, because she knew if she sent it to me in Israel the kibbutz would swallow it up. I think my mother must have spoken to her about it before she died. As if she knew what I might need when I grew up . . . I wasn't afraid of what I was doing at first. I felt guilty for leaving him, but the drive to do and see something new was too great for me to feel fear and going to Chicago felt like . . . like,' and she closes her eyes then, 'like going towards my mother. In the beginning I stayed with her old aunt and she would tell me stories about my mother when she was little. It was so weird . . . I saw my mother everywhere in Chicago. I'd walk around the city and see her face in the mirrored fronts of the sky-scrapers and in the reflection on the lake. It was as if she was with me.'

'And your father?' Ramsi asks her. 'He must have contacted you.'

She laughs. A short laugh. A laugh that stops somewhere between sadness and cynicism. 'Oh, yes, my father wrote to me at my aunt's house. I remember exactly how I got the letter. I was still in bed when my aunt knocked on the door with the letter. She said, "Sarit, here quick, this is from your Abba . . . Open it quick."

'I took it from her and said, "Later." I pretended I was half asleep so that she would leave the room. She would have liked to have stood over me while I read it . . . The minute she walked out I ripped it open, of course.'

In the semi-darkness of the porch at the Inn of the Turquoise Bear there is silence between Ramsi and Sarit. He doesn't ask any more questions. He doesn't say, 'What did the letter say?' His silence in and of itself denotes his question and he sits and waits, while Sarit bends forward in an unfamiliar pose, her arms wrapped round her body as if bracing herself to remember the words of Max's letter.

Sarit,

I have never been very good at expressing my feelings in words. Your mother was better at that. No doubt if she were still here she would write a better letter than I am about to write. But then if she were here I am sure there would have been no need for this in the first place.

When you were born, on my birthday, I told your mother that however little we had on the kibbutz, for the first time since Germany I felt rich. The ghosts were still there, of course, even with your mother's love, even with you, even with my art. When Ima died I was haunted. Crazy as it may sound, sometimes when I dreamt about it I thought it was the Nazis who had taken her too. I saw them grabbing her and dragging her away from me. Later in my nightmares it was not the accident in the tank that had taken my right arm, but them.

The kibbutzniks tried to convince me I had to carry on after that. I'm sure that you remember some of that . . . But they couldn't stop me from sinking into an abyss. It was you, Sarit. The day you brought your easel into my room and painted a picture of Ima in her red dress next to me. Do you remember? I carried on for you and because I had promised Ima that I would. You were everything. You and your talent were all that mattered to me. They still are.

I do not want to waste reams of paper expressing my disappointment, my anger and my outrage. You are aware of them I'm sure. So I will say only this. Make arrangements to come home, Sarit, and not another word will be said about this. I will treat it as the craziness of a badly behaved teenager and you will carry on with the army, with your painting here and next year with art school at Bezalel. I give you my word that I will not mention this aberration ever again.

If you have completely lost your mind and do not intend to come back by then, please don't write to me again, Sarit.

If you stay away I can no longer consider myself to have a daughter. They will have taken you like they have taken everything else. The choice is yours.

Come home, Sarit.

Abba

'Abba, Abba, talk to me. Abba, Abba, please talk to me. Tell him to come to the phone, Dani. You have to get Abba to the phone.' . . . 'He won't come, Sarit. He told me not to ask him again.' . . . 'But I'm not dead, Dani. I've just gone away for a while. Please try just once more.' . . . 'I tried, Sarit. I swear I tried. He said he has lost and hoped and hoped and lost all his life. He says he can't do it again. He keeps . . . he keeps breaking down . . . I'm telling you, Sarit, you need to come back if you want to talk to him . . .' . . . 'Dani, please. Tell him it's someone else on the phone. Don't tell him it's me. Please. I have to speak to him. I have to tell him I want to study here.' . . . 'Study there? Sarit, are you crazy? I miss you. I need you.' . . . 'Dani, get my father. We'll talk about us later. I do want to hear what you have to say, but not now. I need my father. Please go and get him. What time is it there? He'll be back from the fields . . .' . . . 'No, no, Sarit, he hasn't worked in the fields since you left. We can't get him to do anything. He just sits there all day. Rivka says he needs a teacher to help him learn to paint with his left hand. But he doesn't answer. He hardly eats . . .' . . . 'Dani, did you hear me? Get my father to the phone. Tell him it's . . . tell him it's Madame from Jerusalem. He'll come to the phone for her. I know he will' . . . 'Abba, Abba, it's me. It's Sarit. Abba, I . . .' . . . 'When shall I send someone to collect you from the airport, Sarit? Tomorrow or the next day? Do you have the money for the ticket . . . ?'

'Abba, I want to talk to you. I've learnt so much about Ima

here. I feel as if she's with me.' . . . 'Wonderful, Sarit. You can learn about Ima from me. You only have to ask. Now give me your flight details. This call is expensive.'

'Abba, I need to talk to you. I want to go to the university here. Just my undergraduate degree . . .' . . .' . . . Undergraduate degree, Sarit? Are you crazy? An art degree in America when we have Bezalel?'

'No, Abba, not art. I can always go back to that . . .' . . . 'What, Sarit? I don't think I heard you right . . .' . . . 'I said I want to do a degree in science, Abba. I have the grades. Can you send me my school certificates? Can you? Will you send them to me, please? Abba, Abba, can you hear me? Are you there? Abba. Abba . . . Dani get him back. Now, please.' . . . 'No, Sarit. He won't. He says the subject's closed. He says he's lost you.'

'Abba, please listen to me, please . . . please . . . Abba . . . Dani, should I come home to visit?' . . . 'Only if you're going to stay, Sarit. You'll make him worse otherwise. I've learnt to live without you after two years, but he never will . . .' . . . 'But Dani, listen, I thought I might come for our birthday. It's been two years. He must be used to it by now.'

'No, Sarit, he's not. He's dealt with it by shutting you out. Don't you understand? Everyone he's ever loved has left him. For God's sake, Sarit, you're his child and I'm telling you this stuff. He's your father.'

Father. Daddy. Abba. Dear Abba, I wanted you to know I have been accepted into medical school here at the University of Chicago. The selection process was tough. There's a lot of competition so perhaps if you knew how difficult it was you might be proud of me. Proud of me? Of course you wouldn't. This wasn't what you wanted for me or for yourself. It was the opposite of what you wanted for me, wasn't it? I'm sorry I am not the child you dreamt of.

Dear Max,

Sarit has been accepted as a junior resident at Northwestern Hospital. I thought that you should know. I wanted her to write to you herself, but she has given up because you never respond. She is doing so well academically but emotionally she seems to have shut down. She gives nothing away about her private life. She is living on her own and I don't see enough of her now. I worry about her. It's impossible to get her to open up. She has followed in her mother's footsteps in a way, in the medical world, but she's not like her in temperament, Max. She seems so much more like you, from what I remember of the time I visited you and Gaby on the kibbutz and from what Gaby used to tell me of you. In the past, I have asked her to write to you again, but now I don't dare broach the subject with her any more. Max, at least write back to me. Let me know at least for Sarit's sake that you are alive and well.

Dear Lily,
Thank you for keeping me informed. Tell me, does Sarit still paint?

No, Max, No. I can't say that I've ever seen her paint.

Dear Max,
You don't reply any more. Why not?
Yours
Lily

Dear Max, Max, Max . . .

In the cooling night air of the New Mexico desert Sarit is aware of a jacket laid over her shoulders. She turns round. She says, 'Oh. Was I shivering? I think I must have been . . . I . . .'

And Ramsi says, 'Sarit?'

She looks up. 'Yes.'

'Sarit. Do you still miss your father after all these years?'

In another setting she might not have answered. Had it not already been almost pitch black she might have felt the need to hide. Had she not gone so far down the path of truth she might have tried to turn away, but here and now she swallows hard and in a quiet voice she says, 'Do I still miss him . . . ? I think,' she says the words slowly, 'I think that's probably like asking him if he still misses his right arm.'

And then some moments later she says, 'So yes, that's how things have been. I have heard from Dani over the years, but that's all. And even when he does write, he's a voice from another world. Like the painting he sent me. I can't hang that painting . . . I just can't. You know, the one we talked about before. That half-unwrapped oil painting.'

'Yes, Sarit,' he says '. . . I know the one you mean.'

The painting, the sand and mineral painting practised by Native American artists in Arizona and New Mexico is an art that, like sculpture, is both tactile and visual at once. In Santa Fe, in the forecourt of a small public garden dripping with red bell flowers, his long shiny black hair loose around his shoulders, his dark-skinned face intense with concentration, a young Native American man is kneeling, leaning forward on the ground, letting the dark-red crushed sandstone run through his bony fingers on to the canvas. Oblivious, apparently, to his onlookers, in crushed sand and powdered minerals he paints the landscape of his home. With finely powdered sandstone of ochre and of earthy green, with powdered chalk that he takes from the little dishes laid out by his side and sifts on to the canvas. With the orange of cinnabar, the red of hematite, the ultramarine of lapis lazuli that he takes between the tips of his fingers, letting a little fall here, a little fall there to shade and shape and change the meeting of the horizon with the russet, honey mountain ranges. As he works he sings. A sweet tune in the dialect of Navajo, with words that speak of longing and of home. Words, of course, that Sarit and Ramsi don't understand. Words that they can only feel.

With his right hand the young man reaches for a tiny pot and takes from it a pinch of yellow that is almost gold and sprinkles the final dramatic touch on his creation, depicted now in sand and crushed powder on the ground. He turns and points at the dish of yellow gold. He beams and in his broken English says, 'You know what is this?'

Sarit and Ramsi shake their heads. He says, 'It called fool's gold. Made from orpiment. People believe it real gold,' and he laughs out loud there on the ground before his masterpiece.

'Where is that?' Ramsi asks, touching the very edge of the sand painting with his foot.

He points upwards and westwards towards the massive range of mountains and, proud, he says, 'The place I born.'

By the side of the dishes with the powdered sandstone, chalk and ochre, by the side of the hematite, the lapis lazuli and the gold for fools, lies an empty dish. He points to it. He says, 'For gold . . . real gold . . . From you nice people. Very expensive material. Expensive to make painting,' and Sarit and Ramsi both reach into their pockets, take out some coins and three dollar notes between them and bend to put them in the artist's pot.

Without brush or pencil, without knife or chisel, with only his fingers and crushed minerals the Navajo artist has created the clear defined lines of his birthplace. And bending over him, curious about his art, Sarit says, 'But it's a waste. If the wind picks up your picture will be blown away.'

He says, 'No problem. This art not mine. Come through me. Through my body. Tonight I wipe it away and start again tomorrow. No problem to wipe away my home. I can make it again,' he says. 'So easy,' and then, placing his hand on his chest, 'My home in my heart. I never lose it . . . It never leave me, even if I try. Look,' he says and in the swipe of his hand the horizons, the earth, the mountains sprinkled with fool's gold are all gone. Brushed together by the Navajo artist, poured away into a large glass jar and he throws his head back and laughs out loud. 'No problem,' he says. 'You try now,' he adds, beaming, beckoning to Sarit to sit down by him on the ground, offering her *tabula rasa*.

And Ramsi says, 'Go on, Sarit. Why don't you try?'

She kneels down there in the shade, under the poplars. She puts her hand in the stone vessel that contains the powdered red sandstone. She lets the grains run between her long slim fingers, rubs the sand between her forefingers and her thumbs on to her palms. And just as she had bent over the Navajo artist watching, now Ramsi bends over her and watches as she lets the sand fall to create a new beginning.

She begins. She does. This is a start, a hint in red of what could come. But with only a few grains of her painting spilt Sarit feels herself begin to sweat. She turns to Ramsi, looks up and says, 'I think that's enough of storytelling for a while . . . It did feel good against my hands, though.' And then, 'Come on, Ramsi, shall we go?'

And perhaps Sarit is right. Enough stories have been told in Santa Fe. The sculpted woman half covered in pebbles in the courtyard of a gallery, the dark bronze child with his mother on the bench, the turquoise painted doors of the Taos pueblo have coaxed and cajoled first Ramsi, then Sarit into the sharing of confidences here between the mountain ranges that might otherwise have stayed cocooned. Confidences that from their place of depth and darkness have drawn them closer to one another.

And as the knowing has grown, so too has the intimacy that has crept up on them with their words, with their truths and with their stories. An intimacy that excites and alarms all at once as it begins to change the shape of things. An intimacy that in its turn changes the essence of their knowing of each other, in their room at the vine-shrouded inn in the sun-light of the afternoon. For the Bible's choice of the words *to know* is no coincidence. No coincidence at all, because with the words that have flowed, the understanding of the other that seeps through them now is heady. An understanding, a knowing, that opens and liberates, that is erotic and arousing all at once.

'I need to know,' he says, his hands on her hair against the pillow, pulling, not hard but as she likes it, 'what you would do . . . if you were completely free? If anything were possible? What would you want?'

Only a split second's hesitation before she says, 'White sheets . . . sheets . . . just like this.'

'And then? Yes. Go on. Tell me,' he says, hands pressing down on the curves of her shoulders, which he feels then with the side of his face that is rough by now, by the middle of the afternoon.

'You,' she breathes. 'On me. In me. Us . . . like this . . . in the light . . . in colours. Messy, slippery.'

'Wet paint?'

'Yes,' she says, not knowing of the blood-red sand still in her nails and on her fingers and the patterns that it makes on the skin of his back.

He says, 'Yes . . . Go on.'

'Just thick colours,' she says, 'on us. Here. Everywhere.'

Everywhere. With his hands he repeats what she has said.

And he is lost with her now in the colours that she wants.

She says, 'You can feel it, can't you? What I mean?' She takes his hand.

'Yes, yes, I can,' he says.

'Look.'

'Where? Tell me where.'

'Here and here . . . Now here.'

The paint, the thick, wet melting of their colours. The play of shades. The flow and the feel of them. The depth and the fall of them. The shading and enlightening of one another. And in the melting the loss. The loss of self that must come with the gain of the other. A loss that enriches as it takes. As it gives back. Gives over to the sounds. Of words broken now. Of breathing. The breath's shape. Its art. Breath that curves and climbs in waves of heat. Long, slow curves of breath. Short, hot lines of breath. Intense and sharp. And hard.

'Too much?'

'No . . . no . . . not too much.'

In the flow of shape and heat and sweat, she half shakes her head. Hair wet against his face. 'And . . . you?'

She feels his answer. Thinks she hears his 'No . . . no . . . not . . . too . . . much.' She hears his 'Now . . . I know . . . Sarit . . . I know . . . now'.

They know. Not all. But more. He does and so does she . . . more . . . and . . . more . . . the darkness in the light. The light, the white in darkness. 'I think, Sarit . . . I think . . . I know . . . I love . . . I . . .

'Me too . . . the more I know . . . of you . . . the more I know . . . I want . . . I love . . . I . . . do.'

THIRTY-TWO

Has there ever been a time when woman has not wondered how the shape of her life might have been if the slant of her eye, the slope of her nose, the curve of her lip, of her hip, of her breast had been other? At the turn of last century, long before the choice to defy nature was acceptable, when the changing of faces was illegal and in the realms of the occult, the frustrated Victorian woman in her boned corset, in her stifling skirts, her hair stiff and unmoving must have stood, puffing, powdering, touching her face by the looking glass and wondering. In the twenties, the thirties and the forties, before the mirror of her dresser, the wealthy blue-blooded aristocrat in her evening finery, with her red lips, her black silks and her pearls must have cocked her head and wondered too.

In painting the jet black of kajal on to their eyes, the lesser wives of Rameses II surely wondered whether their images would have been carved next to his into the face of the pink rocks at Abu Simbel if they too had known the beauty of his favoured wife, his beloved Nefertari.

And not just through the years, but even now, is there anywhere a woman who does not ask herself 'what if?' The cleaning woman scrubbing bathroom floors will get up from her knees and, standing looking in the mirror above the sink, will ask herself what if she could afford the change, the lift, the tuck of her employer? The fearful woman, when no one is around, will move with stealth towards the mirror in the hall, will see the hooked nose, the crows' feet, the droopy skin and ask herself, 'What if I had the courage? Would it change my luck? Would it change the way I feel?'

And even the woman satisfied with her work, with her life and with her lover will at some time ponder her reflection, questioning other lives that might have been with different faces.

Even Juliann, dressing for November's end in her shiny black lined raincoat with its black fur collar, pulling on her knee-high black leather boots, even she that morning stood in front of the mirror in her bedroom, applied her deep and dark-brown lipstick, looked at her broad features, then pulled the skin of her cheeks backwards and upwards and asked herself, 'What if . . . ? What if I really did want Dr Kleinmann to lift my face? How would it be?' and then, letting her hands drop, laughing, saying to herself, 'You big old fool . . . you're happy as you are,' she calls goodbye to her Siamese cat, walks to the lift and down into the underground garage attached to her high-rise.

She would have liked to have walked to Sarit's surgery. She felt the need to stretch her limbs. Even in her early fifties arthritis was beginning to threaten and the rheumatologist had said she ought to walk, to stretch, to move as much as possible. But a walk alone in the city or the suburbs was ill advised for Juliann. And on the rare occasions when she did choose not to take the car, as she went on her way she was not exactly ill at ease, but wary. Because in truth, however low-key her behaviour, after eighteen years in her profession it would have been impossible for her not to have been recognised from time to time by frequenters of the more unsavoury circles in the city of Chicago and its suburbs.

And whereas in Sarit's profession to be known by one's clientele for one's skill and expertise could only be a good thing, in Juliann's line of work anonymity was infinitely preferable.

She had arrived exactly on time at the surgery so that she would not have to sit in the waiting room but that morning, as fate would have it, Sarit had been held up with a small child at the children's hospital. A child healing slowly, both on the inside and the out. So Juliann had little choice but to sit in the chaise longue, thumbing through copies of *Harpers*, *Elle* and *National Geographic* that Emily had bought to keep Sarit's patients entertained. Alone in the room, for she had made sure she would be the first patient of the day, Juliann looked round at the boxes of plastic coloured cars and trucks and dolls on the table. She noticed too that the walls were almost bare save for some of Sarit's certificates, framed in black in a corner of the room.

Sarit Kleinmann . . . Fellow of the American College of Plastic and Aesthetic Surgeons.

Sarit Kleinmann, Fellow of the American College of Paediatric Plastic Surgeons . . .

Juliann waited for Sarit. She waited because Sarit had a reputation as a brilliant surgeon and because she had flawless character references.

And while she sits and waits, and flicks through magazines, Emily with her pixie look and short blonde hair puts her head round the door. She says, 'I've just had a call from Dr Kleinmann. She's running a little late, but she should be here in ten minutes.'

'Great,' Juliann says. 'Thank you.'

'Oh, and by the way, would you mind having a medical student sit in on your consultation today? She's with us for the week.'

Juliann thinks fast, then, gracious, smiles and says, 'Look, I hope you'll understand, but I think I'd feel too self-conscious. Would it be OK to say no?'

Emily hides her surprise. She says, 'Sure. Absolutely fine. It's your prerogative.' And as she walks back to her desk in the hallway she questions her own judgement, for this woman, when she had called to make her appointments, had seemed anything but tentative and shy.

Juliann, some minutes later, sees the tall figure of Sarit walk past the door. She hears her say, 'Who's first, Em?'

'The Professor. Professor Stocker. It's her second consultation. Here are the notes.'

'Interesting. Let's get Debbie in on this one.'

'No. She doesn't want a student watching.'

'Why not?'

'She feels self-conscious.'

'How odd. I didn't get that impression from her at all.'

Sarit, not in a white coat but in her uniform of black trousers and white shirt, goes to the waiting-room door. 'Good morning. Will you come with me?'

Through the heavy oak door, across the mirrored room Juliann follows her to her desk. Sarit signals for her to take a seat, sits down herself. Juliann's eyes are drawn to the Japanese paper lamp one side of the desk, her fingers are drawn to the pile of magnetic paper clips on the other. She pulls them to her.

Sarit says to Juliann, 'So what can I do for you?' She doesn't say, 'Ah, so you've come back. Does that mean you've decided to go ahead with surgery?' That would not have been Sarit's style. But she recognises the 'Professor', of course, not just because of the deep-brown of the lipstick and the hair, but because of the memorable conversation they had had on the nature of disguise. She recalls how she had not wanted the conversation to end, how she could have sat and talked for hours to this patient.

Juliann lifts her shiny black coat from her lap, stands up and uninvited goes to hang it on the coat-stand by the door. And walking back she says, 'I never told you who recommended you to me, did I?'

'No, but does it matter now you're here?'

Amused by the bluntness of the doctor she carries on. 'I was recommended by Barbara Sacks. She's married to a colleague of mine. You did a superb job on her lids,' she says, touching her own rather heavy eyelids. 'You remember Barbara. Policewoman. Short blonde hair in a bob,' she says, outlining the shape of a bob against her own face.

'Yes,' Sarit says, 'I remember.'

'Great woman,' Juliann says.

And Sarit starts then to grow puzzled as to why the Professor is not coming straight to the point and says again, 'Yes, I remember her. So what can I do for you?'

Juliann looks her in the eye. She says, 'I have done my research, Doctor, and I have come to the conclusion that you are to be trusted.'

'Trusted? How do you mean?' Sarit asks and laughing then she adds, 'You mean I won't do a chin implant when I'm supposed to be doing a facelift?'

'No, I don't mean trusted in that way. I mean trusted with confidential issues.'

'Well, of course,' Sarit says, thinking now that she has understood that a woman of the Professor's standing might not want the world to know she's been under the knife. And so she says, 'Confidentiality is crucial . . . Especially in this business where people don't always want to publicise what they've had done,' she adds and then she says, 'So, how can I help you?'

'Yes, well,' says Juliann, building castles out of paper clips, 'I think I need to tell you why I'm here.'

'Yes?'

'It isn't for myself.'

On the odd occasion this had happened. Just as a relative of the prospective patient might from time to time go to a shrink and say, 'My son, my friend, my daughter has a problem and doesn't dare to talk to you himself,' so once or twice a friend or a relative had come to Sarit with a photograph and had said, 'This is my mother, my daughter, my sister, my friend . . . What can you do for her? She wouldn't come herself.' So now Sarit leans across her desk and, thinking of the waiting room that would soon be full to bursting, trying to speed things up, she says to Juliann, 'Do you have photographs of someone you'd like to show me?'

'Yes, Dr Kleinmann, I do. Or at least I have one photograph. But if you have a few minutes, I do have a story that I'd like to tell you first.'

Sarit looks at her. She says, 'I'm tight for time.'

Her brusqueness, though not unexpected, makes Juliann laugh. She has heard not just about Sarit's expertise but about her manner too. She says, 'First things first,' and she holds out her hand. 'I'm sorry to have deceived you. I'm not a professor. Just plain old Juliann Stocker.'

Sarit does not lift her hand to shake Juliann's, nor does she speak. Unmoving, she sits in her swivel chair while Juliann reaches into the pocket of her black patent bag, removes a card from her wallet and hands it to Sarit. She takes the white card with the gold-embossed insignia, looks down at it and reads '*Juliann Stocker. Special Supervisory Agent, Federal Bureau of Investigation*'.

With a deep breath Sarit takes in the information. She looks up, thick arched eyebrows raised above grey eyes and slowly says, 'Well, I suppose I don't see any reason why an FBI agent shouldn't want to have a facelift too,' and she laughs then. A Sarit laugh that lights her up, a Gabriella laugh.

And Juliann, seeing the radiance of her smile, seeing that for a moment she's relaxed, says, 'Look, Dr Kleinmann, the truth is this visit is not about surgery for me. And I'm sorry I had to be dishonest, but under the circumstances I had no choice but to be thorough in my research.'

'What circumstances? Profess . . . Mrs . . . I mean . . .'

'Juliann, please.'

'What circumstances, Juliann? What research?' and as she speaks it crosses Sarit's mind that for the first time in her medical career some patient somewhere is about to sue her. Before waiting for Juliann's answer Sarit lifts the phone. She says, 'I need a coffee, Em,' and then to Juliann, 'Coffee?'

'Milk, one sugar, please.'

And Sarit looks her in the eye as if she now were the professor waiting for an answer from her student and she says, 'I'm waiting.'

Juliann runs her hand through her short red hair. She clears her throat. She says, 'I'll be as brief as I can . . . As you can see from my card I'm with the FBI.' She stops. 'Um, look . . . I'm sure your doors are soundproof, but would it be possible to have a little music in here? Just in case.'

Sarit looks at her as if she's lost her mind. Not sure if she's making a fool of herself by following Juliann's orders she walks over to her stereo system and, her tone sarcastic, asks, 'Anything in particular I can offer you? Jazz, country and western, classical?'

'Some Mozart would be great to keep my brain sharp.'

'Mozart? But of course,' she says, sarcastic.

And as the sounds begin to fill the room Emily is standing at the door with two cups of coffee on a tray and a 'What in heaven's name is going on here?' look on her face.

Sarit beckons her over to her desk with the tray. She says to Emily, 'The Professor,' and she lays the faintest hint of emphasis on the word 'Professor' . . . 'The Professor,' she says, 'feels more relaxed talking about her surgery with music in the background . . .'

Her back turned, under her breath Emily says, 'What?' and, baffled, leaves the room.

Juliann sips her coffee. She says, 'So, Sarit, here goes . . . We, when I say we, I mean the federal government and the FBI . . . we are currently working with a young woman. She's twenty years old and the main witness for the prosecution in a major drugs conspiracy case we've been dealing with. It's probably the biggest drugs ring here in Chicago since the Black Gangster Disciples in the early nineties. She herself was not involved in any criminal activity, but her boyfriend was in charge of the ring's operations and, to cut a very long and horrible story short, she saw him just after his colleagues had stabbed him and . . .'

Sarit interrupts her. She says, 'Juliann . . . what on earth are we talking about here? Is this some kind of hoax?'

'I wish it were. Unfortunately it is one hundred per cent authentic and it's a very sad case . . .'

The telephone rings. Sarit answers; Juliann hears her say to Emily, 'They'll just have to wait.' She hangs up. 'Go on,' she says.

And against the background of the Mozart, against the pathos of the violin, surrounded by mirrors left and right, in the grey light that comes in through the floor-to-ceiling windows Juliann says, 'Well, anyway, to keep it brief, she was a crucial witness. The only one apart from the doorman. She didn't witness the crime directly but she saw the others leave and found her boyfriend on the kitchen floor with stab wounds to his chest and face. By the time she got there he was dead.'

In a medical context Sarit has seen much that is gruelling and ghastly. But stories of blood and maimings wreak havoc with her. They drag her back, paint pictures in her mind of flesh that hangs from bloody arms. Juliann thinks she sees Sarit change colour. She says, 'But you must be pretty familiar with this kind of stuff. Chicago's such an ugly place for crime.'

And now, as Juliann speaks, behind her desk Sarit feels the weakness in her knees. 'Yes,' she says in a low voice to Juliann, 'I've seen plenty of kids who've been stabbed or shot. Go on.'

And Juliann, making a chain of paperclips, says, 'Felicia, the girl we're talking about, had been pushing her boyfriend to leave the drugs scene for some time. He was Italian, from Palermo and involved with a group that imported drugs in ceramic urns. The stuff originally came from Asia . . . not the urns, the drugs, I mean. It was a clever set-up really. They used an art gallery on Milwaukee as a front . . . People assume the drugs scene here is exclusively South American these days, but it's not true. There's a lot of stuff that still comes in via Italy.' As she speaks for a moment Juliann examines a chip in her reddish-brown nail polish that matches her lips and her hair. She looks up at Sarit. She says, 'Anyway, we had been watching the boyfriend for some time. We had approval to bug the apartment. We had wires, taps, the lot and we were just waiting to accumulate enough evidence to indict him and his colleagues when they murdered him. We think,' she says, 'that his colleagues had begun to consider him a danger. They knew he wanted to get out for Felicia's sake . . . she threatened to break off the relationship if he didn't change his life and they also knew we were on his tail, so basically he was becoming a liability to them.'

Juliann carries on. She says, 'Anyway, we had the apartment rigged up, though we didn't keep twenty-four-hour surveillance. I wish we had.'

And Sarit as she listens thinks, 'This is like some kind of a radio thriller . . .' and interrupting Juliann she leans across her desk and asks, 'But what on earth does any of this have to do with me?'

'Of course,' Juliann says, 'this preamble must be confusing for you. Let me move a little faster . . . You must be wondering why I'm telling you this story. We've arrested and charged two of the top guys and we're hoping for a conviction. As I said, Felicia is a crucial witness for us. She refused to talk at first. She had run home to her parents' place and just would not say a word. I sat with her for hours and hours to get her to open up . . . I knew she was important for us, not just because she'd been a witness, but also because she knew her boyfriend's murderers. Alessandro, that was the boyfriend, used to take her to bars and restaurants with them from time to time and so of course she would have absolutely no trouble identifying them. She also knows where everything is including his address book with all the numbers of his contacts in Palermo. She's an extremely bright girl, an art history student and she understood precisely the machinations of the operation.'

And Sarit, almost forgetting why she is here, why Juliann is in her surgery, but caught up, following the story says, 'So what's happened to her?'

'Well, of course it transpires that she'd received a telephone threat from a member of the gang. They basically let her know if she gave evidence she wouldn't live to see another Chicago snowfall. That together with the shock factor is why she wouldn't speak. She knows exactly who they are, but at first she was so terrified she even denied that she'd witnessed anything. I got her to talk in the end and we promised we would protect her if she would agree to testify. We offered her the Witness Security Programme . . . Do you know what that is?'

'I think so,' says Sarit. And she does know, for through the grapevine she had once heard of another medical colleague approached to work with the FBI to change the identity of a top-level criminal who had agreed to cooperate with the prosecution.

'Basically,' says Juliann, lifting the tortoiseshell hand mirror from the desk and checking her lipstick to make sure it hasn't smeared, 'the Wit Sec is a radical programme designed to protect crucial witnesses who are in serious danger . . . Felicia wasn't happy with the programme as we offered it to her. It would have meant her leaving the state immediately and virtually disappearing off the face of the earth. She didn't want that. She wanted to cooperate with us, but not on our terms. She was terrified . . . or rather I should say she is terrified. And understandably. Because, to be honest, though we wouldn't tell her, we also think she's at high risk. We're about to videotape her testimony in case anything happens to her between now and the trial . . . It's set to take place in six weeks, but it might well be delayed . . . Anyway, as I said, she wouldn't accept the strict rules of the Witness Security Programme, so we offered her a watered-down version of it . . . well, sort of watered-down. We have her living in a ghastly place awaiting the trial and . . .'

'And what?' Sarit says.

'We have made a commitment to her to protect her after it's over too. We don't just drop our witnesses like that . . .'

'So . . .?' says Sarit, although as she says it, as she shapes her lips into the circle to pronounce the question 'So?' there is a growing and uncomfortable realisation, then a shocking certainty, about the nature of the request that's on its way.

'We want to ask you, Dr Kleinmann, to work on Felicia's face and change the way she looks as soon as the trial is over. She has grown paranoid about being traced and this is what she wants from us in exchange for agreeing to testify. We have given the matter a huge amount of thought, as you can imagine, but we've now agreed that we need to give her what she wants.'

'And,' says Sarit, sitting forward, chin in her hand on her desk, 'without your agreement she won't testify and you're afraid you won't get a conviction.'

'Right in one, Dr Kleinmann. You ought to be working for us full time.'

'Thanks, but no thanks,' Sarit says and then, 'Look. This is crazy.'

And Juliann pulls on her mental hiking boots and says, 'The FBI in Illinois has gone through this procedure once in recent years. It was also a case where the witness was crucial to us but risked being killed if he testified. In that case he was a top guy and so he had nothing to lose by cooperating with us. We changed everything about his identity including his face. His case was totally different from Felicia's, though. He really wanted to go on the Witness Security Programme. In fact, he begged us to put him on it . . . it's a very expensive and complicated business, you know, having to create an entirely new life and identity for someone.'

And Sarit says, 'Juliann, are you really asking of me what I think you're asking?'

From the other side of the table Juliann fixes her gaze on Sarit. 'Yes,' she says, 'I am.'

'I see.'

'It's very straightforward,' Juliann says. 'We want you to create a new image for Felicia.'

Sarit shakes her head. She says, 'No, wait. You're going far too fast for me. Let's just assume for a minute you are authentic . . . that this story is true . . . why me, Juliann? Why have you come to me? There are hundreds of plastic surgeons in this state.'

'Ah,' Juliann says. 'Now that's an easy one.' She does not try even to appeal to Sarit's vanity because, paid to be intuitive, after two meetings with her she understands enough to know that Sarit's ego is not fragile, that flattery will get her nowhere. She knows, because in Sarit's dress, in her demeanour, there is no hint, no trace of vanity at all. And so she speaks the truth. She says, 'Felicia is no ugly duckling. She's a lovely looking young woman and we want to do it right. I came to you first of all because I had seen the work you had done on my friend Barbara and several other patients since then, of course. And secondly because it seems you do a lot of aesthetic and reconstructive work with children and adolescents, and although Felicia, of course, is not a child . . . she's twenty . . . somewhere between child and woman, right now she's in a fragile mental state. Also, she insisted on a female surgeon. She seems terrified of men at the moment.'

Sarit gets up, walks around the room, turns back to Juliann, who swivels round to face her. Then she says, 'I have two things to say, Juliann . . . One . . . this is not my kind of thing. Not at all. And two . . . I have patients who've been waiting for forty minutes out there.'

'Doctor . . .'

'Sarit . . .'

'Sarit, this is not a game. It's a federal crime and a personal tragedy that we're dealing with here and we need your help,' and then drawing on the resources she has she says, 'Do you remember when you were twenty? Do you remember how uncertain one feels at twenty even with a normal life? You were probably still protected by your parents like I was and like Felicia thought she was. Imagine having all that suddenly ripped away from you . . . One minute you think the world is a fairly safe place. You're surrounded by your community. The next minute you're out there. You're vulnerable, at risk and on your own.'

Sarit listens, swallows hard. Juliann carries on. 'I want you to think about it, Sarit. You can't say no to that. Although unfortunately there isn't that much time. We're going to need an answer from you almost immediately.'

And Sarit holds up her hands and says, 'Look here, Juliann, if you are who you say you are I understand the delicacy of your position . . . But I can't even begin to consider her case without spending a considerable amount of time with her. And to be honest I don't know if I want to do that. I've never heard of a case like this one before,' she says, challenging Juliann.

Juliann looks Sarit in the eyes. She uses what she has. She says, 'It's rare . . . but it happens . . . although it's obviously not something we would want to shout about . . . But we're on the right side of the law. As you know, in South America it's the other way round. It was the criminals who got their faces changed all the time to hide from the Secret Services in the late forties there and early fifties. And can you imagine how many ageing Nazis must be hobbling around Brazil and Argentina with changed faces?' A pause and then, 'Just think of that, Sarit.'

Sarit shivers, clears her throat. 'I try not to think about things like that,' she says.

'I understand,' Juliann says and of course with her knowledge of Sarit's background she does understand. Far better than Sarit can even begin to imagine. She says, 'That kind of thing goes against justice. What we want from you, Sarit, is to help us do something to protect Felicia and to promote justice,' and standing up, smoothing her black skirt, she says, 'I'll leave you to your work now. And to think about all this. I'm sorry I had to deceive you before. I genuinely am. But I'm sure you understand my reasons. I needed to check you out first. I make no secret of that,' and then, moving towards the door, she says, 'I don't need to tell you that this must stay confidential . . .' and then again, 'I want you to think about what I've said. I'll call you in the morning. In the meantime if you need me you have my card.'

Sarit doesn't walk over to the door with Juliann. She stays standing where she is. So that Juliann has to call across the room to her, 'Sarit, this is important to a lot of people,' before she turns her back, lifts her shiny black coat from the hook and walks out of the door, without even having shown Sarit the photograph.

And Sarit nods slowly and sits down, leans back in her chair and is sitting there still quite stunned, quite drained when Emily puts her head round the door and says, 'What in God's name was that all about? You've been in here with her for hours. Can I send the next one in right now?'

'Give me five, Em, will you?'

'OK five, but no more, Doc. They're climbing the walls out there. Everybody needs a piece of you, you know.'

'Oh yes, Em,' she says, 'that much I do know.'

THIRTY-THREE

Herein lies the irony of the thing. For so many years Sarit had looked to no one for help. At twenty, she had stolen from the kibbutz at dawn, letting only the waking birds in on her decision. On the wooden floor of the studio Max had created for her she had let her paintbrush smear a flesh-coloured stroke where it fell. She had left it there. And on the other side of the Atlantic she had opened her scientific textbook without asking of a single soul, 'Could I? Should I? Is it right for me to change the direction of my life?' And though it seemed that the idea of plastic surgery had come from outside herself, from the professor who once had said, 'Phenomenal manual dexterity, Kleinmann . . . you ought to cut,' the decision to pursue paediatric and adult plastic and aesthetic surgery had been made without the help of her great-aunt, without the help of fellow students or of friends from the world she had abandoned. Her decision to repair and to re-create had been as solitary as her kibbutz life had been communal.

In her paediatric practice, despite the teamwork involved, the ultimate decisions were hers. In her adult cosmetic surgery she alone decided to break or not to break, to lift or not to lift, to cut or not to cut. Fearless, first she looked her patients in the face, then made her decisions. And yet now, being asked by Juliann to change Felicia, Sarit did not, would not, could not agree to so unusual a request without seeking help from others.

'Sarit . . . Juliann's on the line. She's says you're expecting her call.'

'Yes, put her on.'

'Sarit. How are you?'

'Good.'

She waits for Sarit to say, 'And how are you?'

There is silence where the question might have been.

'So . . . I hope you've had enough time to think.'

'Not enough. But I suppose I can give you half an answer.'

'Yes?'

'I will see her for an initial consultation . . . but if, and I say *if*, I agree to see her a second time there will be several conditions involved.' As she speaks Sarit dislikes the sound of her own voice. She dislikes her tone, knows that she sounds precious, as though she were putting herself and her skills on a pedestal. As though she were one of those plastic surgeons she so loathed, who walked around with puffed-out chests and viewed themselves on a par with God.

Under Juliann's desk the FBI's fat cat who has seen and heard it all, who knows more than all the wire taps put together, creeps over to her legs. With her stockinged foot she strokes the arch of his back. She says, 'So, what are your conditions Sarit?'

'First of all,' Sarit says, 'she absolutely must be seen by a psychiatrist to make sure she is fully aware of what she is asking for and what the repercussions might be.'

'We've been through this, Sarit. She has already been seen by one of our departmental psychiatrists.'

'Look, this is the way I work, Juliann . . . you are totally free to consult someone else. No hard feelings. I can recommend a good plastic surgeon in Hinsdale, outside the city. A man, of course.'

The cat wraps its tail round Juliann's ankle. The tickling of a cat's tail against your skin makes it hard to think straight. Juliann bends down, reaches under the desk, strokes the animal, then pushes it away. She says, 'Give me a minute, Sarit, will you, please? I'll call you right back,' and she puts down the receiver. She walks over to the coffee-stained sofa.

She throws herself down and cranes her neck backwards to think.

For a moment she contemplates beginning the procedure of finding a suitable plastic surgeon all over again. She thinks of conducting yet another in-depth background search, she thinks of the intricacies of finding out about his life, the places he frequents, the way he spends his free time. She thinks of the charade of the first visit to the surgeon and of the difficulties of the explanation during the second. She considers too the challenge she would face persuading Felicia to see a male surgeon. In her mind she weighs that scenario against the increased risk of involving another expert linked to Sarit in the picture. She considers too the number of people who might already know, for though Juliann has asked Sarit to keep the matter confidential, she is under no illusions. Sarit will undoubtedly have confided in a friend or two within the medical world and sworn them to secrecy. She will almost certainly have confided in her lover too. Even Juliann in her time has indulged in the odd post-coital indiscretion. For where in the world is there a woman who loves without the pillow talk?

In her office, before she calls Sarit back, Juliann considers the time element too and the proximity of the date set for the trial. She walks over to her desk again, picks up a pen for support, picks up the phone. She dials the surgery number. She doesn't say, 'Hello,' when she's put through. She says just, 'What are your other conditions, Sarit?'

Despite herself, despite the fact that she is not at all sure that she wants to be propelled down this dense dark alley, with Juliann's question, with her asking, 'What are your other conditions?' Sarit cannot help but feel triumph's flicker in her gut. She says, 'My other condition is this . . . if, and again I say *if*, we decide to go any further with this, I will need to involve another expert in aesthetics. It's too much responsibility for one person.'

'You mean another plastic surgeon?' asks Juliann.

'A plastic surgeon perhaps . . . or, I don't know . . . an artist who can advise me on how to change Felicia's look and retain her beauty at the same time.' And as she says this Sarit is quite suddenly overwhelmed by an unfamiliar feeling of need. A need for him, for Ramsi both in a professional capacity and in a way that she has never allowed herself to need another human being.

The cat scratches at Juliann's stockings for attention. Juliann tries desperately to clear her head. She says, 'Sorry, Sarit. Are you saying you want to involve two more experts in this, even before you make a decision?'

Sarit has regained her composure. She says, 'You've got it, Juliann . . . and I can tell you something . . . any plastic surgeon worth their salt would do the same.'

On one end of the phone Juliann takes out a match and a Marlboro, desperate to go out into the stairwell where she goes to smoke several times a day, as if she were a naughty school-girl in this non-smoking building. At the other end of the line Sarit stands up with her handset, begins to pace her surgery, so that were one to take a film shot, first of one woman, tall, dark and purposeful in black and white, then of the other, a strong, stubborn redhead in black and green, they would have looked like two high-powered businesswomen involved in negotiations of an entirely different nature.

Sarit stands by the window. She looks out at Chicago's sky-line. She says, 'Look, this is not your everyday request, Juliann. And to be honest I have never before been asked to work on the face of a woman who already has near perfect propor-tions. Not that I've seen her, but that's what you've implied.'

From her desk drawer, from a file, Juliann takes out Felicia's photo. She looks at it again. She says, 'Oh yes. You're right on that one. She is beautiful . . . as far as beauty can ever be objec-tive, of course. But I'm sure there are things you can do, Sarit. You're an artist after all.'

Sarit ignores her comment. She says, 'Look, I'm not sure I

want to do anything at all. We'll have to take it step by step. You know where I stand now. So this time the ball is in your court.' She says this not as a ploy, not to bait Juliann, but because she means it, because despite some inexplicable lure, a part of her too would feel relieved to hang up now knowing that the ordeal was over before it had begun. She carries on, she says, 'Look, Juliann, if you decide to go elsewhere I will understand. I won't charge you for the time. Because even if the psychiatrist is happy for me to go ahead and even if I can find a way to help Felicia, after that I need a long hard think to see how the whole thing sits with me.'

Juliann chews on her pen, wishes she were smoking. Beneath the desk the cat prepares once more to loop his tail and trap her ankle. By the window Sarit waits. In her anonymous, unfamiliar surroundings in some godforsaken Chicago suburb Felicia stares up at the ceiling. With a mixture of sadness, determination and ambition Juliann thinks of her. In the US government offices the prosecutors drown under piles of documents. In their cells, despite the initial almost irrefutable findings at the detention hearing, the colleagues of the late Alessandro Rinaldi want to plead not guilty to the charges of racketeering involving murder. Patrolling his neighbourhood, the policeman who found Alessandro's body hopes for recognition and a job with the FBI. And in her office Juliann breathes out a sigh and with it this: 'Sarit, this is a very risky business on my part. A calculated risk, of course. The whole idea is that it is kept so low-profile that it has no profile. So here's the deal. You and I will meet somewhere suitably private for cocktails. We'll down a few Bloody Marys and you can tell me all there is to know about the two people you feel you need to involve in this. And we'll take things from there. How does that sound to you?'

And Sarit says, 'Juliann, after this conversation the alcohol part sounds perfect. I'll pass you on to Emily and we can make a plan.'

'Fabulous, Sarit. Fabulous,' says Juliann and she grabs the fat and furry cat from beneath her desk and lifts him into her arms in one fell self-congratulatory swoop.

THIRTY-FOUR

The fantasy of fresco was never far from Ramsi's thoughts. As a teenager, as a young sculptor in his twenties, as a maturing artist in his thirties and his forties he had been drawn by fresco only as an onlooker. He had travelled once, alone, from the Côte d'Azur to Florence and in the darkened silence lit by flames of prayer he had stood in awe in the Brancacci chapel of Santa Maria del Carmine before the fresco of Masaccio. In Santa Maria Novella too, for ages he had stood before the painted stories told within the fresco of the Trinity. And he had reached up, then, above his head as if to touch a dove that flew in colour from the masterpiece and wondered how it must be to own the talent of a sculptor and a painter all at once. Behind him an older woman in a purple shawl had seem him yearn to touch the bird and said, 'You know, they shouldn't attribute these frescos to one artist alone . . . the sculptors worked with painters and the painters worked with sculptors,' and then whispering, getting closer to him, she added, 'But that's not the way it goes down in the history books . . . the biographers were paid to give one man all the glory.'

In a moment the woman had disappeared amongst the tourists and the worshippers, but the thought, the idea of the sculptor working with the painter, creating bas-relief in synchronicity, had stayed in Ramsi's mind. The reality, though, of working with other artists had eluded him, for a loner works alone. An introvert hoards ideas within, shares them not as they unfold, but only in their final form, only once they are solid enough for him to hide behind them. And though Ramsi had never been able to reach out far enough, he had dreamt, as we all do at some time in our lives, of the horizons he might have touched had his personality been other than it was.

And even though he had only once seen Sarit touch art, her fingers coloured with the stains of crushed red stone in Santa Fe that stained his flesh in turn, he knew not just from the pictures of changed faces that he'd seen, but intuitively and by the way she touched him, by the shapes she traced on his skin, that her art was pure and that if there had been a way to void the past, both his and hers, then together they might have made art with the creativity, the depth and the intensity with which they had begun to make love.

He thought of this not for himself alone, not just for the two of them together, but for Sarit and for the wish that grew in him that she should rediscover all that she had once had. And so in the beginning when she came to him, when she held his hands in hers across the table in the moody little crêperie on Clark Street, swore him to secrecy, told him the story and said to him, 'I know you only like to work alone, but would you just see her with me?' Ramsi had said yes for Sarit. He had said yes not just because he wanted to help her, but also because he wanted to draw her further into his world. He had said yes in the beginning for the fantasy of fresco.

And for more reasons than one Juliann had agreed to Ramsi's involvement. She had assessed the risk of exposure and disclosure to be no greater than if Sarit had consulted her medical colleagues. In some ways perhaps the risk was less, because from the hospital canteen to the wards and back again word could spread like virulent bacteria.

Juliann knew too, for she of course had done her research, that Ramsi was an acclaimed sculptor, a loner, who shunned publicity and so she was convinced that the help he would give to Sarit would be that of an aesthetic purist prepared to support his lover in her work. She had questioned Sarit in depth. She had asked her why she needed to involve outsiders and had said, 'This isn't body art, you know. It's serious stuff.

I mean, do you usually ask your lover how you should change people's faces?' but in truth she was able to see why the changing of Felicia would be daunting.

'She's going to be some project, Sarit,' Sammy Schwarz had said, for Sarit had insisted that he should see her first. There was little point, she had said, in her meeting with the girl until Sammy had checked her out.

'How d'you mean a project, Sam . . . ?' Sarit had asked. 'Mentally or physically?'

'Physically first of all,' he said, leaning against the back of his sofa, feet in once white socks up on the coffee table as he talked with her on the phone. 'You'll see for yourself. She's like Botticelli's *Venus* . . . you know, that perfect, pure, blonde beauty. Except with corkscrew curls. She has those proportions that are meant to denote objective beauty. But mentally too this is a really tough one, Sarit . . . I mean, she's been through . . . or rather she's still going through total hell.'

'Sam . . .' Sarit says, 'you're trying to tell me to stay away from this, aren't you?'

As he answers her he weighs each word. He says, 'No. I don't believe I am saying that. The girl's obviously not in a good place. She's distraught. In her shoes who wouldn't be? She's definitely showing some signs of early post-traumatic stress syndrome. She's grieving and she's afraid and she's isolated all at once. But I do think she's rational. Between the bouts of crying I saw a highly intelligent young woman . . . She's a real mixture. In some ways she's mature and in some ways she's unworldly . . . she's been very protected by her family. But she's totally in touch with reality and, as far as I could see, aware of the implications of her decision.'

He stops talking for a moment. And on the other end of the phone while he thinks, he wipes his glasses with a hand-kerchief the colour of his socks.

Had she seen him Sarit would have laughed, but impatient now she says, 'Go on, Sam.'

307

'Look, ask me if it would be better if she waited and the answer has got to be yes. But that's the catch 22, isn't it? Part of the reason she's distraught is her fear of what could happen to her which, given the nature of these monsters and what they did to her boyfriend, seems pretty legitimate to me. So she's got to know where she stands. She's got to see a way forward.'

And intense now, intent on getting Sammy's answer, Sarit says, 'So what are you saying, Sam? Cut to the chase. If you were me would you do it if you could or wouldn't you?'

He says. 'Yes, Sarit.' And then again, 'Yes, I think I might. On balance I think I would. Women change their faces these days for much lesser reasons than this, don't they? You know that only too well,' and his tone lightens. He puts on a silly high-pitched voice with a Chicago accent and says, 'Ooh, I'd like a new nose this morning. Let me call up Dr Kleinmann. Ooh, my lips look a little thin. Let's get a pout this week instead of a new Mercedes sports. Let me call up Dr Kleinmann.'

Sarit laughs, says, 'Glad to know you hold my profession in such high regard,' and then, 'What shall I do, Sam? Tell me what to do.'

'Ah, now there's a question for a therapist. What shall I do? I can't answer that one. Only you can say if you feel up to the task from an aesthetic point of view. And that's got to be a serious concern. Look, Sarit, for what it's worth, I've given you my opinion. I think she's traumatised but sound of mind underneath it all. The one piece of advice I can give you is that for Felicia's sake you should make a decision quickly . . . because if you do decide against it . . . and you might, she'll have to go through this whole process all over again . . . and I can tell you one thing, this is what she wants, and Juliann and her people will give her whatever she needs to keep her happy. They need her. If she refuses to testify their case is history.'

'Hm,' Sarit says. 'Yes, I'd thought of that.'

'And another thing, Sarit. I'm pretty sure she'd want to have it done at this point even if they didn't want her to testify. Even if they dropped the case I guarantee that girl would not be walking around here or anywhere else with the same face for too much longer . . . Talk to Ramsi, Sarit,' Sammy says. 'Get his opinion or get another plastic surgeon involved and then decide. But it's your call. I'm only a layperson but I think this is a job for a real artist.'

The artist, the sculptor on his way to help Sarit, walks towards her surgery. A brisk walk, with direction, his hands in the pockets of the worn dark-brown suede sheepskin that he wears unbuttoned over his navy sweater. He is unused to midday light and midday commerce and in the open air, in the centre of the city, where people look one another up and down as they stand and wait to cross the street, he is somehow out of place. So that there is an incongruity, a sense of anachronism about the classical sculptor walking in the throngs of people past the Gap, past Starbucks, past Banana Republic towards the Bloomingdale building. Ramsi Riyad belongs in the nooks and crannies and wooden stairwells of his home behind the red engraved door on Wells, in the dark corridors of the Art Institute, in the untidy loftiness of Albert's foundry. He does not belong in modern architecture, in mirrored buildings, in shiny modern elevators.

On his way up to the eighteenth floor he is first to walk into the glass elevator, which within a minute is filled to capacity, and he finds himself in the corner at the back, crushed on one side against a teenage girl with acne on her chin and in the crease of her cleavage, and on the other pressed side to side against a young man with a tiny child strapped to him, hidden in the sling to the front of his body. Pressed against the young father while a woman wearing too much musk says, 'Let me take a little peek.' The father shifts his position slightly so she can peer inside the sling. 'Ooh,' she says. 'So cute. What a gorgeous boy.' The father smiles. 'A girl,' he says. 'Marissa.'

The woman says, 'What a beautiful name.' Ramsi turns away.

'Eighteenth floor . . . Who wanted eighteenth?' The voice jolts Ramsi from his other world and he begins to push his way out of the elevator.

Along the corridor he turns right as Sarit has told him to do, walks past the doors of doctors, dentists and of dermatologists till he reaches room 1803. On the side of the oak-panelled door he notices the tiny wooden oblong container that Jews nail to their doors and that has been there since long before Sarit took over the office. The minute mezuzah that he knows contains a scroll with 'Honour thy father and thy mother . . . Thou shalt not worship idols' and the rest of the Ten Commandments written in Hebrew on parchment in black ink.

He looks at the plaque on the door. Dr S. Kleinmann. He feels a swell of pride. He rings the bell. She opens. She takes his hand. He strokes her cheek.

'Hello.'

'Hello.'

She smiles at him. That smile. A new setting for the two of them. A new chapter.

Emily has been sent out for the afternoon and Sarit walks past her empty desk ahead of Ramsi. He moves behind her to the door of her surgery. 'May I, Doctor?' he asks her on the threshold. She crooks her finger, leads him over to a huge, ornate, bronze-framed mirror on the wall. In front of the mirror she stands behind him, puts her hands on his cheeks. 'Anything you'd like me to change for you?' she asks.

In her hands, he looks at himself. His own rugged, dark-skinned, unpolished, bearded face between her sculpted hands. He says in his heavy accent, his deep, thick voice, 'Nothing . . . Don't change anything at all. If we could stay just like this I would want to change nothing, Sarit.' And he takes her hand and brushes it against his mouth. She runs her finger over his lips feeling the ridges and the roughness, and she stands there holding his face still, holding the two of them there in that moment, as if their physical stillness might stop time. He says, 'This reminds me of something my sculpture teacher in Alexandria once taught me . . .' and in Arabic he quotes at her, '*Bos enta nahat fi batne yadi.*'

'What does it mean?' she asks.

He says, '"See, I shall not forget you, for you are sculpted in the palm of my hand" . . . I think it's from Isaiah.'

'You scholar,' she says and takes her hands from his cheeks as she speaks. At that moment, at the time when Sarit says to him, 'You scholar,' outside the building a black limousine with tinted windows pulls up opposite the main door. The passengers in the back might have been a wealthy mother and daughter accompanying one another on a shopping spree. They might have been patients coming to visit their doctor for a consultation. Or they might have come for a post-surgical follow-up appointment, the younger woman's face shrouded to protect her from the elements and from embarrassment.

Autumn was at its close and the air, if not quite cold enough for woollen scarves and balaclavas, was on the verge of it at least. So that as Felicia walked head down across the pavement through the revolving doors into the building, as she stood with Juliann in the elevator where Ramsi had been pressed some minutes before next to the father with his child, one of the shoppers stared at her, at her round blue eyes peeping out above the shrouds and to herself she said, 'Oh Lord, the cold is really on its way. I'd better get myself some winter gear.'

And as Juliann and Felicia are travelling up in the elevator, as Juliann is saying to her, 'You're all right, aren't you?' in Sarit's surgery she and Ramsi have moved away from one another at the mirror and he is pacing slowly round the room, touching other mirrors, framed certificates, avoiding children's toys, just as she in Albert's foundry had touched the pots, the wax, the clay, the bronze and avoided the thick and furry paintbrush.

With the ring of the bell, Sarit goes to answer the door, ushers Juliann and Felicia into the hallway and Ramsi, standing by Sarit's desk, hears a deep, mature woman's voice saying, 'Sarit, this is Felicia.'

He hears Sarit say, 'Nice to meet you, Felicia. Can I get you a coffee or some water?' Of Felicia's voice, though, he hears nothing. No response. He stands alone and waits. As though he were listening to a radio programme, he can do no more than conjure up the girl's nod, her shrug or the shaking of the head. He hears Sarit say, 'Go on in, Juliann. You know the way. I'll get the coffee. I'll be through in just a minute.'

And seconds later an assertive woman with hair and lipstick to match her voice is moving towards Ramsi, holding out her hand with its stubby fingers and saying, 'You're Mr Riyad, of course,' and behind her, over her shoulder as he shakes Juliann's hand, he sees the frightened eyes of the thin figure standing by the door and shrouded still in grey.

Sarit walks in with coffee. Ramsi looks at her. He takes her in. He thinks, 'She has a presence, this woman that I'm with. She really does.'

Juliann says, 'Oh, and this is Felicia, Ramsi.' He nods. He doesn't see the weak half-smile Felicia gives beneath the shrouds, but he does see some humour in the situation. As though he were being introduced to a mummy, for Felicia has not yet begun to remove her scarf. Juliann pulls out a chair for Felicia. Sarit moves to sit at her desk, with Ramsi just behind her, ready to observe, putting his hand to the pocket of his denim shirt, about to roll a cigarette through force of habit, before he remembers where he is. And Juliann says, 'Felicia, remember I told you about Ramsi and that he would be here just to observe today and to help Sarit.'

She nods and Sarit, smiling, pointing at Ramsi says, 'Just ignore him, Felicia. We'll treat him like a medical student.'

Looking at Sarit pouring coffee from a perspex pot, listening to her voice, Ramsi thinks, 'How interesting. Her tone is

312

gentle with the girl. I've hardly heard her speak like this before
. . . as though she's speaking to a child.'

Sarit says to Juliann and Felicia, 'Take milk and sugar if you
want it.' She has forgotten to offer coffee to Ramsi.

Felicia takes off her dark-grey hooded winter coat. She
wears ill-fitting black jeans and a worn green sweater. She
begins to unwind her woollen scarf. She moves slowly as she
does it, as if reticent, as if the face she is about to show were
disfigured, scarred or burnt instead of beautiful.

From different angles both Ramsi and Sarit are watching.
Waiting. Felicia feels their eyes on her. In Ramsi's mind as soon
as he sees Felicia uncovered, as soon as Sarit begins to speak
to her, their work together on the fresco in bas-relief begins.
Sarit looks at Felicia, thinks, 'She's beautiful. Yes, she's really
gorgeous,' and she turns back to Ramsi for some silent
acknowledgement of what she sees. Ramsi looks at her and
nods.

Turning back to Felicia, Sarit says, 'I don't need to ask you
what the situation is, Felicia, because I already know a great
deal, but tell me a little about your meeting with Dr Schwarz.'

Felicia is weighing up Sarit. She wonders why she wears
no make-up, why she wears no jewellery save for her silver
sports watch. She wonders too if the immediate and surprising
sense of trust she feels in Sarit's presence is just desperate and
misplaced.

And the silence Sarit gives Felicia in which to think, the
silence that no one tries to fill, is Ramsi's haven. Now he can
fall back into known territory, sitting, as if in Kingston Mines,
studying Felicia's face, using it as an *objet d'art*. For now, even
with the others in the room, with his creativity he is alone,
but later, as soon as he begins to talk to Sarit about Felicia's
face in his ideas he will be both inspired and constrained by
her input, in the way that one great artist cannot help but be
both inspired and limited when working with another.

Felicia sits up very straight. Beneath the porcelain complexion the girl looks drawn. Her saucer eyes are rimmed with red. And the frailty of her that he sees is not so much in the contours of her face but rather in the expression behind it.

Sarit says to Felicia, 'Dr Schwarz says the two of you had a good meeting.' Felicia shrugs. Sarit asks, 'You didn't like him?'

Her thick blonde corkscrew curls falling over her face, Felicia says, 'He was OK. He kept asking why I'm going to have this done . . . because I am, you know,' she says, her voice rising, 'I'm going to . . . whether it's you or someone else who helps me. And I told him why . . . he kept going on that he was trying to make sure that I'm doing this for the right reasons. In the end he said he understood . . . so I don't want to answer any more questions from you. Please. Do you know how many questions I've answered in the last few weeks? I can't any more. I just want to be left alone. If you're going to help me, please, let's just get on with it.'

Sarit sips from her coffee, says, 'Look, Felicia, I don't want to make you go through the whole thing again, but I need to hear your reasons for myself. It would be unethical for me not to.'

The girl exhales a sigh, as if to say, 'Again? Must I really go through all of this again?'

But she begins to talk and as she does so Ramsi watches.

'Look,' she says, her voice at first controlled, 'I'm like a vegetable. I can't sleep, I can't think . . . I . . . I've been through all this stuff before with the first shrink and then with that other shrink you made me go to,' she says, turning to Juliann. 'What more do you all want from me? Just tell me for Christ's sake . . . What do you want to know? That I'm terrified? That I'll curl up and die if you don't help me and I have to walk around like this?' And leaning on her hands, she puts her head on the desk, so that her hair falls over her arms.

In a gentle tone of voice Sarit says, 'We need to talk if I'm going to help you, Felicia.'

Felicia lifts her head. From where he sits Ramsi thinks she's going to cry. He sees it by the ripples of the muscles, by the movement in her neck as she swallows. But Felicia fights the tears. She says, 'Doctor . . .' and she clears her throat.

'Sarit.'

'Sarit, I need . . . to look different . . . I don't just want to . . . I need to. It's all I can think about. As well as . . . as well as . . . you know . . . Alessandro,' and then the whisper, then the changing of the face that Ramsi sees, the movement upwards of the full cheeks, and not the suspicion this time, but the certainty that she will weep.

'I . . . need . . . to . . . look different. What's the big deal about that? You . . . you change the noses of these vain little pussycats who have nothing more to worry about than being pretty and we're talking about my life here and . . . and you're hesitating. Do you understand? Or don't you all care if I'm killed . . . like him? Is that it . . . ? I warned him about it, you know. I knew what would happen . . .' She sobs. She says, 'And now . . . I'm warning you. They'll find me if I walk around like this.'

From the side Ramsi sees his lover stretch her arm out to the girl, he sees her press a paper handkerchief into Felicia's hand, the practical gesture, an excuse for an emotional one. He watches and feels proud of Sarit. A little as he had felt when she had stretched on tiptoes readying the lines of her sailboat. Sarit doesn't say to Felicia as she cries, 'Wait a few moments. You don't need to talk now if you don't want to,' because she has understood, as Juliann had done at the zoo, that despite the girl's distress she needs to seize the moment. And so she says, 'So, Felicia. Talk to me.'

'I can't any more,' Felicia says as the tears flow, as she twists and twists the paper tissue in her hands, then tears it into shreds. 'For all I care I could die in that godforsaken place they've put me in.' She turns to Juliann, a half-apology on her face through the tears.

And by way of explanation Juliann says to Ramsi and Sarit,

'You know we've moved Felicia to a secure location till the trial.'

They nod. Felicia, now unprompted, in a tone of voice half desperate, half sarcastic says, 'But one day, one day, who knows I might just want a life again. And I can't have it with . . . this . . . this . . . face . . . can I?' she says, prodding herself in the cheek, almost digging her nails into her own skin. 'And I'm not stupid, you know,' she adds, turning again to Juliann. 'I know the reason you've videotaped me talking about what . . . what I saw . . . and . . . and what I know. It's in case they bump me off before the trial . . . all that stuff you gave me about being worried in case I forgot the details of my story. I'm not stupid, you know, Juliann . . . So you've got what you want from me and when I ask you to help me to save my own skin all I get is more questions.'

The eye of a sculptor, the eye of the sculptor who watches Felicia is drawn not just to two dimensions but to three, not just to the face as it seems straight on, but to the movement of its lines and of its shadows, to the possibilities and permutations that they bring. As Felicia speaks Ramsi watches her face in movement, the altering poses of its angles and its shapes. In his intellectual mind he knows he is here to help Sarit to change the face he sees, but still, in this room, he cannot yet think of change. He cannot help but do what he has always done and sculpt her in his head the way he sees her now.

And Sarit, still sipping coffee black and bitter, leans across her desk and once more says, 'How do you think I can help you, Felicia?'

The girl, though not aggressive by nature, snaps, 'Why are you playing this game with me? You know exactly how you can help me. You can change the shape of every goddamned thing on my face.'

At first Ramsi is of no help to the girl for as he sculpts in his mind he changes not one single thing. In his head he uses not terracotta but clay that is chalky white. He moulds the

316

clay, bends it with his wooden tools, his wire loop to shape the lips, the cheeks, the nose and eyes. And working in his head the words that form are those that Sammy Schwarz had used. 'Botticelli's *Venus* . . . hm, she's not so far from that.'

'Do you think,' asks Sarit, handing the tortoiseshell mirror to Felicia, 'that you are beautiful?'

Felicia turns her head away, puts her hand up to reject the mirror. 'I don't want to look,' she says. 'Everything has changed for me. I don't care if I'm beautiful or not. I care if I'm recognisable.' And then, in a quiet voice, almost a whisper, as if she knows she shouldn't say it, 'If no one helps me I'm going to end it.'

No one speaks. In the room there is total silence save for the ticking of the clock. No one moves. No one opens their mouth until Sarit asks, 'Is that a threat, Felicia?'

Ramsi looks at Sarit, the concentration on her face, the need to understand the motives of the girl. And once more the rush he feels is powerful. A rush of love? A rush again of pride? Pride that Sarit is able to touch the core, for she is right, of course. If Felicia is threatening suicide then her state of mind is indeed too fragile for her to say with certainty that she dares to change the way she looks.

And Felicia, perhaps honest, perhaps just clever, wipes her tears, pushes her curls away from her face with the flats of her hands and says, 'Look, it wasn't a threat. I'm sorry. I didn't mean it. I just wanted to shock you into taking me seriously. What I mean is I'll die inside with fear and paranoia if they don't get me first,' and then, lowering her head, she says, 'I can choose to give up on life or I can choose this way,' and before the sobs begin again she says, 'I think that Alessandro would have wanted this way for me.'

Her head is down as she says that, as she blurts out again, 'Alessandro would have wanted this way for me,' so that though he cannot see the expression in her eyes, Ramsi has a view of her profile and her forehead from a different angle and that part of her too he can fashion in his mind. The high forehead that for a moment has taken him aback, that demands nothing new of him. Nothing new at all. For so many times before he has smoothed out clay to sculpt a forehead that was high.

Sarit stands up. She says not a word but from a small antique table behind her desk she takes her camera. She walks over to Felicia and begins to click. She says, 'Stand up, Felicia,' and from the left she clicks, from the right, from the front, from above and from below. Ramsi watches and imagines Sarit as a photographer. He can see it. Sarit, free-spirited in faded jeans and a loose white cotton shirt, her camera slung over her shoulder. He can see it far better even than he can see her as a surgeon. With the clicking Felicia relaxes just a little. As if she thinks that with each click Sarit's acquiescence has increased. And the thought that crosses Ramsi's mind then is this one: 'Sarit's going to want us to work together from the photographs now we've seen Felicia once. Of course, that's the way she'll want it. That's how she works. I know it is,' and suddenly, without knowing why, he feels disturbed and disconcerted. As if in front of Juliann, with Sarit squatting on the floor at Felicia's feet, he wants to blurt out, 'We can't work from photographs alone, you know.' He wants to say, 'You need the real material to create a fresco. We need the girl in front of us. We can't do it any other way.'

But it is Juliann and not Ramsi who speaks. It is she who asks, 'Dr Kleinmann, how are you planning to use these photographs you're taking?'

'I'm not planning anything yet in this case. But in general what I do is scan them into the computer and make changes so that I can get a pretty good idea of how the patient will look after surgery . . . I mean, once she's healed.'

'I see,' says Julian. 'Well, I'm sorry to be difficult, but you can't do that with Felicia.'

'Why not?' says Sarit putting her camera down on her desk, then sitting down herself.

318

'Because we don't want photographs of the way Felicia's going to look hanging around anywhere. It's just not a good idea.'

'But we'd destroy them afterwards,' says Sarit.

'No, I'm sorry. This whole thing has got to be about minimising risk for Felicia now,' she says, leaning across, putting her hand on the girl's arm. 'Having any paper or computer image of the way she's going to look is dangerous. Isn't there another way for you to work?'

And before Sarit can answer, from behind her she hears Ramsi's voice. Ramsi who has said not one word, but who answers for her now and says, 'Yes, I'm sure there's another way to work,' and then, looking at Sarit, 'You can just concentrate on the individual features. You and I will talk it through. I'll be able to visualise what will work as a whole and what won't.'

Sarit looks at him surprised. Not because of what he has said, for she knows that Ramsi can sculpt faces in his head and visualise the outcome even before he starts. But she is surprised to hear his voice at all, because for once she had almost forgotten he was there.

She does not answer Ramsi directly, but to Felicia she says, 'Felicia, I am not going to commit myself right now, but tell me, do you have any ideas about how I could help to change your image?'

Sarit is kneeling down beside Felicia and when she asks the question, when she says, 'Do you have any ideas how I could help to change your image?' and then adds, 'Here, take the hand mirror and let's talk,' this time Felicia takes the mirror from her and patient and surgeon begin to exchange creative thoughts. Sarit's voice is quiet now to match Felicia's. Ramsi lets the words flow over him and turns the picture of the two of them into a silent movie in his mind. The girl tracing the lines of her own face, Sarit touching Felicia's face, the picture of Sarit's hands on Felicia's face, holding the mirror at different angles, nodding and shaking her head. A glimpse of Sarit's own profile reflected in the mirror. A glimpse of Felicia's face reflected in another mirror on the desk. A glimpse of lives fragmented and reflected. And with the soundless pictures comes an opportunity in Ramsi's mind. An opportunity for Ramsi and Sarit to create, to build together, work together, weave together.

The weaving begins in his studio on Wells Street in the early evening, cross-legged on the floor where they sit by the low dark table.

'Show me,' he says. One by one she hands him the polaroid photos. Front view. Right view. Left view. Pursed lips. Open lips. Head up. Head down. He holds each one in his hands for a long time.

She says, 'I have my ideas. But what do you think? Is there anything at all I can do with her that isn't going to make her lose all she has?'

He says, 'Tell me what you think, Sarit.'

'I wish she was ugly.'

He laughs, puts his hand on the curve of Sarit's bare shoulder, covering her tattoo. 'You're funny,' he says.

'Hm,' she says, and then, 'Well?'

'Yes, I think there's plenty we can do. She's beautiful, but it's not a mysterious beauty. There's something we can do with that.'

She notices the *we*. She doesn't mind it. She too is in the spirit of the fresco. 'So don't be cagey, Ramsi Riyad,' she says and, as if by way of persuasion, kisses him on the side of the neck. 'Tell me your ideas,' and then, as an aside the artist in her speaks. She says, 'What material would you use if you were sculpting her?'

'Sculpting her?' he says. 'I suppose that skin would lend itself to ragou . . . you know the chalky white clay . . . or to porcelain . . . Yes, porcelain would be better still. Anything else would be too dark,' and as he pronounces the word, 'dark,' a shadow crosses Ramsi's face.

Then, as though playing a card, he puts the photograph of Felicia face down on the table and is silent for a moment. Then he says, 'I can't do it. I can't work like this just from photos. That's not art. I need the real thing in front of me, Sarit.'

'You mean Felicia?'

He nods.

'But you've seen her . . . and you sometimes work from photos and sketches too. I know you do. So do I. I work from the computer images I create of the way she'll look when I've operated. That's how I see the whole of the way things will be. It's even more important if I'm working on more than one feature.'

He says, 'Yes, but this time you can't do that.'

'True.'

'So, I rest my case . . . we need to see her again,' he says . . . 'maybe here.'

She looks at him. 'Why?'

He answers her question with a question. 'Do you honestly feel you've spent enough time with her to think about radically changing her face if you're not going to be using all your modern tech stuff?'

She thinks for a moment. 'Maybe not,' she says. 'I suppose I'll have to use you as my computer.'

'My point exactly,' he says.

She pokes him in the ribs.

'Ouch.'

'So come on, Rams. Let's talk about creation. What's your bottom line?'

'For you to change the form of the cheekbones . . . sculpt them almost.'

'Hm . . . I thought so too.'

'Great minds . . .'

'Perhaps.'

'Partner.'

'Perhaps.'

'I hope.'

'Me too.'

'Like a fresco.'

She laughs. 'I never thought of that.'

He says, 'So ask Juliann to organise something.'

'She'll say no.'

'So ask till she says yes.'

'Yes,' says Juliann.

Sarit raises her eyebrows.

'I've sussed out your personality, Sarit. If you can't do it your way, you won't do it at all.'

Sarit laughs. The Gabriella laugh.

Juliann says, 'But not in Ramsi's studio, Sarit. No way.'

'Why not?'

'Because I've brought her downtown twice and we can't do that again. It's just too risky. I probably shouldn't have done it in the first place but she categorically refused to see a surgeon out of state.'

'Then what?'

'You'll have to come out to where we have Felicia. And you'll have to make it fast. We need to get things moving.'

'I'm doing what I can, but I still have very mixed feelings about this, Juliann. I'm just not sure I want to do it.'

'Get sure, Sarit. We're not playing art class here,' and then, 'I'm sorry. I don't mean to snap. I'm under pressure. We all are. Can you drive out with me tomorrow night?'

In the back of the car Sarit says she wants to sleep. 'There's a blanket back there,' Juliann says.

'Thanks.' She lies down, her long legs bent. She covers herself in the red tartan, scratchy wool.

On the highway at night with the unknown ahead of them there is little talk at first, till in the street-lit blackness against the background of the blues, Juliann turns to Ramsi in the passenger seat and says, 'So, Mr Riyad, are there sculptors in your family?'

'No.'

'So where does it come from?'

'My hands,' he says.

In the back Sarit stifles a laugh.

Juliann is not intimidated. She has spent her life dealing with complicated characters. She asks Ramsi, 'So what inspires you?'

'Women.' Ramsi reaches his hand over the back of his chair to talk to Sarit. She takes it. She laces her fingers between his.

Juliann says, 'I love the *Nadia* series, Ramsi. What inspired that?'

Ramsi lets Sarit's hand go. The road ahead is empty. Juliann picks up speed. 'My daughter,' Ramsi says.

Felicia is not in a good frame of mind when they arrive. They have driven through the southwestern suburbs, each one more dismal and depressing than the next, till they reach Lemont, with its dull uniform town houses and mid-rises, and its feel of mediocrity. They walk up the path towards a non-descript brick building. Juliann unlocks the front door, they take the lift up to the fourth floor and inside Juliann calls out, 'It's me. It's us.'

No answer. She says to Ramsi and Sarit, 'Wait here a moment,' and leaves them standing in the hallway. The paint on the walls is an eggshell colour. The carpets are wine and grey and flowery. The lamp is a cheap designer model trying to look expensive.

'Depressing,' Ramsi whispers.

'Really depressing,' Sarit whispers back. 'What the hell are we doing here?'

'Come on in,' says Juliann, beckoning them in and then, as though she were a nurse talking of her ailing patient, 'She's not having the greatest day.'

On the edge of the single bed, on the thick wine-coloured spread that matches the curtains that match the flowers in the carpet Felicia sits in pyjamas and a white robe. The artist's model waiting, staring at the poor copy of Monet's *Water Lilies* ahead of her on the wall.

'Hi, Felicia.'

She turns her head towards them. 'Hi.'

On her behalf Sarit feels an overwhelming sense of loneliness and isolation. A sense of identification with the girl, with the young woman cut off from warmth, from love in some strange room somewhere. Ramsi looks at Felicia and feels his gut twist. As though he were making a visit to some young woman in an asylum.

Sarit says, 'OK, Felicia, shall we get down to business?'

The girl looks at Sarit, her expression pleading. 'I'm waiting. I've been waiting for you all day,' she says.

In the middle of the room they place a high-backed chair and ask Felicia to sit down. Ramsi stands on one side of it, Sarit on the other. Juliann goes to sit on the bed, leaning back against the flowery wall, next to the stuffed donkey that Felicia has brought with her from home.

'Do you mind,' Sarit asks Felicia, 'if we talk about your face as if you were a work of art?'

'Anything,' Felicia says.

'She is a work of art,' Ramsi says.

She smiles up at Ramsi. The weak smile again. 'For you two . . . yes, that's probably what I am. So I suppose you'd like to sculpt me.'

'Yes,' he says, 'if there had been time. In porcelain.'

She closes her eyes. Sarit and Ramsi kneel down on either side of her. 'You go first, Rams,' Sarit says.

Close to Felicia's face, businesslike now, he says, 'Look, if you want to retain her beauty, the way to do it is not to touch the proportions.'

'Thanks for telling me,' she says, sarcastic.

He touches Felicia's chin. 'But you could make her stronger here.'

'An implant,' says Sarit.

He makes a sign to Sarit with his fingers bent, a sign of force, as if to say 'stronger'. 'You could give her some more strength here.'

Sarit says, 'Not too much.'

'No, a little . . . just more definition.'

Sarit puts her finger on the slope of Felicia's nose. Felicia notices how her skin feels soft. She wants Sarit to stay there with her hands on her face, to soothe her. She has to stop herself from reaching up to grab her hand to hold it there. Sarit says, 'This nose is perfect. This is my biggest challenge. What can I possibly do here?'

'A bump?' he says.

She laughs. 'Are you crazy?'

'A slight one,' he says. 'It will look beautiful . . . dignified even.'

'The jury's out,' she says.

He says, 'There is no other way.'

Sarit takes her hand from the slope of Felicia's nose. She places her palm on the left side of the girl's cheek. She asks Felicia, 'Are you OK?' Her eyes still shut, the girl nods.

Ramsi puts his palm on her right cheek.

'Her cheeks are rounded enough for me to work with,' Sarit says. She runs her fingers down the girl's face as if sculpting, as if heightening Felicia's cheekbones. 'Ah yes,' she thinks, 'cheekbones. They will change it all.'

'Cheekbones,' he says. 'You can take away from here. She'll look regal.'

'Yes,' she says, 'that's the one thing that I feel confident about.' Across Felicia's face the tips of Sarit's and Ramsi's fingers touch. For a brief moment Felicia feels almost safe. The child with her parents wiping her grazed cheeks when the big boys have pushed her over on the gravel.

'My eyes,' Felicia says. 'What are you going to do about them?'

Sarit laughs. 'We're getting there . . . any ideas?'

She says something in Italian. '*Come una bambina sei . . .* Alessandro used to tell me that . . . that they're like a child's eye. Round like saucers.'

Sarit says, 'I can't lift the brow. She doesn't have quite enough space between her brow and her lid to hide the scar.'

He says, 'That's not how I see her anyway . . . Do you have a pencil on you? I'll show you how I see things.'

'No,' says Sarit. She says no, not just because she never wears make-up, but because she never carries a pencil of any sort in her bag. She hasn't carried a pencil around with her for years.

Felicia sees her chance. She says, 'Sarit, why don't you wear any make-up?'

Had it come from another patient Sarit might have baulked. She might have said, 'Do I have to paint my face just because that's what's expected of me?' But now she laughs, because from Felicia she doesn't mind the question. She is pleased to hear her engaging, pleased to feel her interest piqued. She says, 'Because I've always been a tomboy I suppose.'

'So why a plastic surgeon?'

'My hands made their own decision.'

And Ramsi, focusing for a moment on Sarit's face, his voice quiet now, says, 'You don't need make-up, Sarit. You really don't,' as though in the room there were just the two of them.

Sarit smiles at him and then changes the subject, for Ramsi's words have reminded her of a phrase that she heard all through her teenage years, a phrase that she hears now in her head: '*Von der Natur geschmückt,*' Max used to say to her in German. 'Nature's given you all the make-up that you need,' and then he'd add, 'You don't need to paint your face, Sarit. Your mother never needed to either.'

And Sarit says, 'Come on, let's get back to Felicia.'

At the mention of an eye pencil Juliann had fished into her bag, had jumped up from the bed with it, and now Ramsi squats there opposite Felicia, on the other side of her with

Juliann's kajal pencil in his hand. 'Can I draw on you?' he asks Felicia.

She nods.

He says, 'Sarit, look here,' and on one side of Felicia's face from the corner of her eye he draws the tiniest line that slants just slightly upwards. Sarit nods. She sees his point and though in her mind she had created almost the same change, the slight lifting of the ligament on the outer corner of the eye, somehow she feels resistance. 'It will be difficult,' she says.

'It wouldn't spoil her,' he says. 'Not at all.'

She looks at him. In his voice she hears an unfamiliar note. Not quite insistence, but more than coaxing. To herself she thinks, 'Maybe it's not that easy to work with someone after all.'

He says, 'It's not so easy to mesh two egos, is it?'

She glares at him. A mock glare. He smiles at her. Sarit stands up. She stretches her arms and legs. She says, 'Felicia, there are possibilities that are not a million miles from the ideas you expressed yourself.'

'Is that a yes?' Felicia asks.

'It's not a yes. But it's not a no either. Juliann and I need to do some serious talking.'

And Juliann who until now hasn't said one word pipes up and, half smiling, says, 'You know what, Felicia, if Sarit won't do it we'll enlist Ramsi's services.' They all laugh when Juliann says that. All four of them and in Felicia's laugh, which Sarit has heard for the first time, she knows that the girl will some-how survive her ordeal.

But as if her laugh has made her guilty, with the guilt one feels when time begins to drag tragedy behind it into a new reality, as if the sound of her own laughter has startled her and been almost too much exertion, Felicia says to no one in par-ticular, 'I'm so tired. I've had enough. I'm sorry. I just need to be alone.'

Sarit puts her hand on the girl's head, says, 'Come on. We'll leave you. I'll talk to Juliann later and you and I will speak again.'

Juliann stands up from the bed.

Ramsi says, 'But wait, we haven't finished. I haven't given you even half of my ideas.' In his voice there is a note of panic.

'Ramsi,' Sarit says, 'come on, Felicia's tired. You and I can talk at home.'

'But we need . . .'

'Come on,' she says. 'Let's go.'

And Juliann says to Felicia, 'I'll be here first thing in the morning. I didn't even ask you. Did you eat what I left in the fridge?'

Felicia shrugs.

'Go and eat it, girl! You know how to get hold of me or someone else if you need to.'

She nods. A forlorn and lonely nod.

At the bedroom door Ramsi stands there and watches her. Sarit pulls his arm, but still he stays, as if rooted to the spot, as if he were made of heavy immovable bronze.

'Ramsi,' says Sarit, indignant. He moves with her. But as if he has seen something, as if he has seen a ghost he turns back, till she tugs again at the sleeve of his thick sweater.

'What was all that about?' Sarit says to him as they walk up the path with Juliann ahead of them.

'All what?' he asks.

She doesn't reply to his question that questions her, but she says, 'I'm not sure I can do this. Not sure at all; I don't know that I feel comfortable with it.'

He kisses her, opens the car door for her. 'She needs you. You have to do it.'

Starting the engine, Juliann says, 'That's why you've got to help me help her. This is not just about changing a face, Sarit. It's about saving a life.'

A silence and then Sarit says, 'I'm surprised you left her alone there. How do you know she's not going to run back to her family?'

328

'Oh,' says Juliann. 'She can't. That's another thing that's depressing her. We've had to move them as well. At least in the short term till we feel they're out of danger. They are at risk too. Even though we've got the top guys behind bars.' She adds, 'These people have networks inside and out. You can never be too careful.'

They fall into darkened silence then, lit this time not by flames of prayer, but by the street lights on the freeway and later by the night lights of Chicago's skyline.

With Juliann focused on the road a few minutes later Sarit leans forward over Ramsi's seat. She whispers in his ear again, 'I'm not sure I want to do it. I need some time to think.' He starts. She puts her hand on his shoulder. 'I didn't realise you were sleeping.'

'I'm not,' he says. 'Just in another world. What did you just say?'

'Nothing,' she says. 'Nothing at all.'

And she moves away from him, tries and fails to get comfortable again beneath the tartan woollen blanket.

The reality of fresco, of bas-relief, is altogether different from the fantasy. The artist will be so used to his vision alone that to let another's imagination seep into his image, to sit back and watch the brush strokes of another move across his canvas, to watch the paint drip and run and stream into the spaces of his own creativity is at one and the same time an abandonment and an enhancement of the self. For when the artist works in isolation he has control, or thinks he does at least, but involved in the duet with another's skill and soul, neither one nor the other can be sure in any way of how the paint might dry. The fresco inspired by two artists is a love story on canvas. The longing, the desire, matched only by the risk.

THIRTY-FIVE

A lone piano chord sounds out from all four corners of the operating theatre. A chord that echoes in the bright white room and is followed by a deeper note that makes no secret of the music's dark intent.

Single sounds. Dissonant. Untouching. A score scrawled for the night. For this night that is different from all others.

Bright lights that glare and defy Sarit to see the naked truth beneath her hands. The truth that Lauren wants to hear, as she looks at the sketches of a nose, an eye, a mouth, clipped to the silver stand, and muffled from behind her mask she asks, 'Sarit, what are these? You never sketch. Where are the photographs of how she's going to look?'

'There are none this time, Lor. Long story.'

Wide-eyed, she says, 'But why, Sarit? And why are we doing this at night? For God's sake tell me. You told them in bookings you were busy during the day for weeks and that this was a botch job that needed to be put right straight away, so you'd have to do it at night . . . but . . . but look,' and she lays her gloved hand on the green sheets that cover Felicia, 'she's had nothing done before, has she?'

'No . . . But later, Lor. Not now. No more questions. Not right now.' And she doesn't tell her then. Not till later does Sarit explain that it is for its stillness and for its absence of familiar voices that they have chosen the night. Not till later does she explain to Lauren that for the first time ever she will manage without photographs because she has no choice and because she and Ramsi have pored over Felicia's features together and trusting in her own expertise for the parts, she has trusted in the brilliance of the sculptor's vision for the whole.

And now with these first notes of the concerto, the theatre staff glide past one another, preparing the room for work and the figure for the artistry Sarit will bring.

She stands poised above her patient, as though a violinist with his bow before a solo. She takes a deep breath and with the phrases of the music that stream and flow into one, she stills the unfamiliar threat of shaking in her long slim fingers.

Sarit's fingers on Felicia's face. The fingers on the piano, the bass, the violin. All of them together now. And a pulse that throbs through Sarit to the veins of her wrist. The contours of the sounds that cajole her then to start. A sculpting, slow and heavy in the beginning, with the music in the background, as though a lover, sweet and threatening at once.

And above Felicia's long white neck Sarit begins to form a more determined chin. She draws a thin fine line, creates and fills the space she needs to give the face intent. In her mind she sees Ramsi round his fingers in a sign of strength. She hears him say, 'You need to strengthen there.' His dark, rough fingers in a sign of strength in a movement mirrored by Sarit's fingers on Felicia's face.

And then the shorter notes. Adagio first. Staccato then, on the brow and on the eyelids of the girl. Sarit cuts. She lifts. She stitches. With the skill of the composer lifting upwards into change.

Not Sarit alone, but the orchestra holding her. The shrouded women working with her. And Ramsi's rehearsal is in Sarit's mind. His persuasion, the thorough and uncompromising duet that has prepared her for this. His hand that had guided hers as the two had sat with Felicia in her godforsaken hideout. Ramsi's hand on Sarit's. Fingers touching across Felicia's face, as though the two were making her.

With the humming and the ticking in the theatre, Sarit's

fingertips fashion. With the deepening, the softening of the violins, her mood is lightened for a brief false moment.

And as she heightens cheekbones, Sarit brings Felicia to a different time. A different place.

And then the pause. The relief that Sarit takes, sensing that the changing of the truth has kept the beauty of the girl.

The beauty of the music's movement that Sarit asks to hear again. 'Lauren, I need to hear that part again.' The first movement. The violins. The bass. The pace of the percussion and fingers allegro on ivory and on skin. Confident, knowing movements as she sculpts Felicia. The altering, the shaping, the moulding that Sarit's fashioning brings to the girl. The creation of the Roman nose with fine fast movements. And then the plaster as she casts her work. Wet white plaster, hardly different then at all from the genius of the sculptor, casting faces of the past while she sculpts Felicia's future.

The music reaches higher and moves faster. The adrenalin flows unbridled through Sarit's hands as she wraps Felicia as though she were a mummy. The skill of Sarit's art, that will save Felicia's face and perhaps her mind, that will change her life and the lives of others too.

The hands, the arms of the orchestra, of artists fulfilled with playing. The arms, Ramsi's around Sarit when she goes to him afterwards in the early morning, with the fuchsia sun that rises on a lake pretending calm.

On Wells Street he takes her in. He says, 'You did it, Sarit? You did it, didn't you?'

She nods. 'I did,' she says, 'And I listened to Rachmaninov again and again. I could listen to it for hours.'

'I know which one, I'm sure,' he says. There, at home, he plays the music for her. And the sounds, the notes that waft rise, then from where they lie, upwards to between the wooden vaults on the ceiling. She is beyond words. Beyond thought. And then again he says, 'You did it? Just as we said, didn't you?'

Tears in his eyes. The violins and the piano playing with a pathos that hurts. A caress. A calm caress and then, 'I want to . . .'

'Yes,' but slowly. 'I'm in another world.' One moment sweet and gentle, the next, fierce sounds foreboding she knows not what. A love of the music and each other. A depth. Of that there is no question.

As she calls out he is everywhere, even as she aches with the pleasure that runs through her, with the pathos of it all, her face thrown back as the music peaks and slows, even as she calls out with the joy he gives, lips on lips, with the final note in the growing light she sheds the tears that he, too far from her, cannot see or feel. Tears that well, as if on some reflection of the drama of Rachmaninov's deep and dark intent.

THIRTY-SIX

Snow, like sex, like death, like illness, is an equaliser. As snow whitens the sullied, so it shuns clutter and confusion. Its shock of empty canvas is the backdrop for the candid, the blank slate that beckons words and images of truth.

In sunglasses, in a black duffel coat and boots, in the season's first thick covering at the end of the second week of December, Sarit walks fast by herself from Wells Street towards Lincoln Park. She goes not in a falling, drifting, busy snow that blocks her path and her thoughts, but in a heavy, settled, fallen snow that has come in unannounced and surprised the city of Chicago on its waking.

The air, though cold, is not yet icy. She wears last winter's grey woollen scarf and beret and of course her gloves, but not her balaclava. From beneath her beret at the sides one can see her hair has grown and become a little less severe.

She has left Ramsi asleep still, despite the light that filters through from the high green and amber stained-glass windows and falls on his face and on his bedclothes. She has kissed the rough skin of his cheek, his chin, his hand. She has breathed him in and wondered as she walked out of his blue studio door, down the dark wooden stairs, out of the red engraved door on to Wells Street, why for the first time in the months they've been together he has turned from her the night before.

So early that Sunday morning few have ventured where she goes, so that the sheets of white in the park are truly almost blank. She has stopped briefly at home and toyed with the idea of running clothes and trainers instead of boots, until from her balcony she sees how the snow in the park is too thick and the newness, the freshness, the immediacy of the morning's offering is far too tempting, too urgent in its calling for her to give up the pleasure of each slow sensual crunch. She pulls on her boots and heads straight over Clark Street to the park. The grass, often brown and patchy in the summer, is shrouded in snow's blanket. The branches, once bare and skinny, are padded with the layers of crystal flakes. The dirty black of the railings, and the harsh grey concrete of the walls are hidden by a veil of white. Sarit looks around her, smiles and thinks how snow is nature's plastic surgeon.

Always there is a reason for walking alone through the park. As simple, perhaps, as exercise and fresh air. As complicated, perhaps, as the search for inspiration or as pure as the need for contemplation or the consolation lent by nature. Sarit, though, does not consider her walk to have a reason beyond appreciation of the season's first white beauty. She has not thought that she might be making footprints in the snow across the park on her way to breakfast at the Third Coast, to give herself a chance to be alone and to think of what has gone before that Sunday morning. But in recent days in the little free time she has had to spend with Ramsi she has felt troubled, not so much by her own feelings, as by a sadness, a sullenness, a withdrawal she has felt from him. He has often been withdrawn from the world. That is his way. But in his own slow and almost imperceptible manner, over the months he has known Sarit, he has inched towards her. Until now. Until the last two weeks.

In the immediate aftermath of Felicia's operation Sarit herself had felt a sense of achievement and a sense of relief that the ordeal was over once the girl was gone. But as the days went by her mood had been altered both by osmosis, by Ramsi's closing off, and by a troubling disquiet in her soul. And now, as she walked, with the sound of her footsteps, she could not help but hear the echo of her mind. 'He loves me, he loves me not. He loves me, he loves me not.' An echo that she tried to muffle with each footstep.

Had Sarit been asked she might have said that she was walking just to clear her mind for the working week ahead or that she was walking just to be. But no one asked and so in the beginning, that early winter's day, she goes on her way unchallenged.

At this time of the day there is little to see save for a short round man with his hand on the shoulder of a young boy in a yellow anorak straining to control a chocolate Labrador on a leash. On the edge of white Sarit stands tall and still, and looks ahead of her. She looks out across the park at the purity and the possibility of what she sees, for the expanse of snow in an artistic sense is the mound of clay unfashioned, the canvas unadorned.

And as she stands there in one spot on the edge of Lincoln Park, despite the beauty that she sees she feels a strange sense of malaise and of being drawn out of herself. She removes her sunglasses and is drawn almost into a trance by the dazzle from the snow. A hypnotic sparkling dazzle, a gold dust that lures her to the canvas so that, moments later, ahead of her it is no longer bare. Like light beams searching, light beams thrown from her subconscious mind, the lines of a forehead, of cheeks, of a mouth, of a nose and of a neck begin to etch themselves in the snow in front of her. A face she has seen before this. A face she has photographed herself. The cheekbones not yet heightened, the eyelids not yet slanted, the nose that is not yet altered. The face beautiful, perfect in its proportions. Deep pink lips and blonde corkscrew curls that fall across the forehead. The whole as though a Warhol painting splashed in front of her across the snow. She watches the expressions as she has seen them before. The face crying. Pleading. Fearful. Hopeful. The face of a girl, of a young woman, of someone in between. She watches and to herself she nods. A knowing nod. A nod of recognition that for Felicia she did the best she ever could have done. From her right hand she takes the glove as if to touch the face. She hears the small boy in the yellow anorak

336

screeching with delight. She hears his dog barking. She hears a car hooting. In one swift movement the image is erased from the canvas of snow. And she puts her glove back on and moves across the square towards the Historical Society building in the park. At the back of the building, which is square and imposing, at the bottom of the steps that lead the way to its back door is a bench, each one of its slats piled high with a tall thin mound of powder snow. Sarit walks over to the bench and for the sheer pleasure of it runs her leather-gloved finger through the thin mounds of powder, which fall away beneath her touch. With the flat of her hand she sweeps away the snow in the corner of the bench and on its back, till the beginnings of an inscription come into view. Curious, she wipes away the rest of the snow that obscures the sentence and she sees the words '*In Loving memory of our daughter Edna Weiss*' etched into the grey wood. She sits down where she is and wonders about their suffering. The mother's suffering. And the father's. The daughter's too perhaps.

Ahead of her, as she stares out in the direction of the lake now, there is no one. No man with a dog and little boy in a bright yellow anorak. No one and nothing at all in this snow, save for Felicia's face, which in an instant splashes itself again on the canvas in front of her. She knows, of course, that she plays her own part in the painting of the lines and the altering of the shapes she sees, but she is powerless now to stop herself. Just as in the kibbutz children's house at eight years old she had been powerless to stop herself from painting the picture of her mother's face with the strands of light in the darkness on the wall in front of her. In the cold now, just as in the heat then, she half shuts her eyes and uses her long thick lashes as the filters for the lines that she will sketch and impose upon Felicia's face. She sketches high cheekbones over Felicia's. She sketches full lips, then with a sweep of her lashes draws away just a touch from the pout. She sketches the lines of a nose and flutters her lashes to draw the smallest of bumps on the bridge. She changes the angle of her own head to tilt back the head of the girl that she paints now on the canvas of snow. The painting that this time is colourless. An image in black and white, born of the black of Sarit's lashes and of the whiteness of the snow. The girl Sarit sees as she sits on the bench and closes her eyes. The girl who melts from white on white into the smooth and finished coffee bronze, which has taken her breath away before now in a room full of sculptures at Nicole's in River North.

A bronze that sits there behind her, that watches and welcomes, the first time she visits Ramsi on Wells Street. A bronze that makes her want to ask, 'Whose is that? How well do you know her? Does she live close by? Right here in Chicago?'

The face, the one she has seen in clay beneath Ramsi's hands at Albert's foundry on the West Side. The girl about whom she doesn't dare to ask for weeks, until outside the Baha'i temple she says to Ramsi of Nadia, 'Was she one of your harem?' and he replies, 'No, Nadia was my child.'

And here, now on this canvas, as in some ghastly animated cartoon, as though the snow were water, the two faces have swum and merged and melted into one. Felicia's face and Nadia's face. Nadia's face. Felicia's face, changed and starting to heal, as it will be by now. 'No,' Sarit says to herself. 'No, it wasn't like that. Felicia was something completely different for him. She was a porcelain sculpture or a white clay one. That's what he said. Her skin was pure white. Nothing like his bronzes at all. They couldn't have been more different. Completely different types. Stop hallucinating, woman. Don't do this to yourself.'

Her black duffel coat is thick and feather-lined but she shivers where she sits and without the usual energy in her movements she stands to cross the park and walks along North Dearborne to the Third Coast. En route there would have been so much to notice. The tall figure of Abraham Lincoln on his podium, white this morning as though left in plaster, forgotten and unfinished by the sculptor. The intricate hand-sculpted doors of the church on Dearborne, the Byzantine doors of the Three Arts Club, the mosaics on the floor of the lobby where the door has been opened. But as Sarit passes that morning she notices nothing. And instead of walking she plods almost, the lower half of her boots sinking deep into the snow as yet unshovelled from the pavement. The sinking, not just of her knee-high boots in the snow, but the sick and steady sinking of her gut. The deep, awful, unstoppable sinking of her heart as she walks towards the café.

She almost doesn't notice that she has pushed open the door to the main building, that she has pulled open the door to the Third Coast, that she has taken a seat.

She remembers only looking up from her menu, looking up from where she sits in the corner on the worn and muted sofa by the leaded windows strewn with Christmas lights in the corner of the Eastern European-style café.

'What can I get you this morning?'

The waiter is beautiful. Tall and young and strong, his hair long and pulled back in a ponytail. He is white-skinned with a smile that energises, but she hardly notices.

He repeats himself. He says, 'What can I get you?'

She says, 'Oh . . . oh, I haven't looked . . . I'll have a black coffee.'

'And to eat?'

'To eat . . . ? Nothing now. No, I don't want to eat.'

Twice or maybe three times the waiter with the smile refills her mug. He says, 'Can I bring you the newspaper?'

'What . . . ? Oh yes, great.'

The thick bulk of the *Chicago Sunday Tribune* lies there by her side till a woman leans across to her and says, 'If you're not reading your paper, d'you think that I could borrow it?'

'The paper . . . ? Yes. Take it.'

Peering into her mug, staring ahead of her, not caring if time passes, but reliving scenes and shapes and pictures in her head, muttering to herself first in her mind, 'I didn't. He didn't. You're imagining things, Sarit. It's just his style. That's all . . . You would have felt it if it had been more than that,' and then out loud, 'You're losing it, Sarit. Get a grip,' and as the woman next to her with the newspaper turns to look at her as though she were quite crazy, slow and dazed and dizzy, Sarit gets up to leave. She moves towards the door. Running up the stairs behind her, the waiter holds out a slip of paper and says, 'The check. I'm sorry, I think you must have forgotten it.'

She doesn't apologise, just says, 'How much?' and reaches into the pocket of her jeans for a twenty-dollar bill.

She opens the door. 'Wait,' he says, 'I need to get your change.'

She doesn't wait. She hurries from the café. And if she could have done she would have walked now with eyes closed, so that the snow's possibility would not have had a chance to taunt her. Because now, as Sarit comes to a little in the air, she is overcome with the alien, overwhelmed with the unfamiliar clutch of fear. Fear that if she dares to turn again in the direction of the park, to look again at the open planes, from the ground, the truth will glare at her again and mock her.

The park by this time is dotted with the colours of anoraks, with children throwing snowballs, sculpting snowmen, writing names and messages with their boots or their gloved hands. She is grateful for their graffiti at first, for the way they have cluttered her easel. She is grateful too for the clouds that have drifted in, casting shadows of themselves that seem at first to have left no room for creation on the snow. The snow that has been trodden on, trampled, tarnished. And yet between the people, the snowmen and the dogs, she could swear that on the ground ahead of her she sees not images, this time, but words. Huge sinewing words in jet-black paint. She could swear that on the ground as she walks home she can see the words *Nadia Nadia Nadia* that swirl and paint themselves before her eyes.

340

From her pocket she takes her sunglasses, puts them back on, so that by the time she goes to cross the road the glare has died down just a little and Sarit is no longer now sure whether the words *Nadia Nadia Nadia* are painted on the canvas of snow or on the canvas of her mind.

THIRTY-SEVEN

She goes for him. As she runs from her building, after her the doorman calls, 'Have a nice night, Doctor . . . Emergency or something?' His words hit her back, fall off and drown themselves in the swish of the revolving doors and she is out there in the street. The temperature has dropped. Her head and her neck are uncovered. Her hands are bare too. Sarit's hands bare. No gloves to protect them. She walks fast along North Avenue in the dark towards the corner with Wells Street, towards the red engraved door. Her shoes are ridiculous. Not the sensible snow boots she had worn that morning, the morning of the paintings on the snow in Lincoln Park. But black lace-ups with slippery soles. Totally inappropriate for the snow that has hardened to black ice. She slides and skates dangerously in the dark and the cold. Her pager is lying on her kitchen table. Sarit has not forgotten her pager before. Not ever. This time too she had it in her hand, to take with her. But she put it down and left it lying there next to an empty coffee mug when she picked up the envelope with the photograph she had printed out earlier in the day. The computer image of Felicia that Sarit has created, throat dry, fingers trembling over her keyboard at the crack of dawn. The image of Felicia's face as she will be when she is healed with features changed and corkscrew curls and eyebrows dyed a rich and deep dark brown. The image that Juliann had forbidden Sarit to create when she had said, 'No, it's too risky to have that hanging around. There must be another way for you to work.'

But that morning of the Sunday snow Sarit had defied her. She had had to know. And as she sat, her face inches from the screen, she had superimposed Felicia's new features on to the old photograph of her in simulation of the operation she'd performed. And for a few moments Sarit was still able to tell herself that it was all in her own head. To tell herself again that this was just his style. And the delusion had lasted until she had clicked on to the palette and the airbrush, the only part of the specialist computer programme used to paint and change colour. The only part that she had never used before. The part that was for artists.

The delusion had lasted until after she had changed the colour of Felicia's hair and her eyebrows. It had lasted until she changed Felicia's skin colouring from the porcelain white of which Ramsi spoke to coffee-coloured bronze. And she sat there then, staring at the screen, transfixed, until she literally felt her stomach heave and her arms and legs turn to jelly. Her head thrown back, her eyes closed she had cried out into the emptiness, 'No. Please no. Not again. Not this again.'

She had cried out with these words that went so far back, so very far back in her life, because the 'No', the 'Please no. Not again', went all the way back to then, back to the time when she had felt her talent used and manipulated before, when she had felt her right arm used by Max to create his art. To fuel his life. To banish his demons.

She has spent years and years running from this. Trying to be her own woman instead of having her right arm ripped from her, used by another, cleaved to his shoulder and his life, to recreate what he had lost.

And now with the computer image in her hand and in her head, she ignores the 'Don't Walk' sign and starts to cross the road. A car swerves. Against his closed window the driver screams, 'You lunatic.' Sarit is not thinking. As she tries to run, slipping, towards Ramsi's studio she has no words in her. Instead there is the black and red swirl in her head that is the explosion in preparation. Perhaps that is why she doesn't feel she is freezing . . . because of the red heat in her head.

343

She pushes open the engraved door. Presses hard on his bell. Hard and for a long time. She pushes her face against the black iron bars while she waits. She feels them hard and icy, marking the skin of her cheeks. She wants them to hurt her. Her teeth want to chatter but they are clenched. She rings again. No answer. So she rings other bells. She rings the bell of the neighbour who wears pyjamas. And the bell above. The one below. From the intercom three voices come at her all at once: 'Yes,' 'Yes,' 'Who is it?' Not Ramsi's voice but other voices calling out into the icy air, 'Yes,' 'Yes,' 'Who is it?'

'Let me in,' Sarit says. The neighbour in her pyjamas presses the buzzer to open the gate. Sarit runs up the wooden stairs, past the freezing pond where a rainbow fish, once beautiful, lies gasping. She bangs on Ramsi's door. Again and again. In her head together with the red she sees the wooden floorboards that gave her splinters in her fingers. She sees the sculptures, the heads that she blocks out as she bangs and bangs till her knuckles hurt.

'For Christ's sake. What the hell's going on? It's eleven o'clock at night. He's not there, for Christ's sake.'

'What?' Sarit turns round, stopped in her tracks.

The woman wears a thick dressing gown that she holds closed over her pyjamas. She says to Sarit, 'You know where he'll be. At Kingston Mines. Now calm down,' and then, staring at Sarit, 'For God's sake, woman, you'll freeze your tits off like that. Want me to lend you some clothes?'

'No.'

She's down the stairs already. Down the snow- and ice-covered wooden stairs. In the street. In a cab. Outside the door of Kingston Mines. Fighting her way past the coats, through the noise, the heavy smoke that night in the packed room. Smoke that moves from the front of the room, where she sat with Lauren on the night of the Koko Taylor music. Smoke that thickens as it moves back to the point of the triangle where Felicia had sat caught up in her fight with her boyfriend. Begging him to get out. To live a clean life. To get his act together before he ended up dead.

'Don't be crazy, Felicia. Dead? I promise I won't die.'

The thick smoke towards the furthest point of the triangle in the back corner of the room, where Ramsi sits puffing, looking out at nothing, his beer almost untouched. Before she reaches him she stops in her tracks, getting her breath back.

He looks up, surprise on his face. 'Sarit.'

She stands over him.

'What's wrong with you? Your lips are blue. Sit down.'

'I don't want to sit down,' she says. 'I have something for you.'

'Sit down, Sarit.'

The chair she pulls over to him screeches across the floor. The waitress is on top of her before she has a chance to open her mouth, standing there in her checked apron, bags under her eyes, a pencil behind her ear. 'What can I get you?'

'Nothing.'

She raises her eyebrows, backs off. 'Jesus,' she says.

Sarit reaches into her pocket, pulls out the envelope. She throws it on the table.

The music is noisy. Heavy, dissonant, disturbing drumming. Ramsi picks up the envelope. 'What's this?'

'Open it,' and she laughs a hard, angry, unsmiling laugh. Not her laugh now. Not Gabriella's laugh.

'What the hell has got into you, Sarit?'

His hands, strong, dark-skinned fingers that pull the photograph from the envelope. Wrong side up, so that at first all he sees is the back of it. 'What's this?' he asks again as he turns it over, before he sees. 'What . . . ?'

How long does he sit there after that, holding that photograph in his hand, Sarit breathing heavily, leaning over the table towards him, saying, 'Well, what do you have to say to it? Say something.' And Ramsi, not hearing, staring, bringing the photograph up to his forehead. The mature bearded man in his fifties with his forehead against the photograph.

The music is loud enough so that Sarit shouting at him can be drowned out, so that only he and the waitress and the people at the next table can hear her shouting, 'What were you thinking, Ramsi? What were you trying to do to me . . . to us . . . ?' She pulls him by the arm. 'We're leaving. Get up. Now. We're getting out of here now.'

In Kingston Mines some of the drinkers close their eyes, move their bodies to the rhythm of the music. Others try to interact, yelling over the music, and some stare at the tall, striking, short-haired woman dragging the dazed bearded man behind her through the noise and the smoke, through the club, outside into the street.

Sweating in the cold on the pavement, the red swirls in her head pouring out now, like blood from her mouth, she shouts at him, 'You're going to tell me you didn't know, are you? Huh? Ramsi, tell me that. Say, "I didn't know, Sarit, what I was doing to you." Go on.'

She's up close to him now, where he stands against a lamp-post, the ugly spotlight on his black eyes, with him there gripping the photograph. And as she speaks, Sarit's breath comes out in the air in short, sharp, icy puffs of anger. 'You knew. Of course you knew. Who do you think you are, Ramsi . . . God?'

A group of young men in woollen hats walk past, moving fast, huddled forward against the cold. One of them calls to Sarit, 'Jesus, woman, about to come on or something?'

They pass. Ramsi lifts his head. And quietly, in a voice just loud enough for her to hear he says, 'Sarit. Do you . . . do you know where to go to find her?'

A silence and then, 'What did you just say?'

And he asks her again. So that the second time she knows that he has really said it, that he means it when he says, 'Sarit, do you know where to go to find her?'

And she yells at him. She says, 'Are you crazy? Are you totally out of your head? Maybe you'd like to publish her photograph in the paper . . . *Wanted* . . . *Girl dead twenty years ago*,' and she reaches for him, lunges towards his hand. 'Give it back.' And in the icy cold with her frozen hands she pulls at the photograph. Between clenched teeth she says, 'Give . . . it . . . back . . . now.' She pulls. He grips. She pulls harder. And then it happens, there outside in sub-zero temperatures on the street outside Kingston Mines. With Sarit pulling in one direction and Ramsi in the other, in a jagged ugly scar the face rips and splits itself in two.

And they are both there, each one of them with half a photo in their hand. Sarit with Felicia's eyes and her forehead. Ramsi with Nadia's neck, her chin, her nose. Both of them are stunned and silent, till in a loud whisper he says, 'Do you think I knew? Do you honestly think I knew what I was doing?'

'Go on then,' she says, quiet now, light-headed with emotion, with fatigue and cold but goading him, 'Tell me, Ramsi. Say, "I didn't know what I was doing. I had no idea what I was making you do." Say it.'

And he looks at Sarit now, straight at her. For the first time that night his coal-black pained eyes are on hers and he says, 'Sarit, I don't know if I knew. I just don't know . . .' and then in a whisper, 'I wasn't using you, you know . . . You do know that, don't you?'

And she just stands there, under the ghastly unforgiving glare of the lamppost outside Kingston Mines, Sarit rooted to the spot at first. And in a loud whisper she says to him, 'Oh, yes you were. You were using me, Ramsi . . . to bring her back. Like you've been trying to do all your life,' and she shouts then, 'So now you have what you need from me, stay away.'

And with that Sarit is gone, almost slipping on the ice as she turns and heads down the midnight street, walking fast at first, not thinking to look for a cab. And as her fingers have begun to numb, as the ice has begun to wrap the branches of the trees, so, as she begins to run, minutes later on the skin of her face, somewhere between her cheekbones and her mouth, the streams of tears she does not feel begin to freeze.

THIRTY-EIGHT

She rifles through the drawers of her cupboards, of her desk, of her bedside table in the early hours of the morning. She throws jeans, sweaters, scarves, books into a suitcase. Others she throws on to the bed or to the floor. For a moment she leaves the room for a glass of water, comes back, stands at the bedroom door, her hands to her head.

The word in her head is 'Refugee'. 'Sarit Kleinmann, you are a goddamned refugee,' she says, 'just like the others.' The others might have been Ramsi and his family, refugees from Alexandria. They might have been Max and the boatload of starving men with whom he landed in Palestine. The others might have been both of them. Max and Ramsi, refugees from themselves, each one seeking asylum in his talent. And at the door of her bedroom she stands there and says to herself, 'I'm a goddamned refugee too.'

Later that morning, expressions hidden behind green masks, Sarit and Lauren work. Under her breath Sarit says to Lauren, 'I need to talk to you.'

She lifts her head and stares at all that she can see of Sarit. At her eyes and the top of her cheekbones. 'What's up?' she says. 'You look like death this morning. Are you sick?'

Head down, Sarit says, 'Would I work if I was sick?' And then, 'I've left a message on Sam's machine. I need to talk tonight. To both of you.'

'Give me a hint,' says Lauren, watching the movement of Sarit's fingers.

Sarit says nothing. Not a word. And again Lauren says, 'A hint, Sarit.' Still no response. For Sarit works this morning with great focus. In that, Lauren recognises nothing strange. But she is grateful, because today Sarit will not notice how Lauren uses only her right hand to pass her what she needs. She will not notice that she hardly moves her left arm, which is bruised and sore beneath her white coat. Because Lauren will take years to believe the truth that writes itself in black and blue on the surface of her skin.

And Sarit today, will be oblivious to Lauren's pain, for now she is so engrossed, she works with such a passion, as though behind each snip, each stitch, there were so much more. As though, in their finality, these stitches mattered not just to her patient's life but to her own. She works knowing that the shape she has drawn is daring, new and irreversible, knowing that this change she sews is not on the cupid's bow of lips alone.

Later that night the bar Sarit chooses is dark, unknown and unlikely. A Bucktown bar that was once a home and now has nothing in its exposed brick walls but low tables, low sofas and candles with low flames. So that as Lauren and Sammy sink into their seats next to Sarit in their corner far away from other drinkers on this Monday night, the three see only one another's faces moving in and out of flames and shadows.

Sarit has drunk not beer this time, but two glasses of Beaujolais before Sammy and Lauren arrive and since morning she has eaten almost nothing so that when, each holding a glass of wine, they say to her in unison almost, 'Well? Well, why have we been summoned?' her voice is on the edge of slurred as she answers them, 'You're my friends.'

Lauren looks at Sammy. Sammy looks at Lauren. Tripping over one another's words they ask, 'What's wrong, Sarit?'

'Wrong?' she says. 'Wrong? I'm not sure that's the way I'd put it, but . . . I need another glass of wine.'

She begins to stand, to walk round the corner to the bar. But as she rises Lauren grabs her arm and pushes her back down on to the sofa. 'No,' she says, 'no. You've had enough to drink. Tell us what's wrong with you.'

From where he sits it is not Lauren but Sammy who sees the deep shadow that crosses Sarit's face. 'Yes, Sarit,' he says, 'what's wrong? Tell us why we're here.'

She leans back, slides down, her head against the low curve of the sofa. She closes her eyes, bites the inside of her lip. She says, 'To say goodbye.'

'To what?' Lauren says.

'You heard me, Lor,' she says.

His voice low and slow and gentle as if talking to a patient, as if scared that she were hovering on the edge, Sammy says, 'I'm sorry, Sarit. We're not with you.'

'To say goodbye to me,' she says. 'That's why you're here.'

And Lauren, steadying her voice, says, 'Sarit, have you lost it?'

'Lost it?' she says as if asking the question of herself. 'No,' she says, shaking her head, her tone vague and unfocused. 'No, I haven't lost it, but,' and she leans forward now, beckons them closer, so that their heads, the heads of all three of them, are almost touching as though they were conspirators, and in a loud whisper Sarit says, 'But I am leaving. For a while at least. I have to leave.'

'Leaving what, Sarit? Leaving where?' says Lauren, her high-pitched voice cracking just a little now with the strangeness of it all, with the otherness of seeing Sarit like this, and she shakes her arm and asks her, 'Are you sick or something? Tell us.'

Sarit shakes her head. So close to Sammy that he feels her hair against his cheek.

He takes her hand. He says, 'Sarit, please, what is this all about?'

In a tone of mock conspiracy, in a pretend whisper as if making light of the half-truth she has chosen to tell her friends, Sarit says, 'I'm afraid. Just like Felicia was afraid. She's passed her fear on to me, I suppose.'

They are still, all three of them for a moment like those gold and silver tinfoil clowns who make believe they're statues till they move an inch or two, till they dispel illusions as they raise an arm, a hand, a brow. It is Sammy who moves first to take his glasses off, to wipe them on his shirt, to say, 'Are you serious, Sarit?'

'No, I'm making it up, Sam. It's the kind of thing I enjoy making up. Isn't it, Lauren? Why don't you tell him that this is just my idea of fun.'

'Be nice, Sarit,' says Lauren, in the midst of it all feeling sorry for Sam, feeling sad for him.

'Where did this come from, Sarit?' he asks. 'You're fearless. You're the tough one.'

'Yes, well,' she says, 'we all crack sometimes, don't we?'

Sarit looks around her. It's quite ridiculous, quite unnecessary to look around here in this empty out of the way bar, where she's never even been with Ramsi, but she cannot stop herself.

'What are you afraid of, Sarit?' Sammy asks her.

'That's not an intelligent question, Sam,' she says.

'Tell me, Sarit.'

And now, slipping from half-truth into fabrication, not prepared to talk of love or of betrayal, she says, 'That . . . that they might come after me and try and find out where she is.'

'Do you know?' he asks.

She shakes her head and then again he asks, 'Do you know? Tell me the truth.'

'No,' she says. 'I don't. I swear.'

From round the corner a waiter with a huge silver cross round his neck appears. 'Can I help you with anything else?'

'No,' Sarit says. 'Unfortunately I don't think you can.'

Puzzled, the waiter walks away. The light of the candles moves with him, crosses Lauren's face, catches her as a deer in the glare of headlights staring at Sarit. Sarit lays her hand on Lauren's. A gesture so unlike her. She says, 'Lauren, I should never have told you. You know nothing. Do you hear me? I don't tell you anything but the medical history of the patients on whom we operate, do I? Do I, Lauren? Do I?'

Lauren shakes her head, silky white-blonde hair falling over eyes that have begun to tear.

'You called Juliann of course?' asks Sammy.

Sarit nods.

'What did she say?'

'That she's sorry I feel like this. That this is the last thing she wanted. That she did everything to protect me, which is true, and that she's as she sure as she can be that I'm perfectly safe. She said she wasn't surprised, though. She said distress was contagious.'

Her mood, her demeanour, so far now from that of the bright-pink feathered flamingo, Lauren says, 'But I thought they were behind bars.'

And Sam answers for Sarit now. He says, 'They are, Lor. But I guess they must have their friends . . .'

Sarit lights a cigarette. And now she carries on unprompted. 'I wasn't alone last night when I packed. Juliann made sure of that,' and she gesticulates to infer a presence in the direction of the door. 'And I'm not alone now either.'

'Sarit,' asks Sammy, 'this isn't a game, is it?'

She glares at him. 'You're a shrink. What do you think? How can you even ask me that?'

He says, 'I'm sorry, I didn't mean I . . .'

She backs down. She says, 'No, I'm sorry, Sam, for getting you involved in this.'

And in a whisper then, a frightened whisper, Lauren says, 'How long do you need to stay away?'

Sarit's tight-lipped sarcastic laugh turns into a sad one. She inhales on her cigarette and shrugs her shoulders.

'Where will you go?'

Another shrug.

Sammy looks at her. He says, 'Where will you go, Sarit?'

'I don't know, Sam,' she says. 'But Juliann will know where I am.'

Sammy watches her mouth. He reads her subtext. He says, 'I get it.'

Lauren's voice is almost hysterical now as she speaks. She says, 'Sairit.' She still says it all wrong. She says, 'Sairit, what do you mean? Of course you know. You have to know. Tell me,' and she shakes her arm.

'Lauren, shh,' says Sammy. 'She's right. It's better if she doesn't tell us right this minute.'

'But what about our patients?' Lauren's question is desperate. A plea almost. She bites the cuticles at the side of her nails.

'They'll live without me for a while, Lor. They'll have time to reconsider. Or they'll go to someone else.'

'And the children?' Lauren asks.

Sarit looks away from her. She can't quite bring herself to answer.

The wineglasses are almost empty. The light of the candles has grown weak. And Sammy says, 'What can I do for you, Sarit?'

'Just remember you know nothing, Sam. I have never confided in you if you get my drift. Or in you, Lauren. I never should have given in to your nagging.'

Crying openly now, Lauren nods. Sammy nods, a little overcome himself by now, his voice a little choked when he asks her, '*Do* you know how long you'll be away?'

The candles flicker, threatening.

She shakes her head.

He says, 'And Ramsi?'

She bites her lip. She shuts her eyes again. The flame from the candle almost dies. In their corner they sit in semi-darkness.

'Sarit,' he says again. 'What about Ramsi?'

Still nothing.

'Sarit, does Ramsi know?'

She lifts her scarf from beside her on the sofa. She does not speak. But the psychiatrist is trained to understand all that is unspoken. All that has no need of words. The psychiatrist, compassionate and intuitive as he is, can see the soul even in the darkness.

THIRTY-NINE

Anonymity in a city that is not your own can be exciting, enthralling and intriguing. Anonymity in a city that you cannot call your own can be isolating, lonely and depressing. At first no one will gossip about you. No one will judge you by your past. No one will make demands on your skills, your emotions or your time. By the same token, of course, no one will care. Sarit, in the very early morning stepping off the El Al flight in Tel Aviv, hauls her worn brown leather holdall on to her shoulder at the top of the aircraft's stairs, follows the other passengers down the silver steps and, exhausted and numb as she is, to herself she says, 'The dawn of anonymity.' In the strictest sense of the word, though, her state of total and utter anonymity lasts only as long as it takes for the passengers squashed against one another, holding on to leather straps above their heads in the transfer bus to arrive at the terminal of Tel Aviv's Lod Airport. Her anonymity lasts only as long as it takes for her to reach the front of the queue where the passport control officers in their murky green army uniforms sit behind the glass screen of their kiosks waiting to check and log and punch and stamp. She chooses the line marked for foreign passports.

The young girl with the braces and the protruding chin looks at Sarit's passport. She looks down at her computer. She says to Sarit in Hebrew, '*At kvar hait baaretz?* . . . have you been here before?'

Sarit answers her in English. She says, 'Yes . . .' and then, knowing that they know, 'I was an Israeli citizen.'

'You mean you are an Israeli citizen. You have your Israeli passport with you?'

'No.'

'Where is it?' The girl tries to hide her surprise.

'I didn't bring it.'

'When were you last here?'

'About twenty years ago.'

The girl slips back into Hebrew. She says, 'Just a minute. Please stay here.'

Frazzled, thirsty, impatient, Sarit stands there, angered by the fat Southerner in tomato-red trousers and matching shirt who waits behind her tutting. She turns round. She says, 'Look, this is not my fault, so stop complaining.'

The fat red woman is shocked by Sarit's abruptness. The young girl slips back into the booth.

A bald, bespectacled, anaemic-looking man in grey appears round the side of the kiosk. In Hebrew he says to Sarit, 'Could you come with me?'

Sarit in one way had expected this. The thought that she would be stopped and questioned had crossed her mind and then left it in the labyrinth of other confused, conflicting, jumbled thoughts of the previous few days. Back in the eighties, back when she had left, for a young officer to be abandoning her country, robbing them of her talent, was little better in the eyes of the authorities than being a fugitive from justice.

In the room with the tourist poster bursting with the colours of the Galilee in spring, the bald man says to Sarit in Hebrew, 'When was the last time you were here?'

In English she answers, 'Twenty years ago.'

In Hebrew he says, 'Why don't you carry your Israeli passport?' and she succumbs to speaking in Hebrew that after all these years feels strange and unfamiliar on her tongue.

'I made my life in the US,' she says. 'My mother was American. I carry a US passport.'

'You are married? You have family?'

'What does that have to do with anything?'

'Please . . . I need an answer to my questions.'

355

'No,' she says.

'What is your profession?'

'I worked as a plastic surgeon in the States,' and then, 'Can I have a glass of water?'

'Tap water,' he says and goes to fill a paper cup from a tiny sink at the back of the room. From behind she notices how his trousers seem to fall off his body.

He asks, 'So why have you come back?'

'All these questions are ridiculous,' she says.

He says, 'I'm sorry. You choose not to carry your Israeli passport. We have no choice but to check a few things out before we let you into the country.'

'What is it that you want to know?' she says. 'I need to sleep.'

'Why are you here, Ms Kleinmann? Why now after all these years?'

She doesn't answer immediately. And just as Ramsi had done when she turned up at his studio and then at the foundry, just as he had asked her twice, 'Why have you come?' so the balding official says to Sarit again, 'Why are you here?'

'Personal reasons.'

'You have family here?'

'Yes.'

'Where?'

She gives him the name of the kibbutz.

'Ah yes. Up north. It's beautiful. Is that where you'll be staying?'

'No.'

He frowns. He asks, 'Which members of your family live there?'

'My father.'

'His name?'

Sarit sighs. 'Max Kleinmann . . . what difference does this make?'

'*The* Max Kleinmann? The artist?'

'Yes, *the* Max Kleinmann,' and then, unable to help herself, 'How do you know of him?'

'How could I not know of him?' he says, not looking up from his screen. 'I come from a family of art lovers. My father was a collector.'

He types into his computer, waits for its response. A minute or two pass. He says, 'You were an artist too?'

She sighs. She says, 'Yes,' in a tone that indicates boredom with his questions. 'I was an artist. Now that you've discovered I wasn't an axe murderer, can I go?'

The man looks at her. He sees more than tiredness and jetlag. He says, 'A few years back this would have been a big drama, you know. To let you back in after you left like that when we wanted you as an officer. We'd have wanted to know every detail, but things have changed. We're happy to have you here, Miss Kleinmann,' he says. He opens her passport, stamps it once, twice, three times, then escorts her to the neon-lit baggage hall. He says, 'Sorry for the inconvenience,' and as he turns away he divests himself for a moment of his official role and he thinks, 'That woman must have some kind of broken love story.'

So that Sarit's arrival in Tel Aviv has begun with the strangest sort of anonymity. In the strictest sense of the word she is not now anonymous. Her name is known and logged and noted, and yet this tall woman with the short black hair, the high cheekbones and the grey eyes standing with her trolley and her suitcases in the taxi queue, this woman who in English in the grey early morning says to the driver, 'Tel Aviv centre please,' is without doubt alone and unconnected in the city.

'Where in Tel Aviv?' the taxi driver asks in the thickest and heaviest of Russian accents.

'Can you recommend a hotel?'

'How many stars?' he says.

'I don't care,' Sarit says. 'I'm tired.'

'So just tell me. How much you want to spend?'

'I don't care,' she says.

He says, 'I know a good small hotel near the sea. You like?'

'That's fine,' she says.

'So where you are from?' he asks.

'Chicago.'

'Oh God,' he says. 'It is much too cold to be there. It's better here even with all our problems. You can die there from the cold.'

'Yes,' she says. 'You're right. You can die there . . . from the cold.'

FORTY

Schachor, schachor, schachor . . . pronounced as it is written. The heavy Hebrew word that all at once means dark and darkness, pitch black and blackness and in the dead of night. The word *schachor* that unlike the English bleak or black or blackness bears with its sound no lilt, and in its name no 'L' that hints at a chink of openness, that hints at the moment of weakness when it might just drop its guard and let in the 'L' of light.

Sarit's studio apartment, a large room sparsely furnished, with paint that peels from the walls, is in almost total darkness. Were she to have got up from her single bed, were she to have stood on the balcony beyond the floor-to-ceiling window or to have bent to pull up the rusty lock and open the french doors, she would have felt the mildness of the night wind on her face. Were she to have looked upwards she would have seen the winter stars and ahead of her she would have seen black interrupted only by the message of the lighthouse.

Instead she sits on the edge of the bed staring at the nothingness on the empty wall opposite her. She allows herself neither the release of sleep, nor the pleasure of the wind on her face. She has not bothered even to undress. In the first week she has spent here sleep has come in snatches, and always in the daytime.

So that even in the hours of daylight, when Sarit might have had the chance to shut out blackness, she suffers it instead and keeps the frayed green curtains drawn. Her suitcase is not unpacked but open, spilling over with clothes or shoes where she has dragged things from beneath them. Without the light, as she sat or lay there she would not have been able to read her watch and even if she had, the hands would have told the time not in the Middle East but in the Midwest, for consciously or subconsciously she has left them on Chicago time. On Ramsi's time.

So that at three in the morning where she is, in the third-floor apartment of the simple square Bauhaus structure in a tiny Tel Aviv cul-de-sac built in a hurry and without attention to detail in the 1940s when immigrants from the Holocaust cried out for housing, Sarit has little sense of the hour, nor does she care. And if she has not changed the hands of her watch, nor has she allowed her body's clock to adjust itself to the movements of the Middle Eastern sun, and the little hunger that she feels begins to gnaw always at the wrong time of day. In the night now, on the edge of her bed, she feels her stomach's emptiness and neglects it. The effort of going to the fridge and taking out the carton of milk that in any case is turning sour, the effort of going to the cupboard and removing the packet of cereal is too great. Instead she sits and in the heaviness and lethargy of limbo she stares at nothing.

In limbo since she's been here she has spoken not one word of Hebrew. In the taxi, in the hotel on the first two nights, in her brief search for an apartment, even when her neighbours knocked on her door to introduce themselves she has spoken only English. She has said, 'Yes, I'm American. From Chicago.' She has said 'Thanks, but no thanks' to their offers of tea and coffee, of cake and conversation. And, not wanting to be asked, not wanting to formulate the answers even for herself, she has left them standing at her door wondering where and who and how and why. So that when the woman from the apartment across the way, hefty, unkempt and holding her child against her hip, comes to Sarit's door more out of curiosity than out of warmth to say hello and receives no more than a curt rebuff, she hobbles back down the stairs to the couple on the floor below. She knocks on their door and she says, 'Have you met

360

that arrogant American bitch upstairs? She thinks she's too good for us. Who is she? What does she want here?'

And the couple, an older gentle pair of Czech refugees with paintings on their walls and little in common with the unkempt woman, say, 'Yes. We tried to say hello to her too and she was curt. But perhaps she's suffering in some way. She just looked lost and out of place to us . . . As if she didn't know quite what she was doing here.' And the woman with the baby just went, 'Humph,' wiped her child's nose with the back of her sleeve and stomped back up the stairs. And the Czech couple in their turn, met the Russian pharmacist in the lobby and said to him, 'Have you spoken to our new neighbour? Sarit, the American woman upstairs.'

And he said, 'Yes, I introduced myself. I asked why she was here and she just said "for professional reasons". Then I asked her what she did and she said something like "Too compli-cated to explain . . ."'

'I wonder why she's here alone. Must have left her husband or something. Anyway, she didn't want to talk to me. I've only seen her once. Seems like she just sits up there all by herself,' and he raises his eyebrows in a question and smiles and nods at the Czechs, and before he leaves the building then, before he steps out into the little leafy cul-de-sac on his way to open up his pharmacy, he turns back. 'You ought to find out who she is,' he says. 'She's certainly a dark horse. That's for sure.'

Total darkness, total blackness, though, unless it leads to death, just cannot last for ever. Not so far removed from pitch black are the deepest darkest shades of midnight blue and grey. The grey that follows blue, before the Middle Eastern red that ends the deepest night. The silver grey of Ramsi's hair and of his beard. The charcoal grey of the pencil that she uses in her mind for the lines of his face and his neck and his shoulders that sketch themselves on the wall ahead of her as she sits there, staring, hoping, longing for the return of black and its oblivion. Longing for the return of nothingness. Because

361

though on the surface of things grey might seem bland and dull and dreary, depending on its shade, it has the power to inflict great pain and struggle in its attempt to drag you from your blackness. Sarit does not want the grey. She wants neither the pain of it nor does she want to see his face on the wall ahead of her. His face that on its own has sketched itself, not begged for and then welcomed as her mother's face had been on the kibbutz wall. But Ramsi's face, unwelcome now for the pain and the ache of desire that it will bring. And on the edge of the single bed with its thin mattress and worn springs she curls up on her side in a foetal position and her mouth against her arm, so that the words are muffled as she speaks, she says, 'I needed you, Ramsi Riyad. I did. Why did you do this to us? Why . . .' and she jumps up onto her knees on the bed and like a child she begins to bang her fists on the pillow.

In the early evening, once she has grown quite exhausted by her own emotion, she hears a knocking soft and unwelcome on her door. A knocking that stops and then starts again. She stands up to answer. She does not think about the way she looks, her hair a mess, unwashed for days, her face and her white T-shirt grey and tired. She goes to the door. 'Yes,' she says to the little elderly Czech man in his ill-fitting trousers, held up by braces over his freshly ironed shirt, who stands there and says, 'I'm sorry to *bozer* you.' He says 'to *bozer* you' not 'bother' you, for when he speaks English his Czech accent is strong. 'I'm sorry to bozer you, but my wife and I, we would love that you come to us to drink somesing. We are happy you are here. We love to have young company.'

'I'm sorry I . . .'

'Young lady' – because from where he stands Sarit at forty is still young – 'Young lady, you do not need to answer questions . . . We just would like to drink some coffee with you. My wife said I should tell you she has already made it downstairs.'

362

'But I can't. I . . .' She touches her T-shirt, suddenly aware of the way she must look.

'Young lady,' he says, 'we really do not care what you are wearing to drink a cup of coffee,' and almost as he speaks the word 'coffee' she smells its aroma that to entice her has begun to waft upstairs.

She says, 'OK. I'll be down in a minute.'

'Good,' he says. 'We wait for you. We are on the ground floor.'

He turns away. She turns inside, looks at herself in the old cracked mirror, says, 'Oh my God.' She drags a cleaner T-shirt from a case and with it a black sweater falls to the floor. She cannot help herself. She lifts the sweater and buries her face in it. She breaths him in.

Some minutes later, in the bathroom, she splashes water on her face, puts on a clean T-shirt and follows the smell of coffee to the Czech couple's home.

Their apartment too is dark. Not in the way of hers, but in the way of old people with a lifetime of belongings, of heavy tables covered in lace cloths, of grandfather clocks, of deep dark armchairs and memories.

'My wife Irena,' he says.

She smiles from where she stands by the stove, her eyes kind and tired, her hair fine and grey and in a bun. She says, 'Yes, we met on the stairs. I am Irena . . . You are Sarit, aren't you?'

'Yes.'

'Please sit.'

And so they sit, the three of them, at the large kitchen table. Peter holds out her chair for her. She is glad they have chosen the kitchen. A room with natural wood, dim light and the warmth from an Aga cooker is just about all she can bear after a week of nothingness, a week of only her own company. They are a godsend, these old people, because they sense that questions are unwelcome, that they will surely send Sarit running back upstairs. And so as they ply her with caffeine and home-made biscuits the two of them talk at her. Together, finishing each other's sentences, anticipating each other's train of thought, so that in the end she hardly knows which words have come from whom.

'We are from Prague . . . We've been here since the forties. The story of where we came from and what happened to us, I'm sure you know. But this country has been good to us. Hard, mind you, but good to us. Friends are like family here. And we needed that, didn't we? To feel like family. To have other people to talk to, because after what happened there, you know, Irena, she couldn't have children, so there is just us and sometimes still when we think about it, it is hard. But we don't think about it, do we? Not very much. There is so much to do. Now we're older, we have the time for hobbies. Before when Peter worked in the pharmacy . . . Before when Irena worked in the school we were just too busy, but now we can do what we love. I hope I don't disturb you with my piano ever, Sarit. You must always tell me if you hear it too much up there. Peter blocks it out. He doesn't hear my fumbling on the keys any more . . . No, I don't block it out. It's background for me, when I'm reading. She plays beautifully. I love to hear my wife play when I'm reading or I'm painting. He paints well. No, I don't. Not so well. Just what you see on the wall. My memories of Czechoslovakia. Nothing special. Only watercolours. With oils I would make too much mess and I'm not talented enough. I think for oils you must be more talented than for watercolours. I paint in light colours, you see. Almost never dark colours. It would be too sad. I don't like dark-brown or grey or black.'

Grey or black. *Schachor* . . . the *schach* that is the shadow of the word. The *or* that is the light. So that *schachor* might mean to shadow the light. And the shadow can lift itself slightly, inch by inch from the light. And the black can begin slowly to let in chinks of the 'L' of light. In the early morning, a pinkish light thrown in by the sun, as it wakes the sea, as Sarit stands on the balcony, her arms around herself in her short white bathrobe, and watches the movement of the water. The Middle Eastern winter water. A thick navy-blue, with pieces here and there of turquoise and the white of foam, the grey and black of gulls and crows that tease and plait and play till the wind picks up. Till the sky comes closer and the strokes of blue grow heavier and thicker. Faster, deeper, more threatening, meaningful and frightening. Strokes that draw Sarit further in, as balanced on a rickety chair, naked where her robe has fallen open, her torso, her arms, her hands, are splattered with the paint from the huge thick brush strokes. The brush strokes of the sky, the wind, the water and the sunlight. Thick and fast and furious brush strokes on the huge wall in front of her that once was white. And the *or*, the light from the word *schachor*, the light that seeps through from the blackness into her room and to her soul. The light that comes with the rising of the sun, the brewing of a storm and the strong smell of coffee that wafts up the stairs and underneath the door of the apartment rented by the artist Sarit Kleinmann.

FORTY-ONE

The old man wakes alone in his one-roomed low-roofed house. He stretches to the sound of the waking birds, dresses in a white shirt, cotton trousers, fastens his belt, bends with difficulty to fasten his sandals and makes his way to the communal dining room for his breakfast. He smiles at the robust elderly woman in her white apron laying the long tables. '*Boker tov, Rivka* . . . Good morning, Rivka,' he calls.

She comes closer to him. 'You're so early today, Ben,' she tells him.'

He says, 'I didn't tell you? I'm going to Tel Aviv for a couple of days. Even an old man like me needs sometimes to smell the city, don't you think?'

From the counter he helps himself to rye bread, white cheese and cherry tomatoes, goes and sits at the end of one of the long rough wooden tables. Rivka brings him a mug with black coffee, comes and sits down next to him. 'You're serving me?' he asks her. 'What's so special about today? We celebrating something?'

She shrugs and smiles, pushing strands of hair behind her ears as if she were a young woman still. No matter that her hair is almost silver white. She asks him, 'Why don't you take Max into the city with you, Ben? It would do him so much good. He would get out of here for once, maybe even get some different inspiration.'

'Believe me, I've tried. You know I have. He reminded me he was there a few months ago. He said he doesn't need to see Tel Aviv or Jerusalem any more. He said his mind gives him all the inspiration that he needs. I told him the colours

in the city were different. That they would broaden his reper-
toire.'

'And?' she asks.

'You know what he said? He said he had enough colours
in his palette to last the rest of his life and beyond. He asked
me, "Who needs the city to get blown up by a bomb?" And
he said that if a bomb blew off his left arm we would force
him to learn to paint with his feet.' Ben laughs. He says, 'And
you know what, Rivka, he's probably right. I think he's shown
us that if you are an artist in your mind you can never get
away from it . . . You know what I mean?'

The little that is left of Ben's hair is grey and soft and fuzzy,
cropped close to his head so that as he speaks Rivka wants so
much to touch it. He looks at her, his face at first breaking
into a dark-brown crinkled smile. A smile that leaves him when
he says, 'Max doesn't want to come with me, Rivka. We must
just let him be.'

'What will you do in Tel Aviv?' she asks him, spreading thick
white plaited bread with butter.

'Drink coffee at Mersand with the old refugees, eat some
cake. Put on a little weight.' He pats his stomach. 'They have
the best strudel there. Do you remember when we went that
time?' he asks, his eyes lighting up with the memory of the
taste and the occasion. She nods. He says, 'I'll visit a little with
my niece and her children too. She's driving all the way here
to pick me up. I'll talk a little, walk a little, buy a present here
and there, wander in and out of the shops on Dizengoff and
the galleries on Gordon. You know, Rivka, I'll enjoy and I'll
remember a little how it used to be when I was young.'

'Yes,' she says, 'I think a lot, Ben, how things were when we
were young and how things might have been. We have to take
our chances when we have them, instead of thinking they will
come again.'

She looks at him. He looks away. He chews slowly, stands
up then from the bench and in the lush green greyness of the

Galilee winter he slowly makes his way through the kibbutz, along the gravel pathway, past the laundry, past the school-rooms, past the building that was once the children's house, where he stops and nods, remembering the feeling of his bare feet on the wooden floors, the sound of the puffy night-time breathing of the children as he walked between the beds to check that all was well. The children who have stayed in his mind all these years are the ones who used to wake at night as he dozed on his chair by the door. The pale wiry little blonde boy, the cry-baby who would tell him the stories of his nightmares about crocodiles and ghosts. The fat little girl who woke up begging for sweets and chocolates in the middle of the night. And the dark child with the pale skin and the long, thick lashes. The one with the paintings above her bed, the one who never cried, even when she wet her bed, even when her mother died.

'Max,' Ben had said in the first years, the years before Max learnt to paint again, 'Max, won't you go to America and visit her perhaps? The kibbutz would pay. You know they would. And Chicago, you loved it when you went with Gaby. It's a wonderful city if you don't go in the dead of winter. So why don't you go, Max? For your birthdays perhaps?'

Sometimes he would ask the question twice or three times. He would say, 'Max. Say something. Answer me.' But then he would look at his friend. The grey face. The pursed lips. The nothingness in place of his right arm. The expression he wore like the children who'd had nightmares.

And once, just once, when he had decided to let the subject drop, when he thought that Max would never answer him, he heard him say, 'Too painful, Ben. I can't expect that you will understand. But she made her choices and she's gone. I have to live with it. After Berlin I had to live with it and when Gaby died I had to live with it, so now I will also manage. So I'm asking you. Not again. Don't talk about it with me again. The paint has dried, Ben.'

'All right, I hear you, Max. But let me ask you just one more question. What if she came here to visit you?'

'Visit here?' he says. 'Visit?' he asks, as if considering. 'Visit her own father for a day or a week and then leave again for a year? Like she's a stranger. Not my flesh and blood. No, Ben. Please.'

And Ben had sat and watched his friend and listened, outside the children's house, and at a loss for words he had gone to lay his hand on Max's arm before he realised that he sat on the wrong side of him on the bench. He had given up then, said nothing more and the two men had fallen into silence.

And now, in the car with his niece on the way to Tel Aviv, Ben rolls down the window to let some air into the conversation and lets his niece Ruth chat and chat: 'The children . . . talent . . . music . . . best at violin . . . prize for maths . . . the children . . . so good-looking . . . proud . . . the children . . . top grades, great sportsmen . . . so proud . . . and you, Ben, what do you want to do in Tel Aviv? To wander? Fine, I'll leave you to wander and then you'll come and see the children? But will you be all right alone?'

Ben turns from the car window, through which he watches Tel Aviv's winter that looks so much like spring and, only half joking with his niece, he says, 'You talk to me like I'm ninety, Ruthie, I'm only eighty-two, you know. I'll be just fine.'

She lets him out on the corner of Frischmann and Ben Yehuda Street. At Mersand he orders black coffee with the Viennese strudel of his childhood. He sits in an alcove at the tiny round table by the window, sipping, seeing no one he knows that day, but feeling at home there, surrounded by the babble of voices, of old people speaking Yiddish, German and Czech, Polish and Hungarian. And as he listens he thinks of Max, thanks God that he is not haunted by the past as Max is, that unlike Max he travelled to Palestine with his mother, his father, his uncle, his aunt and his brother before the SS could kick and bang and break their front door and their spirit.

He wipes the crumbs from his mouth, brushes them from his crisp white cotton shirt for even at his age he is still proud and he walks outside and towards Dizengoff Street. He walks slowly in and out of shops, sensing the disquiet, the uneasy stillness that precedes the new intifada.

On Gordon, though, as if the street were from another world, the atmosphere is altogether different. Brighter somehow, lighter somehow, for this sloping street is scattered with the young in sloppy winter sweaters, hands cupped round mugs of steaming coffee, outside on terraces under awnings of ivy even now on this January evening. The street is scattered too with the careful aesthetics of art and sculpture galleries.

Ben makes his way up the hill, wanders in and out of galleries, admires the miniature bronze sculpture of a face that's cracked in two, the face of the same person that on one side has young smooth skin and on the other skin that's old and wrinkled. In another gallery he is drawn to the picture of a coffee house with a well-dressed clientele, the ladies in their hats and high-necked dresses clutching the handles of their bags. A *Kaffeehaus* that reinforces his vague and blurry childhood memories of Vienna as Mersand too had done. As he walks out, on the last stretch of road up the hill, in the early evening now, he begins to feel weary, begins to think that the time has come to call his niece and tell her he is ready now to leave. At the top of the hill, outside a gallery that through its open door buzzes with the conversation of wine drinkers at an opening for new artists, Ben finds a phone booth and calls her. 'I'll be twenty minutes,' she tells him. 'Wait for me inside there. It's getting far too cold for you outside.'

'All right, all right,' he says to her. To himself he smiles and says, 'What do they know from cold in Tel Aviv?'

He looks at his watch, then makes his way inside the gallery. He is a small man and to see the paintings he has to squeeze his way between the people with the wineglasses and the brochures in their hands. They move to let him through, for despite the brusqueness of their manner these people have a certain respect for the young and for the old. As if all the young people were their own children and all the elderly their parents.

He walks past a wishy-washy watercolour of the Jerusalem hills. Amused, he listens as behind him, in the face of the work of these new artists, one of the gallery owners attempts profundity. 'I think he shows great promise,' says the pompous Englishman, 'though of course he hasn't quite yet come into his own. I don't believe an artist can really know where he's going till he reaches his late thirties.'

'*Slicha, slicha*, excuse me . . .' Ben squeezes his way out from between the people and walks round a corner to the other end of the white-walled gallery. As he moves he hears the pompous-looking man say, 'Yes, most impressive. They really are all quite spectacular for new and undiscovered artists.'

In this area of the gallery that is a little quieter, a little less dense with people and with paintings than the area by the entrance, Ben has a chance to stand back a little and view the artwork on the walls. A huge painting of an elephant almost white on white, his trunk and tail and saddle encrusted with bright semi-precious stones and a painting on the furthest wall. In an alcove tucked away. A painting that Ben has surely seen before. A navy-blue and turquoise painting of the sea, the waves crested with splashes that might have been whitecaps and might have been seagulls, and the odd splash of a black crow here and there.

He stands there, surprised by what he sees, watches the water move within the canvas, watches the waves ebb and flow and tell their story. He is struck both by the beauty of the work and by the strangeness of the situation, for it has been so long now since Max has allowed any of the old paintings still in his possession to be shown in Israel or abroad. And though in recent years the art he has created with his left arm has still been good enough to exhibit and to sell, Max has shaken his head at the meeting of the kibbutz board members and said, 'No, I will not sell this stuff. None of it. It is worth nothing except to me. You can sell it when I'm dead.'

So now in this gallery on Gordon, in front of the painting, Ben is confused at first, uplifted then, for there would be no one happier than he, if behind the backs of all of the kibbutzniks Max had decided once more to take his rightful place in the world of art. He walks up to the painting, touches the thick strands of colour. Behind him he hears a voice, 'Bevakasha Adoni, al tiga ba-tmuna . . . Please, Sir, don't touch the painting.'

He turns round, embarrassed to be admonished at his age by the gallery owner, who stands there, tall and thin with a glass of pale wine in his hand.

'I'm sorry,' Ben says. 'It's just that the artist . . . Max Kleinmann, he's my best friend. I live on the kibbutz with him. I . . . I had no idea he was exhibiting again. I'm so happy to see it.'

The gallery owner laughs, condescending, and speaks to him as though he thinks that he's dealing with some slightly demented old man, as though he thinks Ben is hallucinating, hovering on the edge of senility. He says, 'Anyway, it's better not to touch the paintings. But if you'd like something to drink, we have orange juice and lemonade too . . . Over by the door.'

And as he walks away from Ben, he turns back to look·at the whitecapped, gull-capped sea and thinks, 'You know, perhaps the old boy's not so stupid. It really does look like a Kleinmann. That's a good selling point.'

Amongst the groups of people he looks for his partner, the skinny, thin-lipped redheaded woman with whom he owns the gallery. He says, 'Maaya, you know that anonymous artist Kobi brought in, the American who painted the sea over there. He has almost exactly the style of Kleinmann. I was just standing looking at it and that's what came to mind. We must use it in our PR.'

And Maaya nods and smiles. 'Aha. So now you believe me,' she says, feeling a sense of one-upmanship that it was she and not her partner who had discovered this talent, albeit vicariously through the agent.

And whilst they are talking over there by the door, Ben has crept up closer to the painting of the whitecapped sea and looked for Max's initials, cursing all the while that his eyesight, even with his glasses, makes it hard for him to see close up. On the painting there are no initials, of course, for Sarit has fear and dread of recognition rather than desire for it. But somehow Ben convinces himself it is only his long-sightedness that prevents him from reading the initials of Max Kleinmann and that in the swirls and the movement of the water there must surely be an 'MK' somewhere.

He checks his watch again and sees that he must leave. Behind him he hears the voice of the gallery owner, who speaks with confidence and nonchalance to a prospective customer, pointing at the painting of the sea. 'Yes, this painting here is quite spectacular. It lifts you up and draws you in, if you know what I mean. It has so much of the artist Max Kleinmann in it. You remember his work?' he says and notices as he speaks that Ben is still there next to him. 'In fact, this gentleman here, a friend of Mr Kleinmann's himself, actually mistook it for one of his old paintings, didn't you, Sir?'

Ben turns round and nods, amused to be used as part of the gallery owner's sales ploy. The fat client cocks his head from left to right, checks his gold Rolex. He says, 'You know, I love it. But I saw the price in the catalogue. I'd need my wife's approval for a such a major spend.'

'No problem. I quite understand. I'll take a Polaroid of it for you. You can take it home and show her. And if it's not sold by then, you can come back for it . . . Bring your wife with you maybe.'

'A wonderful idea,' says the fat man with the scarlet tie. And the gallery owner stands back and with his Polaroid he clicks.

He pulls the photograph out and as he's shaking it dry the client says, 'You say the artist is anonymous. Why is that?'

'I really couldn't tell you. I only know that he's American and was discovered by a friend of a friend. Another artist's agent came in with the piece and refused point blank to tell us anything about this artist. Here we are,' he says. 'The photo's almost dry.'

And Ben taps the gallery owner on the arm and says, 'I also want one.'

'I beg your pardon?'

'I said I want a photograph too. I am also interested in the painting.'

At first the gallery owner is irritated, for he cannot in truth imagine that this old man in his sandals could afford artwork of this ilk, but suddenly he thinks, 'Aha. Yes. Yes. This old boy's creating interest here,' and he says, 'Of course. With pleasure. Here we go.' He clicks again and within a minute Ben is leaving the gallery walking out into the street towards his niece's car shaking the wet polaroid photograph in his hand. The photograph of the painting that he's so sure has been created by his friend Max Kleinmann.

'Max Kleinmann,' Ben says, smiling, as they walk in the early evening towards the members' lounge of the kibbutz, 'do I have a bone to pick with you, my friend?'

'A bone?' he says. 'So what is it, then?'

Ben looks at him and wonders why even after years some images just never cease to shock. He wants to say to him, 'Max, why did you never agree to an artificial arm? You're such an aesthete in every other way. They can make such wonderful ones these days. They're made by artists . . . sculpted to fit your body,' but he doesn't say it. He doesn't dare, for he has tried before and now has understood how Max has grown to see his missing arm as some kind of metaphor for his life.

And so, half smiling as they walk, he says to him, 'Why didn't you tell me you're exhibiting again, Max?'

'What?'

'The painting in Tel Aviv on Gordon. Your painting. I saw it.'

'Which painting? What are you talking about?'

'Max, you and I have been friends for a lifetime. Why the secrets now? I'm happy for you. The time had to come again.'

Max stops still beside his friend on the gravel under the willow tree close to where Sarit at eight had first found out about her mother's death, close to where the sunflowers are still planted and grow every spring in the shape of an unfinished S.

'You know, Ben,' he says, 'maybe old age is turning you a little crazy. Do I know what you're talking about?'

'The painting,' he says again, 'the one you gave to the gallery on Gordon.'

'A little *meschugge* you are, Ben. A little nuts. You know I will never sell a left-handed creation.'

As he speaks, so very sure of himself, as if all knowing, Ben taps on the pocket of his shirt where he keeps the photograph he has brought back from Tel Aviv and has shown that morning to Rivka, who has said, 'My God, Ben, I think you're right. Good old Max is trading on the quiet. This could belong to no one else. It has his fingerprints all over it . . . And that turquoise . . . do you remember that turquoise . . . ? This calls for celebration . . . but no . . . no you have to do this carefully. He might be upset that we know. You know what he's like. Still such an artist's temperament. Be careful, Ben.'

'How long have you known me, Rivka? Don't you worry.'

And so Ben, wearing kid gloves, Ben, once so used to coaxing children, says to Max, 'It's all right. Keep it to yourself if you feel more comfortable that way. I'm pleased for you. That's all. And you know it looked wonderful hanging there. It really did. As if you had been reborn or something. Max. Tell me. When did you paint it?'

Standing beneath the willow tree, his face half shaded by the weeping of the branches, in a quiet voice Max says, 'Ben, in some ways it was a rebirth to paint with my left arm. I knew at least that the vision was still there. But you know damned well that I've never sold my left-handed nonsense. So why are you playing with me? If this is one of your psychological games to encourage me, Ben, leave it. Drop it. I'm OK, Ben. I'm OK as I am.'

Ben stands close to his friend. He pays attention to every word, but as he listens, so he reaches into the pocket of his short-sleeved shirt, removes the photo from it and as Max is saying, 'I'm OK, Ben, I'm OK as I am,' he presses the photograph into his hand. 'Here, look . . . I got them to take a picture of it,' he says. 'See how good it looks there on the wall. There were people looking at it and commenting on it.'

Max laughs now and Ben stares at him. He is laughing not because of the picture itself for he has not yet seen it, but because of the lengths to which his friend has gone. 'Ben, I'm right. You're crazy,' he says as he too reaches into his shirt pocket for his glasses. As he unfolds the silver arms of his spectacles, he takes the photo from Ben and steps out away from the shadow of the tree into the early evening light. His back to his lifelong friend, he looks down at the photograph. And slowly, without lifting his eyes, he walks away, transfixed all the while by the thick white caps, the black streaks of the birds, the movement of the waves that even in their two dimensions seem to stand out from the photograph like a sculpture waiting to be touched. Huge and heavy waves. Waves that come closer as they speak and spray and startle. Tumultuous, tormenting waves. Transparent waves in navy-blue and the turquoise over which they'd always argued.

'Turquoise, Sarit, why would you use that colour so much? You use too much of it as if the whole world were gay and happy.'

'But, Abba,' she had said, her hand not moving, not painting strokes but still holding the brush to the thick paint on the palette, at the easel where they sat by the banks close to the stream, 'I love this colour. It makes me smile.'

Max on his knees painting turquoise for her, left-handed, round the skirting boards of her new studio, making his concessions, speaking with brush and paint. Believing words redundant, forgetting how Gabriella had said, 'Max, you should tell her how you feel. She's the kind of child who needs to hear these things.'

Working hard, varnishing, keeping vigil into the night. And now, a night twenty years later when Max cannot sleep, when he lies awake, tossing and turning, the photograph clutched in his hand in the darkness. Switching on the lamp next to him and knowing without question because of the turquoise, because of the style, because of his gut.

'Ben.' He shakes him as he sleeps. Unable to find a torch he has made his way to Ben's house in the darkness knowing the ground's moves and dips and crevices as a blind man does. 'Ben . . . wake up.'

'Huh? What, what's wrong? What's happened? Is there a siren?'

'No. No siren. Don't worry.'

Max sits by him on the bed.

'What's wrong with you?' Ben asks. 'It's the middle of the night.'

'The painting,' Max says.

Ben has to haul his thoughts back from daytime into night. He is quiet for a minute. Then he says, 'I knew you did it, Max. Don't worry that you didn't tell us. That's why you're waking me, isn't it?'

'It's not mine.'

'Then whose?'

'Tell them . . .' He clears his throat and starts again. 'Tell them, Ben . . . tell the gallery to find the artist, will you?'

'What, Max? I don't understand. You sound confused.'

'Tell them to find her. And please, Ben, don't ask me questions. Just tell them to find her. I need to see . . . I need to meet the artist. I think we need to talk.'

FORTY-TWO

Pain can be the writer's quill, the painter's brush, the sculptor's clay, his wood, his marble. In the beginning, though, Ramsi was unable to create. Like a man crippled in joints and bones and organs, he lay and stared upwards at the ceiling. The pain was such that turning left or right or sitting up he winced almost, or bit his lip.

There was no self-pity in it and certainly no drama for there was no one in the room to see the sculptor suffering. His feelings went beyond words and thought, and at first even beyond vision. For though pain can fuel creation there is a point too at which paralysis hovers, at which, the very antithesis of itself, it moves in and out of the psyche threatening the essence of the creative spirit and the images forming in the mind. Only once before in his life had Ramsi felt such pain and he was taunted now by its familiarity.

It came this time in waves. The first welling on the freezing night when in the ugly yellow of the street light he had stood and watched Sarit turn from him, run from him as best she could on ice. And it had come, too, in that moment when he had looked down at the ripped and jagged photograph that he held. But that had been a different pain . . . a sharp and searing wrench as though a nerve ending causing one more moment's agony before its death. A wrench followed by a numbness that lasted a day or two, when he could neither sculpt, nor cast, nor polish. On the second day he had called Sarit late at night and, getting no reply even in the early hours, he had braced himself and walked the five minutes in the freezing cold to her building. The night porter in his black uniform had sat up straight when he caught sight of Ramsi, as though he thought he were some vagabond walking in off the street, for at two o'clock on a winter's night few residents invited guests to visit. Beneath his eyes Ramsi had dark circles, his hair hung unkempt over his forehead and when he asked for Sarit Kleinmann, he neither prefaced his request with a 'Hello', nor did he punctuate it with a 'Thank you' or a 'Please'.

The night porter said, 'It's a little late to disturb a resident, Sir. Is he expecting you?'

Ramsi had not corrected the doorman by saying, 'she not he . . . You mean, Is she expecting me?' but had merely said, 'Apartment 2604. Could you call and say I'm on my way up?'

'2604 . . . 2604 . . . now wait a minute. Isn't that the doctor? Yes, Sir, I think it is . . . I believe she's out of town. I'm sure I saw her leave with her bags as I come on duty. Yes,' he said as he tilted his head back a little, as if readjusting things to try and find the memory, and confident now in his recollection, no longer afraid that he will be reprimanded for waking her, for the form of it he adds, 'But of course I try for you, Sir. Just a moment.'

But even as he dials, without a word Ramsi walks away and after him the porter calls, 'Hey, I's dialin' for you.'

Ramsi does not turn back but in a gesture of apology he holds his hand up behind him.

There would have been little point in him waiting there in front of the desk to hear the outcome of the call for in the instant when the porter had said 'out of town', there and then Ramsi had known. He didn't need to ask, 'For how long? Do you know? Did she say? Did she leave a message?' No, at that moment Ramsi needed to ask none of these questions. Winded by the porter's words as they hit him in the stomach, winded by 'she's out of town', in that instant Ramsi was sure of Sarit's reasons for leaving. He knew that she was gone and he knew the why of it.

In the bitter cold and the wind outside the building he goes to sit on a large stone beneath a tree where in the fall, the spring, the summer lovers often sat. The stone was huge, uneven and earth-grey, and though the street was too dark for him to see its colour or its sparkle he was aware all the time of its roughness beneath his hands. Hands that he pushed against the stone's jagged edges so that where he pressed, on his palms indentation marks appeared. And as he felt the comfortlessness of the stone, in that moment too he felt its message, its possibility and its offering, and he knew what he would do.

As he stands he feels dizzy, nauseous and afraid. He has to bend and steady himself before he can make his way along the street.

And even though he has stood up from the stone and is moving towards home, still he feels its sharp rough edges on his skin and out loud as he walks fast, battling wind and the beginnings of a snowfall, to himself he says, 'Albert, Albert, I must call Albert now.'

As if an intruder he bursts into his own home, as if about to ransack the place, letting the red door, then the blue door slam behind him, repeating over and over again, 'Albert, I must call Albert now,' and with no regard whatsoever for the hour, he leaves a message on Albert's answerphone. He says, 'It's me. Ramsi. Call me as soon as you get this message. I need stone or marble. You have some there. I've seen it. I want to come and get it.'

And he lies there listening for the sound of the telephone as though at three in the morning Albert might call him to discuss the quality and the availability of stone. He lies waiting for the break of day and with the filtering of the first light through the window, still in his clothes he gets up, turns on the water at the kitchen sink, the tap running full blast, splashing him, as he fills a mug, gulps the water down, not considering bread or fruit even for a moment before he moves towards the door. Outside seeing how the snow is piled high on his car, seeing how the ice has frozen on his windscreen, he begins to walk through the streets in search of a taxi. He might, had he looked north, have seen a yellow cab approaching but he no longer wants to look behind him and looking straight ahead he sees only the odd car passing and the truck that throws out grit in an attempt to de-ice the roads. Roads that have about them that early morning feel that allows both for thought and for the anticipation of the movement and the madness of day.

Ramsi seems after a few minutes to forget that he needs a taxi, he seems to forget exactly where he is going, though not for a moment does he forget what he is looking for.

On Dearborne he passes a construction site, a half-finished apartment block and a courtyard strewn with huge great lumps of stone, some half covered in snow. And walking, searching through the courtyard he looks around him. By a massive rectangle of stone he bends down and with both hands in their fingerless gloves he rubs the side of the stone, lets the thin covering of ice fall away to reveal a piece of marble almost black. 'No, not this,' he says to himself. 'Too dark. Too black,' he says, as if, had he wanted it, the stone would have been his for the taking. And looking up then he sees the yellow taxis begin to pass in front of the construction site and in the back of a cab he gives the driver Albert's address on the West Side of Chicago. The driver, in a fur hat with flaps that come down over his ears and tie beneath his chin, turns back to Ramsi for a second and in a strong Eastern European accent says, 'I do not like to drive over there. It's rough, but if you must go I will take you.'

'Yes,' Ramsi says, 'I must.'

As he bangs on the concrete iron of the front door of Albert's home cum foundry it is still only seven in the morning. Through the spyhole Albert sees him. He opens up. His red eyes redder even than normal, his white hair more dishevelled, he says, 'Why are you here at this time? It's freezing. Come in.'

Ramsi is beginning to push his way past him already, through the huge workshop with bronze, wax and plaster sculptures strewn around in all stages of casting, into the room at the back where the furnace is, the room where in the past Albert has stored different coloured, different textured slabs of stones. But now Ramsi sees only the furnace, huge and black and steaming like a witch's cauldron, and turning back to Albert, a look of panic on his face, he says, 'Where's the stone? You used to have stone here. I saw it. Did you move it outside?'

'Sold it,' Albert says, standing at the door, facing him. 'All of it, to one guy. A retailer.'

'What d'you mean? You can't have sold all of it. I need some, Albert. There must be some outside.' The tone of his voice is desperate and he goes as if to push his way towards the door again.

But Albert grabs him by the arm and stops him. 'There isn't any stone, Ramsi. What's got into you? You don't carve stone,' he says, standing blocking Ramsi's passage.

And as though he were a drug addict starting to shake without his fix, Ramsi says, 'I need some stone.'

'What for?'

'Please, Albert, show me where to go.'

Together they drive to the stone yard. Out towards the sub-urbs, along the highway by the side of trees and lake on this snowy morning in Albert's red rusting Chevrolet Cavalier with the foam stuffing protruding through the seats. At first neither of them speaks. Ramsi's state is that of the agitated poet, inspired, compelled, but bereft of pen and paper. He closes his eyes, to begin his work in his head, to begin to visualise.

Albert glances at him, sees the tension on his face. 'What's this all about, Ramsi?' he asks.

'Don't ask me, Albert . . . I can't . . . I don't want to . . .' and then, 'But thanks for driving me.'

'No sweat.'

And then in an attempt to change the subject, to make some

sort of conversation, Albert asks him, 'How's the woman?'

'Gone, Albert,' he says.

For a second Albert takes his eyes off the road. 'You left her. Just like the others,' and then, looking straight ahead again, 'Shame. I would have hung on to that one. Not beautiful exactly but there was something about her. Can't say exactly what. Quite liked her myself,' he says and he laughs a nervous laugh that falls on heavy silence.

Ramsi turns away to stare out of the window.

They say nothing then to one another, till they pull into the stone yard, till they step out on to the concrete, covered with a thin layer of snow and lined with the hangars and garages that serve as workshops for stone sculptors and storage places for the stone.

From one of the garages a young man in jeans and a dark fleece sweater walks towards them. 'Albert,' he says and slaps him on the back. 'Good to see you. I was working. Been up since six. I heard the car. Wondered who it was.'

The man looks at Ramsi. Albert says, 'Oh, Guy, this is Ramsi Riyad.'

And Guy, though he says no more than, 'Good to meet you,' cannot help but let surprise register on his face. On another day, on any other day depending on his mood, the recognition might have amused or annoyed Ramsi, but this morning, immune to it, as Guy speaks to him Ramsi is struck only by the familiarity of the man's accent. By the guttural 'r' that a layman might have thought to be French, but that Ramsi in a syllable or two recognises as Israeli.

'I need some marble,' Ramsi says. 'Or stone.'

'How much?'

For a moment Ramsi stands quite still. And in a movement that hurts him, in a movement that heralds both the beginning of the end and the end of the beginning, Ramsi holds his hands apart, rounding them as though cradling thin air. 'This much, I suppose . . . yes . . .' and he bites hard on his lip.

'Yes. This much,' he says, his hands still in the air. 'I think this is what I need.'

'Three feet or so?' says Guy.

Ramsi nods.

'And width?'

Again Ramsi says nothing and Guy, patient as though talking to a child, asks him again, 'Width, how wide do you need it?'

'This wide,' he says and then, turning to Albert, gesturing again, 'this wide, don't you think?'

'How would I know, Ramsi?' and then, aggrieved for being kept in the dark, he says to him, 'I don't know what you need it for, do I?'

And Guy thinks, 'It's true what they say about him. He's a deep, dark type,' and out loud he says, 'Come with me, Ramsi. We'll find you something.'

Behind him Albert and Ramsi walk across the snow-covered cobbled stones. In and out of garages Ramsi follows him, running his eyes and his palms over different slices, mounds and slabs of stone and marble. 'Too light,' Ramsi says, 'too dark . . . Too rough . . . Too sugary.'

Till Guy says to him, 'If you can tell me what it's for I could help you better.'

Albert has wandered off and so they, the sculptors, stand there together in the hangar for Guy, the provider of stone, is a sculptor too and again he turns to Ramsi and he asks, 'So what's this for?'

Ramsi is about to tell him the truth. The words are there waiting to give life to his intention, but in the way that an idea shared and spoken becomes a harsh reality he cannot yet quite bring himself to mouth them and so instead he says, 'It's for an abstract piece.'

'I see,' says Guy, though of course he doesn't.

He leads Ramsi to a slab of creamy Indiana limestone. Ramsi kneels down by it, lets his hand slide across the smoothness of

384

its side, studies the fine veins as they run through it, as though a vet examining an animal. And he thinks to himself, 'Yes, yes, this is it . . . This is right, I have to have this piece.'

He looks up at Guy. He says, 'I'll take it.'

'How much of it?' he asks.

'This much,' says Ramsi, his arms stretched widthways across almost the whole piece of stone, about three and a half feet across, just a little longer than the height of a small child.

And Guy says, 'You'll have to take the whole piece. It's not worth my while hacking off a foot or so,' and he moves to the door of the hangar and calls to Albert, 'He's found what he needs. We'll get it into the back of your car.' And then, turning back to Ramsi he adds, 'Unless you want to work here. You could sculpt in one of the garages. A lot of our sculptors do. We don't charge much.'

'No,' he says, 'I need to be at home.'

When the stone has been loaded from a trolley into the car, in Albert's Chevrolet with the piece of creamy Indiana limestone, with Ramsi suspended somewhere between vision and creation, somewhere between the first bout of pain and the worst of it, Albert asks him, 'Have you ever carved stone?'

'In Alexandria,' he says, 'when I was studying.' He sees the dusty shelves with rows of Greek and Roman busts, with copies of the heads of Caesar and Marc Antony, with rows of other naked plaster men with muscles well defined. He hears his straight-backed professor, for whom sculpture was discipline as much as art, saying to him, 'Stone carving is about taking away till the truth reveals itself to you, Riyad. You might say that stone and marble aren't your medium, but if you want to call yourself a sculptor you have to learn to sculpt and carve with them as well. You never know. One day you might need the skill.'

Today of all days he needs it, the stone sculptor's training. Bent over the slab of Indiana limestone in the courtyard in front of his apartment with the carving tools that Albert has lent him on the ground by his side. In the cold, close to the fishpond, dressed in one dark-coloured sweater over another, his hands bare now, he bends to pick up the fiercest chisel, the point chisel, from the ground.

Slowly he straightens up and moves back. He raises his left arm way above his head, so that the blow, that first blow of the chisel on stone, will come at it from a height. The first blow that on stone is so crucial. Not like the beginnings of a clay sculpture where if he has taken too much away he might add more, but the first heavy hacking blow on stone, that falls irreversible, separating, deafening and dramatic.

A blow. A thud. A heavy piece of limestone that, hurt and broken, splits and crashes to the ground giving life and new possibility to the stone that it has left behind.

A second blow. And then a third. And Ramsi working, legs and back and shoulders straining, the sounds of exertion coming from his throat, ignoring his neighbour as she marches out of her apartment, a coat over her pyjamas. 'What on earth . . . would you stop? You crazy man!'

At times turning his head from her, at times not even hearing over the next two days, as he coughs and coughs, breathing heavily, not wearing a mask to protect himself as he should, inhaling the cold air, the dust, the pain, hacking at the slab of stone, as he hollows with the sharp, the searing teeth of his point chisel, as he sculpts with the fierce unforgiving edge of the chisel that is flat. Cold and hot and sweating, determined and afraid all at once and the neighbour tries a different tactic now, comes up to him spluttering in the dust and the noise saying, 'Ramsi, stop this. I can't take it any more. I really can't.'

He looks at her. She sees his black-rimmed eyes, pained eyes pleading. 'Please,' he says. 'Just this. I have to do it. I have to finish. Another day and I'll be done.'

She walks away, comes back some minutes later with a mug of tea that she sets down by the fishpond. 'Cover your face. The dust is dangerous. And then get a life,' she says.

He is trying. Ramsi Riyad is trying hard to get a life. With each blow, each cut, with each muscle that he flexes to lift a chisel, to hollow and to shape the stone, with each bead of sweat that pours down from his neck to the small of his back beneath his sweaters, with each scrape of rasps and files moving across stone, changing and shaping, Ramsi Riyad is fighting hard to get a life.

Pieces of stone that litter the ground around him everywhere, his thumb and his first finger sore and open from the rasps. His hands raw and red from the files and from the cold. The lifting of the bouchard, the chisel used by Ancient Egyptians once their heaviest work was done, once the stone or the marble had begun to give birth to their vision. And now it is Ramsi who lifts the bouchard, carves out the final pieces from the inside of his sculpture, not feeling the hunger or the thirst he ought to feel after three days of very little food or drink.

A hardness, a harshness, a roughness in his sculpting, that with the start of the polishing of the art he has created in two pieces of creamy Indiana limestone he must change into a different movement. Gentler, closer, as if the tempo of a symphony slowing down.

He stands back when he has finished, wipes his hands on his clothes, brings them to his face, unshaven now for days, and he shakes his head there by the sculpted limestone. He might, once he had polished, have engraved the sides of his sculpture with images denoting links between this life and the next, as his forefathers had done. He might have inscribed columns of poetry or of prose beneath the lid in a decorative imitation of the practices of old kingdoms. But on this piece of work Ramsi wants only beauty and simplicity . . . to keep the creamy white stone as pure as possible. And so the symbols, tiny hieroglyphics, a thread of running water, a bird, a hand, a leaf, an arm that make up the name, the one name he engraves with a tiny silver tool on its left side will come not now, not straight away, but only once the lid is on his sculpture.

He hardly notices when snow and darkness begin to fall together. And he knows not in his mind but in his hands and in his fingers that his work is done. Swaggering with exhaustion, in his studio he moves from the door to the muslin curtains at its far end. He pulls them back and stands there leaning on a table, blinking, staring at his work. At copies and originals, at busts and almost life-size figures, at finished polished bronzes, at unfinished terracotta pieces. Some of people he has met along the way, some of models he has found at Kingston Mines, but most of her, most of the little girl, the child, the teenager, the young woman he has tried for all these years to keep alive. He stands there, his eyes moving from one sculpture to the next as if hunting for something, as if there were an urgency in his task. He moves as if towards one sculpture, a life-size piece of a small girl, but inches from it, close enough to touch it, he turns his back, walks over to his chest of drawers. From the bottom drawer, from under a pile of winter sweaters, he takes out an old worn leather album, turns to the back page and from underneath a photograph he removes a tiny yellowing scrap of newspaper. In his hands where the rough and heavy stone had been he holds the flimsy cutting, forces himself to look at the faded face of the little girl, forces himself to read the words of the announcement his mother had placed in the paper without him even knowing, '*Nadia Riyad, adorée par Maman, Papa, Grandmaman, Grandpapa . . . Née le 30 juin 1972, morte le 5 octobre 1978.*' Again and again he reads the faded newsprint and not once as he speaks the words out loud to himself does his voice break or crack or falter. Not till he has taken the newspaper cutting with him in his hand, not till he has walked outside again and has placed the piece of paper on the inside of his sculpture, on the inside of the coffin he has sculpted, does Ramsi's throat begin to tighten. Not till he has knelt down on the ground in the snow that falls on him

388

and leant over the side of the tiny sarcophagus, his head bowed forward, does Ramsi begin to lose control of his emotions. Only then does he begin to sob and sob, quite unaware of his neighbour, who stands at her front door and watches him as though she were a mourner at a funeral.

FORTY-THREE

<figure>⬦ divider ornament ⬦</figure>

Through the rain she sees the lemon groves, the orange groves, the fields of yellow-green bananas ripening. In recent years she would not have seen foliage tumbling over fruit as art, but now as she drives, to calm herself she turns to look, she sees these unripe fruits through the window and she paints them in her mind.

In the back of the Beetle she has rented she has thrown her worn brown leather holdall with the jeans, the T-shirts and the sweaters she brought with her from Chicago. And on the very first stretch of road from Tel Aviv, the stretch that leads towards the airport, she looks down at her hands on the steering wheel and thinks of the way that she is going.

She has been given directions, but still she feels unsure of the route and she finds it hard to read the road signs. Not just because of the rain that falls on her windscreen, but because her brain cannot decide whether to focus on the directions in Hebrew or in English. At first it is the Latin alphabet that draws her eye. English after all has been the language of Sarit's professional life, if not the language of her dreams, but the further north she drives, the closer she comes to the airport so the English letters seem to fade and as though they were subtitles in a film it is the Semitic swirls to which her eye is drawn.

She pulls in at a petrol station, rolls her window down a little, jumps out in the rain without pulling up the hood of her grey sweatshirt, goes to fill her tank. From a Mercedes sports next to her a handsome tanned man trying to stay in middle age and dressed in a rainproof jacket steps out, sees his window of opportunity. He walks up to Sarit. He says, '*Ani eesse lach* . . . I'll do it for you.'

She doesn't say, 'Thanks, but no thanks,' as she did to the man in the multicoloured shirt in Kingston Mines and many more besides. For no reason in particular she lets him fill her tank. She runs inside to pay. Coming back she says in Hebrew, '*Ani baderech hanechona le airport* . . . am I heading in the right direction for the airport?'

He lifts the nozzle from the petrol tank. She notices that his hands, as suntanned as his face, are on the verge of wrinkling too. She considers saying, 'You ought to stay out of the sun,' but she refrains.

Standing there he says to her, 'Yes, this is the way . . . But you're not leaving, are you? You have to stay and have coffee with me. Or at least take me in your suitcase.'

One leg in the car, flirting just a little, Sarit says, 'Sorry, there's someone waiting for me.' She gets inside, closes the door and winds up his window of opportunity.

Imbuing her comment of 'There's someone's waiting for me' with his own meaning, to himself the tanned man says, 'There's someone waiting for her. Now that does not surprise me.'

The airport comes a few miles down the road from the garage. She's listening to the radio as she drives. An Itzhak Perlman, virtuoso . . . Chanson sans Paroles . . . that the rental company has left in the CD player. As she approaches the turn-off to the right towards the airport, as if in rhythm with the music's staccato phrases the rain beats still on the windscreen. She lifts her foot a little, slows down with the music. Sarit looks to her right. She thinks of where she's come from, she thinks of him, allows herself the images, the wrench, the pain, then turns back to the road straight ahead of her, the road straight north, obscured from view in part at least by weather.

She grips the wheel, feels it cold beneath sweaty palms, leans over to turn up the volume. She drives faster as if the symphony of speed and rain and music might block out thought. She opens her window and for a minute or two lets the water fall into the car on to her arms and her wrists. She looks up again towards the signs that lead her in the direction of Haifa. For years she has read nothing in Hebrew except for Dani's notes, except for the letters that the Czech man from downstairs had brought to her several weeks after she had painted the mural of the sea on her wall, after she had gone almost in a trance to buy an easel, brushes, paints and canvases. In the weeks that she had lived on Peki'in, the little leafy cul-de-sac that faced the sea, despite herself she had grown fond of Peter and Irena. Not that she had any real desire to come out of herself or socialise in any way. But the aromas of bread baking, of coffee brewing, of goulash stewing continued to waft up the stairs, bringing with them invitations that she come down and join them. And because in the mornings she was often unable to eat, because when she woke she felt not only a sadness, but a sickness too, on some days by the time Peter knocked Sarit would be too hungry to resist.

On other days, though, on her worst days, she would open the door only a crack and so he came to judge Sarit's moods by the angle at which her door was open. So that he might go back down to his wife and say, 'She opened only a couple of inches. She won't come visit us today,' or, 'You know what, she opened the door almost like a normal human being. She'll come down and have the stew with us. You'll see.'

He knew to tread carefully with Sarit. The first time he smelt paint, saw life and colour in her flat, he just nodded and said, 'Very nice,' in a way that did not beg reply. But the second time, when beyond Sarit he saw the sea in mauves and pinks and purples, the sea in grey and white and black and turquoise against the backdrop of the terrace that looked out on to the Mediterranean, he said to her, 'Ah, so we have an artist in our midst. Now I know why you are here. To paint our country. I didn't know you were a kindred spirit.'

He said 'our country' and not 'your country', to paint 'our country' and not to paint 'your country' for not once had Sarit spoken a word of Hebrew to the couple, not once had she talked of her childhood or given any hint of a life before Chicago and when Irena asked, 'So tell me, why did your parents choose "Sarit"?' she said, 'My mother spent time here before she married and liked the name.' The couple had nodded together in their dark apartment filled with aromas, with watercolours and with the past. They had nodded and had half believed her story.

Peter, though, had been excited to discover this complicated, closed-off and mysterious woman a 'kindred spirit'. He had waited till a day when her door was opened wide, when the light flooded in and uninvited he had walked past her between her paintings as if a visitor at a gallery. He had said, 'Young woman, you're quite something,' and in a sudden gush, a mixture of generosity, of awkwardness and affection, with a wave of the hand and without looking at him she had said, 'Look, take a couple of them if you want. They're getting in my way.' That was all she had said. Just, 'Look, take a couple if you want. They're getting in my way.' That was all it had taken. Just those few words to change the colour and the course of things. Because it is in truth remarkable how very little it does take. A sprinkle of salt or cinammon to change a taste. The lowering of a light to change a mood. The touching of a hand to change a life.

And then, a few days after Sarit's painting of the sea in turquoise, mauves and pinks and purples, in grey and black and white had been propped up downstairs against the wall in Peter's and Irena's apartment, he had asked Sarit, 'Tell me, would you ever show your stuff?'

At the time, at the moment when Peter put the question to her, Sarit had been at their kitchen table with Irena ladling goulash on to her plate and she had sat there with the steam from the bowl of stew that rose into her face and had said,

'Show my stuff? I don't know . . . I . . . I don't think it's up to much . . .'

They laugh together. Peter and Irena. The elderly Czech couple. He says, 'Not up to much. I don't think we agree . . .' And then, not knowing anything but struck by something, drawing on insight or intuition, he had said, 'You could always exhibit anonymously.'

She had looked up then and he had read her expression.

'The anonymous artist,' he had said and laughed. 'You see.' And he had banged on the table, delighted by his epiphany. 'Now we have it. Now we are getting to the real artist's personality.'

The stew had burnt her tongue. She had felt the pain of it, the pain of the artist who feels the need for anonymity and she had gulped down water.

Peter had said nothing more, but some days later when Irena met Sarit in the darkened peeling lobby in a hushed voice, an excited tone she said, 'Don't tell him that I told you, will you? He wants to tell you himself . . . but his friend, he has a friend, an agent . . . to cut the long story short . . .' and she had squeezed Sarit's arm and done a tiny little jump on the spot there in the run-down entrance to their building. 'Well . . . a gallery on Gordon wants to show those two paintings of yours. The ones of the sea.'

Beneath her fingers Irena had felt Sarit's arm go rigid. She had shaken her a little and had said, 'You're not happy with this? Please don't tell me that.' Sarit had not answered that question, had not responded to the enquiry about her happiness but, a note of panic in her voice, she had asked Irena, 'Has Peter handed them over already?'

Sarit's paintings, anonymous as Peter had promised, had indeed been handed over so that a couple of weeks later she had heard Peter climb the stairs, she had heard him call, 'A piece of strudel, young lady. A special delivery,' and through the door, no more than half opened, he had handed her the tray and on it the fresh strudel and the poorly sealed crumpled cream envelope addressed merely to 'The American', and he had said, 'The gallery sent this to my friend . . . about you. He said your cheque is inside. He really wants to meet you. He says an artist can't be anonymous to his agent.'

Sarit wondered if Peter had steamed the envelope open to have a look and tried to seal it again. She could not help but smile to herself at the thought of him and Irena standing there, whispering to one another, holding the envelope over hot, steaming water. By the door of her apartment she had thanked him as he hovered and had said, 'Perhaps I'll be down later.'

She had watched his face fall in disappointment at the fact that she wasn't going to read her letter on the spot and in his company, until triumphant he remembered and he said, 'Oh, of course, I'll have to translate the letter for you. It's in Hebrew.'

And Sarit had answered, 'Thanks, but no need.'

'What?' he had asked. 'You're not interested in what it says?'

'Yes,' she says, 'I am, but I can manage.'

Thoroughly confused, Peter limps back down the stairs. She makes herself a hot tea on the rusting stove. She puts on a heavy black turtleneck and she goes and she sits there on the balcony in the fraying wicker chair in the winter sun with the letter in her hand. She runs her index finger, the long slim index finger of her right hand, along the V at the back of the envelope, opens it slowly, knowing as she had done as a child, as she had done when Gabriella began to talk of loving and of loners, knowing though she knows not what.

At first the money order that flutters to the floor offers light relief. She bends to pick it up, sees that the amount is written out in ink pen and in dollars. 'Nine hundred and fifty dollars,' and she laughs out loud with no one but the sea to hear her. A laugh not of derision but of incredulity that anyone should want to pay for what she's painted. Astonishing, really, that Sarit should laugh with incredulity and pleasure even at a cheque for a few hundred dollars, when only weeks before her patients had been prepared to pay her many thousands for the talent and the vision in her hands. The hands, the grey eyes that turn then to sheets of paper from the envelope. And she feels as she begins to read in Hebrew as one feels when after time in bed with some illness, weak and blinking, one first ventures out into the light, into the air to tiptoe back into all that is familiar. She blinks. She reads the top sheet.

Dear American artist,

I enclose a cheque and a letter from the gallery. I'm sure someone will translate it for you. As Peter must have told you I would like to meet you at the earliest possible opportunity. I think there is much that we can do together. In the meantime I will respect the privacy of the artist and leave the decision to you.

Yours,

Kobi Yeffetz.

And then the sheet beneath it, a copy of the letter from the gallery to the agent.

Dear Kobi,

As you will see from the cheque we have sold both of the seascape paintings you brought in. I knew as soon as I saw them that the artist had true talent. The way a customer describes his work is that he paints as if he were painting for his life, as if the colours were running through his veins on to the paper. The paintings not only went very quickly, one before and one after the exhibition, but *Turquoise*, as I have called it, seemed to cause quite a stir. We had photographed it for an old customer, a collector, and also for another older man. The collector called and bought it the morning after the exhibition. The older man didn't seem the sort who would invest in art . . . A kibbutznik from up north. But he had made some comments about your artist's work being similar to a Kleinmann. I laughed at the comparison but you know the more I look at it, the way you can almost touch the colours, the more I see he had a point.

To cut a long story short, the kibbutznik called the next day and said he may be interested in buying the painting but that he had to know who the artist was. I explained that we had sold that particular piece but that the artist was going to keep on producing work. I told him all I knew . . . that he's American, somewhere in his late thirties, early forties and wants to remain anonymous. When I asked why he was so insistent on knowing the artist's name he said that a friend of his was sure he recognised the work as that of someone he had known many years ago.

All that aside, as you know, I would very much like to meet the artist myself. I think he has a future and in this very tough market I don't say that lightly. I very much look forward to seeing more of his work.

Regards
Maaya

In winter, in the Middle East, the weather can be hot and cold at once. So that on the balcony, on one hand, the one in which she holds the letter, Sarit can still feel the warmth of the sun, and yet on her other side she sits cold and shivering in the shade.

She remembers that, the shivering and the sweating on the balcony, the hot and then the cold, as she drives on, as she passes the airport and drives alone northwards some days later. And in her mind, in black ink on the cream crinkled writing paper, she sees the words 'He paints as though he were painting for his life'. She sees the signs for Haifa and branches off, driving up and down the steep hills of the town, till at the foot of a street almost vertical, she brakes and looks upwards to her right. Upwards towards the eighth wonder of the world, the gardens almost perpendicular hanging with every shade that any artist ever has or ever will mix on his palette. At the foot of the hill in the rain that now is lighter Sarit steps out of the car and turns to look up at the sloping overflowing gardens. She stares though not just in awe at shape, design and colour, but she looks upwards too towards the Baha'i temple that she cannot see, the temple that she knows is hidden behind the gardens. She stares and in her head she hears him say, 'I'm not so good at this, Sarit, you know.' She hears herself replying in a whisper, 'No, no, me neither . . . Not at all.' She puts her fingers to her face in the rain that falls hard now. She remembers the feel of his hand on her wet cheeks the night when she had cried in Soul Kitchen. She remembers too the way he had run his finger down the bridge of her nose and had said, 'Your Barbra Streisand nose.' Through the water that might be rain and might be tears she laughs, then shakes her head. 'Laughing and crying at the same time. Ridiculous,' she says. 'I'm like a goddamned rainbow.'

As she walks back to the car, in her mind she sees the post-card of Michelangelo's *David* that she picked up from the doormat of her hallway in Tel Aviv a few days before. She sees herself turn it over and read the words on the back in Juliann's handwriting.

> Dear Sarit,
> Here with our mutual friend. She's feeling better and looks great. We both agree Michelangelo has nothing on you.
> J

Back behind the steering wheel now, on her way further north, she stops at a little Israeli–Arab roadside café. She orders pita bread with falafel but shuns conversation. She wants her own company though not her own thoughts. In her faded jeans in this down-and-out little eaterie by the side of the road she looks so much at home.

In Hebrew with an Arab accent the owner, overweight and friendly, asks, 'Where are you going?'

'Up north,' she says.

'You visit Zfat?' he asks. 'The artist place?'

'Yes,' she says to keep him quiet and looks back down at her food.

'Beautiful art there,' he says.

She drives on alongside green, alongside Arab villages perched on hills and small Israeli towns. Sarit does not turn off at Zfat, the ancient town that takes art back to the Bible, that believes artistic creation to be the very essence of life. It's enough for her to know that it is there. Instead she follows the signs towards Ein Hod, a community of cobbled streets with engraved benches and sculptures in front gardens and galleries. There too she might have driven past the turn-off, but curiosity draws her in, as does the need to pause. She parks the car outside the village. The rain has stopped and she wanders at twilight through the narrow cobbled streets, past a house where a young boy sits on the step by an open front door in his navy duffel coat and plays with plasticine. Past another house with gold and silver oblong pieces that swing and chime, touching one another, moving away, then touching once again, making music in the wind. Down a path that leads to a gallery in a home where, as Sarit walks in, to her right a woman in her sixties sits at a table and watches a child sketch stick men next to her.

She looks up at Sarit. 'Feel free to wander around,' she says. Sarit recognises her accent as German or Austrian. She walks into the back of the gallery, looks around. Her eye is caught by the painting of a marriage, the two figures under a white canopy, faceless but facing one another on the verge of a new life. 'The artist was inspired by Chagall,' Sarit says.

'Yes, all his life,' the woman says.

'Is he living?'

The woman bows her head. 'No,' she says. 'He died last year at ninety-seven . . . He was my father . . .' And then, lifting her head again, smiling now, 'But we keep the gallery in the family . . . It's been ours for four generations.'

Sarit nods. The woman says, 'I have a small poster of the painting. Fifty shekels only. Would you like it?'

Out of the gallery at twilight back up the cobbled streets of Ein Hod with the poster of the faceless couple that she has bought she knows not why. And this stop here, in this community of artists, was the last on the way up north. Because Sarit has stopped at the garage, at the Baha'i temple, at the Arab café and now here, and on the road there comes a time when even in the face of the unknown, even in the face of feelings that are mixed, tied up in one another, one must choose either to go on or to turn back.

She does not need to read the directions that lie on the seat beside her. The landmarks might have changed, but the way has not. Perhaps for the sake of timing too she has stopped en route, because now she drives in dimming light and to arrive in blackness will be easier for her than to arrive in light, for she has no plan exactly. And following the plan she doesn't have she turns right, drives along a narrow wooded road to the entrance, where at the sound of her car a soldier, a gun slung over his arm, walks out of a portakabin to let her through or bar her way.

She winds down her window. He bends down, looks in, says, '*Erev tov* . . . Good evening.' He wears the green uniform with a stripe on his shoulder.

'Good evening,' she says . . . 'Can I drive in?'

He says, 'Ah, you're American.' He asks, 'What have you come for? The guest house?'

She knew she would be asked why she had come but she hadn't known how she would answer. She's happy for his prompting. 'Yes, for the guest house,' she says.

He smiles.

She thinks, 'He's half my age.'

He opens the iron gate. He says, 'Welcome, we hope you like our kibbutz.'

'*Our* kibbutz, *our* kibbutz,' just as Peter had said, '*Our* country. You've come to paint *our* country.' As she drives towards the main door over and again she says these words to herself, not just because what the soldier has said has struck a chord with her, or because she would like to have told him the truth, but because repeating the words fills up her mind and leaves no room for fear.

She doesn't recognise the front entrance, the low modern building, the lounge with the plush red chairs and gold-studded armrests and the ornate engraved glass and oak coffee tables. She doesn't recognise the bar to her right or the desk to her left, from behind which a young girl calls, 'Yes, can I help you?'

She walks over, looks at the girl. A redhead, seventeen or eighteen, fresh-faced, on the verge of it all. Sarit speaks in English. 'I . . . I . . .' and then she can't. She stops. She clears her throat, 'I need a place to stay for the night,' she says.

The girl laughs and says, 'You sound like Mary.'

Sarit catches her breath, wondering if this young girl has a sixth sense. She says, 'So do you have a room in the guest house?'

'Yes,' she says. 'Sure we do. It's pretty quiet at the moment. I'll take you there in a minute. But don't you want to eat first?'

She looks around her. 'Where do guests eat?' she asks.

'With the kibbutzniks,' the girl says, 'in the communal dining room.'

'Oh,' Sarit says, 'no, I'm not that hungry. I'll just go to my room.'

'Fine. Can I have your passport and a credit card?' and then, 'You know you can get a drink or some chocolate from the machine behind the bar if you want.'

Sarit hands over her American passport and her card. The young girl looks. She says, 'Kleinmann. That's funny. We have someone here on the kibbutz called Kleinmann. An older man. You should introduce yourself.'

'I'm just going to get a drink,' Sarit says. She turns her back, walks over to the drinks machine close to the bar. She tries twice or three times before she can steady her hand enough to slip the coin into the slot and pay for the Coca-Cola that she doesn't want.

She goes back to the desk, signs the credit card slip. The cool and soothing can in one hand, her holdall in the other, she follows the young girl to the kibbutz guest house. The way is paved, the building is modern and unfamiliar in its shape. And in that there is a sense of relief for Sarit, as if the newness, the strangeness, the lack of familiarity in all of this will allow her to forget that this is the place she came from and the place that she has come to. Until then, on the steps, behind the girl who holds open the glass door for her, Sarit stops and turns round, as if it were a person who had called her name. A person rather than the scent that had moved towards her and engaged the memory of her senses. The scent of the wind, of the earth, of the stream. The smell of apple orchards, lemon groves and eucalyptus leaves that stops her in her tracks right there on the steps before the guest house door.

'Here we are,' calls the girl. 'This way . . . Is your bag too heavy for you?'

And Sarit says, 'No. I'm fine,' and follows the girl inside, upstairs, into the small and fairly spartan room not unlike the picture of Van Gogh's room at Arles, with a single bed against the wall and a single empty chair beside it.

The girl hands Sarit the key. She says, 'Breakfast is any time from 6 a.m. There are signs to the dining room,' and then, 'Rest well . . . you look a little tired,' and she walks out and shuts the door behind her.

We have all had nights like this. Nights when chasing sleep

is wasting time. When if it comes at all it does so in fits and starts and bursts of disturbed and sweaty semi-consciousness that exhaust more than they rest.

Sarit's night bears images of arms and hands and fingers, straining, reaching, grasping, holding, with the sounds of banging and of shutting as though a window had been left open in the wind. So that in the morning there is no delicious transition from sleeping to waking, no single moment of waking, but only a time when she knows that her eyes are sore, that her head is heavy and her body tense. She sits bolt upright, throws off the sheets, jumps out of bed and searches for the car keys that she finds on the chair under her pile of clothes. She holds the keys, tries to recall the route to the car park. She plans how she will make a dash for it, how she will run from the guest house to her car and drive south again, so that no one but the girl at the front desk will ever know she's been here. For a fleeting moment she plans her escape and then she puts the keys back down.

In the bathroom she switches on the light, for dawn has not yet broken. Where she stands at the sink, the window that had been left open bangs shut, swings open again and stays there in the wind that has come in a gust but stilled itself. She feels a vague wave of nausea, stands with her hands on either side of the sink, breathes in deeply as she straightens up, caught by her reflection, which looks back as if to challenge.

She dresses in her jeans, grey sleeveless vest and corn-blue sweatshirt. In the early morning air that has not yet taken leave of darkness she walks down the stairs out of the guest house. Without thinking of the way she walks. She looks up at the sky. She had forgotten that here stars stayed out till morning. She passes the laundry with the turn-off to the studio, she passes what was once the children's house, but she doesn't stop, for she is afraid now to break her momentum. She passes the signs for the dining room, which she doesn't need to read and she finds herself a little dizzy, a little breathless in front of the dining-room door. She pulls the handle back, walks in, turns to her right, to where the long self-service counter still stands. She takes a plate, helps herself to chopped tomatoes and chopped cucumbers, to a piece of rye bread and a cup of tea.

From behind the counter a round woman with a net over her hair says to her in English, 'Eggs?'

Sarit shakes her head, mutters, 'No thanks,' but makes no eye contact.

The woman stares as though there were some vague flutter of recognition. She says, 'Do you want a table by yourself? Or are you OK sitting with the kibbutzniks? They'll be in soon.'

Sarit chooses the empty table in the right-hand corner of the room.

As she walks, her tray that has very little on it feels heavy in her arms. Behind her she hears a few muted morning voices. She doesn't turn her head to look. She sits down, takes her plates from the tray, begins to chew the bread, to sip the tea, which soothes her throat. She has no idea how long she has been sitting there. Two minutes, five, perhaps fifteen, whilst the volume of the voices has grown with the steady stream of kibbutzniks who have come into the dining hall.

From somewhere in the hall comes a crash, the dropping of a tray, the clanging of cutlery, the smashing of cups and plates and saucers. Sarit cannot help but turn then and catch a glimpse of long tables filling up with bobbing heads, though she does not notice those that turn in her direction. She looks down again, plays with the salad on her plate, not knowing where she will go from here. A minute passes, maybe two until behind her she feels a presence. She does not panic. She does not feel the coursing of adrenalin through her body as she has done before. Instead she feels almost calmed, as though behind her there were a healer with his hands above her head. She turns. She looks up into the face of a tall man, once skinny, with pale eyes disbelieving and blond hair turning grey.

In Hebrew he says, 'I'm seeing things.'

She looks up at him. She doesn't need to ask if she is seeing things. She knows the face that she has drawn. Her voice is shaky. 'Dani.'

'Sarit?' he says.

And he is a split second away from throwing his arms round her, when his instinct tells him not to, when he feels that she wants at all costs to avoid a spectacle and so he stops himself and sits down there next to her on the bench. He says, 'I can't believe it. You didn't say . . . we didn't know . . . You're crazy.'

For the first time in two days she laughs. It feels good to release the tension in her face. She says, 'You always thought I was crazy.'

'Yup,' he says, 'I did and now I know. When did you get here?'

She tells him and and they bow their heads there at the table, talk in the quiet voices of complicity, for within seconds though she doesn't voice it he has understood what is to come for her. She takes his hand, squeezes it so hard that the gold band on his finger digs into his skin. He says again, 'Sarit, I can't believe it,' and turning to face her then, he adds, 'Those cheekbones . . . I would have recognised them anywhere.'

He cannot ask the questions one might normally have asked. He cannot say, 'Why have you come?' or 'How long will you stay?' for these questions, both of them, hide so much more behind them. And so he says, 'My God, Sarit, we have twenty years to catch up on . . . twenty years . . . you have to meet Deborah and the kids and . . .'

She asks him about his children, remembers their names, their ages from the birth announcements he had sent. He answers her, but somehow it is he who is more distracted than she, as if there were a silent agreement between them that he would take on Sarit's anxiety now that she was there. And she is asking him something about Deborah, about how a city girl likes life on kibbutz, when Dani nudges her, his elbow against her arm, when he says, 'Over there, Sarit.'

405

She looks up, follows his gaze, to the self-service counter, to where he points towards the back of a tiny woman in a white overall leaning forward, towards a child tugging at her hand, towards a man with a mug of tea and a piece of rye on a red plastic tray, a man who walks as upright as his years and the weight of them will allow him, slowly, with his food, towards his table in the far corner of the room. With her eyes she follows his movements, though she might then have said to Dani, 'What are you pointing out? What is it you want me to look at?' for she would never have imagined him like this. In her mind the years had not bent him, slowed him down or turned his hair from black to white, and yet she knows from the tumult in her own body that there is no need at all to ask, 'What are you pointing out?' She knows not just because posture and years gone by are no disguise, but because of the way he carries his tray in his left hand, his right sleeve missing, his shirt sewn together by his right shoulder, as if he had grown into the contours of this body, as if this were no aberration, but just another way to be.

And Dani, sensing that Sarit will not move from where she is, says, 'Stay there, Sarit. I'll be back.'

In those moments in between, in those moments before Dani comes back, thought is thwarted by sensation. The dry mouth, the quick heart, the weak legs, and then him standing there, by the long wooden bench at the long wooden table. And Dani in between them carrying a tray, hovering as though about to say, 'Sarit, this is your father,' as if about to say, 'Max, here she is.'

She does not move at first from where she sits. She looks up at him. He down at her.

'Sarit.'

She nods and stands up.

'Sarit . . . I . . .' He reaches out, puts his hand on her shoulder.

She cannot lift her hand to his. She cannot say, 'Abba . . . Abba.'

Nor, as Dani moves out of the way and her father moves unsure towards her, does she return his embrace. Instead she stands there numb and stiff against him, so that for him, for Max, it is as though he were showing affection for a sculpture.

He lets her go, stands at arm's length from her. He says, '*At niret . . . Niret yafa . . .* you look quite beautiful.' In his voice there is a tremor. Perhaps the years. Perhaps his life. Perhaps the moment. She does not answer him. She thinks only, 'You look old.' She does not thank him for what he has just said to her, but on her face she has a weak half-smile as if she has just been paid a compliment by some total stranger. She stands there not knowing where to put her eyes.

'Right then, let's eat,' says Dani, rubbing his hands together.

She tugs his sleeve a little. He understands. He sits down between Max and Sarit. Max leans across Dani. He says, 'When did you arrive, Sarit?'

'Last night,' she says, looking towards him, but not at him.

'Where did you sleep?' he asks.

'In the guest house.'

'They made you pay?'

'Of course,' she says.

'Ridiculous,' he says. 'Ridiculous.' His voice a little more confident, a little stronger now that there is a practical issue on which to focus. 'You should have told me you were coming.'

Inside her something twists. She looks down at her plate, forces herself to eat a forkful of chopped cucumber. And Dani says, 'Don't worry, Max. I'll sort things out. I'll get them to credit your card, Sarit. We can't let you pay to sleep at home.'

The twist again. The food that she can hardly swallow. The cutlery that she puts back down on the plate, before she stands up and she says, 'It was a long drive last night. I'm going back to my room to rest,' and she nods at Dani, half shuts her eyes and walks towards the door of the dining room.

And Dani next to Max watches as he lifts his cup and tries once, twice, three times to bring it to his mouth. He puts his hand at the top of Max's back and rubs. He says to him. 'Are you all right?'

'Of course,' he says.

'It will be OK, Max. You need some time to break the ice. You'll see,' he says. 'It's normal. Let her go and sleep a little.'

On her way back to the guest house she doesn't think, 'What should I do? What was the point? We have nothing to say to one another.' She doesn't think these thoughts in words, but she feels them in the tightness and the twists in her breath and in her body.

She draws the curtains. She shuts the window in the bathroom or thinks she does for it is left open just a chink. She flops down on the bed and she sleeps as though anaesthetised. A heavy drugged morning sleep far more to block out the here and now than to make up for the night before. A sleep that begins to release its hold with a half-dream of canvases on easels of all sizes and on each one a picture of Gabriella's face, her mother's face asking, hoping, smiling and cajoling. This time there is a transition from sleeping into waking and with it sounds outside her door. A scuffling and a setting down. She waits a few minutes, drags herself up, opens the door a chink to see a tray with a salad, some bread, a sliced orange and a glass of cold milk. For a moment she hesitates, then lifts it, takes it over to the bed, where she sits with the tray on her lap and begins to eat, for it has been a day now since anything substantial has passed her lips.

She combs her hair again, splashes water on her face. That afternoon the shadows underneath her eyes are dark. She walks through the kibbutz, in her jeans and her trainers, this time in broad daylight. She passes the stone statues of mother and child as one, of the Queen of Sheba on her camel. Looking around her, checking to see if anyone is watching, she stops and touches the stone that glistens in the cool sunlight, feels almost guilty as though she no longer has a right to the sensation of this stone beneath her fingers. She walks along a path that is shrouded by trees. Old and gnarled and knowing trees that darken the way. Her white trainers are brown and muddied from the rain the ground has saved in recent days.

She has not questioned whether the house will still be there. She has just assumed it. But she has forgotten that it was made only of wood and that even at the time she left there was talk of rebuilding it.

The trees move their branches back on to a clearing and in its space stands the house of her childhood. In brick now, instead of wood, red now instead of ochre and yet its shape, the proportions of its face so much the same, so that she knows, so that she can tell that they have built it for Max thinking that he has had enough, that he must be put through as little change as possible. She knocks on the front door. No reply. She tries again. She waits. She turns the handle and walks inside. And although the material of the house is different, the floor tiled, the brick exposed, it feels and smells the same, like a person matured and wearing different clothing. Hung on the wall in the living room is a painting Sarit has seen in progress. The half-face in thick oils, the portrait of Max's mother ravaged by the Nazi dogs, the one that she had watched him painting the day Gabriella tried to teach her the concept of 'mitboded' . . . the concept of being a loner.

She turns from it, looks up above the fireplace and stops. She blinks, bites her lip, then smiles up at her mother's face, not in strands of light in her imagination, but in oil paints and from the photographs in her father's memory.

She stands there, quite still, remembering. Then she puts her hand up as if blocking light, opens her palm and closes it in front of the painting, catching the memory of her mother.

She is about to walk through the narrow hallway towards the bedrooms then, but she turns instead and leaves, back along the muddy way that twists and bends. Only the branches of the trees have forks left and right, but the road itself offers no turn-offs to the walker and so within moments they come upon one another there. Father and daughter walking towards one another.

'I was looking for you,' he says.

'Oh,' she says. She does not need to add, 'And I for you,' for he can see from where she's come.

He makes no secret of his staring. In hers she tries to be more subtle, for she is shocked by his ageing.

They stand there, awkward with one another, in the middle of the path. He asks, 'How long will you stay?'

She hasn't decided. She doesn't know, but on the spot she says, 'Oh, I don't know. A couple of days perhaps.'

'So we have time,' he says, bent over just a little, and then, 'Sarit.'

'Yes.'

'I liked the painting . . . Of the sea. I saw a photograph of it.'

'Who brought it to you?'

'Ben,' he says.

'Oh . . . Ben,' she says. 'Yes, Ben.'

And the images of him, the sounds of him, of his voice and his footsteps on creaking floorboards have begun in her mind, when they stop within her there and she looks at her father. Properly. For the first time. Calls him by a name for the first time since she has seen him and says, 'Is that it then, Abba? I think I get it now. You're pleased I'm here because of the art. Because you can see I've started painting again. Wonderful,' she says, 'I should have known, of course. How stupid of me.'

'Sarit,' he says, his slow feet in the mud of the pathway, the light from between the branches falling on his weathered face, 'Sarit, we . . . we need to find a way to talk.'

She looks down at the ground, then lifts her eyes towards him and in a quiet voice that comes from a place she didn't know that she could reach, she says, 'Have you only just decided that?'

And she leaves him with that question then. Not waiting for an answer as she walks past him on the path.

With legs of lead he goes towards his home where, in the living room, he will look up at the painting of Gabriella and the painting of his mother, and in the hallway he will look up at the paintings of Sarit that line the walls and fill the bedroom in which she would have slept.

And she, Sarit, walks towards Dani's house to meet his family and on the way, close to the laundry, she sees a white-haired woman hanging white sheets that flap in the wind. Between the sheets the woman stands and stares ahead of her and as Sarit moves closer, she calls out, 'It isn't, is it? It really is.'

Sarit walks up to her. The white-haired woman takes her hands. She says, 'Sarit. The naughtiest girl in my class. They told me you were here.'

'Hello, Rivka. How are you?'

And Rivka laughs. 'How am I? Now that's a question . . . Sit and talk to me a little.'

They sit down together on a low stone wall. 'You look wonderful,' says Rivka. 'How is it to see your father?'

A silence and then, 'I don't know, Rivka.'

'Time,' she says. 'You need time. Both of you.'

'I don't know. Maybe too much time has passed. I don't know that I can.'

'You can,' she says. 'If we want to we always can . . . He said that "I can't" stuff too. He said "I can't" when we told him to learn to paint with his left arm. It wasn't till after the stroke that it began again.'

'He had a stroke?' she says, there on the low stone wall.

'A mild one. You didn't know?' she asks. 'No, of course you didn't. He told us not to contact you about it. He said it wasn't right to expect you to come after all these years. But he was lucky. It was in his right side. He drags his leg a little. I don't know if you noticed. The doctor said the stroke might have

411

paralysed his right arm, but' – and she laughs – 'as he didn't have one, that was no problem.'

Sarit laughs too. She cannot help herself and Rivka says, 'That smile. Your mother had that smile,' and then she adds, 'It was so strange, really. Before the stroke he had struggled many times to paint with his left hand and I think he had almost given up. But afterwards it just all seemed to flow out of him. No one understands quite why . . . But then I don't suppose it matters. When you rediscover something you love, I don't suppose it matters where it comes from, does it?'

FORTY-FOUR

We cannot force ourselves to feel. The heart has a mind and a memory of its own. The heart can make its own decisions. Sarit wants to know so she might feel. She wants to ask her father, 'What was it like for you? How was it to be without your only child?'

And yet she cannot ask these questions of him. Anger and the sense of loss have built their fortress and where she goes so they walk with her. As she stands by the stream she puts her questions to the winter water. Not to her father, but only to the water can she say, 'How did it feel for him without his only flesh and blood?' She looks to the depths and the ripples for an answer and she finds none. She turns to the weeping willows, to their bark and to their foliage for an answer. There is none there either, though somewhere in their shadows, in their movement, she sees her mother's face again.

He finds her there by the banks. Close to a bench he says, 'If you want to sit here for a while we could.' He sits at one end. She at the other. She looks straight ahead of her.

He leans towards her, his left side turned in her direction, the fingers of his hand threaded through the slats to stop himself from reaching out. 'We need to talk,' he says.

'Do we?' she asks.

He says, 'Are you happy, Sarit?'

'Please,' she says. 'It's taken you twenty years to ask me that.'

He bows his head. A minute passes. A fly buzzes round his face.

As upright as he can be against the back of the bench he says, 'I hoped you'd come.'

She remembers being six here and tugging at his arm, dragging him in to swim with her. She remembers the croaking of the frogs, the jumping of the fish, the silhouette of an otter slipping into twilight. She has forgotten though how her father said, 'Sarit, please, promise you won't ever leave here.'

Max is silent next to her, waiting, hoping to distinguish the words in his head from the buzzing of the fly. Waiting for them to make coherent shapes that he can understand before he speaks them, for words never were his medium.

She looks at the trunk of a huge oak tree with a hollow in its centre. She says, 'I see Ima's face everywhere.' She says it not because it is her father to whom she speaks for even though the winter's day is mild, she is shrouded still in frost, but she says it because of the truth of it and because he happens to be there.

'If she hadn't died . . .' Max says.

'Yes, then what?' she asks him.

'Then . . . then . . . she would have helped me find a way.'

'A way to what?' she asks.

'To be a father.'

She stands up, walks to the edge of the bank. She peers over the edge and watches the fish jump up and disappear again, making circles.

'Sarit,' he calls.

She turns round to face him, her hands in the pockets of her jeans. 'Yes.'

'I want to know about your life. About love and friends and work.'

She has not yet come this close on purpose but now she walks up to him. She stands over him almost and in a quiet voice she says, 'You have no right.'

He does not show the hurt, the pain. He says, 'I have no right . . . but, but . . . you cannot stop yourself from wanting.'

She moves away a little. She thinks, 'No, that's true. You cannot stop yourself from wanting.'

414

She goes back towards her father, sits cross-legged and picks at the grass, which is damp with rain. She says, 'You really didn't care after a while, did you? You just got used to a world without me.' She says it not because that's what she believes, but because she needs to challenge him.

And what Max wants to say to her, to his daughter, here on the edge of the banks by the stream that flows into the River Jordan is, 'Got used to life without you? Oh no. Not that. Not for a single day. I pushed you away because I was too afraid that you'd get used to life without me. I was too terrified of the loss of you. And if I couldn't see you here, right here in front of me, then I wouldn't know if you were letting go . . . If you had gone. But I found a way not to lose you. To . . . to keep you close, even though you weren't. It was the only way I knew.'

He does not speak these words out loud. He sits there on the bench looking at his child, and together with the sadness he feels a sense of pride. Pride at the strength of her, pride that she has come from him and Gabriella. For no matter if the mistakes we make with them are grave, we will still see our reflection in the faces of our children when they're grown.

And as he looks at the grey eyes and their lashes long and thick, as he looks at the skin that is pale and clear, at the aquiline of her nose, at the bones of her cheeks, her face, his daughter's face becomes all the faces of her that he has painted over the years. The faces he has struggled with in secret in the first years. The ones that he has ripped up in frustration because his left hand would not dance the way his right hand did. The ones then that have begun to paint themselves as though she, her face, had begun to guide his hand the way that his hands had guided hers when she was small.

She lifts her head from where she's sitting on the grass. She looks at him, his skin more patterned than a leaf now. She says, 'Abba, that's what happened, isn't it? You just got used to life without me.'

'No,' he says, 'no, Sarit . . . I . . . I kept you with me.'

She doesn't know how he means it or what lies behind the words 'I kept you with me.' And yet she knows only too well what it means for a father to try all his life to keep his daughter with him, though she's not there by his side. Of that she knows enough from Ramsi.

By the stream she might have said, 'Kept me close? Don't make me laugh. You wouldn't come and visit me and you wouldn't let me come to you until it was too late, until I didn't want to any more.' She wants to say that to him, but when she looks up she sees him, tired, leaning against the back of the bench, his eyes closed, his face tilted upwards towards the moment of weak sun that has dared to venture through the crack between two dark and heavy clouds. And so, there by the banks, she asks him nothing more.

Not till the next day does she know what Max was trying to make her understand when he said, 'I kept you with me.' Not till she goes back alone again to her father's house to stand before the portrait of her mother and moves from the living room into the room that would have been hers, had he asked her even once, had she ever come to stay.

She stands there in the doorway and on the walls in canvases unframed she sees the child, the girl, the young woman. She sees what her father had been struggling to express. She sees his time, his pain, his trouble and she watches herself. She watches her expression change from one canvas to the next, from a frown, to a smile, to a stillness as if in the sequence of a film. And yet it is not Max's efforts, his struggles, her father's struggles that move her for their own sake. And she feels no joy or pleasure as she looks. This art, his art, his portrayal of her does not, cannot now, bring her joy.

Not that Sarit has ever known art as pleasure unadulterated. Not that a painting has ever been just a painting. And for her, of course, whether in strands of light, in clay, in flesh, on snow, a face could not be just a face. And so these images

416

of herself around her here are so much more than that. They are accordions, with her face painted at the handles at each end. Accordions that stretch out in time and space to make their music bitter-sweet. To tell their own story. To bestow their own gift.

Because as she stands there, her head upwards before the images of herself, as she swallows hard, fights at first for control, and gives in then to the lonliness, the longing and the pain, it is not because of the aesthetic beauty of the art that Sarit begins to cry. It is not for Max's struggles that the tears stream down her face, as she wraps her arms around herself, as if protecting, as she stands there swaying, saying out loud, 'My God, this hurts. Do you know how much this hurts? Goddamn it, Ramsi. I hate this. I hate it. I . . . love . . .'

No, it is not for Max's pain, nor for the beauty of the art itself, but because of the gift her father now has given her that Sarit has begun to lose control. Because of the way the light falls in his paintings, the way it sheds itself on her own story, guiding her, showing her, begging her to understand a father's longing for his daughter. Because of the way the light in Max's paintings shows her that, if a one-armed man tortured by his history will learn to paint with his other arm so as not to lose his child, so as to keep her memory with him, then a sculptor eaten up by years of guilt and grief, consumed by years of pain, will stop at nothing in his desperation to keep the memory of his daughter by his side, to take pride in her as she grows from a little girl to a young woman. He will let his subconscious mind race and trample over what is right, what is rational and reasonable. He will allow it to lead him to the edge, where tortured by the precipice he can see destruction, desolation and new loss.

FORTY-FIVE

———⟡———

At the edge of the precipice, spent from the sculpting and the sobbing, kneeling over the sarcophagus, Ramsi runs his hand along the marble's side, feels with his fingers, with their imprint where he has engraved his child's name in hieroglyphics. *Nadia, Nadia, Nadia,* the name that comes from the Arabic word *Nahat. Nahat* . . . to sculpt. *Nahat* . . . a sculpture that is Ramsi's acceptance. Acceptance that might be his end and might be his beginning. Acceptance that might or might not let him leave his holocaust behind him. For days then, afterwards, his neck, his face around his beard remain unshaven. He does not dress, he does not venture out. His mind knows no way forward. But with all the anguish and the angst that the creative spirit brings, it has a power too to work for the artist, for the sculptor, to speak for him and speak through him, when he cannot find the strength himself. His creative spirit has the power to drag Ramsi yet again from where he lies, to lead him, his hands, his fingers to the pinky, grainy terracotta clay. To help him as he finds the sketches that he needs, as he rummages for them in the drawer that smells of cedarwood, beneath the green kimono that Sarit had worn the day she posed for him.

He stands before the tall thin wooden sculptor's stand, before this clumsy clump of clay and of their own accord, his hands begin their work now on the mass. His thumbs moving it, his fingerprints marking it, rough at first as if nothing fine, nothing delicate or beautiful could ever come from this. And yet for this work he cannot be rough or desperate or angry. For this piece that makes him bend to see his sketches, for this piece that makes him slow, he must be careful, close and concentrated. And in his artistry, not with chisels now, but with tiny tools, with little wire loops and cocktail sticks and the tips of his own fingers, he must re-create not just the strength of bones and joints and knuckles, not just the details of veins and nails and the smoothness of skin but the grace of fingers too. Of her fingers. Of Sarit's fingers, long and slim and intertwined as they were when she lay there on the beige velvet chaise longue covered with the purple raw silk throw. And on the inside of her hand, as he moves round his piece to sculpt her palm, he draws the line, the life line that cuts in, that breaks and mends again. And more than this, more than shape and grace and lines, there is the movement of the piece that he must find. The movement of her hands that he will fashion till with the pain, the yearning and the longing that he feels for her, they transcend beauty, art and image, till beneath his hands hers speak with the life that he has offered them. Till Sarit's hands come alive and speak to him through his work of art, just as they speak to him in life.

He stands there now, bent over them. He cups them in his palms, the wet terracotta against the dryness of his skin, then presses his own hands against them, against his work and he destroys it. He pushes one sculpted finger against the next. He ruins the angles, the shape, the lines. He lifts the piece from where it stands and pummels it, returns it to the clumsy lump of clay that it once was, as though his work had never been. Not again,' he says in disbelief. 'Not another icon . . .' and he hurls the clay on to the floor and into the emptiness cries out, 'Is it too late again . . . ? Tell me it's not too late . . . please, Sarit.'

FORTY-SIX

They are not, this time, November fields. Not the fields of late autumn where the black crows fly, but the fields of early spring with blue tits and robin redbreasts and the tern that fly now overhead. The yellow this time is not fading, but so close to bursting forth. The sun is neither hot, nor melting into evening, but the warmth of it is rising into day. They walk so slowly to the open spaces for to carry his easel and his paints the man needs all his strength. The brambles and the undergrowth through which they have to pass are still there, but on their legs they feel no nettles. In each other's company the two are calm and peaceful as though soulmates.

Through the flitting sunlight they walk to the open fields of endless possibility. He follows her. Not she him. She sets down her own easel. 'Here,' she says. 'This is the best place. Put your easel here next to mine.'

He smiles, begins to set his easel down. She watches him as though he might need her help for he is old now. Very old. But in the fresh breeze, surrounded by the beauty of his home and in her company, Max feels strengthened, as though the end were the beginning. In front of her she sets her canvas on her easel. By her side she puts her palette and her paints. He does the same.

She asks him, 'Doesn't it feel funny just painting with one arm?'

Max says, 'You only paint with one arm, don't you?'

She giggles. 'Oh yes. I do.'

'What will you paint?' he asks her out there in the open air.

'Not telling you,' she says.

'OK,' he says, 'that's your surprise for me.'

With his left hand he squeezes tubes, he pours his turps, he blends, he mixes paints. Beige and white and mustard, even mauve when she is there, though he has to lean over and borrow from her palette, for he has not used mauve in years, nor did he imagine he would want to.

'Go on,' he says. 'Tell me what you're going to paint. Point it out to me.'

'I can't,' she says.

'Why not?'

'You'll see.'

They fall silent there, the two of them in the April fields. So that the only sounds one hears are the birds, the brushing of the grass blades against one another, the brushing of the paints on canvas.

She asks him, 'What are you painting?'

'It's a surprise too,' he says, 'but in lots of different colours.' He tries again. He says, 'And you?'

'A picture in my head,' she says.

He laughs.

For a moment she looks cross. 'Don't laugh at me.'

'Not at you. With you.'

'Hm,' she says.

He looks at her hands. He thinks they will be as beautiful as her mother's are. He studies the way she holds the brush. He does not need to bite his tongue to stop himself from telling her the right way. For Max has long since realised there are many different ways.

She says, 'You can guess what I'm painting. . . .'

He lays down his thick brush, walks closer to her. He sees the outline of two faces touching in pink and black and brown.

Excited, she says, 'Do you know, Saba? Do you know, Grandpa?'

'I know,' he says.

'Tell me, tell me now,' and with her elbow she almost knocks her easel over.

He steadies it with his left hand. His worn and brown and wrinkled hand.

'Tell me now,' she says again.

He goes back to his own easel. He teases her. He says, 'Well, you live with them.'

She giggles. 'Yes, I do. I do. Does that mean I'm a good painter? Because you can guess?'

He smiles at the way she lisps. Like her mother used to do. He notices she holds herself before the easel as her mother did.

She says, 'Saba, I don't know if I'm going to be just a painter.'

He looks at her. The shiny dark hair. Her father's dark skin. His coal-black eyes. He asks, 'What would you like to be, Gaby?'

'Em . . . em,' and she giggles again. 'I might want to be two things like my mummy. A painter and a doctor,' she says.

'I see,' he says.

She says, 'Saba?'

'Yes.'

'Why don't we live here?'

'Because,' he says, his eyes not now on the child, but on the canvas.

'Because what?'

'Because the painting turned out in a different way.'

'What? Saba, what?' She puts her brush down now. In the expanse, the wind, the warmth of the yellow, pinkish mauve he feels her tugging at his sleeve. She says, 'I want to live here.'

He says to her, 'You did, you know, when you were very little with your Ima. Just you and Ima.'

'I know that,' she says, indignant, as though he has taken her for stupid. 'My Ima told me . . . So why can't we live here now?'

He dips his brush into the paint. Somewhere he adds a

stroke of indigo. 'Because,' he says, 'because at home you can learn to paint with Ima and to sculpt with Abba in the same house, can't you?'

'Oh yes,' she says, and then, 'Anyway, my Abba was too sad without me. That's why he came to find me.'

'Yes,' says Max, 'but not just you. Your Ima too . . . He came to find your Ima too.'

Remembering, he adds a swirl of yellow to his painting. Thick and warm suggestive yellow. He looks at Gaby, but he doesn't say out loud what he is thinking. He doesn't say to her, 'Your Abba didn't know about you till he came here. Your Ima didn't tell him till she saw him.'

He turns back to his work. From time to time he looks at hers out of the corner of his eye.

'Saba?' says the child.

'Yes?'

'I like it here with you.'

He does not speak. He cannot. But he puts down his paintbrush. With his left hand he strokes her shiny hair. And in his imagination, with his right hand he paints a swirl of brilliant white. One swirl. Then another. In his mind in the April fields next to her he paints the final swirl of thick and brilliant white.